She became his soul mate and first love, but can he and she escape a destiny that was decided before they were born?

In 1920's Florida, an abandoned baby boy grows up under a cloud of mystery, adopted by two strong southern women who try to protect him from his family's secrets and heartaches. But even their best intentions and deepest devotion can't hide the truth forever or soften the fate that faces both him and the girl he loves.

Augusta Trobaugh's unforgettable novel speaks of loyalty, loss, the difficult choices we make in the name of family, and of courageous hope, each inspired by the fragile and painfully longing music of life, a song that seems to come from beyond the moon.

"[Augusta Trobaugh is] is a writer of extraordinary talent and skill."
—*BOOKLIST*

Other Augusta Trobaugh Titles From Bell Bridge Books
Praise Jerusalem!
Resting in the Bosom of the Lamb
Sophie and the Rising Sun *
River Jordan
The Tea-Olive Bird Watching Society
Swan Place

*Also available in audiobook, narrated by the late Rue McClanahan, star of *Golden Girls*

Music From Beyond the Moon

by

Augusta Trobaugh

Bell Bridge Books

Bell Bridge Books
PO BOX 300921
Memphis, TN 38130
Print ISBN: 978-1-61194-124-1

Bell Bridge Books is an Imprint of BelleBooks, Inc.

We at BelleBooks enjoy hearing from readers.
Visit our websites—www.BelleBooks.com and www.BellBridgeBooks.com.

10 9 8 7 6 5 4 3 2 1

Cover design: Debra Dixon
Interior design: Hank Smith
Photo credits:
photo-© Teresa Yeh | Dreamstime.com

:Lfmb:01:

Dedication

For Dr. Raoul Mayer—
Thank you for saving my life.

Chapter One

1924, Love-Oak, Florida

Dawn had not yet arrived, but the rain had ended and the eastern sky turned a fragile, golden pink. The clouds moved away, revealing a moon still hanging in the sky and casting a silver sheen across the quiet lake.

All night, the storm lashed the land, shredding the palm fronds and blowing water from the lake up onto the sandy road. But now, a new dawn had come, and the storm was gone, leaving the earth fresh scrubbed and chastised.

In the deep brush of palmettos behind the main house of the old fishing camp, the air was still thick with the breath of heavy rain, and from time to time the soft cries of a night bird pierced the moist silence— perhaps an owl perched high in a water oak, grateful for the end of the storm and watching intently for a tender mouse-morsel to scurry from the sanctuary of the flooded palmetto fronds below.

Tree frogs pulsated the air with their mesmerizing thrumming, and water lapped in the estuary as the tide changed. From a distance, a bull alligator bellowed three times in quick succession and then fell silent. Closer, another sound, only softer—a newborn baby whimpering in troubled slumber.

Moonlight filtered through the Spanish moss that hung from the rain-soaked limbs of ancient water oaks and decorated the side of the old house in random, ghostly shades of silver. Where the paint had long ago peeled away, specks of weathered wood showed through, and the screen door to the long back porch hung slightly off-center, as if balancing against the tilt of the house on its concrete block foundation

At the base of a silvery-trunked cypress tree off to the side of the house, a child, a small boy—barely a toddler—sat with his knees drawn up under his chin, his eyes wide, watching for anything that might come at him from out of the damp darkness.

The woman had put him at the base of the tree, pressing down on his shoulders and shaking him slightly. "You stay right there. You hear me? Don't you move a single inch! And yes, I know the ground is wet. But you just do as I say."

She lifted her hands from his shoulders and taking a biscuit from a paper sack she had carried inside of her blouse, she pressed the biscuit into his hand and then walked away from him toward the house, reluctance slowing her steps. He watched as the pale triangle of her skirt disappeared behind the house.

"You stay right there, you hear me?" she repeated over her shoulder, but in a softer voice, almost a voice that said "goodbye," but without the words. "You be a sweet boy, honey." Her golden-honey-toned words melted away into the darkness beyond the palm fronds and the tall grasses.

While his eyes clung to the swinging skirt as it moved away, a noise in the palmetto bushes startled him, making him want to cry out for the departing figure. But he knew the storm was gone, the rain and wind had stopped, and she had said for him to be quiet, so he made not a sound, not even when, from among the dripping palmetto fronds, he saw deeply tanned hands—big hands!—separating the fronds, followed by a face— but not the face of any monster he had ever dreamed in his short, nonverbal life. This face had eyes that were soft but black and almost lifeless—the watchful eyes of a hungry alligator? And a hooked nose above a stern mouth. In the wet, black hair, a single white egret feather. No doubt whatsoever in his childish mind. He knew this creature, a beautiful, magical creature from the stories he had heard. He wanted to cry out to the face, but the cry caught in his throat, and he remained silent.

Instead, the boy listened as the woman's departing footsteps ceased and her knuckles rapped loudly on the screen door of the house. At the same time, the creature-face disappeared, moving backwards silently and finally dissolving into the poisonous black-green of the undergrowth. From nearby came the low, throaty growl of a panther, but not a growl to threaten—more of a sound coming from deep in the massive chest to comfort and to say, "I am here, and I will not leave you."

The woman's knock on the leaning screen door of the old house was the last thing the boy heard, because in spite of the sadness of watching the woman walk away from him and the surprise of seeing the magical creature in the brush and the feeling of the wet, wild grasses against his skin and hearing the soft growl of the panther—despite all of these things, the heaviness of his eyelids became too much to bear. His body softened slowly, and he relaxed against the base of the tree, still watching for the beautiful creature-face in the palmettos and with the panther speaking its comforting growl. So he remained where the woman had put him and told him to stay, and despite everything, he drifted away into a deep, sweet sleep and into dreams where the creature-face smiled at him and the panther's growl was a peaceful lullaby, and where the grass and the trees were soft and dry. And for the rest of the night before that dawn, he did not awaken. Not even when he dreamed human voices, one so familiar and another so foreign to him, and a flashlight beam that came wavering toward him from the back of the house. Not even when strange, trembling arms lifted him out of the wet grass and carried him away. Not even when the biscuit dropped from his uncurled fingers and rolled away into the underbrush.

Chapter Two

"We can bathe him after a while," a voice said. "Let him sleep for now."

"What we should have done—is cleaned him up right away and put something on all those mosquito bites. Calamine lotion," another voice said, and both were women's voices. "Makes me sick, that does! That baby so filthy and all those nasty old bites on his legs."

"Let him sleep," the other one admonished. "We'll have plenty of time to clean him up, but sleep's the best thing right now. Doc said so, and he ought to know."

"But he needs something to eat," the other protested. "Looks like he's been starved half to death. And that diaper! Goodness!"

"I know. It smells just awful, but it sure doesn't seem to be bothering him." A long hesitation then and the other woman saying, "Maybe he's used to it being that way." Another hesitation and then the finalizing words, "Doesn't matter right now. Doc said let him sleep. You just go on in the kitchen and put on a pot of grits. This child will be hungry when he wakes up, and we can get that nasty diaper off and give this baby a good scrubbing."

"What I don't understand is why Doc didn't come right on over here, when we called him and told him we had a little child some woman just walked off and left in our yard!"

"He has his reasons, I'm sure. Maybe he's gone out looking for the mother."

"Almost scared me to death! That knocking on the door before good daylight even, and us seeing that poor woman, and her pointing to the tree where we found this baby. And then us trying to ask her about it, and her simply disappearing into thin air!"

"Well, we'll hear from Doc soon enough, I expect. But in the meantime, we have to take care of him."

"I think he needs a big dose of castor oil, right off the bat," the other one exclaimed. "Needs a good dose to get him all cleaned out."

"No castor oil!" The words were whispered in an angry manner. "That's always your answer to *everything,* and I'll not stand by and see you torture this precious little thing with it. No need to 'clean him out,' because maybe he hasn't had anything to eat in a long time. Leastwise, that's the way it looks. So you just go tend to those grits, like I told you to."

"And why do we keep calling it *him*, is what I want to know."

"Well, we don't know, but it sure looks like a *him*."

"You gonna look in that diaper to see for sure?"

"No! We'll just leave it alone until we get a bath all fixed. It's too nasty to look, until we can take it all the way off. Now please go on and fix those grits."

Following the whispered fuss between the two women, the child sensed footsteps retreating and heard a mild and fading grumbling. A door closed softly, and only then did he open his eyes.

The room was dim, despite the fullness of the sunlight on the other side of the drawn shade, and the one finger of sunlight that came through the side of the shade held the promise of a hot summer day ahead. He sat up, rubbing his eyes and searching for the skirt he had watched disappear into the dark. Trying to reach for it, press his face into it.

But there was no skirt. He had not stayed where she told him to stay, so maybe that's why he couldn't find the skirt. Tears, far warmer than the long finger of sunlight, tried to come, but he choked, swallowed, pushed the tears away, and made not a sound. •

As if she had heard his silent cry, one of the women came back into the room. She was short and round and wore a white chenille bathrobe with a huge peacock woven into the front—a gold, green and blue peacock with a rich crown of delicate feathers on its head. In fact, the peacock seemed to mirror the woman herself, because her head was covered in fine, golden curls, each one a perfect corkscrew. Her curls didn't stand up as high as the peacock feathers, but they bounced and quivered as she came across the room to the bed where the boy was lying. She gazed at him with sad blue eyes, the curls bobbing softly, then she moved forward, gathering him into her arms. He pushed against her, but she held him, and still, he made not a sound. But, in a breath that was little more than a stifled sob, he inhaled her scent—talcum powder and some aroma like lemons. Or watermelon. And from the soft curls came a perfume he had never known before. Later, he would learn that it was lavender.

Her warm, tender body held him and rocked from side to side, in sadness, in comfort.

Again, he pushed against her, but not quite as hard, and she simply gathered him back, pressing him into her soft warmth.

"There, there," she crooned, rocking him back and forth. "You're all right, honey. Don't you cry now. Fiona's here, baby. Fiona's gonna make everything all right. And Glory's here too, so—you poor, nasty, smelly little thing—don't you fret! Fiona's here. Glory's here." The words he didn't understand had the hush of a benediction.

"Glory!" she called over her shoulder. "Put on the kettle and get that washtub ready. We're gonna wash this child." To the child, she added softly, "Can't abide the smell of you another minute, little one!"

When the large, galvanized tub had been put onto the screen porch and half filled with water, Glory lifted the huge kettle from the stove, and using her apron as a protection against the hot handle, she poured the steaming water into the cold water in the tub and swished her hand through it, to check its temperature.

Fiona carried the child to the porch, holding him so that he was mashed securely against the garish peacock on her ample bosom. "That's good," Glory pronounced, wiping her wet hand on her apron. The child stood silently while Fiona and Glory started peeling the dirty clothes from him, tugging the dirty shirt over his head and bending his nose in the process. But still, he made not a sound. When they came to the diaper, they struggled against the terrible smell and discovered, to their dismay, that the soiled fabric was firmly adhered to his skin in the back. Discreetly, Glory lifted the front of the diaper away from the child's bulging stomach and peered into it. "Boy," she pronounced. "But we already figured that anyway." Fiona made a few tugs at the stuck fabric in the back of the diaper, bringing forth the first sound he had made—a low whine of anguish.

"Lord have mercy! We'll have to soak this off him," Glory pronounced, and the boy looked at her closely, as if he agreed. He studied her dark face—far darker than the face he had seen in the bushes—and breathed in the musky aroma of her body. Her black skin was shining with perspiration as she bent over the tub of water that was to be his bath. Then he studied Fiona again, as well, the pale skin and blonde, corkscrew curls and the faint aroma of lemons from her hands. Silently, those hands lifted him into the warm, soapy water, and while Glory sponged his arms and shoulders, he studied her face—how the whites of her eyes were the color of coffee with milk in it—the way his mama liked her own coffee. Studying Glory's face, he could also see his mama's face as she bent over a steaming cup, blowing into it, and smiling at him.

"It's too hot, honey," he heard her golden voice say.

"Hot!" he repeated.

"No, honey," Fiona soothed him. "It's not too hot. We wouldn't put you into a tub if the water was too hot." Still, Glory reached down and swept her fingers through the water, just to make sure that the boy didn't have a valid complaint.

"It's just right," Glory pronounced, satisfied. So while the boy soaked in the tub of warm water, Fiona began slowly prying the filthy, dried diaper from his tender skin, bit by bit. Once it was off, she dropped it, dripping, into a trashcan and lifted him out of the tub.

"We have to get some fresh water now. Start all over again."

So they wrapped the child in a towel and dumped the bath water right out onto the floor, where it streamed off under the banisters and fell into the hydrangea bushes surrounding the porch. Glory poured in fresh water and added another large kettle of steaming hot water from the stove. Again, she swished her hand through it.

"That's good," Glory said, and Fiona removed the towel and deposited the child back into the tub. From there, the two women soaped down every inch of him, rubbing his soft skin with their warm hands, scrubbing his matted hair softly with their fingernails, soaping his arms and bloated stomach, cleaning him all the way to the pink toes and the bottoms of his feet, concentrating especially on the grime behind his ears and on the back of his neck and the tender, reddened skin where the diaper had been. And the whole time they bathed him, they murmured rough words of anger at first and glanced at each other, clucking their tongues. Finally, the clucking stopped, and their words became soft and comforting, little whispers that were almost like small songs. They even smiled a little.

"Well, what a handsome little fellow!" Fiona exclaimed. "Who would have thought his hair would be so blonde under all that dirt?" Once again, she lifted him from the tub, and Glory wrapped a clean towel around him.

"What're we gonna use for clothes to put him in?" Glory asked, with irritation in her voice. "Can't just let him run around wearing a towel, for Heaven's sake! And what're we gonna use for a diaper?"

"I think he's 'most too big for diapers," Fiona mused. "But I'm not sure. We better tear up an old sheet and use that anyway."

"We still got some of Mr. J. Roy's old shirts in the closet," Glory added. "Those'll do for clothes 'til we can get him something better. At least he'll be clean and dry."

"Yes," Fiona agreed. "Somebody might as well get some use out of them." And all the time they were talking, Fiona was rubbing down the small, pink body with a clean towel, and then she got a bottle of hand lotion from her dresser and rubbed the lotion all over him, right up into the edges of his hair, where his neck and ears were bright pink from being scrubbed, and on the reddened bottom where they had peeled away the diaper. The lotion felt smooth and silken on his tender skin, and he liked the aroma of it, the softest perfume-and-soap aroma and the lavender he'd smelled in Fiona's hair. He rubbed his hands over the lotion she had smoothed on his distended stomach and smelled his fingers.

"Feel lots better, don't you?" Fiona asked. "Tell you one thing, you sure do *smell* better." But the child had already forgotten about the glorious scent of the lotion and was gazing through the screen door toward the back yard. He lifted one hand and pointed to the yard, whining softly. Fiona and Glory watched him silently. Then Fiona acknowledged his meaning. "I know. I know," she crooned. "You want to go look for her, I reckon, but she isn't there, honey. She isn't there."

Glory spoke up. "You gotta say it so he can understand. You gotta say, 'She's gone bye-bye.'"

"She's gone bye-bye," Fiona repeated, and the child moved his eyes from the door and gazed at her with a solemn expression.

"That's right," Fiona said. "Gone bye-bye, honey. So you stay here with us, okay? She'll come back. You just be good and patient, and she'll come back."

"You ought not to tell him that," Glory whispered. "We don't know that for sure."

"It's okay," Fiona assured her, but Glory clucked her tongue in disagreement. Then she sighed. "I'll go get one of them shirts," she said. "And calamine lotion for the mosquito bites."

"See?" Fiona said to the child. "It's going to be all right!" Her voice was bright and musical, as if she were reading a fairy tale to him. He glanced once more toward the screened door and then heaved a small sigh, as if he had finally given in to her words.

They dabbed calamine lotion on the mosquito bites on his legs and arms and then diapered the boy in part of a torn sheet, fastening the makeshift diaper with safety pins.

"Better try to find something like rubber pants to go over that diaper," Glory suggested. "Else, the minute he wets, everything he's got on gonna be wet, too."

"We need to make a list of things," Fiona said. "So we can go in town in a little bit and get whatever we need. But of course, we don't know how long we'll have him here with us, so we don't want to spend too much."

"One of us better go and one stay here with him, leastwise until we get some of them rubber pants," Glory said, and Fiona nodded in agreement. In the meantime, Glory had brought a soft old shirt from the closet, and when Fiona shook it out from its folds, she caught—for the least little moment—the faintest aroma of J. Roy's shaving soap. *Funny that his smell should still be in this shirt, despite it being washed and put away for so many years!* she thought, but she said nothing. Strangely, she felt her eyes fill up, but she didn't know whether it was because of J. Roy's aroma still on the old shirt or whether she was feeling the sheer joy of taking such a pitiful little boy, cleaning him up, and putting him into fresh clothes. Regardless, she blinked away the tears that threatened to come, put the man-sized shirt on the child, rolled up the sleeves until his small hands appeared and then buttoned the front, which went all the way down to his toes.

"Well. That's all we can do for now," Fiona sighed. "Now let's get some good food into him. Lord only knows when he last had something to eat. 'Cause no telling where his mama came from, but not from around here, that's for sure. And no telling how long she'd been traveling. A long way, I should think, from the looks of her. And out in that awful storm, to boot."

The women both remembered again the thin, rain-soaked woman who had knocked on their back door long before dawn. Remembered her anguished face and heard her whispered words, "I'm sorry to bother you folks so early." That was absolutely every word she said, but then she had pointed toward the tree and put her hand over her mouth, as if to stop herself from speaking further.

While Glory stood at the screen door, with the porch light shining behind her, Fiona picked her way across the yard and found the child asleep. When she turned to ask the woman what was going on, the woman was gone.

"Where'd she go?" Fiona called to Glory.

"Don't know," Glory hollered back. "Didn't see her go. Just disappeared!" And then Fiona had gathered up the child, surprised at the weight of so fragile-looking a little thing, and carried him into the house. *Time to find out what this is all about later,* she thought to herself, because her entire attention was turned to the child who was in such an obviously miserable condition. While Glory held the door open, Fiona carried him inside and put him on her own bed, where he mumbled and turned onto his side, his small mouth making slight sucking sounds in his sleep. Fiona pulled a cotton quilt over him, over the filth and the wet clothes, as well. And immediately, they phoned Doc—the only person they knew to call— and he said for them to let the child sleep, and he would come by to see him as soon as he could. In the meantime, Doc would see if he could find out anything about the mother.

"Grits are probably done by now," Glory said, breaking the reverie of memory for them both. "They'll be easy on his stomach, and a soft scrambled egg will be good, as well. But I still say a good dose of castor oil would do him just right."

"Forget that, Glory. I simply won't permit it."

"Well. Don't you go blaming me if he gets so stopped up he ends up with a fever."

"He won't."

"Won't get stopped up?"

"Won't get stopped up *or* get a fever."

All this time, the child looked from one to the other of the women, looked not with the typical curiosity one would expect, but with a calm, reassured expression, as if he knew, despite their fussing with each other, knew in some strange, nonverbal way that those strange women had been right. Everything was going to be okay.

What he didn't know—couldn't know, at his tender age—was that his vision of the skirt would fade away so quickly, and that he would not consciously think of it again. But he also didn't know that deep in his heart, where he couldn't see it or even know it was there—or that it wasn't—*something* was gone, and that nothing would ever be the same again.

Chapter Three

Fiona carried him into the kitchen, where the simmering grits perfumed the air with the aroma of corn and milk, and where Glory was humming "Victory in Jesus," the hymn she always seemed to be humming. Fiona left him standing by one of the kitchen chairs while she went into another room and returned, carrying two large encyclopedias. These, she placed in the chair and spread a clean kitchen towel over them. Having thus made a high chair, she lifted the boy and sat him on the books, pulling the chair up snug against the table.

"You better stir some cold milk into those grits," she directed Glory. "Else they'll be too hot, and he'll burn himself."

"I know, I know!" Glory said, and then she went back to humming as she stirred milk into the bowl of grits. The enticing aroma became too much for the boy, who suddenly rapped his hands against the table top and whined, the corners of his pink mouth turned downward at such an exaggeration, Fiona almost laughed. But a hungry child was certainly no laughing matter, she sternly reminded herself.

"Hurry up!" Fiona said in an urgent tone. "This little thing's probably starved half to death."

"Reckon does he know how to use a spoon? Or should we do it for him?" Glory asked as she placed the bowl of cooled grits in front of the child. But before either woman could figure out whether to let him feed himself or to do it for him, he grabbed the bowl, tilted it up against his mouth, and started sucking the grits right out of the bowl. The two women watched him in amazement, but he paid no attention to them, other than to glance at them briefly over the rim of the bowl.

"Well, I guess he don't need no spoon," Glory said at last. Then she laughed. "Him eatin' just like a little pig!" And, in fact, she was right, as the child's grunts of pleasure filled the kitchen, and when the bowl was empty, he licked all around the inside of it and then set it carefully on the table. Butter from the grits shone on either cheek, and a solid line of stray grits rimmed the edge of his newly shampooed hair.

"Here—give him these," Glory said, putting a plate piled high with fluffy, golden scrambled eggs on the table in front of him.

"We shouldn't give him too much, right at first," Fiona said.

"Well, you're the one said we had to feed him," Glory argued back. "Besides, I don't expect he'll eat more than is good for him."

The boy stared at the eggs, then leaned forward and sniffed the plate suspiciously.

"Lord have mercy!" Glory whispered. "Reckon he don't even know what that is?" And she was right—but the boy picked up some of the eggs carefully, between his thumb and forefinger and lifted it to his lips. He stuck out his tongue and tasted the eggs, then he popped them into his mouth.

"M-m-m!" he murmured, and Fiona and Glory looked at each other and smiled.

A single, loud *THUMP!* sounded at the back door, and the smiles disappeared from Fiona's and Glory's faces.

"It's Old Man!" Glory exclaimed. "He was supposed to come by and mow the grass. I forgot all about that—and that grass is way too wet anyway, after the storm. And what're we gonna tell him about . . ." She fumbled, not knowing what name to call the child. "What'll we tell him about this child?" the last two words, she whispered, as if afraid to speak them aloud. "Maybe we ought to put him in the bedroom for now?"

"No," Fiona said. "We don't have to tell Old Man anything at all, and besides which, we haven't done a single thing wrong. You just remember that. This child's mama just up and left him right in our yard. We didn't have a thing to do with that. It's not like we kidnapped him or anything. And you're right—that grass is way too wet to cut, so what's Old Man doing here?"

While the women had been talking and speculating about the child who was now sitting at their table, wearing smears of congealed grits in his hair and the remnants of scrambled eggs on both cheeks, he had been looking from one to the other of them with mild curiosity—perhaps as if he had never heard human voices before.

"We shouldn't talk about his mama like that—not right in front of him," Glory said, and Fiona nodded her head, looking anxiously at the boy, to see if he understood anything of what they had been saying. His breakfasted face showed nothing, and Fiona wondered if perhaps he didn't really understand that he had been left.

When Glory opened the door—and the child saw Old Man standing there—the boy came as close as he had ever come to actually smiling. His eyes sparkled in some kind of silent amusement, and while he would not have had words for what he saw, he knew that this was the face he had seen looking out of the palmetto bushes in the dark—the same kind eyes, the same soft mouth. But the dark head was now devoid of the white egret feather.

Fiona noticed the familiar way the child and Old Man gazed at each other. "You know this little boy?" she asked Old Man. "You know who his mama is?" But Old Man simply stared at the boy, his dark eyes warm and yet wary, as his Seminole eyes always seemed to look.

"You know him?" Fiona repeated, speaking louder, as if Old Man were hard of hearing. But just as Old Man shook his head slowly, *no*, the phone in the hallway rang.

"That's probably Doc," Fiona said, and she hurried into the hall to answer. "Maybe he's found out something about . . . the mother." These last words, she whispered, glancing anxiously at the boy, who was still gazing raptly at Old Man. While Fiona went into the hallway, Old Man and the child continued to stare at each other, and Glory stood, transfixed, watching them.

"You know this child?" Glory asked, repeating Fiona's question.

Old Man's eyes then shifted to her, and he paused for a long moment before he shook his head. *No.* But Glory was almost positive that she saw the smallest smile on Old Man's lips just before he shook his head.

"Well, we just don't know what to make of it." Fiona's voice carried down the hallway. "It's a boy, and he's fine. Eating well, and we've gotten him cleaned up." Another long pause. Then, "Okay. Thank you. We'll expect you then."

Fiona came back into the kitchen, where Glory was looking at Old Man, and Old Man was still gazing at the boy.

"I don't really know why you're here this morning," Fiona said to Old Man. "That grass is so wet, you'll kill yourself trying to push that mower through it." As always, Old Man said nothing. "Well, if you're so determined, just go ahead and try cutting it." And then, seeing the slight glint of concern in the dark eyes that turned from the boy and looked at her, she added, "We'll take good care of him."

As Old Man went out to find the lawn mower in the shed, Fiona and Glory looked at each other.

"He knows *something*," Glory whispered. "He ain't saying nothing, but he surely knows something."

Fiona wiped off the boy's face with a dampened kitchen towel and lifted him down from the chair.

"So what'll we do with him now?" Glory asked, and it was certainly a valid question, because neither of the two women had any real experience with children, particularly one this young. In fact, both Glory and Fiona were childless, something that had caused much quiet grief to Fiona when she and J. Roy were younger.

For years, she had watched hopefully for signs of a pregnancy every single month. But without fail, she was disappointed, and finally, bitterness filled her to the brim. Privately, she railed against her own body. What was wrong with her? Wasn't she a woman? She had breasts and a womb, and she also had a compelling, almost overpowering hunger for a child, but no child came—not a single one. Not even a hint of one, not even a pregnancy that failed before fruition. Nothing. For years, she privately endured great, soul-tearing sobs of frustration, always deep into her pillow and always when J. Roy was gone. And never once did she say anything to him about her private grief.

Silently, desperately, she actively—and shamelessly—encouraged the activity that might have produced a baby. She made three hand-sewn nightgowns of the most delicate batiste, with the neckline cut lower than the pattern called for and edged in the finest lace, and the whole time she stitched them by hand, she hummed to herself and imagined J. Roy lifting the gown gently over her head and cradling her in his warm arms—she moaned appropriately, but in her heart, she was screaming silently, *A baby! A baby! Please, God, a baby!* She also sent away for perfumed body powder that was more expensive than anything she had ever used before—sent away for it because she was too embarrassed to go into the local drugstore or department store and buy it herself, and every night, she powdered her freshly bathed body generously underneath the batiste gowns and prayed, *Let your fragrance help me make a baby!* She would spray sweet cologne on the bed sheets and light candles on the dresser, and all the while, J. Roy snored peacefully in his chair, with the evening news murmuring on the radio.

Then she would lean over his chair, letting the neckline of the gown fall open and kiss his soft mouth to awaken him to the fragrance of scented soap and expensive powder, rub her clean, soft face against his whiskers, and lead him, groggy but happy, into the bedroom. But still—no baby.

She sent away for three bottles of Lydia E. Pinkham's Vegetable Compound, because she had heard somewhere that there was "a baby in every bottle," and she downed it hopefully. The bitter herb drink left her slightly more relaxed, but still not pregnant. For Fiona, there was no baby, not even in a bottle of Miss Pinkham's famous formula.

Finally, Fiona's hunger for a child actually bypassed the means of becoming pregnant and moved ahead into predicting the gender of the nonexistent baby, the baby she would surely have, one of these days. For several months, she slept on her right side and with a pink ribbon under her pillow, which was supposed to produce a girl baby. Then for several more months, she slept on her left side with a red ribbon under her pillow, supposed to produce a boy baby.

But still, no baby came.

For whatever reason, J. Roy seemed not to notice any of this flurry, even though he happily enjoyed the fruits of Fiona's efforts. He simply smiled more than was usual and went right on with his quiet life, leaving every morning to go to work at the docks and coming home late every evening to shower the dirt and grease from his body and then to collapse, exhausted, into a chair in the living room. On a nearby table, a radio spun out the news, and he said he was listening, but any time Fiona looked into the living room, J. Roy was asleep in the chair. And there he would stay, until she had bathed and powdered herself, dutifully swallowed her dose of Miss Pinkham's Compound, and gently awakened him and led him into the bedroom.

Years passed in this manner, and as she and J. Roy grew older, the pain of her barrenness began to diminish, as if her agony of *wanting* had been so strong and so terrible, it could not be sustained. Strangely enough, there was some form of strange comfort in the giving up, and she was happier than she had been in years.

Life settled into something closely resembling contentment. J. Roy went to work on the docks, Fiona made curtains for their kitchen, baked bread, and braided rugs for their living room and bedroom. Sometimes, she braided rugs for which she had no floor space, and in those cases, she simply placed one rug on top of the other. And that is the way her life was passing—with rug upon rug upon rug.

The only break in Fiona and J. Roy's routine came once a year, when they spent a week at a fishing camp in central Florida, where J. Roy indulged himself in his favorite activity. From before dawn until after dark, he was out on the lake in a rented boat, fishing. During those times, Fiona walked along the lakeshore, sat quietly reading in the shade of a live oak, and on occasion, she briefly wondered how on earth her life had turned out the way it had. She certainly wasn't unhappy, but she surmised that life was supposed to move forward in a fluid way, and her life seemed to have gotten stuck in some sort of an emotional backwater. She could never find a way out, and on occasion, she wondered just how many braided rugs she could make in a lifetime and how high they would pile themselves over the years. And who would get them when she was gone.

But suddenly, everything changed. Fiona and J. Roy went on their usual summer week at the fishing camp one summer and learned, to their surprise, that the owner was putting it up for sale. Even though she and J. Roy said not a word aloud to each other, the one meaningful glance between them confirmed that they both wanted the same thing—this small piece of tropical paradise. Fiona thought that perhaps her enthusiasm for the venture arose simply because it was something different—just that simple. Here was a direction. Here was work she could do. Here was a new start, something into which she could pour all of the pent-up energy of her failed expectations.

Once she and J. Roy paid out every single cent of savings they possessed for a down payment and moved to the small cottage at the camp, J. Roy seemed to sense Fiona's enthusiasm and endless energy, so soon after they had moved, he started spending his days out on the lake, leaving the success or failure of the camp to her and her alone. She shouldered the responsibilities willingly, remembering all of the years J. Roy had left home long before dawn to work all day on the docks while she sat at home, braiding rugs she didn't really want or need.

And so, for almost fifteen years, Fiona had run the fishing camp on Love-Oak Lake, and almost from the beginning, she had a miracle— Glory—to help her. In fact, only a week or so after she and J. Roy had moved into the main house of the camp, Glory came walking down the sandy road and knocked on the back screened door.

"Mr. Greever down to the store said you all could probably use some help, so here I am," Glory announced, and because J. Roy was off fishing, Fiona was left alone with the decision of whether or not to hire that thin, unsmiling young woman. But before she could even think, she was arrested by Glory's pronunciation of the word "store," which simply came out as "sto." And "help," which came out simply as "hep." But Glory certainly didn't see anything unusual about her pronunciations, of course.

"The *what?* And *do* what?" Fiona had asked, not familiar with a Mr. Greever and also not too certain about what a *sto* really was. Or *hep*, for that matter.

"The sto! The sto!" Glory had insisted. Finally, she snorted in disgust and yelled, "Where you'uns go to buy yore bread!" Then, for some strange reason, Fiona began to giggle, trying to hide her laughter so as not to hurt this strange woman's feelings, and Glory stared at her struggle and hesitantly placed one foot behind her, so as to be ready to run at a moment's notice. Her eyebrows drew themselves down, and for a brief, frightened moment, Glory hoped beyond hope that she looked ferocious enough to scare this crazy white woman. But the more Glory frowned and shook her head both in fear and confusion, the harder Fiona had to try to suppress her giggles, and at last, she failed completely. Giving off a raucous snort that made Glory jump, she simply released the heavily suppressed laugh, and it felt wonderful to her.

Glory stepped backwards, her eyebrows shot up in surprise, and she stared at Fiona with the whites of her eyes showing, until, at last, she chuckled and snarled at the same time. "I done heard me all kind of stories about you crazy white people," Glory sputtered, "But I ain't never heard nobody laugh so hard! Are *you* crazy, Miss Fiona?"

And that honest question had been the very beginning of an on-going duet of laughter and sharing of hard work and deep companionship that Fiona was more grateful for every day of her life.

Back then, when Glory and Fiona had been working together only a few weeks, Glory came up with the idea of a Fish House Restaurant on the end of the pier. "Mr. J. Roy ain't gonna do nothing 'round here but fish," she had pronounced. And there was no judgment at all in her words. To Glory's mind, she was simply stating an all-too-obvious fact. "You know that, and I know that. So us might as well make use of all them fish he catches."

Fiona listened carefully to Glory, because even that long ago, she had learned that Glory's mind was really the most magnificent and practical thing about her. And making good use of the fish J. Roy proudly brought home was something that appealed to Fiona in another way. Rather than thinking that J. Roy wasn't doing much to help around the camp, Fiona preferred to think that he was having some kind of a reward—for all those long-before-daylight hours he had spent on the docks, dragging heavy anchor chains and with his aching feet squishing in wet boots. J. Roy would be pleased about providing fish for a restaurant. He could go fishing every single morning and have the satisfaction of knowing that he was helping out in a most important way.

So Fiona listened to Glory's suggestion, and soon she arranged to have a small restaurant built at the land end of the pier, mostly of uneven—inexpensive—boards, outfitted it with a monstrosity of an iron stove they bought from an elderly lady in town, and brought in three small wooden tables and chairs to go with them, to go on the dock outside of the kitchen door. Glory took over the restaurant from the day it opened, and almost immediately, her good fried fish, French-fried potatoes, homemade coleslaw and sun-steeped sweet tea brought so many customers every weekday noontime that people were lined up along the shoreline approaching the old dock, waiting for openings at the tables. Some of the people, too impatient or too hungry to wait for a table, received their fish and French fries steaming hot and piled high on paper plates at the back door, handed out in sullen obedience by Jubilee, Glory's eight-year-old niece from down the road.

Some years later, J. Roy passed away. Simply had a heart attack when he was all alone in his little boat out in the middle of the lake he loved so much, and no one knew what had happened until he failed to come home with his usual copious catch of large-mouthed bass. All night long, the police were out on the black lake, using lanterns to look for the boat and J. Roy, and when dawn came, they finally towed the boat to the dock, with J. Roy's body covered with a black tarpaulin. And Fiona, standing on the dock, with Glory holding on to her arm, could only look at the large catch of bass and think of how proud J. Roy would have been to bring them home to her.

Despite the tears she choked back, Fiona was glad that J. Roy had died doing what he loved the most—died facedown in a small boat filled with his catch. And not on some dark, smelly pier where the only thing anyone would think about was how they could make up for the strong back that was no longer able to carry anything.

After J. Roy died, Fiona asked Glory to move into the main house with her—right into J. Roy's own room at the back of the cottage. Fiona and J. Roy had opted to have separate rooms because of his snoring and her incessant wakefulness. Too, by that time, Fiona had given up any hopes of conceiving a child, and she had hand washed the batiste nightgowns, folded them carefully in tissue paper, and put them away in the bottom drawer of her dresser. It was a funeral, of sorts. But J. Roy, in his typical, easygoing fashion, had made no mention of their separate bedrooms, had simply accepted that Fiona needed her sleep, since she was working so hard to make the fishing camp a success.

So when J. Roy died, Fiona invited Glory to move right into J. Roy's room, after they had packed up his clothes and put them into the hall closet. Since Glory had been living with her sister for many years, she was delighted to have a room of her very own, away from Jubilee, who seemed to hit her "petulant teens" quite early—or, as Glory called it, her "pouting time."

"Lordy! I'll be *SO* much obliged to be away from that child's heaving sighs all the time and rolling her eyes at every single thing her mama and I say to her!" And Jubilee felt the same way about being away from Glory, who watched her like a hawk and criticized almost everything Jubilee put her hand to. Still, Jubilee came to the restaurant every weekday noontime, to hand out the "to go" plates.

To Fiona, Jubilee always seemed pleasant and well mannered, but with Glory, Jubilee reportedly resorted to her sighing and eye rolling. And Glory seldom gave her even a small smile. The minute Jubilee showed up at the restaurant, Glory simply loaded her down with work and then ignored her, except to criticize her efforts. Fiona sometimes felt sorry for Jubilee, and on occasion, she slipped a quarter to her, as a token payment for her hard work. But Fiona always had to hide that from Glory, who insisted that children should work and not be paid for it.

"Listen, she's got a roof over her head and food in her belly, and that's a gracious plenty!" Glory would proclaim from time to time, usually when she suspected that Fiona was slipping some small change to the girl.

Regardless of their quiet disagreement about Jubilee, they lived and worked well together. Glory did all of the cooking and ran the restaurant, and Fiona made reservations for the ten small cabins that stood in a semicircle around the southern end of the lake, and kept the cabins and the grounds spotlessly clean.

With the restaurant in mind, Fiona had quickly arranged for Mr. Owen to take over J. Roy's fishing duties. A retired hardware salesman, he lived in a small house at the far end of the lake—a house he had inherited from his mother. He agreed to provide the fresh fish for the restaurant—mostly Love-Oak Lake's acclaimed bass—just as J. Roy had done. A quiet, amiable man, Mr. Owen was delighted to be compensated well for fishing every day, and he also felt compelled to do as the Bible said and try to help provide for a widow. So, he happily and faithfully provided copious amounts of fish for Glory's deep-fat fryer.

With all the fish they could use provided, Fiona and Glory managed to bring in enough money to live comfortably, if not extravagantly, and business both in cabin rentals and in the restaurant picked up considerably, thanks to hard work and the events of the times. Because originally, most of the cabin rentals had been for retired businessmen from Montgomery and Atlanta and Jacksonville, but as automobiles became more popular, whole families started coming to the fishing camp, and Fiona added a few picnic tables under the live oak trees, and a small playground—just two rope swings hung from the sturdy limbs of the same trees. Then she made improvements to the concrete-block shower house, which made up for the tiny, toilet-and-basin bathrooms.

But now, while Fiona and Glory stood in quiet confusion about what to do with that little boy, and totally inexperienced as to how to care for him, he answered their unasked questions by putting his head down on the table and gazing up at them sleepily and with heavy eyelids.

"Reckon we ought to put him back to bed?" Fiona asked. "He didn't get much sleep." Glory added, "He's plumb wore out, is what he is," so Fiona gathered him up, and he slumped sleepily against her shoulder. For a long time afterward, Glory remembered the new look in Fiona's face at just that moment—the softening of eyes that were usually sharp and watchful, like the eyes of a hawk, but eyes that suddenly seemed deep and almost liquid in their blueness.

Fiona had no more than put the child back into her bed when the doorbell rang. "That'll be Doc," she said, but when she opened the door, she was surprised to see that Doc looked somewhat haggard and frazzled. But maybe that shouldn't have been much of a surprise at all, because everybody in town and around the countryside—wherever Doc's patients lived—knew about the Doc and his wife, Myra, having lost their infant daughter so recently. Word had it that right after the funeral, Myra had taken to her bed and hadn't been out of the house in the several weeks since that tragedy.

But Fiona would not hurt Doc by commenting on his appearance, other than to be silently concerned for him. Perhaps his disheveled appearance was the result of his worry over Myra and his grief over the loss of their only child. So she simply said, "You been out looking for the mama of this child I told you about?"

"Oh . . . no," he answered, seeming distracted. His salt-and-pepper hair was mussed, a state she had never seen it in before, and he had deep pouches under his eyes. "No," he repeated. "No."

"He's in here," Fiona said, leading Doc into the bedroom. The child was sound asleep, and Doc sat down on the edge of the bed and took a watch out of his pocket. After placing a gentle hand on the child's forehead, he lifted the limp wrist and looked at his watch, pulled back the sheet Fiona had put over the child, and examined the mosquito bites on his legs. Lifting the edge of the sheet-diaper, he examined the red, irritated-looking skin.

"He's got a good appetite," Fiona offered. Doc said nothing but then sighed and placed the sheet back over the sleeping boy.

"He's around a year and a half old, maybe closer to two. And you say the mother just walked away, once she showed you where he was asleep under the tree?"

"That's right." Fiona glanced at the doorway, where Glory stood, drying her hands on a dishtowel.

"Disappeared!" Glory pronounced. "Just disappeared like she'd never been!"

"It wasn't *that* dramatic, Glory," Fiona objected. "When I went out into the yard and found the child—and that was right after the storm let up—the mother must have just walked away. The yard light and the porch light don't shine that much around the other side of the house, so we didn't see her go. Neither one of us."

Doc sat back and once again studied the sleeping child. "Was she maybe about so high?" He indicated a height with his hand. "Maybe blonde hair?"

Fiona and Glory looked at each other blankly.

"We didn't see her," Fiona repeated. "You think you may know who she is?"

"No, not really," Doc said, but once again, Fiona and Glory glanced at each other, and Fiona was frowning slightly.

"If you do, I wish you'd tell us," Fiona said. But Doc got up off of the bed and slipped his watch back into his pocket.

"Not really," he repeated.

"We washed him," Glory added, unnecessarily, as if she wanted to get the conversation and the questions turned in another direction. "He was in the awfulest mess you ever saw—so dirty and stinking!"

At that, Fiona shot a glance at Glory, because Fiona didn't like the word "stink" in any form, and since Glory knew this, she glared back at Fiona, as if daring her to say anything unpleasant in front of the doctor. "So what I want to know is this," Glory went on. "How come that mama to decide *us* was the ones to leave this baby with?"

But no one could answer her question.

So the doctor studied the child for a long, silent moment, with Glory still going on about the disappearance of the woman, and the more Glory talked, the more fantastic her story became, until she had it down that the woman they thought they saw may have been a *haint*—a dead mother who came back as a spirit to see that her child was being cared for.

Fiona only halfway listened, because she was well accustomed to Glory's fantasizing and spiritualizing almost anything she was talking about. But Fiona was also watching Doc—noticing the slight tremor in the hand that held the watch and wondering about the dew-stained cuffs of his trousers. Wondering too, if he knew something about the child's mother, and if so, why he didn't say anything. Maybe he wasn't sure and didn't want to suggest something that might not be true. But he still looked worried. "You all right, Doc?" she asked, above and over Glory's mournful recounting of the fantastic haint-mother story.

"Oh . . . yes." Doc seemed to come back from a deep daydream. "Well, I guess we'll just have to wait and see if she comes back for him." But Fiona heard something in his voice that she had never heard before—what was it? A tone of remorse? And why?

"Ain't coming back!" Glory pronounced, interrupting Fiona's thoughts and clearly caught up in her own fantasy story. "Her's a *haint,* and she ain't coming back!"

Doc ignored Glory's thready voice and stood up. "Will you let him stay here?" he asked, and somehow, his question surprised Fiona. "If not, about the only thing I can do is take him to the authorities for you. They'll find some kind of child welfare agency to take care of him. I think there's one in Gainesville."

Fiona tried to say something about that, but she found that her mouth just wouldn't work. All she could think about was Doc carrying the sleeping child away, could clearly see his soft, pink arm dangling over the Doc's shoulder and the sweet, blonde head resting against Doc's neck. *Some kind of child welfare agency to take care of him. I think there's one in Gainesville.* Doc's words echoed ominously in her ears.

Doc added, "But it will have to be right now, I'm afraid. Myra and I are going up to Jacksonville to visit her sister, and we're leaving in a couple of hours."

At that moment, something completely new arose in Fiona's breast—something so strange and fierce and protective that she not only found that her mouth was working again, but her response came out almost as a bark. "Of course he can stay here! This is where his mama wanted him to be—Heaven only knows why, but she brought him to us."

"Haint!" Glory whispered from the doorway.

"Well, that's fine then," Doc said, eyeing Fiona in a somewhat surprised manner. "He seems to be healthy, but if you have to take him to a doctor while Myra and I are gone, you'll have to go to Dr. Martin over in Brooksville. But as I say, I think he's just fine. Good appetite, sleeping well . . ." He smiled at the child, who had slept all the way through the brief examination and the conversations. "I see you've put some lotion on those mosquito bites, but I'll write down the name of an ointment you can get at the drugstore for that rash in his diaper area. And if you remember anything else about the mother, you let me know next week, when Myra and I get back."

"Thank you," Fiona said. "I hope you and Myra have a safe trip. It will do her good to see some of her family again."

Glory made no further mention of a haint, but when she glanced at Fiona, she had a look of a horrified apology in her eyes. After Fiona closed the front door behind the doctor, Glory whispered, "Oh, I'm so sorry! I never thought a single thing about the Doc and Miss Myra losing that little baby girl."

"I know you didn't, Glory," Fiona comforted her. "And I'm sure he didn't think a thing of it."

"I shouldn't have gone and said nothing about *haints,* not in front of the Doc."

"Well, I'm just glad Myra feels like taking a trip at all. Far as I know, she hasn't left the house since they lost that baby. A trip will do her good."

But Glory was shaking her head, and Fiona thought that she was still admonishing herself over her careless words about *haints*. But that wasn't the case. "He seem kind of *funny* to you?" Glory asked.

"Yes, a little bit," Fiona admitted. "But he and Myra have been through a lot, and he probably is still pretty worried about her."

"Mebbe so, and mebbe he suspects something about the . . . mother. Else, why would he ask those questions, especially after we said we didn't really see her."

"I don't know, Glory." At that moment, Fiona felt both exhausted and exhilarated, and she shook her head as if she were trying to clear it. "Well, we have things to do, so why don't you stay here with . . . *him* . . . and I'll go into town to the drugstore and get what we need?"

"Get some of them rubber pants," Glory reminded her, and Glory, as well, shook her head, as if to clear it of anything confusing or unpleasant. "I'm still so sorry about talking about *haints*."

"Nothing we can do about it now," Fiona replied. "And truthfully, I don't think Doc noticed. Seemed like he had other things on his mind."

"Well, it looks like we're gonna have this little boy with us—don't know how long, but we're sure gonna have him with us a little while, anyway. Sure do wish we knew his name," Glory mused.

"We'll *give* him a name," Fiona exclaimed, and her face brightened immediately, as if giving the boy a name was the most surprising thing she had ever thought of. She bit her lip for a moment. "We'll call him Victor—for that hymn you're always humming, 'Victory in Jesus.'"

"Victor!" Glory said, tasting his name. "It's sure enough a pretty name. Strong too. And after my favorite hymn. Can't be nothing wrong with that. Sure can't be." Fiona nodded, but the one phrase that stayed with her, playing over and over in her mind, was *If the mother comes back for him.* And maybe Doc did know more than he was saying. Else, why would he suggest the height of the mother and possibly the color of her hair? It just didn't make any sense, but she decided not to try to discuss it with Glory anytime soon. At least not until Glory got over all her talk about *haints.*

"Victor!" Glory said the name softly and smiled at Fiona. "I surely do like that. Now I'll go make us a list for you to take to town." Glory went into the kitchen, still muttering the new name under her breath and chuckling.

Moving almost in a businesslike manner, Fiona put on one of her Sunday dresses and pressed her black hat down over her corkscrew curls. She moved around quietly, so as not to awaken the sleeping boy. *Victor!* She would have to get used to having a name to call him. And she truly liked the name. It was bright and beautiful, the kind of name you might shout joyously when the sun came up over the far edge of the lake, lifting upwards into a faint wash of gold and pink clouds.

At such a thought, Fiona went to the bed and studied Victor at leisure—his soft, blonde curls, full pink cheeks, the lazy sweep of blonde eyelashes against his skin. And she breathed deeply of him, intoxicated with the perfume of soap, of cleanliness and contentment that arose from his body. He was clean, he was beautiful, and he was sleeping peacefully— and all because of what she and Glory had been able to do for him.

At the last, she peeked under the edge of the diaper—still dry, still clean thank goodness, but she had better get on along to the drugstore and buy some things he would need. Torn sheets and old shirts would do only for so long.

In the kitchen, Glory sat at the table with a piece of notebook paper in front of her and the lead tip of a pencil in her mouth as she concentrated.

"You about got that list ready?" Fiona asked.

"'Bout so, but I sure don't know what all we're gonna need, 'cept diapers and some kind of shirts. And them rubber pants, of course." Fiona took the list. "Now if he wakes up, just rock him or something, until I get back."

"Should I try to take him to the potty?" Glory asked, her brow furrowed in concern.

"You could try it, but be careful you don't scare him about it. He might not even know what an indoor bathroom is, so don't just plop him on the potty, and for Heaven's sake, don't flush it, whatever you do!"

"Don't you be gone too long," Glory reminded her. "Makes me sort of nervous, not knowing when he's going to wake up, or if he knows anything about using a potty, or maybe he'll start crying for his mama." The last word, she spoke almost in a whisper, so that the sleeping boy wouldn't hear her. "And I won't know what to do!"

"I'll come back as fast as I can," Fiona assured her.

So, list in hand, Fiona started out of the house, thinking that she was really glad that, presently, there were no visitors staying in any of the cabins and that the restaurant was always closed on Mondays. So neither Fiona nor Glory had to worry about keeping up the business while they got accustomed to their new roles as . . . what? Not parents. Not even grandparents. Just two womenfolks who were going to take good care of a little boy who had nobody else to do that for him.

"Don't be gone too long," Glory called once again, and that's how Fiona knew for sure that Glory really was nervous about being left alone with the little stranger-child. *Victor.*

The small town of Love-Oak, Florida and the lake itself got their names because some anonymous person—probably way back in the early 1800s—couldn't spell.

Because when the earliest white settlers moved into the area and found the beautiful, pristine lake in which "those renegade Seminoles" had fished for years, they decided to call it Live-Oak, after the huge forest of moss-draped trees surrounding it on all sides. But when that name was finally written down, the nameless recorder of information wrote "Love-Oak" instead, and that became the name of the small settlement that sprang up around the lake's southern border, as well as the name of the lake itself.

The settlement prospered, and word went out into the surrounding communities about the good fishing in Love-Oak Lake. So before long, people came long distances in wagons and buggies, bringing canvas tents in which they slept while they spent days fishing. Those were people who lived too far away to make the trip to the lake and back in only one day.

And Bernard Smith, who, at that time, owned all the property around the lake, as well as the lake itself, saw a possibility for cashing in on such a great fishing spot. Originally, he tried charging a fee for people to fish there, but the lake was too large, and he could not walk all the way around it every single day, collecting a pittance from the few fishermen who didn't manage to hide in the brush when they saw him coming.

So Bernard Smith built ten small, one-room cabins around the lake, and he rented them out to people who wanted to stay overnight.

The cabins were certainly nothing luxurious, lacking any indoor plumbing at all, and just large enough to hold a double bed, a tiny drop-leaf table and a small ice box. The icehouse in town delivered fresh ice for the boxes every other day, which the guests filled with bologna, bread and soft drinks they bought at the grocery store in town. The only running water was provided by a hand pump located between cabin numbers Five and Six, and each cabin was supplied with a china pitcher and large bowl for bathing.

Eventually, Smith built a shower-room out of concrete blocks, and at the end of a long, hot day of fishing, the fishermen lined up for the shower, carrying their own bars of soap and towels over their arms. A few years later, Smith added small half-bath bathrooms onto the backs of three cabins, putting flush toilets and washbasins with running water into small, closet-like extensions on the backs of the cabins. Those particular cabins became so popular, he upped the amount he charged for the "luxury" cabins and eventually built tiny half baths at the back of every cabin. The common shower-room remained the same, and when wives started accompanying the fishermen, he designated a two-hour block of time in midmornings for "Ladies Only."

For himself, Smith built a cottage, right at the end of the line of smaller cabins, so he could keep an eye on everything that went on. The cottage had a small living room, a large kitchen, two bedrooms and one full bathroom. But the best features of the cottage were the wide front porch and the smaller, screened-in back porch. This was the house and the entire fishing camp that Fiona and J. Roy had bought when Smith's grandson inherited the camp and finally decided that he didn't want to run it himself. He had hired people on two separate occasions to manage it for him, but in the end, he was happy to sell it to Fiona and J. Roy.

On that morning years later, Fiona walked along the road that led to the small town of Love-Oak, only a sandy trail that ran between large sweeps of palmetto bushes, scrub pines and an occasional live oak tree, the one for which both the town and the lake were supposed to have been named. As she walked, Fiona could hear the faint scurrying away of creatures in the bushes—blue-tailed skinks and chameleons, and perhaps a land crab or two, but the noises didn't bother her. Instead, she was thinking about going into the drugstore, like she had done so many times before—she was a woman everybody in town already knew—but this time she would be buying things that were really outlandish for the needs of two women, living alone—diapers and child-sized shirts. What was she to tell people?

If the mother comes back. The same words echoed over and over in her mind.

Well, she certainly wasn't going to tell people that some strange woman she had never seen before in her life had simply deposited her child in the back yard and disappeared. That would never do, because what if the mother didn't come back, ever? Why, that little boy would grow up being known as someone whose very own mama simply walked away and left him with perfect strangers. No! So . . . what to say? And what had Doc already said, and to whom?

By the time Fiona walked past the small, beach-style houses at the edge of town, a story was formulating itself in her mind. Suppose she told people that Victor was her great-nephew? Fiona certainly had an older sister who had lived in Gainesville until she passed away a few years before, and that sister did have a daughter, one Fiona had never actually met. The daughter now lived somewhere out west—Colorado maybe? Wyoming? Fiona couldn't remember, even though she had sent a sympathy card to the daughter when her mother died. But Fiona had never been close to her sister—eleven years separated them, and by the time Fiona was only around six or seven years old, the sister had married and moved away.

Well, suppose she did tell a story about Victor being her great-nephew? That would do, wouldn't it? But what if the boy's mother came back? Fiona shuddered at the thought and surprised herself by whispering, "Please, God! No!" to the sandy road and the stunted palmetto fronds and the high, wispy clouds. Because now that she and Glory had gotten him scrubbed clean and had fed him, and Fiona had held him in her own arms, she couldn't bear the thoughts of that woman taking him back and letting him get into such terrible shape again. Take him back and not love him? The very thought almost broke Fiona's heart.

So as she walked, her footsteps became more like marching and less like strolling, and her jaw jutted out a considerable distance, so that by the time she reached the makeshift sidewalk at the edge of town, she had made a firm decision—no matter what, she and Glory were going to keep that little boy. That Victor. No matter what! So as soon as Doc and Myra came back from Jacksonville, she would ask him not to tell anyone about how the child had come to stay with them. She would tell him that Victor was her own great-nephew, and that she simply hadn't recognized her niece in the dim early morning light. That's what she would say, and that would be the end of it.

When she opened the door to the drugstore and the small bell above the door rang out—sounding almost joyful, as it always did—Fiona saw that Mrs. Owen was behind the counter—the very Mrs. Owen whose husband provided fish for Glory to fry. Fiona's steps hesitated, because, like everybody else, she knew that Mrs. Owen was one of the nosiest women who had ever lived. Always asking questions she should have been embarrassed to ask but didn't have enough sense to realize that she was overstepping her job—which was to wait on people and ring up their purchases. She took her work far beyond that and, for example, if someone bought skin ointment, Mrs. Owen always wanted to know exactly what kind of itch they had and—worse—exactly *where* the itch was located! So that when any of the ladies in town had a need for truly personal items, they always peeked in the window, watching for a time when Doc Adams, the pharmacist, would be behind the counter, and not the nosey Mrs. Owen.

"Why, Fiona! How on earth are you, darlin'?" Mrs. Owen's happy voice rang out just as soon as Fiona entered the store. "I haven't seen you or Glory in the longest kind of time. You all doing all right?"

"We're just fine, Roberta," Fiona replied, keeping her face in a careful and neutral state but offering the smallest smile, for courtesy. Fiona took a deep breath and continued, "We've got my niece's little boy staying with us . . . for a while, and I need some of this ointment for his diaper rash. Doc wrote it down for me."

She handed over the paper, and Roberta Owen studied it carefully, her lips pursed in mock concentration.

"Your niece's boy, huh?"

"That's right," Fiona replied, again being careful to keep her voice level and steady.

"He gonna be with you long?" Roberta asked, her eyes glittering in anticipation of being able to repeat Fiona's news to anyone who would listen.

"We don't know, right now."

"How come he's with you all?" Roberta came right out and asked, all the while reaching up on a shelf behind her for a tube of ointment. Fiona hesitated. She hadn't thought of anyone asking that question specifically, but in only an instant, Roberta herself gave her the answer.

"His mama sick or something?"

"Yes, that's it," Fiona breathed. "She's right sick, and Glory and I said we'd take care of him until she's better."

"What's wrong with her?" Roberta asked, wrapping the tube of ointment in a piece of white paper and tying it with string.

"Uh . . . woman trouble," Fiona said in a whisper, and then she set her lips tight, as a signal that she wouldn't be more specific. Mrs. Owen's eyebrows went up, but even as nosey as she always was, she certainly wouldn't press on such a topic. Such details would have been too much—even for Mrs. Owen.

"And where does she live?" Roberta asked, cutting the string with such rapt attention that it seemed she wasn't paying a bit of attention to anything Fiona had to say. But Fiona knew better.

"Up near Gainesville," Fiona lied.

"That's a right long way away," Roberta commented, handing over the packet to Fiona.

"Yes, I know," Fiona said, taking the ointment and turning to leave. "Just put this on our bill, please."

"I hope your niece gets better soon," Roberta said as Fiona went out, accompanied by the delighted ring of the bell. "Awful big job, taking care of a baby," she called to Fiona's back.

Once Fiona was outside on the sidewalk, she walked purposefully toward the mercantile store, although with all her heart, she wanted to stop outside of the drugstore and catch her breath. But Roberta would be watching, so she walked resolutely ahead.

At the mercantile, she repeated the story to Alma Anderson, the clerk, someone who was also a member of Fiona's Bible class at First Baptist, and Alma clucked her tongue appropriately about Fiona's niece's illness, while wrapping up a parcel of two dozen diapers and three soft cotton shirts that looked to be about the right size.

"We'll have to put her on our prayer list," Alma commented.

"Who?" Fiona asked before she could catch herself.

"Why, your niece, of course," Alma smiled. "We'll pray for her speedy recovery."

By the time Fiona started home with her parcels, she had almost come to believe the story of her great-nephew as the absolute truth. She would have to be sure to tell Glory about it just as soon as she got in the door. And then she began to wonder if perhaps, in her absence, Victor's mother had come back for him, had felt so horrible about deserting him and leaving him in the hands of absolute strangers that she had run all the way back, sobbing and crying, "My baby!"

Fiona quickened her steps and moved with a greater resolve, her heart thudding dully in her throat and her imagination providing the vision of a hand-to-hand fight between herself and the unfortunate mother of the boy. As she envisioned this struggle, she felt a surge of the most terrible anger she had ever felt in her life. *NO! I won't let her take him! She deserted him, and she can't have him back! He's mine!*

As her quickened steps carried her along the sandy road, the edge of the house came into view. She could see the bright water of the lake, feel the freshening breeze on her face. *Is he still there? Oh, God! Please let him still be there!*

Somehow, her mind raced forward to the house, to the bedroom, to her own bed, where she would—*Please, God!*—find him sleeping peacefully. But at the same time, her mind also raced backwards to her own childhood, when she grew up in another little town not too far from Love-Oak.

On a day long ago, she had been skipping down a sandy trail she'd played up and down a thousand times before, but this time, she came face-to-face with a Florida panther. She knew what it was immediately, because she'd heard the tales—mostly from the few Seminole people living nearby—about the panther and its magical qualities. And truthfully, for a moment, she didn't know whether she was looking at something out of a dream-story she had heard or if she were looking at a real panther, something she had never seen before. She had gone absolutely blank at that point, breathing in only the stark aroma of her own fear. The panther, with two small cubs on the path behind her, stood stock still as well, and the panther and the girl stared at each other as if neither of them could believe what they were seeing. Then the panther lifted back her lips, showed her yellow fangs, and growled softly in her throat. Behind her, the cubs that had been cavorting with each other in complete unconcern suddenly stopped and stood, frozen, watching their mother and the child, as they faced each other. Instinctively, Fiona, even at that tender age, had known not to run, had known that any sudden movement would trigger the mother panther into an attack.

"I won't hurt your babies," Fiona whispered to the panther. "I promise, I won't hurt your babies."

The panther glanced behind her only once, to assure herself that the cubs were still there. For long moments, they all stood, gazing suspiciously at each other, and finally, the panther lifted her lips again in a halfhearted snarl, and then turned and seemed to disappear as quickly as a puff of smoke into the thick, low palmettos, the cubs tumbling clumsily behind her. Fiona didn't move a muscle until the slight rustling in the bushes ended. Then and only then did she begin shaking, and she turned and ran—back to the safety of her own house, her own yard, her own world.

And now, all those years later, Fiona was walking down a similar sandy road, but for the first time, she knew exactly how that mother panther had felt about her cubs. Because right in front of her, just beyond the window frame of the house ahead, the child . . . *her* child was sleeping or sitting at the table, and as she hurried forward, she felt that her lips had lifted into the smallest possible snarl a human mouth could manage.

She came across the yard, looking around to see if Old Man was still mowing the grass or trimming the bushes. The yard was neat and trim and all of the fallen palm fronds from last night's storm had been cleared away. But she saw no sign of Old Man—only the results of his work.

Glory met her at the back door, took the parcels out of Fiona's hands, and as if she had heard Fiona's question before it could be asked, she offered, "He's still asleep. You reckon he's okay?"

"I imagine so," Fiona replied, but her heart gave a strange lurch, and after Glory put the parcels on the kitchen table, they both went to the door and peeked into the bedroom, where Victor softly snored in a deep sleep, lulled by a full stomach, a clean body and sheer exhaustion.

"You get them rubber pants?" Glory whispered.

"Yes," Fiona answered, closing the door without a sound.

"Maybe we ought to try and put them on him now, while he's still sleeping. That, or else he may wet your bed."

"There are worse things than a wet bed," Fiona smiled. *Like a bed without J. Roy in it. A bed without this sweet baby in it. A bed for my old bones to rattle in all alone.*

They went back into the kitchen and opened the parcels. Glory took a diaper from the pile and shook it out.

"You know how to fold this right?" she asked Fiona.

Distracted, Fiona merely nodded, and Glory frowned. "You got to fold them different for a boy," Glory said. "Got to put the thickest part in . . . front."

Still, Fiona said nothing, and Glory studied her face carefully, but Fiona didn't seem to notice.

"You say you know how to fold a diaper right . . . for a boy?" she asked.

"M-m-m-m-huh," Fiona murmured.

"Well, how'd you learn how to do that?" Glory pressed.

"Did you pay Old Man for the yard?" she asked, instead of answering Glory's question.

"I did. Gave him his money and thought he would go on back home or at least to the Trading Post, but he didn't. Sat out there on the back steps for the longest kind of time. Made me uneasy, it did. 'Cause whether you like it or not, he knows something about that little boy. About Victor."

"You think so?"

"I *know* so," Glory insisted. "You'd see it too, if you'd only pay attention. What's the matter with you? Look like you're dreaming or something."

"You think Old Man knows something about our boy," Fiona repeated, just to let Glory know that she wasn't entirely caught up in dreaming.

"Yes—especially with him being down at the Trading Post his people set up beside the restaurant. He probably knows all kinds of things about every single person—Black, White, and Indian—in this whole town. Maybe in this whole county."

"Did you ask him about it?"

"Sure did," Glory bragged. "Went right out and sat down on the steps beside him, after he'd been sitting there for a long time. Asked him right out, but you know Old Man—he never said a word. Just looked at me with those black eyes. Gave me the heebie-jeebies, I tell you! And then he just got up off the steps and walked away. Didn't say a word."

Fiona listened silently. "That's pretty much the way he always is," she offered. And then she took a deep breath and turned to Glory. "Listen, I told folks in town that he . . . Victor . . . was my sister's grandbaby. My great-nephew."

Glory frowned and shook her head. "How come you to do such a thing?" Glory raised her voice, and Fiona shushed her and nodded her head toward the bedroom door.

"How come you to do such a thing?" Glory repeated in a rough whisper.

"Because I won't have him be known around here as a child whose very own mama ran off and left him with strangers."

"But that's exactly what did happen. And besides, you think he's gonna be here long enough for anybody to say anything about him?"

"Not *think*, Glory—*hope!*

"Something sure changed in you in that little bitty time it took you to walk to town and back," Glory announced.

"I guess so," Fiona admitted.

"That sure is one big job you're wanting to keep coming your way. And the thing I still don't understand is *why* that mama brought him to *us* in the first place. Far as I know, neither one of us ever saw her before in all our lives."

"I don't know. But she *did.* Came right to our door and knocked on it and then showed us where he was."

"Maybe Doc can find out something," Glory said. "Maybe he already did."

"I don't think he had time," Fiona said, hopefully. "He and Myra were leaving for her sister's in Jacksonville right away."

"I wonder did he take time to call the sheriff?" At that thought, they both stared at each other in silence. Finally, Fiona said, "But if everybody thinks it was my niece who left him here, there wouldn't be any need to get the sheriff involved."

"But Doc knows the woman was a stranger. We told him she was."

"Well, maybe she really *was* my niece, and I just didn't recognize her. Don't know how I could, because I've never seen her. Not even when she was a baby." Again, the two women were silent for a long while, and Glory said, "That what you're gonna tell Doc when he gets back?"

"Yes, it is." Fiona searched Glory's face, but she could see no expression that would tell her whether or not Glory thought it was a good idea.

"Maybe," Glory finally said, "Maybe after a while, you'll think that's the gospel truth." Fiona nodded, and Glory went on, looking deeply into Fiona's eyes, something she rarely did. "On the other hand, maybe it really was your niece brought him. That would certainly explain why she came right to our door. If that mama was a complete stranger, it just wouldn't make any sense for her to leave that little boy with us. Couldn't you call your sister and ask about it? Find out if the mama was your niece?"

"My sister passed away a few years ago," Fiona explained. "We hadn't seen each other in a long time. Talked on the phone long distance once in a while is all. And the daughter—Lord! I don't even remember her name. But come to think of it, I guess she was born about the time J. Roy and I bought this place."

"So she would be seventeen or eighteen years old now," Glory mused. "Old enough, anyway."

"Yes," Fiona agreed. "Old enough."

Chapter Four

Glory made a fresh pot of coffee, and she and Fiona sat at the kitchen
table, silently—each with her own thoughts. Glory was wondering what it
would feel like not to know Jubilee, her own niece, and the thought was
not entirely unpleasant. Fiona was thinking about Glory's
pronouncement—*Maybe after a while, you'll think that's the gospel truth.*

"Glory, how come you never married and had a family?" Fiona's
question came right out of the blue, and it startled and surprised her as
much as it did Glory.

"What you talking about?" Glory almost snarled. Because Glory
wasn't at all patient with questions that had nothing to do with whatever
she had been thinking about at the time.

"I said how come you never married and had you a family?" Fiona
repeated. "We've been together for all these years, and I never knew."

"Nothing for you to know," Glory muttered, bristling as she always
did whenever Fiona tried to ask personal questions that seemed to violate
the unspoken agreement they had about not prying into each other's
personal lives.

Fiona waited patiently, watching Glory sip her coffee and actually
chew it before she swallowed. "And why do you do that?" Fiona blurted.

"Do what?" Glory almost shouted, because her mind had been firmly
engaged in Fiona's previous question, and now another question right on
top of that was too much for Glory.

"Why on earth do you *chew* coffee?" Fiona repeated, watching even
then as Glory's jaws worked on another mouthful of coffee.

"I don't do that!" Glory fumed, suddenly angry, but not knowing
why.

"Yes, you do," Fiona insisted. "You've always done that."

"Then why haven't you said nothing about it before now, is what I
want to know!"

"I don't know," Fiona confessed. "I've always noticed it, but I never
came right out and asked you about it."

"So why're you asking now?" Glory asked, frowning.

"I don't know. Just felt like asking, I guess. And maybe it's because
of Victor," she added. "'Cause whatever *we* do, he's going to do, as well."

"And you don't want him chewing coffee, is that it?"

"I guess so," Fiona confessed. After that, a long silence sat between Glory and Fiona, and finally Glory said, "You think he's going to learn bad manners from me?" Glory's eyes held a look of accusation that surprised Fiona.

"Why, no," Fiona sputtered.

"Maybe you think I'm not good enough to help raise him. That is, if he stays here." Glory spoke the words as if they were a simple fact she had just discovered.

"Why, I don't think that at all," Fiona protested. "I don't know how you could believe such a thing! And he *is* going to stay. I'm sure of it."

"Sure sounded something like that to me," Glory whispered, somehow backing down in her own mind. "And I want him to stay, too, you know." And then, without missing a beat, she answered Fiona's prior question about chewing coffee, which was what had started the whole unfortunate conversation.

"It's 'cause of my mama."

"Your mama?"

"Yep—only coffee my mama knew how to make was camp coffee."

"What's that?"

"You know—where you just dump coffee grounds into a big pot of water and boil it. That's camp coffee."

"And doesn't it have grounds in it?"

"Sure it does. And that's why I got the habit of chewing my coffee."

"Oh," Fiona said, thinking that she had never heard of camp coffee in her life. And she immediately wondered what other things she knew nothing about—like trying to take care of a young child. That was one, for certain, and she wondered if Victor would grow up to be a man who chewed his coffee.

"And about your other question, same answer," Glory said, dragging Fiona's thoughts back to the kitchen table, the two of them sitting there, and the coffee cups in front of them.

"Same answer?" Fiona was having trouble following Glory's mind leap.

"Yep," Glory nodded. "You asked me why I never got married and had me some children, and it's the same answer. It's 'cause of my mama." Fiona waited, knowing that Glory would finish what she had to say, given enough time. "See, my mama had eight chirren, and I watched how her life went, and I promised myself I'd never have that."

"Never have a baby?" Fiona's thoughts flew back to the batiste nightgowns and the perfumed powder and the bottle after bottle of Lydia

E. Pinkham Vegetable Compound. "Never have a baby," she repeated, turning the question into a statement. "But didn't you ever fall in love?" Fiona asked, also remembering J. Roy's warm, gentle hands and delightfully stubbly cheek.

"Love?" Glory asked, as if she had never heard the word before in her life. "Love?" she repeated.

"Yes! Love!" Fiona felt frustrated, but she couldn't have explained why, even to herself.

"Wouldn't allow that," Glory muttered. "Just wouldn't allow that, no way, no how! Wouldn't allow it then, and wouldn't never allow it now!"

Glory spoke with such finality that Fiona merely stared at her.

"But how did you not . . . love?" Fiona asked, at last.

"Just wouldn't allow it, I done told you!"

"That's sad," Fiona said, looking down into her coffee cup.

"No, it's not," Glory fumed quietly. "It's not sad at all—it's smart, is what it is, 'cause loving somebody . . . anybody . . . means you can get hurt awful bad."

Silently, Victor had come to the doorway of the kitchen, and when they noticed him, they saw that he wore a distressed expression on his face and one hand tightly clutching the front of his sheet-diaper.

"He has to go potty!" Glory announced, and she and Fiona quietly rushed him into the bathroom, pulled down the diaper, and put him on the toilet.

"Quick!" Glory said. "Push . . . that down, else we'll all get soaked!"

Fiona was hesitant about touching the boy, but before she could decide what to do, he had pushed himself down so that the resulting stream went right into the toilet.

"Smart boy!" Fiona laughed. "Guess we'll have to take those diapers back to the mercantile and buy some pants for him." As she spoke, she studied Victor's face and Glory's as well. And she thought to herself, *And you think you're not going to love this little fellow?*

"Huuumph!" Glory snorted, as if she had heard Fiona's silent question.

They passed the rest of that first day with Victor in trial-and-error fashion, with Glory making rice pudding for him (which he liked) and oatmeal (which he didn't). All through the day, Victor said not a single word, which Fiona fretted about, speculating fearfully at one point that perhaps the boy was r-e-t-a-r-d-e-d, but Glory couldn't figure out what Fiona had spelled, so finally Fiona whispered it into Glory's ear so that Victor couldn't hear her.

"Retarded!" Glory yelped loudly, and Fiona scowled and waved her hands around in the air.

"Hush!" she whispered viciously.

"He's certainly not retarded!" Glory went on, speaking louder than ever. "Why, you just look in his eyes, and you'll see he understands every single word we say!"

"Oh, Lord!" Fiona winced, but Glory addressed Victor directly. "You know what we're saying?" But he said not a word. Simply held out his bowl for more rice pudding, and after he had eaten his fill, he pointed toward the bathroom.

"See?" Glory asked, gloating. "He's just as smart as a whip." And Fiona just smiled to herself. After Glory had helped Victor to the bathroom and back, he climbed back into the chair at the kitchen table and looked at Glory and Fiona expectantly.

"I got me some beans to gather," Glory said. "Need to have something to cook to go with that fish tomorrow." She looked at Victor. "You want to help me pick some beans?" She spoke loudly, as if perhaps Victor might be hard of hearing.

"If you take him out into the garden with you, I think I'll go have a little rest," Fiona said. "I'm about worn out, what with everything that's been going on. And, Glory," Fiona added. "You don't have to talk loud to him. I think you're right—he can understand everything we say."

"You go on and lie down," Glory said. "Me and Victor'll be just fine." Glory glared at Fiona for a moment and then she raised her voice. "Yep—we'll be just fine, won't we honey?"

Victor's clear blue eyes regarded her solemnly, and then he nodded his head, a movement so small, it was almost imperceptible.

"You're going to take him out in the back yard?" Fiona asked, frowning.

"I'm going to take him with me into the garden," Glory was still smiling at Victor.

"Don't you think that may bring back some kind of . . . memory?" Fiona stumbled to a halt.

"Maybe so," Glory admitted. "But we'll have to deal with that some time or other, so better let it be sooner." With that, Glory picked up her basket and held out her hand to Victor. "Come on, honey—let's go get some good beans we can have for supper."

Victor looked past Glory and her outstretched hand to the back porch door and, beyond that, to the yard where he had been left. *Like a little puppy nobody wanted,* Glory thought, as she studied his face.

"Come on, honey," Glory repeated. "It's okay. You just come on and go outside with Aunt Glory."

"*Aunt* Glory?" Fiona laughed. "And now you're going to be his aunt *too?*"

"If you can be that, so can I," Glory insisted. "Besides, he's too young to know I'm not the same color as him. And when he gets older, we'll make him understand."

To Victor, she smiled and singsonged, "Yes, we will! Won't we?"

With Victor and Glory in the garden, Fiona retreated to her bedroom and stretched out, sighing deeply and breathing in Victor's baby perfume that was on her pillow. *And this time yesterday, who would have thought our lives would take such a turn? And that it would be such a beautiful, beautiful turn? And Glory saying she wasn't 'never' going to allow love in her life. What a trick she has played on herself!* Fiona thought, just before she fell into a deep, peaceful sleep.

When Fiona awakened, she could smell the wonderful aroma of frying chicken and green beans cooking away with pork-fat seasoning. She came into the kitchen, where Victor was sitting right up on the kitchen counter, happily working away at a piece of biscuit dough, and Glory stood between him and the stovetop, making sure that he was not too close to the simmering beans and the frying chicken.

"You had a good nap," Glory said. "And Victor and I picked a right good mess of beans. Smell them?"

"I sure do," Fiona said, but her eyes were fixed on Victor, on his pink arms and legs, the clumsy fingers mashing the piece of biscuit dough over and over again. And on the fair blonde hair and the clear blue eyes. *And how on earth could anyone, especially his own mama, walk away and leave such a child? And who was she, anyway? About "so high," as Doc had asked? And with blonde hair?*

"He's making you a biscuit," Glory said, chuckling. "And I want to see you *eat* it." And when the pan of biscuits came out of the oven, Fiona certainly did eat the one Victor had made himself, a slightly discolored, tough little lump, but he watched her carefully, and his eyes brightened as she smacked and said, "M-m-m-m! That's the best biscuit I ever tasted!"

Victor himself ate an entire drumstick, a good serving of green beans, and two of Glory's biscuits, one with both butter and honey in it. He drank down a small glass of milk. Glory refilled his glass, and he drank that down, as well. Finally, he let out a huge burp. Fiona and Glory both laughed aloud, but Fiona, wiping her eyes, said, "We shouldn't laugh at burping. That won't teach him any manners at all."

"We'll have plenty of time to teach him manners," Glory said. "But we gotta remember he's a boy, and no matter how hard we try, we can't turn him into a little girl."

"What do you mean?"

"I mean that boys do things like burping . . . and worse. They aren't neat and clean like most little girls." Fiona thought about Glory's words, and then she said, "I wish there was a man around here for him to be around, but there isn't."

"Sure there is," Glory protested. "Old Man."

"Old Man?" Fiona yelped.

"Sure," Glory said easily. "Think about it—Old Man is kind and patient and nice to ladies. Those are all qualities we want Victor to have, aren't they?"

"I suppose so," Fiona admitted. "Well, we'll just have to do the best we can, that's all."

"It's all anyone can do," Glory agreed. "But it's getting close to nighttime. Where is he going to sleep?"

"Why, with me," Fiona answered, thinking with relish of the small, warm body in her own bed.

"Won't do for very long," Glory replied. "He needs a bed of his own."

"Yes, I agree. But for now, we'll just have to put him in my bed. We can get him a bed of his own when . . . ."

"When we know for sure his mama isn't going to show up and want him back," Glory finished Fiona's sentence, and they both looked at Victor. Somehow, they would have to learn not to say anything like that in front of him. That night, Victor's first full night with Fiona and Glory, they did put Victor in Fiona's bed. He went without complaint, and when Fiona tucked the blanket around him, he studied her face intently, but with the same bland expression he always had.

"Night-night, honey," Fiona crooned, and then, on impulse, she leaned forward and kissed his forehead, inhaling the warm perfume of his hair and skin. "I'll leave the door open so the hall light will make it a little better in here."

Much later, when Fiona went to bed herself, she slipped between the covers quietly, so as not to disturb the sleeping child. And before she fell asleep, she breathed a silent prayer . . . of thankfulness. She awakened only once during the night, when Victor whimpered in his sleep. Automatically, she patted his back until the whimpering stopped and they both fell into a deep and peaceful sleep.

At breakfast the next morning, Fiona and Glory lingered over their coffee, watching as Victor ate heartily of scrambled eggs and warmed-over biscuits.

"And what are we going to do with him today?" Glory asked, at last. "We both got work to do, you know."

"I know," Fiona sighed. "I've got to get two cabins ready for folks coming down from Georgia for a week of fishing."

"Well, he can't go with me to the restaurant," Glory said. "Too much he can get into there, especially in the kitchen. Hot grease and such as that."

"And too close to the lake for my liking," Fiona added. "So he'll go with me and help me clean the cabins, won't you, Victor?" As always, Victor's eyes moved from one to the other, as they spoke. Then he scooped up the last of the eggs and burped heartily. And right at that moment, Glory and Fiona heard a noise on the front porch.

"Who's that?" Glory asked, an unaccustomed alarm in her voice. And Fiona's heart bumped most unpleasantly.

"The mama?" Glory whispered.

But when Fiona went to the door and opened it, she saw only Old Man's retreating back and at her feet, a small pile of clothes, topped by an envelope.

"Wait!" Fiona called, but Old Man just kept walking away.

The bundle contained two pairs of children's shorts, three knit shirts, and some mismatched socks, but no shoes. All the clothes were clean and sweet smelling but obviously well used. The envelope contained a short note—"Take care of him. Love him. Be god to him." And it was signed, "the Mama."

"What on earth?" Fiona blurted.

Glory took the note from Fiona's hand and read it for herself.

"What does that mean?" Fiona asked. "Be god to him?"

"I think it means be *good* to him. She just can't spell too good."

"But where did Old Man get it? And the clothes?"

"Heaven only knows," Glory answered. "And he'll never say anything, that's for sure. But I told you and told you that Old Man knows more than what he's saying."

"So maybe this means she's really not coming back?" Fiona asked, hopefully.

"Sure sounds like it," Glory said. And then to Fiona she chortled, "Looks like we got ourselves a boy!"

Fiona tucked the note into her Bible, dressed Victor in a pair of the shorts and a shirt—they fit him perfectly—and started out to clean the cabins. Glory headed off to the restaurant. At the pier, Jubilee was sitting near the door to the restaurant kitchen. When she saw Glory coming, she jumped up.

"Did you hear about Doc and Miss Myra?" Jubilee blurted out.

"What about them?" Glory asked, struggling with the padlock on the kitchen door. Under the pier, the lake water lapped softly, a sound that always pleased Glory, no matter that she had a long day ahead of her, standing over a hot stove and frying fish and, she would have added, putting up with a petulant child who didn't want to work at all.

"They came back from Jacksonville already," Jubilee said, and Glory noted the happy expression on Jubilee's face—an expression that was always there whenever Jubilee had some kind of gossip to share. "And they weren't alone."

"What do you mean?" Glory hated to rise to the bait of listening to gossip, but this time, she couldn't help herself. "They just left yesterday. How come they came back so soon?"

"I said they weren't alone when they came home," Jubilee repeated, fairly glowing with the "secret" she couldn't wait to divulge. "They brought back a baby."

Glory stopped fumbling with the padlock. "Brought back a *what?*"

"A baby!" Jubilee chortled. "They got a baby in Jacksonville!"

"And how on earth do you know this?" Glory demanded, thinking that perhaps Jubilee's imagination was working overtime.

"My very own mama told me," Jubilee said with a smack of self-satisfaction. "Doc called her this morning on the phone and told her. 'Cause my mama was the one supposed to be watching out for their house while they were gone, so he wanted to let her know they were back home."

"Where'd they get a baby?" Glory hated herself for asking, but she really meant to know.

"They 'dopted it, Doc told Mama."

"Adopted it?" Glory parroted.

"Sure enough," Jubilee agreed excitedly. "A little girl baby," she added, fairly bubbling with the joy of having such fascinating news to tell. "But there's more," she teased. Glory had finally gotten the padlock off of the kitchen door and swung it open, revealing the dim interior, the huge black wood cook stove, and the faint aroma of the last day's fried fish.

"Well?" Glory was feeling impatient, as she always felt around Jubilee.

"He said my mama wasn't to say anything—not a single word—to

Miss Myra about the baby being 'dopted."

"What? Don't she know?"

"Yess'm, she knows. She *has* to know, 'cause she went all the way to Jacksonville with Doc, just to get that baby. But I think she don't *want* to know they 'dopted it. I think that's what it means."

Glory listened thoughtfully, wondering silently if it wasn't awfully soon to adopt a little girl baby, after Doc and Myra had lost their own baby, and if Myra was in a state where she didn't want to acknowledge where this new baby came from, perhaps she was still too deep in grief to try being a mama again. And maybe that's why Doc had seemed so strange, when he came to check on Victor. They were going all the way to Jacksonville, to get a baby. Must have been hard for him not to say a thing about that. But Glory said none of this to Jubilee, of course. Instead, she went into the dim kitchen, lifting down the heavy cast iron skillets that hung above the stove. When Jubilee tried to follow her inside, Glory stopped her. "You wait out here for Mr. Owen," she instructed. "Got to *have* fish before we can cook fish!"

"But don't you think it's interesting?" Jubilee was clearly disappointed in Glory's reactions to such juicy news.

"No, I don't think it's interesting," Glory snapped. "I think it's none of our business, is what I think!" Chastised, Jubilee sat down on the end of the pier, dangling her feet over the lake and waiting for Mr. Owen's boat to come in, bringing all of the fresh fish for them to cook that day.

Glory took three heads of cabbage from the icebox and began chopping them for coleslaw. Perhaps, to Jubilee, Glory seemed strangely unconcerned about Doc and Myra's new, adopted baby, but in her heart, she was thinking about those good people and the terrible loss they had suffered and praying that this new adopted little girl would heal their wound. And at the same time, she was thinking that Fiona needed to know that the doctor and Myra were back from their trip, because Fiona would want to get in touch with him right away and tell him that the little boy was really her great-nephew, and that the good doctor need not be concerned that he would need to bring the police or the welfare agencies in on this happening. Yes, Glory needed to tell Fiona as soon as possible.

Fiona's walk with Victor in tow to the cabins that needed to be prepared for guests was a slow and sometimes frustrating one, because in one hand, she was carrying the bucket for scrub water and in the other a broom and a mop. So she had instructed Victor to hold on to her apron as they went along the path, and he had obeyed, in as much as he was able. Fiona had noticed that the roughness of the path was hurting his tender feet.

"Next thing we have to get is some shoes for you," she said, but Victor didn't seem to notice what she said. Because, being a toddler, he found absolutely everything along the path to be fascinating, so he had to pick up every small pebble he saw and uproot every weed they came across. Each time he turned loose of her apron and stooped to examine a crawling ant or small shell, she waited patiently, naming every single item for him and hoping that his reluctance to speak was not an indication of any true difficulty he may be having. And the fact that never, even once, had either Fiona or Glory seen him smile. Not even a tiny smile. The closest he had come was the way his eyes seemed to sparkle when he saw Old Man. Whatever that meant.

But after all, perhaps they were expecting too much from Victor. Having his own mama walk away and leave him with strangers was certain to impact him, emotionally, even if he was so young that he would probably never remember anything about that. Perhaps that would be the kindest thing, after all. In the meantime, he was showing a healthy curiosity about almost everything, so Fiona would be satisfied with that.

"That's a pebble," Fiona said to him, as he studied the small stone resting on the palm of his hand. "Peb-ble," she enunciated. "Here," she continued, "Throw it in the lake. That's lots of fun!" Stooping, she picked up another pebble, sounded out the word again, and tossed it into the shallow water near the path, where it plopped into the water, sending out circles from where it fell. Victor studied her carefully, watching the pebble and the concentric rings that it caused, and then he attempted to throw his own pebble, which landed only a few inches from his feet.

"Try again," Fiona chirruped encouragingly, and Victor retrieved the pebble and tossed it once again. This time, it landed in the very edge of the water, and Fiona clapped her hands and said, "Yay! That's much better," she encouraged. Victor looked at her face and then back at the small ripple in the water his pebble had caused, but the expression on his face never changed at all.

"Well, now, let's get going so we can clean those cabins," Fiona said cheerfully. And he followed her until he happened upon yet another pebble, which he had to try to throw into the lake.

"Maybe we'll have to get Jubilee to help take care of you," Fiona mused. "Sure not going to get any cleaning done this way, are we?"

Eventually, they reached the first cabin to be cleaned, and Fiona picked Victor up and plopped him on the unmade bed. She went into the bathroom, being careful to put the bottle of bleach on a high shelf, where Victor wouldn't be able to reach it. He sat on the bed for all of two minutes before he climbed down and went into the bathroom, where he stood for long minutes, watching Fiona as she scrubbed the small sink, rinsed it, and wiped it dry with a spare towel. She moved him out of the small room while she wiped the floor and put down a small rug, and then he moved forward, stepping carefully on the damp floor, picking up the rug and solemnly handing it back to her, as if it were something she had accidentally dropped.

"Thank you, honey," Fiona said. "But it's a rug—it's supposed to be on the floor." He watched her carefully, as she replaced the rug, and then he picked it up again and, unsmiling, handed it to her, watching her the whole time.

"Well, maybe you're right," Fiona sighed. "Maybe we don't need a rug in here after all." Under her breath, Fiona murmured, "We'll have to see about getting Jubilee to watch you for us, leastwise when there are cabins to get ready for paying guests!"

Glory left Jubilee grumbling to herself and scowling, but working at cleaning the fine mess of fish Mr. Owen had brought around, as usual. Glory had to stop herself from laughing at all the fish scales glistening in Jubilee's black hair—scales that flew like a blizzard to accompany Jubilee's grumbling discontent. She concealed her widening smile as she slipped out of the kitchen, went along the dock, and fairly raced down the sandy path to the cabins she knew Fiona was cleaning. She could locate the cabin easily, among the cabins ringing the lake, because the cabin door was open, and she could hear Fiona talking to Victor.

"Now just a little longer, honey—you be a good boy and sit there and watch me. Victor? Victor?" As Glory approached the cabin, Victor came to the doorway, his arms full of clean towels he had unfolded. As Glory went inside, Victor let the pile of towels drop on the floor and followed Glory to the bathroom, where Fiona was still talking to him, as if he were still standing right behind her. "Just a few more minutes, Victor—be a good boy for Aunt Fiona now and stay where I can see you!"

When Glory came to the doorway, Fiona looked up. Her hair was hanging in her face, and she reeked of the bleach she had been using to clean the bathroom. "Where is he?" she demanded of Glory.

"Right here," Glory laughed, moving aside so that Fiona could see Victor standing there, and anyone would be able to see that he was just looking around for something else to get into.

"Good Heavens!" Fiona said. "This isn't going to work! I just can't keep up with him."

"I know you're probably thinking of getting Jubilee to look after him, but you can't do that because I need her in the restaurant." Glory smiled again, picturing all those fish scales in Jubilee's hair. "So we'll have to figure something out," Glory was emphatic about not giving up Jubilee. She wasn't about to be wearing all those nasty old scales in her own hair! "But there's something else you need to know about."

"What *now?*" Fiona asked, dejectedly. "Victor, you come right back here!" she added, and Victor obeyed . . . this time. "Stay where I can see you," Fiona directed. "Oh, Lord!"

"Doc and Myra are back from Jacksonville," Glory said. "And I know you want to get to him as soon as you can, to tell him about Victor here . . . being your *great-nephew* . . . and no need for Doc to get any of the authorities involved."

"Oh, yes!" Fiona sounded relieved. "They're back already? I wonder why?" Then she added, "Can you watch Victor for just a minute so I can go call Doc?"

"Just for a minute, 'cause I got fish to fry and hungry folks willing to pay a good price for lunch. But there's something else you need to know before you go and call him. Doc and Myra 'dopted a little baby girl in Jacksonville, and they've brung her home with them."

"Adopted?" Fiona couldn't think of anything else to say, not without getting into a long-winded discourse about Doc and Myra losing their own little baby girl and Myra needing a good visit with her folks in Jacksonville to make her feel better.

"That's right," Glory said. "Jubilee told me first thing this morning, and she ought to know 'cause it's her own mama supposed to look out after Doc's house while they were gone."

"Adopted?" Fiona said again. "And back from the trip already?"

"That's right," Glory said. And then both of the women realized that Victor had slipped away from them, so they went outside, calling his name. He hadn't gone far—only to the edge of the lake—and Glory took his hand. "I'm glad to see him acting more like a normal little boy should act," Glory pronounced. "Even if it makes things harder for us. Now, you go make your phone call," she directed. "And I'll hang on to Victor until you get back. But hurry!"

On the way to the house, Fiona was trying to decide if she should say something to Doc about the baby girl he and Myra had brought home from Jacksonville. She would rather have heard the news from Doc himself or at least from Myra, but that wasn't the case. This was nothing but pure gossip, for all she knew, and by the time she reached for the phone, she had decided not to say anything to him about an adopted baby—real or not.

When Doc himself answered the phone, Fiona started right in, explaining to him that the little abandoned boy left in her back yard was really her great-nephew, and she was sorry she had acted so surprised and had everyone thinking he was a complete stranger to her. As she spoke, Fiona was surprised to realize that she felt not a single regret about what she was saying. Because for all she knew, it could be true. Although the note Old Man had left with the clothes certainly said nothing to indicate that there was a familial relationship between Victor and Fiona. One just never knew, did they?

Right at the end of Fiona's explanation, she waited for Doc to say something, but he was silent. And then Fiona heard a baby crying in the background—a very young baby, from the sound of the cries.

"Oh," she started in. "I'm so sorry. Do you have a patient or something?" Because she had definitely decided to hear about this adopted baby from Doc himself, or at least from Myra, and not to reveal to them that any gossip was already going around the community.

"Oh, no!" Doc seemed distracted. "That's . . . that's our new daughter!" His voice rose so that he almost sounded as if he were absolutely crowing in pride and happiness.

"What?" Fiona enjoyed acting completely surprised. "Your new *daughter?*"

"Yes. We got her in Jacksonville . . . adopted her in Jacksonville and brought her home with us today."

"Oh my!" Fiona exclaimed, not only because she was really happy for the new parents but also because this would certainly take Doc's mind off of Victor and perhaps any wondering about whether he was, indeed, Fiona's great-nephew. Maybe even make him forget that he seemed to know something about the woman who had left him. "This is sudden, isn't it?" Fiona asked, simply because she couldn't think of anything else to say.

"Well, that was our intention, in going to Jacksonville," Doc explained, and all the while, the baby—sounding like a newborn—wailed disconsolately in the background. "We didn't want to say anything about it until we were sure. Sometimes, things don't go through the way we expect, you know."

"Well, congratulations to you both!" Fiona chirruped. "Give Myra my love, and tell her I'll stop in as soon as I can."

"Yes, thank you. I'll tell her, but please wait to make a visit, if you will. We're kind of new at all this, you know, and we aren't really up for company right now. But thank you very much. Now, I'd better get off the phone and go help Myra," he explained.

"Congratulations again," Fiona said.

"Oh yes—and bring the little boy in for his shots before long," Doc added, becoming once more the reliable physician and not the harried new father.

"Oh, I will. Goodbye now."

When Fiona got back to the cabin where she had left Glory and Victor, they were both throwing pebbles and small shells into the lake.

Glory's hair had come undone from its clasps and was hanging around her face in disarray, and when she saw Fiona, she said, "thank the good Lord you're back—this boy like to have worn me out, just that fast!"

Victor looked up at Fiona and for one brief moment, Fiona thought that he was going to smile. But that was wishful thinking. *Give him time!* She told herself. *Just give him time.*

"You get hold of Doc?" Glory asked.

"I did," Fiona said. "And I could hear the baby crying in the background."

"He say anything about that baby being 'dopted?"

"Yes," Fiona said. "And he said for all of us to give them time to get settled in, before we go visiting."

"Didn't say anything about Miss Myra?"

"No, and I didn't ask," Fiona said.

Glory nodded, and while she said nothing more, she did wonder about what Jubilee had said—that no one was supposed to say anything around Miss Myra about the baby being adopted at all.

And I do wonder why?

Somehow, Fiona managed to finish cleaning the two reserved cabins, all the while struggling to keep Victor in her sight and out of trouble, and her timing was perfect—because the taxi from Wasachoossee pulled up in front of the main house just after she had put away all the cleaning supplies and had gotten Victor to lie down for a much-needed nap.

"Honey," she said as she pulled off his shorts and shirt and lifted the sheet over him, "I don't know if *you* need a nap, but I sure do need for you to take one!" And, tired as he was from throwing pebbles and running around beside the lake and in and out of the cabins, he gave her no trouble at all—simply sighed, turned on his side, and sucked his thumb until his eyelashes descended and swept his rounded cheeks and his breathing became deep and rhythmic.

The "taxi" was really a large car the likes of which people in Love-Oak had seen only recently—a brand new Studebaker Light-Six Touring car, with a real roof (not at all like the open Model T) and that could hold up to six people, including the driver, of course. That car met the train in Wasachoossee anytime there were people coming to the camp, and when the taxi arrived in Love-Oak, the men piled out of the car laughing, juggling armloads of fishing tackle and already lying to each other with fish stories that never happened. The women—if there were wives along, which was quite rare—descended more demurely, juggling hatboxes and suitcases, and touching dainty handkerchiefs to their perspiring faces.

"Oh, goodness! It's so hot!" they first wailed without exception, and Fiona always wanted to snap back, "Well, it's *Florida!* What did you expect?" But of course, she never said that, simply smiled and nodded her head politely at the women, knowing full well that after one long week suffering in the heat, waving away insects with perfumed handkerchiefs, and guzzling gallons of sweet tea, they would probably never come again. And that suited Fiona just fine—probably suited the fishermen husbands, as well. Because while the men happily fished from dawn until dark, the women had little to do except walk along the lakeshore or sit in the shade of the Australian pines, drinking tea, crocheting, playing cards, and whispering complaints to each other. And when it was "ladies time" in the showers, Fiona would usually overhear shocked, feminine screams coming from the little concrete-block house, because that cool, damp place was where lizards by the dozen chose to congregate. Those screams always made Fiona smile.

But this time, Fiona was relieved to note, there were no wives among the group of four gentlemen who piled out of the taxi. Mr. Owen, the same Mr. Owen who provided all of the fresh bass for the restaurant, was waiting, as usual, to help with luggage and to start briefing the avid fishermen about the lake, the available boats, and the amenities in nearby Love-Oak itself. After the driver from Wasachoossee had unloaded all of the luggage and fishing gear, Fiona herself greeted the guests, offering to provide anything additional they might need and advising them of the restaurant and the wonderful food available there for lunch. For dinner, she suggested the restaurant in town, and she always mentioned the Trading Post and how they could get real Seminole souvenirs there. Mr. Owen took over at that point, helping to carry luggage and fishing tackle and already swapping fish stories with the four genial fishermen.

And Fiona, waiting for Victor to wake up from his nap, sat on the porch, rocking and thinking of how satisfying it was for her to know that the reserved cabins were in such good condition for her guests, no thanks to Victor—little scamp! And of course, that also brought up the subject of finding someone to help her and Glory out with Victor—especially during times when they were both so busy.

But soon, Fiona put her head back and closed her eyes. She might as well grab a nap herself, while Victor was asleep. The mere thought of Victor brought a warm smile to her face. *Thank you, Father,* she prayed silently. *Thank you for bringing this wonderful little fellow into our lives. And please help us to survive Your generosity!*

Chapter Five

The rain didn't start until after dark on the day the four new fishermen arrived, which was unusual. In the summertime, rain clouds usually began building up in the heat of the afternoon, scudding along lazily from the west, gathering darker and darker hues underneath, until the air could no longer hold all of the moisture. Then the heavy rains came, usually accompanied by window-rattling peals of thunder, and rain that was a shower-warm deluge of fat drops, pounding the roof and bringing the fishermen who were on the pier scurrying for the safety and comfort of the fish restaurant on the dock or the open doorways of their own small cabins, if they were staying at the camp. Those fishermen who were out on the lake in small boats during the afternoon storms simply endured the rain and thunder, hoping for the sun to reappear and the fish to keep biting.

But that day, the rain had waited until the sun had gone down, and Fiona was glad that the fishermen had been able to get in a full day on the lake. Victor was already safely in bed, and Fiona and Glory were sitting on the front porch in comfortable silence, shelling butterbeans and watching the steady downpour of warm rain. Suddenly—out of the dusk, two people came running toward the porch from across the yard, with soggy newspapers draped over their heads.

Fiona and Glory watched as two strangers—a man and a woman—ran up the steps and onto the edge of the porch, where the overhang from the roof protected them from the rain.

"Whooee!" the man yelled, pulling the soggy newspaper off of his head and dropping it onto the porch floor. "A gully washer, sure enough!"

For a brief moment, Fiona thought that the man may have been one of the guest fishermen who had arrived that morning, but then she realized that he certainly wasn't, and also that none of the fishermen had brought their wives with them. And this woman certainly didn't look like a *wife*—at least not like any wife Fiona had ever seen.

Because when the woman pulled the soggy newspaper off of her head, her hair was the color of Mercurochrome and shone like a neon light, even sopping wet and in the low light of the porch. Further, she was wearing the shortest shorts either Fiona or Glory had ever seen, and high heels that were caked with wet sand. Her blouse was a peasant type, with a gathered neckline that hung far too low, revealing the tops of saggy breasts and clinging to her wet body in almost a burlesque manner.

"Evening, ladies," the man said, as if he suddenly realized that he and the woman had come up onto the porch without even saying hello to the two women sitting there. "Do you mind if we come in here out of the rain?"

"Well," Fiona hesitated for a moment. "No, I guess we don't mind. What are you all doing out in this weather anyway? You live around here?"

"No, we're traveling. Or at least we *were*. Car quit on us," the man said, indicating the road with his thumb. "Damned old hunk of junk!" The curse word and the vehemence in his voice startled Fiona and Glory, and the woman, who had been shaking rain water out of her improbable hair, stared at him and then glanced at the women.

"Honey, you better watch your language in front of these here ladies," she said, with a hint of an apology in her voice.

In that moment, both Fiona and Glory summed up the couple standing before them and glanced at each other, though they said not a word. They didn't need to, because they had both heard that apologetic tone in a woman's voice plenty of times, and Fiona had even used such a tone with her beloved J. Roy on rare occasions when he had become too upset over something to have good sense . . . or good manners.

"You want to use our telephone?" Fiona offered. "I don't think the garage is open this late, but it wouldn't hurt to try."

"Can't pay for no garage," the man grumbled. "And besides," he added, looking at the woman again. "I can fix it myself, probably. Once the rain lets up."

"We'll have to wait until morning, won't we?" the woman asked him, and again both Fiona and Glory noticed the subservient tone in her voice, as if, without using actual words, she was trying to placate the man, trying to diffuse his apparently rising bad mood. Briefly, Fiona wondered if it was the woman's fault that the car had broken down. Had she forgotten to get gasoline for it? Or was he one of those despicable men who, having gotten angry and upset about one thing, seems to spread it around to everyone and everything around him. But her thoughts were interrupted when the woman squealed, "Oh, look at that precious little boy! Hey, honey!"

Fiona turned her head and saw Victor standing behind the screen door in his rumpled pajamas and with his thumb in his mouth.

"Well, hello there!" the woman crooned to him. "Who are you?"

"That's my nephew," Fiona said, and she was surprised to feel the hair automatically rising on her arms.

"Go on back to bed, honey," she said to Victor, and he turned and walked away, obedient because he had worn himself out tearing around the whole afternoon like a little wild animal, and also because he had a stomach full of Glory's good fried fish and hushpuppies she had brought home from the restaurant for him.

"What a precious little boy!" the woman continued to gush. "Did you see him, honey?" she asked the man, who was still looking out at the rain and simultaneously digging in the pocket of his jeans for a cigarette. Once he had lit the cigarette, he turned to look at the screen door, now vacant, that the woman pointed out to him.

"Little boy?" he asked, and his raspy voice sent a chill through Fiona. Glory must have felt the same quiet alarm, because she got up out of her chair, putting the bowl of shelled butterbeans on the porch floor.

"I'll go put on some coffee," she said, casting a strange glance at Fiona, so that Fiona knew making coffee wasn't all Glory was going to do. But whatever else Glory had in mind, Fiona didn't know.

"Oh, I'm sorry," the stranger-woman said, still squeezing water from the soaked hanks of hair around her shoulders. "We haven't even introduced ourselves. This here is Middy—and I'm Starry."

Fiona had never before heard such strange names, but she tried to keep herself from showing her surprise. However, she wasn't successful, because the woman added quickly, "Oh, I know those are strange sounding names, especially when you first hear them. But you see, our last name is Night, so Middy and Starry make sense then."

From the other side of the screen door, Fiona thought she heard Glory talking on the phone, but she couldn't be sure, and besides, she was struggling to catch on to whatever point the woman was trying to make. The woman frowned slightly and continued, "Starry Night and Middy Night—or Mid Night, you see?"

"Your last name is Night?" Fiona seemed unable to find a comprehensive thought in her mind. She wondered who Glory was calling and why.

"Yess'm," the woman explained. "Used to be spelled with a 'k' but after we went into show business, we took that off. Made more of an impression, you see, if we spelled it the regular way most folks know about."

"Starry Night?" Fiona repeated foolishly, and she wondered where Glory had gone and why she was taking so long with making coffee and who she had called on the phone. If anyone.

"Yess'm," the woman smiled. And she leaned her head toward the man. "And Mid Night, too. Isn't that right, honey?" The man didn't acknowledge the woman's words. Instead, he stood leaning against the porch banister, staring out into the pouring rain.

Fiona studied him carefully, wondering what there was about him that made her feel so suspicious and uncomfortable. Perhaps it was simply his appearance, because he was a tall, gaunt man with dark hair pulled back into a scraggy ponytail. The sleeves of his orange shirt were rolled up, revealing heavily tattooed arms—one tattoo a long knife and another a face of some kind. Fiona couldn't make out what it was, under all that dark hair on his arms. His legs were long and encased in jeans that were almost tight enough to have been painted onto his skin. On his feet he wore cowboy boots that were heavily cracked and run-over at the heels. As he stared out into the rain and smoked the damp, bent cigarette he'd pulled from his pocket, Fiona studied his hands—long, thin fingers and dirty fingernails.

The woman—Starry—seemed to have run out of things to say, so she slumped against the other banister, alternately studying her fingernails and glancing at the man—Middy. Fiona took the lull in the stilted conversation as an opportunity for further studying Starry herself. But before her eyes had gone beyond the short shorts and the flabby buttock-skin hanging pitifully out of them, Starry reached over to take the smoked-down cigarette butt from Middy. Snorting, he jerked his arm away from her and flicked the butt out into the yard.

"So . . ." Starry was obviously embarrassed and started casting about, looking for something to say that would carry forth a polite conversation with this stranger who had just witnessed Middy's rude behavior and whose front porch they had invaded, seeking shelter from the continuing downpour. "So how old is your little boy?"

The question sent another flood of alarmed goose bumps over Fiona's arms, and ignoring the question, she got up out of the chair. "I'd better go see what's taking Glory so long with that coffee. And I'll get you all some towels so you can dry off a little bit."

As she went inside, she quietly reached back and slipped the screen door latch into place. There was something *wrong* about these strangers, but she couldn't tell what it was. The woman showed too much interest in Victor, for one thing—more interest than good manners would have required.

Once inside, she also closed the door to her bedroom, where Victor was in bed but not asleep. He glanced up at her but made no move to get out of bed. Silently, Fiona wished that there were a lock on that door, though she had never thought about such a thing before. She went into the kitchen, where Glory had placed coffee mugs on a tray and was filling them with steaming coffee.

"What's taking you so long?" Fiona asked.

"You recognize that woman?" Glory asked, ignoring Fiona's question.

"Why, no," Fiona said. "Should I? Who is she?"

"Blamed if I know," Glory said, putting the sugar bowl and cream pitcher on the tray. "I just wondered if she's the *mama*, come back after Victor."

"The mama?" Fiona sputtered. "Of course not!"

"Well, I just asked," Glory complained. "You only saw the mama one time and that was in a dark yard, so I thought maybe this was *her*, come back for Victor."

"What on earth would make you think such a thing?" Fiona's voice held all of the pent-up frustration she had felt, wondering if that woman would show up again. But then she remembered the note Old Man had brought—the note from Victor's mama that was in her Bible.

"And she was awful interested in Victor," Glory reasoned. Fiona didn't even have time to answer that suggestion before there came a light knock at the back door. Fiona flinched. What if those people, those strangers, had tried the screen door and finding it latched, had come around back? And there was no way in this world that the woman could be the *mama* Fiona had feared. She was much taller than the mysterious woman in the back yard. And the man! For Heaven's sake, he couldn't be Victor's father, not in a million years! Not with that black hair and gaunt build.

The knock at the back door sounded again, and Glory's face told Fiona that the knock was nothing to be alarmed about—indeed, Glory's face showed almost instantaneous relief. Before either of the women could go to the door, it swung open and Old Man walked into the kitchen, dripping wet from the downpour. He was wearing his full Seminole outfit, including the egret feather in his hair, clothes he usually reserved only for his performances at the Trading Post. And that wasn't all he was wearing—because Fiona's one quick glance at him told her that the bulge in his waistband was that terrible knife he sometimes carried. But his face under the dripping, black hair and the sagging egret feather was as calm and beatific as it ever was. Without a single word, he walked through the kitchen and went out onto the front porch. Glory gathered up the tray.

"You called him?" Fiona whispered, as they made their way to the porch.

"Sure did," Glory answered. Then she smiled. "I always knew that having a savage for a friend would come in handy one day!"

"You calling Old Man a *savage*?" Fiona could hardly believe her ears.

"No," Glory admitted. "But he sure does look like one!"

"What'd you tell him?"

"Told him there was some stranger-folks over here, and I didn't like the way they looked at Victor, and he's better be over here in a heartbeat. I knew all I had to do was mention that little boy!"

"I don't know why that is," Fiona whispered, as they went out onto the porch. "But I'm certainly grateful for it this night!"

The porch scene couldn't have been any different than it was when Fiona had left Starry and Middy there alone. Middy no longer leaned in a silent swagger against the banister, but stood almost at attention, his eyes riveted on Old Man, who was standing near them, tall and silent. Middy's tongue flickering nervously across his lips, and Starry had turned pale as a ghost and stood staring, openmouthed, at Old Man as if he already had a tomahawk poised over her flaming red head.

"Have some coffee," Glory said, with a mischievous smile on her face. She put the tray down on the wicker table, but no one made a move to take a cup. Finally, Old Man slowly moved aside and went down to the far end of the porch, where he sat down on the banister, his back ramrod straight and hand at his waistband.

"Maybe we better go, hon," Starry said, putting her hand on Middy's tattooed arm. Middy started to jerk his arm away, but he hesitated, casting another long glance at Old Man.

"Why, you can't go out in this downpour!" Fiona was completely surprised at the words that came out of her mouth, but then she realized that, even if there was no remote chance that Starry could be Victor's mama, she wanted to keep these folks around long enough to make sure they didn't have any claim whatsoever to *her* son. Glory looked at her with a terrible frown, and even Old Man looked surprised.

"Listen"—Fiona tried to recover herself from that unlikely invitation. "You all can stay in the cabin at the far end for tonight," she sputtered. "It's probably a little bit musty, since I wasn't expecting anybody to stay in it, but it's clean and dry, and you can see about your car in the morning."

Starry's mouth hung open, and Middy glanced sideways once again at Old Man.

"We wouldn't want to put you folks out," Starry began, but Middy interrupted her. "We 'preciate it," he said almost in a low growl. Fiona reminded herself that some men ... in fact, most men, she would guess . . . were reluctant to take help when help was offered.

"No trouble at all," Fiona insisted. "It's not locked—Number Seven, all the way at the end. Bed's not made up. But clean sheets are in the closet."

From the far end of the porch, Old Man coughed once, and Glory reached over and snatched up the coffee tray, setting the cups to rattling. Middy and Starry looked at Fiona once again before they went down the steps and ran across the dark yard, toward the lone streetlight that illuminated the very end of the row of vacant cabins.

"Thank you, ma'am!" Starry shouted back over her shoulder, as they disappeared along the dark sandy path in front of the cabins.

"What'd you go and do that for?" Glory fussed loudly. "Now we've got those strange folks here for the whole night."

"We couldn't just send them out into the rain," Fiona argued. "And besides, better to have them all the way down at the end in that cabin than camped out here on our own front porch. And I want to make sure of who they are, before they disappear."

"Well, just be sure we lock all the doors," Glory said. "I won't rest very good knowing such as that . . . *trash* . . . is around. No way in this world that . . . *trash* . . . could have anything to do with our baby!"

As Glory took the coffee tray inside, Old Man approached Fiona.

"I'm sorry we made you come out in all this rain," Fiona said, and typically, Old Man said nothing. Fiona thought that he would leave then, but he hesitated only a few minutes before he went back and sat down on the same banister and looked toward the cabins.

"Listen," Fiona said. "I'm going inside now. Will you come in and have some coffee?"

Old Man merely shook his head, *no.*

"Well, if you're going to sit out here for a little while, I'll leave the porch light on for you."

Once again, Old Man shook his head, *no.*

"Listen, you don't recognize either of those folks, do you?" Because when Victor first came, Glory had been so sure that Old Man knew something about the boy's real mama. And of course, there had been that note Old Man delivered.

But again, Old Man shook his head, *no.*

Fiona breathed a sigh of relief and went inside, closing and locking the door and reluctantly turning off the porch light. But during the night, she awakened, went into the dark living room, and peered through the window at the far corner of the porch. All she could see was the lone white egret feather in Old Man's hair, shining like a candle in the darkness.

As soon as Fiona opened her eyes the next morning, she looked rather anxiously at the small lump Victor's body made under the sheet. Was he really there? Or were there nothing but bunched-up blankets under the sheet? But then the lump moved, the blonde head raised itself off of the pillow, and she was looking into those beautiful, trusting, blue eyes. And how could she have been worried? Old Man spent the night on the porch, and if anyone had tried to come into the house, he would have stopped them. Old Man and his knife. Such comfort!

"Come on, honey. Let's take you into the bathroom," she said in the most matter-of-fact voice she could manage. He went with her obediently, his hand soft and warm in her own. Afterward, she took him into the kitchen, where Glory was stirring the grits. Already, the sweet aroma of fresh biscuits filled the room. Fiona seated Victor and gave him a glass of milk and then she glanced knowingly at Glory.

"Old Man's gone," Glory reported quietly. "Nothing's going on."

"You haven't seen or heard anything from . . . *them*?"

"Not a thing."

"I'd better go down there and see what's what," Fiona announced. "They need to get that car fixed and be on their way." The last words came out in a wishful rush.

"We need to get things settled," Glory agreed. "I got to get on to the restaurant and start cooking."

"And we've got two more reservations coming in today," Fiona added. "I have to get those cabins cleaned and ready."

"Wonder what kind of condition those folks are going to leave Number Seven in?" Glory murmured, and Fiona hoped there would be nothing to do but open the windows to air out the cabin, wipe out the bathroom sink, and take away the linens those people had used.

Fiona left Victor and Glory at the kitchen table, and she walked through the gray dampness of early morning down to cabin Number Seven. She would definitely feel better when the two strangers were on their way and well away from her home . . . and Victor, even though any concern Fiona had about Starry being Victor's natural mother had faded with the ending of the long night. She heard no sound from the other two occupied cabins, and she guessed that the fishermen had gone out on the lake long before good daylight.

She knocked lightly on the cabin door, and it was opened almost immediately by Starry, who, of course, was dressed in the same outfit she had on the night before. Once again, Fiona glanced at the poor, saggy breasts that in years past would have peeked provocatively over the top of the peasant blouse. Suddenly, she felt a rush of sympathy for Starry—it was always sad to see a woman who had depended for her entire life upon her looks—her "sex appeal," she guessed they called it—and then age took over and everything she had depended upon had sagged and wrinkled and become only a gross and ugly shadow of what it once had been. And this woman—this Starry—wasn't really so old. Just *tired,* Fiona thought. Then she also thought, *Used.*

Involuntarily, Fiona glanced down at her own ample bosom. Thank goodness, she hadn't had to depend upon her figure to keep J. Roy happy. As long as he had his dinner on time and his boat for going out onto the lake, he was a happy man. Strange how, once upon a time, she had resented his contentment—had wanted him to need her more, but he never had. Why, he hadn't really even wanted children from her, she supposed. Or at least, if he did want them, he never revealed such a thing to Fiona. Once more, she thought of the years when she had practically dragged the poor man off to bed almost every night, hoping against hope that the result would be a child. A child!

"Good morning," Fiona said, rather stiffly, trying to shake off the memory and at the same time, trying not to stare at Starry's poor, half-revealed bosom.

"Yes, ma'am," Starry said. "And good morning to you, too!" Her voice sounded too bright, and Fiona looked into Starry's eyes, where she saw a slight embarrassment at their last night's dependence upon the kindness of strangers. "Middy's already gone to fix the car."

Fiona hesitated, trying to look beyond where Starry was standing, to see if they were leaving the cabin reasonably clean. Starry saw her glance and she quickly said, "I took the sheets off the bed, ma'am. You got one of them washing machines? But no matter—I can wash them for you anyway. I'm used to doing laundry by hand."

Fiona was surprised—obviously, this Starry-person had some upbringing somewhere along the line—someone who had taught her how to be a good guest, albeit an unexpected and perhaps unwelcome one.

"Machine's on the back porch," Fiona said. "And while the sheets are getting washed, you can come in and have yourself some breakfast." Again, her own words surprised her. But she really didn't mind Starry that much—only that Middy-man and all his nasty tattoos.

"Well, thank you, ma'am," Starry said. "I am right hungry. But I don't want to put you all out—anymore than we already have, that is."

"You won't be putting us out," Fiona said. "Just bring those sheets, and I'll show you how to use the washing machine."

Fiona and Starry came up on the back porch, where the new agitator washing machine stood in modern grandeur. Silently, Fiona took the armload of sheets from Starry and loaded them into the machine. Then she poured in a cup of soap powder and closed the lid. When the machine leaped to life, Starry backed up automatically. The washer hummed and danced on the porch floor, and Fiona made sure that the hose for discharging the water was right at the bottom of the banister, so that the wash water would run off the porch.

"You stay here until it gets going good," Fiona instructed. "If it starts bouncing around too much, we'll have to move the wet sheets around inside until it runs smooth."

Starry looked at Fiona as if she had asked Starry to observe a hungry dancing bear, but as Fiona moved toward the kitchen, Starry stayed right where Fiona had instructed.

"Come on in the kitchen and get you some breakfast—once the machine is running smooth," she directed.

Glory had been watching from behind the curtains of the kitchen window that looked out over the back porch. Fiona always thought that whoever had built the cottage had added the back porch as an afterthought, hence the window that was originally designed to overlook the back yard. As Fiona came into the kitchen, Glory accosted her at once, whispering and snarling, "Have you gone and lost your mind sure enough? Gonna bring that . . . woman . . . right into this kitchen and with *him*"—her head indicated Victor—"sitting right there?"

"It's okay, Glory," Fiona tried to soothe her. "I don't think there's a chance in this whole world that woman is Victor's m-a-m-a." She spelled the word and watched Victor, where he was dipping his fingers into the puddle of melted butter in the middle of his bowl of grits.

From the back porch came the sound of the washing machine, growling unhappily.

"And what are you going to do if she *is* the M-a-m-a? You just tell me that!" Glory was angry, and her jowls shook with the force of whispering that powerful question.

Fiona smiled—the kind of smile Glory had never before seen on Fiona's face, a smile that moved right up to her eyes and filled them with a strange light. But then Glory realized that she *had* seen eyes like that once before—a panther's eyes when she was guarding her cubs.

"Oh, Lord have mercy on us all!" Glory wailed, and Victor looked at her with a slight frown. At once, Glory managed a fake smile that would have fooled any child, except one so young, and still smiling for Victor's sake, but with a snarl in her voice, she whispered to Fiona, "Ain't *nobody* gonna take this child away from us!"

"And seems to me you're the one said she wouldn't allow love," Fiona couldn't resist saying. But before Glory could respond, the screen door to the back porch opened and Starry came in. Fiona and Glory watched her as if she were an unsuspecting chipmunk scurrying around in the weeds, completely unmindful of the danger that might be around her. Starry glanced quickly at the two women who had such strange looks on their faces, and then she saw Victor, who was studying her placidly.

"Oh, there's that sweet little boy!" Starry gushed, and Glory's imagination flew into activity, so that she had an immediate vision of herself and Fiona digging a deep grave at the back of the yard and dumping the lifeless body of this . . . *tramp* . . . into it. Something about that vision was completely satisfying! Starry paused, perhaps still wondering about the strange look on the faces of the two women standing in the breakfast-perfumed kitchen.

Fiona broke the spell. "Have a seat, Starry," she said, ignoring Starry's remark about Victor. Starry did as she was told, and she shifted her stare from Victor to Fiona and Glory, and a little frown crowded between her eyebrows.

"Grits?" Fiona asked.

"Yes, ma'am, please," Starry whispered, stealing yet another glance at Victor. Fiona watched both Starry and Victor carefully, waiting to see any glimmer of recognition from the boy or any sign of undue interest from Starry. But seeing nothing that alarmed her, she turned back to the stove and placed two slices of buttered toast on Starry's plate.

"Eggs?" Fiona asked.

"No, ma'am, thank you," Starry replied.

During breakfast, Starry said not another word, but focused her full attention on the good breakfast she was enjoying.

"You want some more coffee?" Glory asked, and the tone in her voice said that Starry had better *not* want any more.

"No, ma'am, thank you," Starry said, and then she got up from the table, picked up her dishes, and took them to the sink. "I thank you for such a fine breakfast," she said softly, and she avoided looking directly at Glory or Fiona, as if she could feel that the two women were uncomfortable with her being there. Without another word, Starry went toward the back door.

"Where are you going?" Fiona asked.

"Why, I'm gonna hang out those sheets," Starry replied. "Middy will be coming back soon, I reckon, and I need to be ready to go with him."

"Oh," Fiona sighed. Somehow, the thoughts of polite, well-mannered—if not well-dressed—Starry going off with the gaunt, dirty Middy filled her with sadness. And yet she was relieved at the same time.

"I gotta get on to the restaurant," Glory said. "You take care of these breakfast dishes?"

"Sure," Fiona replied. "And after that, Victor and I have to get those other two cabins ready."

"She be all right?" Glory whispered, inclining her head toward the back yard, where Starry was hanging the wet sheets on the clothesline.

"I guess so," Fiona answered. "She's just waiting for . . . him."

Fiona had gotten Victor dressed, and she had to use great patience, because he wanted to put on his own socks, and his determined, clumsy efforts almost drove Fiona to tears. But she was patient, and finally he got the socks on, and only one of them had to be adjusted because he had the heel part on top of his foot. As Fiona straightened it, he watched carefully, and she knew for a fact that he would never make that same mistake again.

And as almost always, Fiona studied him carefully. *And what is there behind those beautiful eyes of yours, Victor? You still don't speak, and Glory says it's because you probably don't have anything to say yet. But surely, you notice everything that goes on around you. Notice that strange woman at our breakfast table. You look and look, and I know that you take in everything around you, but still, you don't say a word.*

And you never smile. I've never seen you smile, not even one time.

Glory stuck her head around the bedroom door. "I'm going to the restaurant now. What's *she* gonna do?" Her head indicated the back yard where Starry had just finished hanging the sheets.

"Why don't you ask her to go along with you—help out some, while she's waiting?"

"I could use some help," Glory admitted. "And beggars sure can't be choosers," she added.

"You're not a beggar, Glory," Fiona said. "If you don't want her help, that's okay."

"Oh, I'll take it," Glory growled. "Take all the help I can get—and anywhere I can get it!"

"Then go tell her," Fiona directed.

Fiona took Victor by the hand. "Come on and help me get those cabins ready," she crooned, and so she gathered clean sheets and a fresh bar of soap from the cabinet in the hallway. Giving Victor the soap to carry, she saw his eyes light up with pride, and she made a note to remember how much he liked doing things to help her, despite his tender years. And his silence. And his lack of a smile.

When Starry and Glory arrived at the restaurant, Jubilee was sitting at the end of the pier, waiting as usual for Mr. Owen, and when Jubilee saw the stranger walking along with Glory, her eyebrows rose in question, but she didn't say a word.

"This here is Miss Starry," Glory said, and her frown warned Jubilee not to ask any questions. Glory herself almost bit her tongue with the revulsion of putting an honorific in front of the name of this . . . trash. But still, this trashy woman was white, so the proprieties must be taken. To Starry, Glory said, "This here is Jubilee, my niece. She's almost a teenager," Glory added, as if that explained everything Starry would need to know.

With that, Glory opened the padlock and swung open the door to the restaurant kitchen. "It's gonna be a nice day," Glory commented. "So you need to get the chairs put out," she said to Jubilee. "And you might want to use the hose and wash out under the cleaning table." That outdoor table on the edge of the dock was outfitted with a spigot and covered in linoleum, and it was where fishermen cleaned their catch and where Jubilee cleaned the fish they would cook that day.

"What can I do?" Starry asked.

"You know how to clean fish?" Glory replied, drawing a sharp glance from Jubilee, whose job that usually was, and the one task she hated more than anything else in the world.

"Why, yess'm," Starry brightened. "I sure do."

"Well then, as soon as Mr. Owen brings in the catch for this morning, you can get started on them." And to Jubilee, she repeated, "Get those chairs outside now."

Jubilee smiled happily and went to the storage closet to retrieve the folding chairs. She was delighted to be relieved of the nasty job of cleaning fish, and silently, she wondered why on earth Glory would give that job to a "guest," which is what this woman, Starry, had to be— probably. She sure wasn't family, and she wasn't a paying guest. That much Jubilee could figure out. But she didn't know anything else about her, and she did know better than to ask questions. So she hummed to herself as she gathered the chairs and began unfolding them around the small tables that were set up on the pier right outside of the kitchen door to the restaurant.

"Better wipe out them chairs," Glory called, and Jubilee rolled her eyes and went into the kitchen for a bucket of warm, soapy water and a rag. Starry stood by, obviously feeling awkward, until they all heard the outboard motor on Mr. Owen's approaching boat. As he cut the motor and allowed the small boat to nose its way into the pier, he threw up a tanned hand and grinned around the stem of his pipe.

"'Morning, ladies," he chirped. "You all ready for a mess of good fish?"

"Sure enough," Glory replied, reaching out and taking the string of largemouth bass Mr. Owen handed up to her. They were so fresh that some of them were still flopping weakly.

"You come back around eleven-thirty," Glory instructed him. "I'll have your plates all ready."

Because that was the arrangement Fiona had worked out with Mr. Owen. She had no money to actually pay him, and truthfully, he didn't really need money at all. He was quite contented with a valid excuse to go fishing every morning, bringing fresh fish for the restaurant, and in return, Glory fixed two plates overflowing with fried fish, hushpuppies, French fries and coleslaw for Mr. Owen and his wife.

On this particular day, Mr. Owen handed over the string of fish, and his eyes swept across Starry, who was standing with one hip thrust out and her shoulders back. Glory noticed this stance and issued a loud "H-u-u-mph!" but Starry didn't seem to notice. Mr. Owen averted his gaze, and Glory noticed that, as well. Mr. Owen was a good man. A married man. And certainly he had lived in this world long enough to recognize a "loose" woman when he saw one, Glory thought.

"Start getting them fish cleaned," Glory snorted to Starry. "And don't you be casting your wandering eyes—lustful eyes! At a good man, a *married* man."

Starry took in her breath sharply. "Why I would never think of doing such a thing!" she objected, surprise showing in her painted-on, uplifted eyebrows.

"Maybe you done it so long, you don't even know you're doing it at all," Glory retorted. Starry didn't say another word, but her eyes filled up, and she took the string of fish in silence. Mr. Owen glanced from one of them to the other, and then he quickly put the outboard motor into reverse and pushed away from the dock.

For the next half hour or so, Starry stood at the outdoor table, cleaning the fish and throwing the intestines and fins into the lake. When she scraped off the scales, she did so almost viciously, and Jubilee, still setting up the chairs and then sweeping off the dock in front of the kitchen door, noticed tears dropping onto the table, in and among all the juices of slaughtered fish. When Starry finished, she took a deep pan full of perfect filets into the kitchen, where Glory had everything set up for dipping, battering and frying the fish. When Starry handed over the pan, she said not a word, and Glory glanced at her.

"That man of yours come back yet?" Glory asked, none too kindly.

"I . . . I don't think so," Starry said, keeping her eyes cast down and determined not to let Glory make her feel any worse than she already did. But she did wash her hands thoroughly at the outdoor table, and after she dried them, she tried to pull up the sagging neckline of her blouse and walked back to the house to sit on the porch, waiting for "her man" to come back with the repaired car.

By the time lunchtime at the restaurant was over, Fiona could hear Starry's sobs coming from the porch. Fiona put two and two together in a flash. Starry's "man" wasn't coming back—repaired car or no repaired car. Fiona went out onto the porch quietly, and while she felt inclined to put her hand on Starry's shaking shoulder, she resisted the impulse. After all, this woman was really nothing more than a stranger. So instead, she simply said, "What will you do?"

Starry hiccoughed and admitted, "I don't know."

Somehow, Fiona's heart went out to this strange woman, and she tried to resist the feeling. Finally, she asked, "You got family you can call on?"

Starry shook her head. "No. No family."

"How about him . . . your hus . . . *him*? Has he got any family you can call?"

Starry tilted her head and looked up at Fiona with misery in her eyes. "He's not my husband," she admitted. "I mean, we're not married."

Fiona tried to keep a neutral expression on her face, but it was hard. "And I don't know if there's any family he has," Starry continued. "Leastwise, none I know about."

"Well, where did you all come from?" Fiona was determined not to discuss Starry's relationship, if any, to Middy any longer.

"Gainesville. And before that, Jacksonville. And before that, Tampa."

"Traveling all around, huh?"

"Anywhere we could get work."

Fiona hesitated only a moment before she asked, "And what kind of work was that?"

"We're entertainers," Starry said, but the tone of her voice belied her true belief in that profession. So she amended her answer. "We got along with little jobs singing in roadhouses and such as that." For a moment, her face brightened. "Middy plays such a good guitar!" But then she added, "When we can't get that kind of work, we get whatever we can."

"And that would be?"

"Anything—washing dishes, waiting tables—that's me, of course."

"And what does *he* do?"

"I really don't know," Starry confessed, looking up at Fiona with reddened eyes and a dripping nose. Fiona pulled a tissue out of her apron pocket and thrust it at Starry. "He just goes out, and when he comes back, he has some money. Not much, but some at least."

The conversation lapsed, and finally Fiona said, "Well, we don't know anything. He may come back yet."

"Maybe," said Starry. "But I don't think so." Her tears had stopped, and she used the tissue to wipe her dripping nose. Afterward, she started to hand the used tissue back to Fiona, but then she reconsidered and simply balled the tissue up in her fist.

"You all have been so nice to me," she said. "And I sure do 'preciate it. But I better be getting on. I'll just walk on along the road and maybe catch a ride. Go on along to the next town or something like that."

"But can't you put on something better looking . . . uh, some *other* clothes before you go?" Fiona had a terrible vision of Starry walking along the side of the road dressed in such provocative clothes—Lord only knows what kind of man would offer her a ride.

"No, ma'am," Starry said. "I don't have nothing better than this. It's what Middy likes . . . liked . . . for me to wear."

"Well, you can't go off looking like that," Fiona insisted. "Come on in the bedroom with me, and I'll see if I can find you something better."

But as they approached Fiona's bedroom door, two things happened. First of all, Fiona envisioned Starry walking along the road with her thumb held out, and although she was dressed in one of Fiona's housedresses and it was way too big for her, her feminine curves would still show through that proper fabric and God only knows who would come along and whisk her away. The second thing that happened was a loud crash from the kitchen.

"Good Lord!" Fiona yelled. "Victor? Victor?" She went running toward the kitchen, yelling his name the whole way and with Starry running right on her heels. Victor was sitting in the middle of the kitchen floor, surrounded by all of the pots and pans he had pulled out of the bottom cabinet. Holding two pot lids, he watched the women running toward him and then he banged the lids together again in a mighty crash, shutting his eyes tight against the deafening noise.

Fiona scooped him up in her arms, and both lids clattered to the floor.

"Oh, Victor!" Fiona gasped. "I thought something terrible had happened to you!"

"Is he okay?" Starry's voice came as a surprise to Fiona, such had been her focus only on Victor.

"I think so," Fiona said. "It's just that I'm not used to having an active little boy around, and I never know what he's going to get into next." The final words came out as a kind of soft wail, and before Fiona knew what was happening, Starry reached over and lifted Victor from her arms.

"I know all about little boys," Starry said. "I had me two little brothers, and if it hadn't been for me, I guess they would have driven my poor mama half crazy. They can get into all kinds of mischief, can't they?" Her question clearly addressed Victor himself, as her voice had gone all soft and singsongy.

Fiona studied Starry and Victor carefully.

"You don't know this little boy, do you, Starry?"

Starry seemed completely surprised. "Why, no, ma'am—but I guess almost all little boys are pretty much alike. And this one is no different, I expect. But I'll tell you one thing, he sure is pretty."

"Yes, he is," Fiona reflected. "But he's had some things happen in his life most little boys don't have to deal with." Starry's eyebrows went up, and she waited for Fiona to continue. But Fiona didn't say anything else about Victor. Instead, she said, "Tell me something, Starry . . ." she started out. "Are you a *good girl?*"

"Ma'am?"

"I said, are you a good girl?"

Starry hesitated, still holding Victor, who had put his head down on her shoulder. Unconsciously, she stroked his hair and started rocking from side to side with him in her arms. "I *used* to be a good girl," Starry finally admitted, and when she looked at Fiona, there were tears clinging to her eyelashes.

"Used to be?" Fiona asked.

"Yess'm. Before I met Middy, I used to be a good girl."

"I think you could be a good girl again," Fiona pronounced, somewhat surprised at hearing her own words.

And just at that moment, Glory came into the kitchen, carrying the smell of frying fish on her clothes. She looked at Fiona and Starry and put both of her hands on her hips.

"And what in the world is going on here, is what I'd like to know!"

For some reason, Fiona and Starry both started laughing, and the more they laughed, the more Glory scowled. Finally, Starry looked right into Glory's eyes. "I'm gonna be a good girl again," she said, and then she went back to laughing.

"Lord have mercy on us!" Glory grumbled. "Lord simply have mercy!"

As it turned out, Starry was right. Middy didn't come back. That, of course, was much to Fiona's relief and to Glory's I-told-you-so satisfaction.

For all of that long, hot afternoon, Starry sat in one of the rocking chairs on the front porch, with her knees drawn up under her chin. She was wearing one of Fiona's staid housedresses, a cream-colored print dress festooned with the palest lavender flowers, a dress that reached almost down to her ankles and that buttoned high enough that no hint of her poor bosom was showing. The dress bunched around Starry's waist, where Fiona had fastened a belt, trying to make it fit Starry's sparse figure.

Fiona, glancing out of the window, envied that small waist, but she was pleased to find that Starry had carefully tucked the dress around her legs. So that sitting as she was doing—with her feet up in the chair—no one passing by could have seen her underwear . . . *if* she was wearing any, that is. And by noticing the mere slope of Starry's shoulders, Fiona could tell that she was still hoping—hoping against hope—that Middy would come back for her.

Finally, without a word, Starry left the chair, went down the steps, and walked away. Fiona and Glory watched from the window.

"Better this way," Glory pronounced. "We got no right messing in that woman's business. So good riddance!"

"I know," Fiona answered. "But there's something I like about her. Don't know what it is though."

"Just what you usually do," Glory huffed. "Take in all kinds of things what ain't got no hope. Just your heart getting in the way of common sense, once again." Then Glory continued. "But I tell you the truth, this place getting to be something for folks getting dropped off and left on our doorstep!"

Fiona ignored Glory's words, and she spoke as if she had been so deep in thought, she hadn't heard a thing Glory said. "She could have been a good girl again. I just know it," Fiona whispered. "And besides, Victor seemed to like her."

"You sure you wasn't just looking for a baby-sitter?" Glory asked.

"Maybe," Fiona admitted. "But there was something or other about her I really did like."

"Wash all that color out of her hair, she might not have been so bad looking. Not so trashy," Glory admitted. "But that's just wishful thinking, and I still say good riddance!"

"I just hope she isn't trying to hitchhike," Fiona said. "I just hope and pray she isn't doing that."

At dusk, Fiona took Victor for a long walk about the lake, where he seemed to be amazed at everything he saw. He threw pebbles into the lake, and when an osprey flew from the top of a nearby dead live oak, he gazed in wonder, his mouth open and eyes bright.

Fiona felt the reflection of his amazement. "Where on earth have you been, honey, that little bitty things like this bring out such wonder in you? Where have you been and who have you been with, that could have you be so dirty and smelly and hungry and not know much about this old world you've been born into?"

Victor looked up at Fiona, as if he could understand every single word she said.

"And honey," Fiona went on. "Why don't you ever smile? Don't you know how? Hasn't anybody ever smiled at *you*?"

Darkness was almost complete when Fiona and Victor returned from the long walk, and as they approached the house, Fiona, as always, found supreme comfort in the yellow light from the small windows—in the near darkness, the light sounded a small song of safety and comfort to her. *Home.* Probably the most beautiful word in the world. And now, she would be able to make that real for Victor, as well. Make him warm and safe and happy. Make him smile. The thought was completely satisfying.

"We're home, honey," she said to Victor, and as soon as the words were out of her mouth, she saw the dim figure of someone sitting in a rocking chair on the front porch. It wasn't Glory.

It was Starry.

Fiona resisted the impulse to rush forward and embrace the stranger—the sad over-the-hill *harlot-woman*, as Glory had called her when Victor wasn't around to hear. Instead, Fiona came up the steps slowly, holding Victor's hand and waiting for his baby legs to negotiate the high steps, and she looked up at Starry as if finding her in the rocking chair was something she had fully expected.

"It's a beautiful evening, isn't it?" Fiona asked, and Starry stared at her for a moment before she answered.

"Yes, ma'am, it sure is pretty." Then Starry added in the same matter-of-fact voice, "I went along the road to where our car was broken down. It's gone."

"Well, we sort of expected that, didn't we?" Fiona asked. Victor had managed to open the screen door, and Fiona said to him, "That's right, honey. Go on inside and find Aunt Glory."

"He sure is a pretty little fellow," Starry said. "Just like a ray of sunshine."

"Yes," Fiona agreed, pleased. And then Starry added, "I don't rightly know what I'm gonna do now."

"You can stay here," Fiona whispered. "You can have that little cabin where you and . . . you all stayed last night. It isn't much, but it will keep the rain off your head."

"But how can I pay you for it?" Starry asked. "I don't have a thing but what I've got on my back." She looked down at Fiona's dress. "Oh, I guess I don't even have that."

Fiona thought for a long moment. "To tell you the truth, we never have had every single cabin filled at one time. Never more than five of them rented out at once. So you wouldn't be costing me anything at all. You could work in the restaurant, help me clean cabins when folks have them reserved. You already know how to run the washing machine. And maybe you could help take care of Victor when Glory and I are busy with other things."

"Oh, I'd like that!" Starry's eyes lit up. "I'm real good with children." She hesitated and then added, "And I can clean fish real good too. You can ask Miss Glory about that."

Fiona had never before heard a white woman give a black woman the honorific of "Miss," but she said nothing. Probably, that Middy character was a northerner, and Starry had picked up some new ideas from him.

"Better for you just to call her Glory," Fiona suggested.

"Yess'm," Starry replied easily. "But you certainly can ask her about how good I clean fish."

"I'm sure," Fiona agreed. "So let's give this a try—you can stay in the cabin at the far end, and we can see how things work out."

"Thank you, Miss Fiona," Starry said.

And then Fiona added, "But if *he* comes back, he can't stay here."

"Yess'm," Starry agreed.

"So if that happens, you'll have to either go with him or send him on his way. One way or the other."

"Yess'm," Starry repeated.

"Are you sure you understand?" Fiona pressed.

"I understand," Starry said, and then she smiled a smile that would have been even more wonderful if it had not been ringed with a deep coating of dark purple lipstick.

"Listen," Fiona started out with a gentle lilt in her voice. "Maybe you don't want to talk about it, but I'd like to ask you how you met Middy."

The sudden smile that wreathed Starry's face lifted the sagging chin line and the painted-on eyebrows, so that Fiona had a quick glimpse of how lovely Starry had been, as a very young girl.

"I used to work for my uncle in his little gift shop in St. Augustine," Starry began. "I was one of four girls and two boys in my family, and my three sisters were all so beautiful, they could have been movie stars—any one of them. And then there was me." Starry cast her eyes down. "Awful hard growing up like that, being the youngest of the girls and me just as plain as a bowl of oatmeal. But one thing I loved to do was take care of my two little brothers. They made me feel pretty!"

Fiona tilted her head to the side, deciding quickly not to dispute anything Starry said about herself. Because whatever her memories of her younger years, it was her own perception, and Fiona knew better than to argue with it. But she certainly knew what she thought—*If somebody had simply shown Starry how to use makeup the right way and told her she was beautiful, even if she wasn't, maybe she would have thought enough of herself not to take up with some slimy man like Middy!*

But now, better to let Starry talk everything out, and then Fiona would know so much more about this woman who would be living in one of Fiona's cabins. This woman who would be around Victor almost every single day.

"That little shop of my uncle's was real nice, and I didn't mind the work at all," Starry went on, her eyes lighting up. "It was a nice shop, and nice people came into it, tourists mostly, I guess, but nice people anyway. But it was hard—waiting on all those people who were going somewhere and doing something. People who had real lives and were only visiting St. Augustine."

Fiona settled back in her chair, listening to Starry's quiet voice and trying to grasp a complete reality in Starry's words.

"Maybe you know how it is," Starry went on. "You see other people and you want whatever it is they have so bad, you almost die inside!"

Fiona reached back in her memory and saw herself walking down a sidewalk and passing a woman who was carrying a baby in her arms, and as the woman passed, Fiona caught a whiff of the baby's aroma—powder and warmth and sweetness—and that perfume made her weak in the knees. *Yes,* Fiona thought. *I know exactly what you mean.*

"Seemed to me like everybody had someplace to go and somebody to be—except me." At that point, Fiona felt that some sort of response was called for, and she said, "You know, that may just be something that happens to most young girls. They don't know what they want, but it sure isn't what they already have."

"Oh, yes!" Starry agreed enthusiastically.

"And that's what you were feeling when you met Middy?"

"Oh yes," Starry repeated. "It was a Wednesday afternoon and nobody was in the shop. I was staring out of the window, watching people go by on the sidewalk and feeling so awful, I just wanted to die. And that's when Middy came squalling along the street on his motorcycle and crashed into the lamppost right in front of the shop!" Starry smiled at the memory, and her eyes seemed to glaze over. "Goodness! What a noise! That loud motor and then the squeal of brakes and the CRASH! against the lamppost. I went running out, of course, and there was Middy, lying on the sidewalk, leaning on his elbow and shaking his head. He looked up at me and said, 'I must be dead, 'cause I'm looking at an angel!' And that's when I fell head over heels in love with him."

"Just like that?" Fiona asked, because she was trying to remember the first time she had met J. Roy, and she couldn't. In her memory, there had never simply been a single day of her life when J. Roy wasn't a part of it.

"Yep—just like that! Him lying on the sidewalk with a big bruise on his forehead and thinking I was an angel—me!—and with all those tattoos running up and down his arm."

"Was he badly hurt?"

"Oh, no. Just the bruise on his head, and after a while, he stood up, got his motorcycle back up on its wheels, and took off down the street. He'd asked me where there was a garage, and I thought maybe I'd never see him again."

"But you did," Fiona said, encouragingly.

"Sure did!" Starry laughed. "A couple of days later, he came roaring up in front of the shop and stopped, and while I was watching through the window, he motioned to me. And so I went out and I got onto the back of that motorcycle, and all he said to me was 'Hold on!' and we roared off and I never went back to St. Augustine again."

"Just like that?" Fiona asked, smiling in spite of herself at the thought of Starry simply running away from everything that she thought was sad and boring—running away by riding off on the back of a monstrous motorcycle and holding on to a large, dark-haired man who was covered in tattoos.

"And did you love him?" Fiona's question came as a surprise to both Fiona and Starry. And Starry stared at Fiona without speaking for several minutes, as if Starry had never thought of that question before.

"I did," Starry said at last. "I loved him a whole bunch."

"Why?" Fiona asked, because she really did mean to know what on earth had prompted a well-brought-up girl like Starry to decide to spend her life with someone like Middy.

"I don't know," Starry confessed. "Some kind of magic, I guess."

From the kitchen came the crash of pot lids banging together and Glory saying over the din, "You're giving me a headache, Victor. A real headache!"

"Listen, Starry, we'll get you all fixed up. We'll make things better for you." Fiona said, and because Starry wasn't quite sure of what that meant, she said nothing else. "In the meantime, let's get you some clean sheets and towels. And remember, ladies' time in the shower house is ten to eleven in the mornings. I don't want you blundering in there when men are using it."

So the two women vacated the rocking chairs and went inside, leaving the ghost of the heavily tattooed Middy alone on the porch with his phantom cigarette.

Glory finished putting all the pots and lids back into the cupboard—where Victor could pull them out again any time he chose—and she watched from the kitchen window that overlooked the back porch while Fiona got out clean sheets and towels and sent Starry walking off down the path to the very cabin where Starry and Middy had stayed the night before.

When Fiona came into the kitchen, Glory snorted, "Well, let me run right out and look all around the yard! Maybe I can find us something else—like a old stray cat or something—we can take in and give a home to!"

During this exchange, Victor, having been removed from the pots and lids cupboard, was sitting at the kitchen table, a half-full glass of milk before him and a cookie in each hand. Glory looked at Victor and her eyes filled up with tears. "Oh! What a terrible thing for me to say! Just look at what a beautiful boy we've given a home to, and we found *him* out in the yard!"

"I know you didn't mean it, Glory," Fiona said in a gentle voice.

"I love him like I carried him in my own body!" Glory muttered, again close to tears.

"And I do too," Fiona added, deciding right on the spot not to say anything to Glory about her determination not to love anything or anyone. Then Fiona looked at Victor, noticing for the first time the cookies in his hands.

"Glory!" Fiona exclaimed. "He's going to ruin his supper with those cookies. Lord have mercy! You're going to spoil him to death."

"I know," Glory said, lifting her chin to let Fiona know she need not fuss, that Glory intended to spoil Victor—but perhaps not his appetite—every single day of his life.Victor gazed blankly at Fiona and then, while Fiona and Glory watched, he dropped both cookies from his hands and held out his arms to Fiona.

"Mama!" he yelped, and it was the very first word they had ever heard him speak.

"Yes, baby," Fiona crooned, taking Victor into her arms and hugging him until he hung, almost limp, over her shoulder. "Yes, baby," she repeated, rocking him from side to side, just the way she had seen Starry do earlier. "Sure enough, I'll be your mama."

Then Fiona studied Glory's frowning face. "And so will Aunt Glory," she added, turning the frown into a silly grin. "And so will Miss Starry, I guess," Fiona added, and with that, Glory's grin disappeared, just like the sun going behind a rain-laden cloud.

"Huumph!" Glory snorted, turning back to the stove. "Don't think she's one bit fit to be any kind of a mama to anybody!" But Fiona kept swaying back and forth, back and forth, with Victor in her arms.

As they stood in the familiar kitchen that day, neither Fiona nor Glory could tell what was ahead of them.But Fiona was determined that Victor would know *love* the way no other child in the history of the whole world had known it. Somehow, she would find a way to make up for his abandonment. Somehow, she would teach him how to love without the fear of love leaving him!

Glory still wore a scowl, but Fiona knew that the scowl was for Starry, and not for herself or Victor or for the daunting task that lay before them. Fiona would make everything right for Victor. She was sure of it. After all, he would have a real mama in her, though she intended to make him call her "Aunt," to support her claim that he was kin to her. Glory would spoil him daily, and Starry—well, whatever she had to give to Victor was yet to be seen. But Fiona knew that it would be something beautiful, something to teach him even more about love.

And it wouldn't be just women who taught Victor—Fiona would see to that. Old Man would teach Victor all of the old Seminole stories, the myths and the secrets. When Victor was older, Mr. Owen would take him out fishing almost every morning, and Doc would take such a special interest in Victor that folks would say that Doc loved Victor almost as much as his very own daughter, Rebecca.

Victor dozed under his gentle to-and-fro rocking against Fiona's warm shoulder, and just before he finally fell asleep, he heard the gentle whisper of water bubbling in the kettle on the stove, almost like the soft growl of the guardian-panther of his dreams. And in his dream, he watched while a skirt—a pale triangle of glowing fabric—disappeared into the darkness.

Chapter Six

From the small table in the far corner of the coffee shop, Old Man—dressed in his full Seminole outfit for spending a full day in the Trading Post next door—watched quietly for the new waitress his grandson had told him about, the waitress who was taking sweet Rowena's place. She didn't see him when he came in, but he studied her carefully. She was so very young, with white-blonde hair and a weak chin, and she cleared away the dishes from the tables where some early morning fishermen had eaten breakfast—gobbling down scrambled eggs and homemade biscuits and slurping their hot coffee, in a rush to get out on the lake.

After she took the dishes into the kitchen, she came back and wiped down the tables with a cloth wrung out of warm, soapy water, moving the dime tip one of the fishermen had left next to the napkin container, wiping around it, and then finally picking it up and dropping it into her apron pocket. When she came out of the kitchen again, she was carrying a tray balanced on one hand and holding a pot of coffee in the other, her face a bland reflection of her rote way of working the tables.

And then she spotted Old Man for the first time.

She froze right in her tracks, her small mouth above the receding chin molded into a startled "O." Her eyes widened, showing the whites all around the pale blue corneas, and she tilted the laden tray she carried to the point where two plates heaped with eggs and bacon threatened to slide off and hit the floor. She quickly put the coffee pot on a nearby counter, rebalanced the tray, and looked around her nervously—looking perhaps for a sheriff's posse to rescue her from the "savage." Seeing nothing other than the other patrons who were huddled in early-morning stupor around their plates and cups, she at last pretended that she didn't notice the old Seminole. Retrieving the coffee pot, she walked toward the table of fishermen who were waiting for their breakfast, but she glanced back at Old Man several times. He returned her glances with his typical blank expression. Blank, yes, but with the deep crannies and wrinkles telling of wisdom, of experience, of kindness, for anyone who had the kind of vision it would take to notice such things.

He did not smile at her, but within only a few moments, she began to feel that she had nothing to fear from this man—and then, as she saw that no one else in the shop seemed to be alarmed by the Seminole Indian sitting there, either, she admitted that in some strange way she couldn't understand, the presence of this strange-looking old man was comforting.

Finally, finally, she approached the table where Old Man was sitting—patient and relaxed and with his large hands folded contentedly across his stomach. "Coffee?" she whispered, still keeping a safe distance away from him and waving the half-full coffee pot. He nodded his head once, and she filled a cup, hesitating only briefly before coming forward and placing it on the table in front of him.

"I'm new here," she said to him, almost as a means of apology, and she balanced the coffee pot against her hip. "I'm Abby," she added, and although Old Man said not a single word, the slow nod of his head told her that he had heard her name. Abby stared at him for a long moment, and then she turned and went off into the kitchen, glancing back over her shoulder only once as she went through the swinging door.

Old Man stirred several spoonfuls of sugar into his cup. If he had been a man who was given to smiling, he certainly would have smiled at Abby's initial reaction to him, because it reminded him so completely of the first time he had come into the restaurant when Rowena, who was now called the "old waitress," had been the new employee.

After Rowena's initial reaction to him in his Seminole getup, a reaction not unlike Abby's, she had become quite comfortable around him. Not because he entered into any conversation with her whatsoever, but simply because Rowena liked to smoke cigarettes. So whenever she had time, she would light up a cigarette and flop down in the chair across from Old Man at the corner table, slipping off her shoes, wriggling her aching toes under the table, and talking. And how she could talk!

Especially, she liked talking to Old Man because he was always such a good listener, and once she realized that he never spoke a single word himself—not to her and not to anyone else—she used to lean across the table and whisper to him, "You know what? I like talking to you 'cause I know you won't never repeat a single word I say. Isn't that right?" In answer to her question, Old Man simply gazed at her with his dark, bottomless eyes, and he didn't even have to nod his head for her to hear the *yes* he said.

"You aren't supposed to sit with the customers," Roy, who owned the restaurant, reminded her sometimes, but the tone of his voice belied his real displeasure. Because no one could ever be displeased with Rowena—not with that lovely, open face and clear blue eyes, not with the soft, blonde curls that threatened to escape from under the edges of her waitresses' cap. Not with her youth and innocence, and not with the soft-spoken voice that had such a strange lilt in it.

"I come from the hills of North Georgia," she told Old Man one time. "That's where I got my way of speaking, and some folks seem to think it sounds funny, but I don't think so, 'cause I sound just like my mama and her mama before her. And my daddy and all his people. So it's like music to my ears!" She studied the silent Old Man for a moment, and then she said, "I'll bet if ever I heard you say anything, it would sound beautiful too—not like what I sound like, but . . ." Rowena drew her eyebrows together and studied Old Man carefully. "But I'll bet your voice would sound like all the night creatures—locusts and tree frogs and those big old bull alligators that sing almost every night in the springtime." Old Man said nothing, nor did the expression on his face change, but Rowena saw a softening in the dark eyes, and she knew that deep inside, where no one else could see it, he was telling her that she was right.

All of the customers—especially the fishermen who came to the lake only for a week or so—had taken very kindly to Rowena, thanking her when she brought their food and refilled their coffee cups, and when she would turn to go back into the kitchen, the eyes of the fishermen would follow her—even the older men—quietly appreciative of her softly curved hips and the way her stockings swished pleasantly against each other as she moved away. But even though Rowena was extremely polite, she was also thoroughly professional, slipping away quickly to avoid a stranger's hand touching her wrist as she reached for her tips.

When Rowena worked at the restaurant, Old Man became so contented at the corner table that Arabella, his wife who ran the Trading Post next to the restaurant with help from their grandson, Dave, complained to him that what few tourists they had coming into their small shop wanted to see a "real Seminole," and that his absence was hurting their business. As always, Old Man said not a word, but he continued to wear his Seminole tribal clothes every day, even though he avoided the Trading Post and stayed at the corner table in the restaurant as long as he wanted.

Finally, Arabella took to telling the tourists, "Listen, if you want to see a real Seminole—an honest-to-goodness real Seminole—just look through the window of the restaurant next door. He's sitting at the corner table. You can't miss him!" So the women tourists would peek in the window, and sometimes, they would even come into the restaurant, moving timidly and taking a table as far away from "the savage" as possible, tittering over their cups of tea and looking his way from time to time with curious but frightened glances.

But one day, only a week or so after Rowena had started her waitress job, three men came in who, clearly, had already begun drinking beer, long before taking out one of the rented boats. Roy peeked out at them through the serving window in the kitchen, shook his head and clucked his tongue. "Crazy!" he said. "Storm come up, they'll all drown." When Rowena took their orders, Old Man watched carefully, and when she left to go back to the kitchen, the men leaned together, mumbling and laughing loudly.

And Old Man watched.

Rowena brought their orders, balancing the three plates along one arm and carrying the coffee pot in her other hand. When she put their plates in front of them, one of the men looked briefly at the other two and crooked his finger to Rowena, signaling for her to lean closer to him—as if he couldn't hear very well or speak very loudly. And Rowena did lean, but then one of the other men slid his hand quickly around her hip and over the roundness of her buttocks. She jumped back, sloshing the coffee in the pot and bumping into and turning over a chair at a nearby vacant table. Frightened, Rowena retreated quickly toward the kitchen, but she was met by Roy, who saw what happened and came barging out of the kitchen to confront the men. But Roy was too late. As soon as he came out of the kitchen door, he could see Old Man, who was standing behind the perpetrator, wearing that same bland expression on his face.

Other people in the restaurant later said that he had moved across the room as swiftly and as silently as a panther in the low brush, grabbed a handful of the man's hair and yanked his head back, exposing the vulnerable throat and the protruding Adam's apple. And poised over that throat was Old Man's long, evil-looking knife, resting against the goose-bumped skin just below the open mouth and the terrified eyes. The two other men had thrown back their chairs in their haste to escape, but they still stood, as if trying to decide how to rescue their friend without getting themselves cut to bits by the crazy savage.

Roy put his hand up, as if he were stopping traffic, and he spoke softly into the complete silence that had fallen over the restaurant. "It's okay, Old Man." The Indian waited for a few more terrifying moments before he lowered his knife and released the hair. The man's head snapped forward, and he half-stumbled, half-scrambled away, putting his hand to his throat, as if to make sure it was still intact. Then all three men ran into each other as they jammed their way through the door, leaving the few other people in the restaurant openmouthed and silent.

"It's okay," Roy said again, and Rowena came out from behind Roy, her smile tremulous and her eyes filled with unshed tears. She put her hand out and touched Old Man's arm. And while she said not a word, something passed between Rowena and Old Man—something like one would witness between a protective father forced into becoming a dangerous father—and a grateful, shaken daughter.

From that day on, Rowena sat with Old Man every chance she got, and she talked to him. How she did talk! And Old Man listened.

"Did you know I got me a baby boy?" Rowena said one morning, and Old Man lifted his eyebrows, as if he couldn't imagine that this lovely child was old enough to have a child herself. "Yep," she smiled, nodding joyfully. "And he's the prettiest little thing you ever saw in your whole life. Just now started walking, and oh, he's so proud of himself! Likes to rise up on his toes, just like he's a little rooster, trying to crow!" Then she lowered her eyes, as if to stop herself from visualizing her beautiful little son and his newly acquired skill. "He stays with Mee-Maw—my mama-in-law—when I'm working," she added, and her face clouded over. "My man—my boy's daddy—don't like me working," she murmured. "But we need the money real bad."

Just then, someone at another table held up his coffee cup, and Rowena went to refill it. While she was gone, Roy came out of the kitchen, enjoying a slight lull in breakfast orders and with a sigh, he took Rowena's seat at Old Man's table. "Shame about her," Roy ventured. "Such a sweet little thing and her married to one of them turpentiners. Sure ain't easy for any of 'em." While Roy talked, Old Man watched Rowena, once again wondering how on earth such a young woman could have a child who was already starting to walk.

The restaurant was doing a good business, as more and more fishermen heard about Lake Love-Oak and Fiona's clean cabins, and consequently, business was good, as well, not only in Glory's fish restaurant on the pier but also in town, at the Seminole Trading Post and Roy's larger restaurant. And now that automobiles were becoming so numerous, Roy had installed a single gasoline pump right in the front yard, further tempting tourists to stop.

Some of the fishermen, or more likely their wives, might come in the Seminole Trading Post, finger the small trinkets without buying much of anything, and wait around somewhat nervously to watch Old Man's grandson, Dave, wrestle an alligator in the pit behind the shop. The wrestling matches were publicized by a large sign nailed beside the door of the trading post— "Authentic Seminole Alligator Wrestling at 10 and 2—10 cents admission." That the alligator was only a very young one didn't seem to matter, for despite the gator's tender years and juvenile size, he bore the familiar scales and black, cruel eyes, and he obligingly opened his mouth wide and hissed on a regular basis, showing the tourists his soft, candy-pink tongue surrounded by a huge set of razor-sharp teeth. The wrestling matches were mainly for show, but they satisfied the tourists. And so when Dave and the alligator finished several minutes of dancing around each other, with the gator's jaw snapping at him viciously, Dave reached around and caught the gator's tail, spinning the young creature around in the fine sand of the alligator pit. At this, the tourists always sucked in their breath, and some of the women screamed, while others tittered nervously. After the wrestling matches, which took place twice a day, the women would sometimes buy key rings made of gator hide or bead bracelets that bore the Seminole symbols for rain, lightning and thunder, or fire. Or one of the fine tapestries of Seminole symbols that Arabella, Old Man's wife made by hand.

Old Man himself never wrestled the gator, and, in fact, never even rang up any purchase from the Trading Post. His sole job was to sit in the corner in a tilted-back chair, wearing his traditional Seminole clothes, watching the tourists and scowling. It was the scowl that entranced the tourists and frightened them just enough to thrill them.

"Look!" they might whisper, believing that the stony-faced old man couldn't hear them, or that, if he did, wouldn't care what they had to say about him. Or perhaps he didn't even understand English.

"Look! A real savage!" That is when he would have to bite his lip to keep from laughing. Sometimes, just to amuse himself, he pretended to sleep, with his head resting on the back of the tilted-back chair, and when any of the tourist women would come close enough, he would snap open his penetrating, black eyes, sending the curious women into shocked squeals. But that was all a part of the business—the business of selling bits and pieces and revered symbols of Seminole heritage to silly white women who would return to their perfect homes in Gainesville or Birmingham or Atlanta telling stories, over dainty cups of tea, to their friends about their frightening encounter with "the savage" at the Seminole Trading Post or in the restaurant.

But despite the way Old Man spent most of his days in what he regarded to be a charade that was disrespectful to his ancestors—whether he was sitting in the Trading Post itself or at his regular table in the restaurant next door—deep in his heart, he knew that someday he would be called upon to make a sacrifice that would honor his ancestors, bring them more honor than any chanting or alligator wrestling or bead making could ever do. He never questioned exactly *how* he knew such a thing, only that the silent knowledge sustained him—bloomed, invisible, in the deepest part of his heart.

So that on one quiet morning when rainy, windy weather had run many fishermen off of the turbulent lake and into the restaurant and the Trading Post, Rowena poured Old Man's coffee with a hand that was shaking slightly, and he looked at her face, feeling in his very bones that something was terribly wrong. When she finished pouring, he did something he had never done before—reached over and gently put his large brown hand over hers, feeling protective and wanting to do anything he could to help her—no matter what was the problem. He had heard people talk about Rowena's husband and family, and he knew that they were turpentiners, only one family among many who had tried to make a go of farming and had failed. The few crops they managed to produce sucked all of the nourishment from the soil, so they turned to turpentining—slashing through the bark of the pine trees, fastening on small cups to collect the sap and laboriously gathering the filled cups, pouring the sap into barrels and replacing the cup to collect more sap. From tree to tree these people went, with the men usually handling the heavy barrels and the women and even small children emptying the cups and cutting grass around the trees. Whole families made their livings that way, so it was no wonder Rowena liked her job in the restaurant. She considered herself fortunate to work in a clean place, and she made good tips because she smiled at the customers and treated them as if keeping their coffee cups filled was the most important thing in her world.

But on that particular morning, there was no smile from Rowena— not even for Old Man—and she gently pulled her hand out from under Old Man's comforting touch and suddenly went so pale that he thought she would faint. But instead, she quickly set the coffee pot onto the table and ran to the bathroom. Roy peered out of the kitchen opening, looked at Old Man, and they both shrugged their shoulders at each other. They waited, unsure of whether to knock on the door of the women's bathroom themselves or to ask one of the lady customers to do that for them. But before they had to make that decision, Rowena came out of the bathroom, with her face newly scrubbed and some color back in her cheeks.

"I'm sorry," she said to Old Man and Roy. "See, I'm getting me another baby." Turning deeply pink at her own words, she took the coffee pot and began refilling cups at a table across the room.

Roy shook his head slowly, as if drawing some comfort from the motion. "As if they don't have troubles enough!" he muttered.

Over the next few months, Old Man accepted coffee from Rowena every morning and tried not to stare at the waistband of her apron. In truth, *birth* had always fascinated Old Man. A miracle, every single time, whether the coming of another child was a welcome or an unwelcome event. He knew that it was a miracle that no mere *man* could ever experience. And more than ever, Rowena seemed to enjoy Old Man's silent company, so that she sat at his table during quiet times, smoking her cigarettes and talking about first one thing and then another. Her son—whom she always just referred to as *my little boy*—was the usual topic of her conversations, whether the child had learned how to eat corn on the cob without her having to cut the kernels off for him, or how he had learned how to sing "Jesus Loves Me" in Sunday School, or how much trouble he was giving to his mee-maw, who took care of him while Rowena was at work. At other times, her words were not so interesting or happy. Her husband and Mee-Maw had a big fuss about the coming baby, with Mee-Maw telling him he should have not have "bothered" Rowena. That he knew good and well it could lead to another mouth to feed. When she told Old Man about that, she dropped her eyes and waited before going on. Then she told Old Man about her husband blaming *her*, telling her that if she was really a good wife, she'd have "gotten herself taken care of."

Old Man knew exactly what she meant, because one of the advantages—or disadvantages—of being a completely silent man was that sometimes the womenfolk simply forgot he was around, and they talked of things he really would rather not have heard. Herb compresses for the painful breasts of nursing mothers, herbal teas to relieve stomach cramps associated with—he assumed—a woman's cycle. And if all of the women he heard talking were Seminole, one topic of conversation might well be what to do when twins were born. The old-time Seminoles—but Old Man did not include himself in that group—insisted that one twin would have to be given away or allowed to die. Because twins were thought to be thunder and lightning—perilous! So on that rare occasion when twins were born, the women would get together and talk about where to take one twin and to whom it should be given. Although too enlightened in the present age to allow a baby to die, they still agreed that one twin must be given away—preferably to someone in a faraway village—to grow up as someone else's own child and never to know about being a twin.

So when Rowena whispered to Old Man about "woman things," he was not shocked or surprised. After all, she was almost like his own daughter, and she spoke of nothing he had not heard before. Still, when she spoke of the child's father wanting her to "take care of it," he knew exactly what she meant, although he had never before heard women speak of such a thing. But there must be herbs a woman could make into a tea—herbs that would make a baby *go away*. Or perhaps something a doctor could do. But of course, he said nothing. Rowena herself brought up the subject of what her husband had asked her to do.

"I couldn't do that!" Rowena whispered to Old Man, leaning over the ashtray on the corner table, and with her blue eyes looking deeply into his dark ones. He nodded his head. *No, Rowena could not do that.*

And so the months passed and Rowena talked and talked, and Old Man listened. On days when her eyes would look as if they were reflecting bruises from inside of her heart, he knew before she even told him that Mee-Maw had been impatient with her little boy—that Mee-Maw had slapped him because he wanted another biscuit, and she had none to give him. Or that he had dirtied his pants, and she had gotten so angry, she made him wear the soiled garment all day long, so that when Rowena came home, his fragile skin was blistered and raw. But Rowena dared not say a word to Mee-Maw. Without Mee-Maw's help, Rowena would not be able to work at the restaurant, and they would all go hungry.

Then there came a day when Rowena ran to the bathroom several times, and she looked so pale and sick that Roy put her into his truck and drove her home. Hastily, he had stuck a sign in the window of the restaurant, "Back in fifteen minutes—help yourself to coffee." During those minutes, Old Man sat at the table, and whenever anyone came in, he pointed to the coffee pot. Two tourists from the Trading Post came to the window and stared at him for long minutes, and instead of pretending to be asleep, he stared right back at them—until their faces reddened in embarrassment and they went away.

When Roy came back, Old Man could tell that he was angry. He tied back on his apron, giving the strings such a hard jerk that they almost broke, and he headed into the kitchen, to fill the orders of people who came in while he was gone. Old Man watched, but he didn't offer to help. If Roy wanted his help, Roy would ask for it.

But when the few customers cleared out, Roy poured himself a cup of coffee and came to sit with Old Man. For long moments, he just sat there, and then he began speaking to the tabletop, "I never saw anything like that in my life," he muttered. "Nasty! Pure nasty!" Old Man, as usual, said nothing but heard everything.

"Rotten *bastard!*" Old Man had never heard such a word come out of Roy's mouth before, not even when orders were mixed up or customers sent their eggs back twice, demanding that they be cooked "over easy" and no other way. "Sitting out on the porch of that old shack, drinking a beer. With his feet up. And *her* trying to work and support them all." Roy heaved a deep breath and hit his fist against the tabletop, sending the ashtray and his coffee cup skittering. "What on earth is going to happen when that baby comes? Works turpentine, he says? Well, he isn't working *nothing*." Red-faced and grumbling, Roy got up and went back into the kitchen.

Old Man sat for a long time, silently, as always.

Rowena didn't come back to work, and Old Man didn't know where she lived. He thought about her though. Wondered how she was doing. Wondered if the baby had come, and what would those people do for food?

About two weeks later, early on a night filled with wind and torrential rain, Old Man thought of Rowena again, of her and her little boy and wondered what the shacks they lived in were like and would they keep out the rain and wind? Because late in that afternoon, Old Man had seen a large bird with a forked tail flying high—very high—and so he knew that a hurricane was nearby. If the bird had been flying low, he would have known that the full force of the storm was coming. But this bird, flying high, told him that the storm would probably pass well away from Love-Oak. And the sign was right, because a tropical storm on the verge of becoming a hurricane had traveled through the Caribbean and into the Gulf Stream, crossing the coastline and passing over land close to central Florida and now blowing against the house where Old Man and Arabella lived.

They had been listening to the radio and sitting in the cozy living room of their small cottage at the very end of the lake and about a mile from Fiona's fishing camp. But over the static and the disembodied radio voice talking about the storm, Arabella was almost positive that she heard a loud growl—or perhaps a high whine—from outside, distinct and separated from the sound of the wind. It was the howl of a panther, for sure, but one had never before come so close to their house. She looked at Old Man for confirmation of what she had heard, but he didn't seem any different than he had been before the strange sound, still intent upon the voice from the radio. It *could* have been the wind, she reasoned with herself. But then Old Man stood up, leaving his chair rocking slightly, put on his rain slicker, and lit the kerosene lamp before he opened the door and admitted the howling wind into the living room.

That wind was so fierce that Arabella got up and went to the door, lending her strong shoulder against it from the inside, so that it closed with a satisfied click. So what she had heard had, indeed, been the panther calling and of course, Old Man went to answer the call. No doubt about it. So she wasn't surprised or distressed. After all, it didn't happen often—hadn't happened in years—but when it did, she knew not to say anything to her husband. It was all very simple, and she accepted it, just the way she accepted everything about her husband.

She would not wait up for him, knowing him as she did, because in some ways, Old Man was what people called one of the "old Seminoles," and his wife had long ago accepted that certain wildness in him—a spirit that could not be completely tamed to hearth and home, any more than she could persuade him to leave the restaurant table in the corner and come back to the Trading Post where the tourists could view him so easily. But Arabella had known him well, even before she married him. She had been only in her late twenties and Old Man already approaching fifty, back then. But Arabella, if she did not feel *love* for him, certainly respected him, and she was a good wife to him. She never demanded conversation—she had known for many years that he was mute—never asked about his coming and going, and certainly never, ever, doubted that if he heard the panther calling to him, he would answer.

So she checked the door, to make sure the latch would hold against the wind, and then she went to bed, pulling the covers over her head to try and shut out the howling wind and pounding rain and didn't worry about him for a single minute. But just as she fell asleep, she envisioned Old Man's craggy face, wet with rain and with his chin pressed against the wind. It was the face she knew, the face she *loved*—especially the wildness in that face, the wildness that could not be tamed in the man.

During the wee hours of predawn the next morning, the wind began dying down, the rain tapered off to a steady, civilized drumming against the tin roof of the cottage, and the water gurgling through the drainpipes had lost its wild sound.

At times like this, when tropical storms surged through the area, Arabella was especially grateful for the stout little cottage they lived in. Because if things had been left up to her husband, they would be living in what Old Man called a proper *chickee*, the traditional, open-sided abode of all of their ancestors, and in the very village where both Old Man and Arabella and all their ancestors had grown up. With a *chickee*, Old Man would have argued, the winds would have blown right through, or, at the worst, would have taken off only some of the thatch on the roof, easily replaced with the plentiful palm fronds so readily available. But with the cottage, he would have to worry about pieces of the tin roof blowing away in the wind, pieces that would be expensive to replace. He conveyed all of these arguments without saying a word, but Arabella had insisted, and so—reluctantly—he built the cottage. And now, so many years later, even the village was gone. Not a single *chickee* remained. What had been their own ground had been purchased by someone unknown, paved over for a parking lot for those newfangled contraptions, automobiles, and his people, except for his wife and his grandson, had scattered, leaving the *chickees* and that whole way of life. No more friendly, safe circle of *chickees*, no central fire where all the village women had cooked together, and no sharing of whatever meat could be had—everything from deer to turtle.

Some of the villagers had moved farther south, into the Everglades, where cars and civilization would never intrude—or so they thought.

In those wee hours just before dawn, Arabella felt the vibration of Old Man's footsteps on the porch and heard the door to the living room open. She got up, pulling on her robe, and went out into the living room where Old Man was standing, water dripping from his rain slicker.

In his arms, he carried a girl, equally dripping but either unconscious or asleep. He turned slowly and put the girl down on the couch, just as carefully as one would put down a sleeping child, and at that point, Arabella recognized Rowena, the little waitress in the restaurant beside the Trading Post, a girl now still wearing only the thin, pink-striped skirt and white blouse she always wore to work.

Arabella hastened back into the bedroom and brought out a blanket, which she spread over the girl before she turned to face Old Man. "What happened?" As she spoke, the girl sprang awake, wild-eyed and looking confused.

Old Man said nothing.

"It's okay, honey," Arabella crooned, and without a word, she went into the hallway and returned carrying several towels. She handed some to Old Man, and then she went to the couch and began trying to dry Rowena's sopping hair.

"I work at the restaurant," Rowena whispered, after she had looked around in a confused state. She saw Old Man where he was standing by the door. "That's how come he knows me," she said, as if she needed to explain to Arabella exactly what was going on. Arabella glanced at Old Man, and he nodded his head slowly. Her gaze went back to Rowena.

"Yes, honey," Arabella fairly crooned. "I've seen you myself. But are you okay? What were you doing out in that storm?" And over her shoulder she asked Old Man, "Where did you find this girl?" But she didn't expect an answer from him.

"It's kind of a long story, ma'am," Rowena said in a whisper, and Arabella noted that no woman, especially no white woman, had ever said *ma'am* to her before. And now here was this soaking wet young woman lying right there on the couch in her own living room, having come from . . . where?

Old Man stood at the door, saying nothing. *Because, answering the panther's call, as he had always done, he had stumbled forward against the wind, and he found Rowena struggling along the sandy road, leaning hard against wind that whipped her hair. She reached out her arms to him, and he gathered her up and carried her all the way to his own home, where she would be dry and warm and safe and where Arabella would know exactly how to take care of her.*

"You just lie there and stay still," Arabella directed. "I'll go find you some dry clothes to put on."

"Oh, no ma'am," Rowena protested. "I don't need you to wait on me."

"Well then, if you feel like it, come on with me into the bedroom, and the least we'll do is find you some dry clothes." As Rowena got up from the couch, Arabella eyed her carefully, watched as Rowena reached out and steadied herself by holding to the arm of the couch. Watched her as she moved, somewhat slowly and perhaps painfully, into the bedroom. As Arabella followed her, she looked once again at Old Man, whose face was a complete blank.

Something happened, Arabella thought to herself. *But I'll never find out from him.* Arabella knew that it was something terrible. Some awful pain Arabella could sense but not understand. To Rowena, she said, "We should have Doc come and take a look at you, I think."

"No, ma'am. Don't need no doctor."

Old Man watched the two women go into the bedroom and close the door, and he wondered what would have happened to Rowena if he had not been out in the storm, if the panther had not so plainly called to him. *And what would come of this? Of what they left behind? What would happen when a young woman's heart died right before his eyes?*

Arabella and Rowena were in the bedroom for a long time, and when they came out, Rowena was wearing Arabella's chenille robe and had a towel wrapped around her wet hair. "I wish you'd lie down for a while like I asked you to do," Arabella said.

"No, ma'am," Rowena argued, and she did look better, with some faint color in her cheeks. "Well, come on in the kitchen—I'll make some coffee for us, and you need something to eat. Something that will sit easy on your stomach. Now what on earth were you doing out in this storm?"

Old Man heard Arabella asking questions, heard the fear and anger in her voice, and he went into the bedroom and closed the door, so that the women could talk in private. When he went into the bathroom to peel off his own soaked clothes, he noticed Rowena's waitress dress soaking in cold water in the sink, and silently, he remembered . . .

 . . . Kneeling in the damp straw of the old pig enclosure down the road, listening to the agonized whimpers of a young girl pushing a baby out of her own body and into the world. His rough brown hands cradled the tiny head as it appeared, and when the slippery body followed, it nestled into Old Man's gentle hands as if that tiny creature had been waiting for all eternity just to be there with him.

 Old Man shook his head, to clear it. Something was going wrong in his mind lately, and for a moment, he couldn't tell whether he was remembering something that really happened, or whether he was just remembering the night *when he was a boy and a panther cub came back to life, right in his own two hands.*

In the kitchen, Arabella poured a mug of steaming coffee for Rowena, adding a large amount of milk and sugar, and put it in front of her. The young woman took it gratefully, blowing into the cup before taking a tentative sip.

 "Won't you tell me what you were doing out in that storm?" Arabella asked, watching Rowena's face carefully. Rowena put down the mug, but she continued to stare into the cup.

 "I ran away from my husband," she finally stated.

 "Can you tell me why?" Arabella urged gently.

 "No ma'am," Rowena answered, looking quite suddenly into Arabella's eyes.

 "Well, do you have a place to go?" Arabella floated the question out into the air just as gently as she could, and waited.

 "I got a place," Rowena admitted. "And I got money to get there, but I think I need some help getting to the bus station."

 "We'll help you," Arabella promised.

Old Man sat in the rocking chair by the window, watching the palm fronds whipping in the diminishing wind. Arabella came out of the kitchen, with Rowena following close behind her.

 "She needs a ride to the bus station," Arabella said, not noticing the glance between Rowena and Old Man. "Can you borrow David's car and take her?"

 Old Man said nothing, but he got up out of the chair, put on his jacket, and left. But as he crossed the porch, his heart was still speaking silently to him. *And what will come of this? The panther knows, but she is not telling us. The panther was there, and she knows!*

"We'll wait on the porch," Arabella suggested. "My husband and David will come for you and take you where you need to go."

"Bus station," Rowena repeated. "I'll have to have a dress to wear, if you don't mind," Rowena said. "When I get to . . . where I'm going, I'll wash and send it back to you."

"No need," Arabella said. "I just wish you'd tell me why you think you have to go away. Maybe we could help."

"Only help I need is to get far away," Rowena answered. So the women went into the bedroom, where they decided on a navy-blue cotton dress for Rowena, and because it was far too large for Rowena's tiny frame, Arabella used a belt to fit the waist to Rowena, and she noticed that from time to time, Rowena's face would go almost chalky white and then color would come back to her cheeks.

"I wish you'd see the Doc," Arabella said once more.

"No, ma'am," Rowena insisted, and so they went out and sat on the porch, waiting to see David's dark car come driving up. Arabella had so many more questions she wanted to ask, but she knew better.

When the car finally came, Old Man got out and held the passenger door open for Rowena, who turned once and looked back at Arabella before she got in.

"Sure do thank you, ma'am," she said. Old Man closed the door and leaned in the open window, studying his grandson who was driving.

"I know," David said. "Bus station."

Chapter Seven

Old Man sat in the restaurant nearly a month after that night, still remembering everything that had happened and watching Abby as she walked lightly back and forth from the kitchen to the tables, refilling coffee cups, serving heaping breakfast platters, removing used dishes, wiping down tables, and pocketing the small tips left for her. As she passed Old Man's table, she extended the coffee pot, and for the first time, he nodded for her to refill his cup. She smiled at him as she poured the hot coffee and then walked away, the coins jingling pleasantly.

Old Man watched her, but he was remembering Rowena and the panther that had called to him on that stormy night, called him to find Rowena in the downpour of rain and the raging wind. Because the panther had not called to him in many years, until that night, and as Old Man sipped from his refilled cup, he found his mind drifting back to the very first time the panther had ever called to him.

He had been only a youngster, no more than twelve at the time, living in the *chickee* with his mother and two younger brothers. And that was the very first time he heard the distinctive but subdued scream, followed by a mesmerizing growl, coming from the deep brush right beside the open-sided *chickee*.

"What was that?" one of his younger brothers had awakened as well.

"It is the Great Spirit," said Old Man without hesitation—Old Man, who back then had not been old at all, and who spoke openly and easily.

"The Great Spirit?" the frightened brother had asked.

"Yes, and He is calling me. The Great Spirit is using the voice of the panther to call me." With those words, Old Man had gotten out of his bedroll.

"Are you sure it's not a dog crying?" the brother asked. "Because if it is, you know that we will hear that something bad has happened."

"Not a dog," Old Man had assured the brother. "Go back to sleep."

"Or maybe an owl?" the youngster persisted. "If it's an owl, don't answer! He will steal your spirit and you'll die!"

"Not an owl," Old Man had assured him. "Now go back to sleep," he ordered once again.

Without making a sound, Old Man had crept far away from the camp

where the *chickees* surrounded the central campfire, far away from the light
of the fire and into the absolute darkness of the palmetto thickets on a
moonless night. As he walked, the ground became softer beneath his feet,
and he knew that he was approaching the edge of the swampland, that he
must be careful not to stumble into the edge of the water itself, where an
alligator might be waiting to grab him, pull him under, and hold him until
he was dead. He stopped walking, and since his footsteps no longer made
even the softest sound, he listened for long minutes, waiting to hear the
panther once again speaking to him. But he heard not a sound.

That's why he was so surprised to look around and see the panther
herself, standing behind him in the water-filled footprints he had made on
the narrow trail. He turned slowly, making not a sound and standing as if
he were frozen, because despite having heard the panther at a distance, he
had never been so close to one before. He studied her eyes, a vibrant
yellow, ringed with black, as if someone had taken charcoal and outlined
those neon eyes, and the eyes reflected *light*, though there was no light for
them to reflect. The ears were stiff and standing straight up, tilted toward
him, as if waiting for him to speak. Old Man, even as a boy, knew all
about the panther and how when the Creator, the Great Spirit, finished
creating everything, He knew that His favorite animal was the panther—
Coo-wah-chobee.

But despite knowing how special the panther was to the Creator, the
boy also could not help being a little afraid of the glowing eyes and the
rigid ears.

Afraid until . . . as the moon came out from behind a cloud, he saw
that the panther carried a tiny cub in her jaws. And as all cubs must do—
even the kittens of cats who lived in houses—the tiny one hung in
absolute stillness from his mother's jaws. But his small hind legs, which
should have curled inward and with his tail tucked between them, were
not curled at all. They were hanging down, motionless. From the powerful
jaws that carried that tiny cub came a softer growl, almost a plaintive plea,
and then, ever so carefully, the panther moved closer to the boy and, with
what appeared to be great tenderness, deposited the cub on the soggy
ground at his feet, where it crumpled and lay still. The mother panther's
eyes met his own startled ones, and as he watched, her eyes seemed to
grow larger and glow even brighter with a strange, yellow light.

"What do you want?" he asked the panther, not daring to make a
move toward the cub. As if answering his question, she nudged the cub
with her nose, moving it a fraction of an inch closer to his feet, where it
lay still. Very slowly and very carefully, with his own frightened eyes fixed
intently on the panther, the boy reached down, his hand coming closer

and closer to the cub. The panther watched him, a soft growl still in her throat and the eyes becoming a more mellow shade of yellow.

"I won't hurt your baby," he whispered. "You don't have to worry."

But it was the boy who was worried. What if the panther sprang upon him, as he reached toward the inert cub? But as his hand moved, only fractions of an inch at a time, and he kept his own eyes riveted on the now milder-looking eyes of the panther, he saw a distinct softening in the animal's whole face. The growl ceased and the large, pink tongue came out and licked the whiskers at either side of the mouth full of terrifyingly sharp teeth.

"I won't hurt your baby," he murmured again, but as his fingers touched the velvet softness of the cub's side, he could feel that the tiny body was already cool. Surely the mother panther must know that her cub was dead, and yet she had called out to him in the darkness. He was sure of it. Slowly, ever so slowly, he slid his fingers under the cold, dead cub and then he lifted it slowly. The tiny head rolled to the side and hung over his hand.

"I'm so sorry," he whispered to the panther. "I'm so sorry, but your cub is dead. I can't do anything." Once again, the panther emitted a low growl, but the boy had become so interested in the cub's small body, he didn't even notice. Because the creature in his hand was a perfect miniature of the mother, and the most beautiful little thing he had ever seen. The tiny mouth was tilted slightly to the side, revealing needle-sharp milk teeth, and protruding between them, a small pink tongue. With his other hand, the boy drew a careful finger across the tiny ribcage, simply in appreciation of the perfect, miniature body, but as he did so, he thought he felt the slightest possible lift to the ribs. His mouth fell open in surprise and delight, and without thinking, he rolled the body of the cub into his other hand so that the head slipped backwards, revealing the throat and chest. The mouth fell open, as well, and so it seemed like the most natural thing in this world for the boy to blow air into the cub's mouth. *Gently! Gently!* he told himself, blowing yet another small puff of air into the cub's mouth, while his fingers lightly compressed the tiny chest, almost without thinking.

Suddenly, the cub shivered and began breathing on its own, the ribcage rising and falling rapidly, the mouth panting, and the lips lifting over the needle-teeth in a small but encouraging snarl. The mother panther watched carefully.

"It's alive!" the boy whispered, trying to resist the urge to shout the good news to the treetops. "It's alive!" This time, he yelled the words, and the sound of his voice went echoing in the swamp, the jubilant words bouncing from the trunk of a nearby live oak to the wide green fans of the palmettos. And his joyous announcement was answered by the twittering of birds in the dark trees, by the scurrying sounds of chameleons and skinks in the deep grass beyond the path, and by the joyful bellow of a bull alligator, far out in the swamp.

The cub, in the meantime, seemed to discover that it was being held, and it began to struggle. The boy slowly placed it onto the ground right in front of its mother and backed away. The panther sniffed the cub several times and then gave it such a firm lick with her mighty tongue that the cub fell over, snarling and meowing in protest. Its eyes now fully opened, a shade of deep, almost muddy blue, and the lips curled themselves back in a lovely, juvenile imitation of a ferocious grin. One of the cub's front paws reached out and swiped in annoyance at the mother.

She gazed at the cub for several moments, and then she cast her eyes back upon the boy. Her own lips lifted back, revealing her terrible fangs, but the yellow eyes still kept their soft look, and so the boy was not afraid, and he stood silently, gazing with complete wonder at the panther and the tiny cub.

At last, the panther gathered the cub into her careful jaw, and casting one more look at the boy, she trotted off into the shrubs. The cub that had been protesting and wriggling had been rendered pliant and still in her mouth, but now with its hind legs tucked firmly under its stomach and the small tail curled inward, as well.

For long minutes, the boy who, all those years later, had grown up and lived life long enough to be called Old Man, stood silently, wondering if perhaps he had simply dreamed everything that had happened between himself and the panther. And right at the moment when he realized that it had certainly not been a dream, he also realized that he must never speak a word of it to anyone, not even to his brothers. Not even to his own mother. And from that very night, he never spoke another word. Not to anyone.

Now, as he sat in the restaurant, watching Abby moving back and forth from the kitchen to the tables, he knew that he would never speak of what he had seen that stormy night a month ago, not even to himself. Not even in the silence of his own thoughts. Because Rowena was a mother, someone who had brought life into the world.

She was magic, and one never, ever spoke of magic.

Chapter Eight

At the same time Old Man was sitting in the restaurant and remembering both that incredible incident from his childhood, as well as the more recent one, Fiona was going into the drugstore, with Victor firmly in hand.

Now that some time had passed, everybody in town knew Victor as her great-nephew, knew him from the Sunday School where Fiona took him every week, knew him from Glory's small restaurant, knew him from almost every place Fiona went. Because she always had him with her, and she enjoyed the comments about his beautiful blonde hair, his chubby, healthy-looking legs, his bright blue eyes and quick manner. Indeed, that very quick manner caused Fiona to hold his hand tightly whenever they went out, for Victor was filled with energy and curiosity about absolutely everything he saw or tasted or smelled or heard.

The only thing that was truly different about Victor was that he had never smiled. Not even once. But most people weren't around him long enough to notice that, for which Fiona was grateful.

"He'll smile when he's good and ready to smile," Glory pronounced. "And not one minute beforehand."

And Starry simply ignored Victor's lack of a smile. Once, she attempted to tickle him in the ribs to make him smile, but Glory put a stop to that immediately. "You leave him alone!" Glory bellowed at Starry, causing Starry to jump in surprise. "Now listen, I'm going to tell you and I'm going to tell Fiona as well. Leave that boy alone and stop trying to make him smile. He done been through some stuff—stuff you don't even know about . . . And we just got to be patient. We got to take him just the way he is and be grateful for him."

And even though Victor was a boy who never smiled, he was also completely fearless, the way of most children his age. Given the opportunity, he would happily have jumped from the pier right into the sun-sparkled water of the lake, with no understanding whatsoever that the beautiful water could become a cruel trap that would close over his head and trap him, without air, beneath its sparkling surface. That terrible fearlessness frightened Fiona more than anything else, and she often jerked awake from a sound sleep in the middle of the night, having survived yet another terrifying dream in which Victor's bright and beautiful head disappeared under the lapping water or his strong, energetic legs carried him deep into the dank swamp, where alligators waited in shallow water for unsuspecting prey. On those nights, Fiona would awaken filled with terror and with her hair dripping in perspiration, and she would hurry into Victor's room to make sure that he was safe and sound in bed.

The months had been long ones, with Fiona and Glory wondering almost every single day if the strange, rain-soaked woman from their back yard would show up again just as suddenly and try to reclaim her son. Try to take their Victor away from them. But then, as day after day and then week after week went by and nothing of that sort happened, both Fiona and Glory lapsed into a sort of gentle amnesia in which they seemed quietly to forget exactly how Victor had come into their lives.

Once in a while, Starry would look hard at Glory and Fiona, as if she wanted very much to ask them something. But she never did ask.

And on that particular day, Fiona had taken Victor with her to the drugstore because Doc wanted her to start giving Victor a tonic, even though his appetite was good and his energy seemingly boundless.

"Just to make sure he's getting all the vitamins and minerals he needs," Doc had said. "A growing boy needs all the help he can get."

And Fiona, remembering that Victor simply refused to eat carrots, no matter how well she cooked them and mashed them up and even tried hiding them in mashed potatoes—resulting in mashed potatoes that were a suspicious-looking shade of pale orange—Victor simply would not eat them, no matter how well hidden they were. So perhaps Doc was right—better to be safe.

So Fiona and Victor went into the drugstore to buy the tonic Doc had recommended, and that's where they saw Myra, who was standing at the prescription counter, grinning and holding her baby tilted up slightly in her arms so that Mrs. Owen could see her better. Mrs. Owen was gurgling and cooing like a crazy woman, and Myra was glowing with pleasure. Fiona approached gleefully, looking at the baby whose face was almost covered by a fancy lace bonnet and who was wearing a gorgeous pale blue baby dress festooned on the sleeves and neckline with even more lace and decorated with rosettes of narrow satin ribbon that trailed across the dress to the very hem.

From within the soft folds of the bonnet, the baby's dark eyes sparkled and the tiny, rosebud lips worked vigorously around an imaginary pacifier.

"Oh, Myra! She's gorgeous!" Fiona exclaimed. "Why, I don't think

I've ever seen such a beautiful baby." All of the good feelings Fiona had about Doc and Myra adopting a baby—especially after their tragic loss—came pouring out, having been put on hold, as Doc had requested. Usually, folks in the community rushed right over to welcome a new baby, but Doc's request for quiet and privacy had been honored, not only out of their respect for Doc himself, but because everyone knew of the tragedy he and Myra had faced with the loss of their own child. But with Myra bringing that sweet baby right out and into the drugstore, there seemed to be no more need for holding in their congratulations.

Fiona and Mrs. Owen both cooed and exclaimed over the baby, and a few other women in the store gathered around to admire her, but the child's face suddenly turned bright red and the features twisted themselves into what almost looked like a snarl. The arms tried to flail within the crocheted blanket and all of the lace on the sleeves of the baby dress, and the knees jerked up violently.

Quickly, Myra put the pacifier back into the baby's mouth, and peace was restored instantly. The baby gazed at her admirers with those beautiful, dark eyes, and she sucked vigorously on the pacifier.

"Rebecca's getting hungry," Myra explained.

"Oh, Myra," Fiona gushed yet again, still holding tightly to Victor's hand as he bounced around like a kite on a string, trying to get away from Fiona's death grip on him so he could explore all of the interesting things he saw on the lower shelves of the store. "She is absolutely gorgeous! I know you and Doc must be so proud."

"Oh, we are," Myra murmured, rocking the baby in her arms and gazing intently into that beautiful little face. But right at that moment, Victor renewed his attempts to wrench his hand free from Fiona, and in a desperate attempt to stop his struggling, Fiona reached down and swept him up into her arms. From his new vantage point, Victor could see the baby in Myra's arms, and he gazed at her long and hard.

"Yes, honey—see the beautiful baby?" Fiona crooned to him. And before either woman could even move, Victor reached out with his left hand and grabbed one of the baby's tight little fists. And held on.

"Oh, no, honey!" Fiona yelped, trying to pry his fingers from the baby's hand. But he was holding on tightly and gazing deep into the baby's eyes. "No! No!" Myra fairly screamed, pushing Victor's hand away somewhat violently, and then carefully examining the small fist, smoothing out the tiny fingers and sending a searing glance at Victor.

"I'm so sorry!" Fiona said. "He didn't mean any harm."

"No harm done, I guess" Myra replied, but she still looked at Victor with genuine anger in her eyes. Fiona, holding Victor's hand tightly against his body, tried to smooth things over by changing the subject, so she went on, swept up in trying to recover the wave of good feelings. "I'm so happy you and Doc went ahead and adopted a baby, after . . ." Fiona's speech tapered off, as she realized she was about to mention the terrible loss. "I mean . . ."

But Myra's eyes glittered in bitter offense, about far more than Victor's innocent grabbing of the baby's fist. "Fiona! Have you lost your mind? This baby isn't *adopted*!" she whispered in a vicious tone, and her eyes filled with angry tears. "How could you say such a terrible thing? How could you?"

With that, Myra lifted the baby up to her shoulder, cupping her hand protectively around the back of the baby's wobbling head. "There, there," she crooned, as if the baby were old enough to have understood the "terrible" thing Fiona had said.

"I'm so sorry!" Fiona backed away immediately, still holding tight to Victor's arm and wondering what her mistake could possibly have been. "I thought . . ."

"Well, you thought *wrong*!" Myra snarled. "This is *our* child, our very own child!" With that, she turned and hurried out of the drugstore, leaving Fiona and the others standing in a shocked silence. Fiona released her grip on Victor's arm.

Finally, Mrs. Owen, who of course had overheard everything, leaned over the counter. "I should have tried to warn you. I guess she doesn't remember what happened to their own child."

"What?" Fiona was still shocked.

And Mrs. Owen continued, "Doc warned some of us about it. Said Myra hadn't gotten used to the baby yet, and we should be careful what we said to her."

"She doesn't *know* the baby's adopted?" Fiona asked, still incredulous and embarrassed.

"I guess not," Mrs. Owen admitted. "Looks like it's going to take her some time. Doc said they'd have a tea, once Myra got all settled in with the new baby. But I don't think we should hold our breath about that."

Victor had begun to squirm in her arms, so Fiona quickly said, "We need a bottle of this tonic." She handed over the scrap of paper on which Doc had written the name. Mrs. Owen took the paper and started to walk behind the counter, but then she turned back to Fiona and said, "Listen, don't feel bad. We've all been kind of tiptoeing around about this. Maybe Myra will get better soon. And if she has that tea Doc was talking about, we'll all get to see as much of that beautiful little baby as we like."

Mrs. Owen had certainly meant for her words to be a comfort to

Fiona, but when Fiona got home with the bottle of tonic, she still felt so miserable that she simply waited at the kitchen table until Glory came in from the restaurant. Tearfully, she told Glory everything that had happened. Every careless word she had spoken. Every look she saw in Myra's offended eyes. Glory listened carefully, but she made no comment, because Glory had lived in the world long enough to know that there are some things that can hurt you so badly, only time will take care of them. She had no words to give to Fiona, to relieve her the least bit.

Victor, happily delving into the pots and pans in the bottom cabinet, hesitated in his noisy explorations and, looking straight at Fiona and Glory, smiled and said, "'Becca!"

"What?" Fiona asked, startled to see a smile, for once, on that usually solemn little face.

"'Becca!" Victor chortled happily and went back to the pots and pans, banging them together so loudly that Fiona and Glory blinked, involuntarily.

"He said *Rebecca*," Glory advised in between the banging of pot lids. "That the baby's name?"

"Yes," Fiona said, wondering how, in the midst of all the confusion and hurt feelings in the drugstore, Victor had managed to pick out that one particular name. "Rebecca," Fiona whispered. "Well, he just doesn't know what he's saying."

"I wouldn't be so sure about that," Glory said, smiling in a strange way. "Maybe he's in love with her."

"In *love*?" Fiona's squeal made Glory twitch. "Why, he's just a baby! What can he know about love?"

"Sometimes, maybe little ones know a lot more about love than us grown-up folks," Glory said in a low, gentle voice. "Sometimes love comes early," she added.

Fiona didn't say anything else, because she knew not to argue with Glory when Glory had that strange, faraway look in her eyes. Because sometimes, Glory thought that she could see the future, and no amount of arguing from Fiona could change her mind. But she kept thinking about what Glory had said—*Sometimes love comes early? Why that's the silliest thing I ever heard!* But then something else came into her mind, something very much like an actual voice—*And sometimes love comes late*. But, being Fiona, she shook off the words she thought she heard, because she knew good and well that no one said such a thing.

Glory and Fiona stood in the silence, perhaps watching and listening for voices from within, but they said nothing more. Glory unconsciously patted her chest. Right over her heart. But Fiona, in her own typical fashion, turned her mind to something immediate and concrete. "You help me give Victor some of that tonic? It's probably going to take both of us to get it in him."

"Well, Lord help us all!" Glory exclaimed, laughing.

And later, when brown splotches of spilled and spat-out tonic were scattered almost evenly around the floor and all of the kitchen cabinets, Glory wiped her bespattered face on her apron and said, "Just keep your mouth shut about this, and tomorrow we'll get Starry to give it to him."

At that, Fiona had to smile.

Starry, of course, knew absolutely nothing about how Victor really came to live with Fiona and Glory, and she had a feeling that there was something about it that Fiona and Glory weren't telling her, but because she had no choice, she accepted the story about Fiona's niece, just as she had been told, and so did everyone else in the community, except for Glory, who knew the truth, and—possibly—Old Man. But they didn't know for sure about Old Man. He never said anything anyway, so they finally forgot to worry about him and what he did or didn't know.

Starry quickly adapted herself to her work at the fishing camp, and Fiona would be the first to admit that Starry could clean a cabin even better than she could herself. Glory, of course, would admit nothing of the sort about Starry's help, but each weekday, when Starry handed over the huge pan filled with perfect filets, Glory glanced at them in approval, but still she said not a single word to Starry.

Gradually—very gradually—Starry seemed to forget about Middy, and the bruised look that had been in her eyes eventually faded away. For clothing, she wore some of Fiona's old housedresses, all still hitched up with a belt, and Fiona worried about that makeshift arrangement in Starry's apparel. Extremes were always suspect, Fiona knew, even if one extreme had been Starry's short shorts and low-cut blouse and the other was shapeless dresses that hung on Starry like flour sacks. The whole idea, Fiona thought, had been to teach Starry something about modesty—in thought, deed, and dress, but the intention certainly hadn't been to make her look like some poor white trash woman the cat dragged in. This called for a compromise, and Fiona pictured in her mind the kind of dresses she would like to see Starry wearing—modest yet somewhat stylish, wholesome and clean, and not too revealing of Starry's voluptuous figure. And as for makeup, Starry wasn't wearing any at all—she had come down from lavender-hued eyelids, crayoned-on eyebrows, and purple lipstick to absolutely nothing at all. That wasn't good either, and Fiona often fantasized about introducing Starry to appropriate makeup, teaching her how to press a modicum of powder onto her nose and to use a brighter color of lipstick—instead of that awful purple—and less of any color.

Sometimes, watching Starry in the loose, belted dresses, Fiona worried that bringing too much pressure on Starry might make her rebel—even though she was a grown woman and probably beyond such adolescent emotions.

When Glory pointed out to Fiona that the Mercurochrome coloring in Starry's hair was slowly disappearing at the very roots, to be replaced by a healthy-looking chestnut brown hair, Fiona resolved that she must take Starry in hand soon—help her find better clothing and introduce her to the kind of makeup *ladies* used.

"Take some time for it all to grow out," Glory pronounced, still speaking of Starry's hair, even though Fiona's thoughts had already moved ahead to better clothes and appropriate makeup. "But when it does, I guess she'll be right nice looking. Mostly."

But Glory's reluctant approval of Starry disappeared on those rare occasions when Fiona allowed Starry to take Victor for a walk along the lakeshore. At that, Glory always snorted in disapproval.

"What if she lets him go out in the lake and he drowns himself?" Glory asked. "Or what if she loses him and he wanders off into the woods and we can never find him? What if she lets him run into the swamp and a big old hungry 'gator gets him?"

"That won't happen," Fiona assured Glory, and Fiona would never, ever admit that whenever Starry had Victor off to herself, Fiona felt somewhat anxious, until she saw them coming home again. Fiona knew that during those long walks, Starry talked up a storm to Victor, and "Lord only knows what all she's telling that child!" Glory would always interject.

But Fiona wasn't really worried, because Victor was so very young, he probably didn't understand much of what anyone said anyway. Too, one day, early on, Fiona had been watering the plants on the porch as Starry and Victor were coming back from a long walk, and right beside the porch, they had stopped for a moment, while Starry bent down to tie Victor's shoelaces. And because Starry kept talking to him the whole time she worked with the laces, Fiona stopped the watering and listened, eavesdropping unashamedly.

"You got to be a good boy," Starry said to Victor. "'Cause otherwise, things just don't go right for you. You hear me?" As Fiona peeked from behind a hanging fern, she watched Victor nod his head solemnly. "You just take me, for example," Starry continued. "I'm learning all over again how to be a good girl, and I hope that won't ever happen to you—well, you're not a girl anyway, so that can't happen—but you know what I mean, don't you? I hope you don't ever give away your love to nobody like Middy—that is, if a girl could be like Middy," Starry amended. "'Cause that kind of person can make you be bad, no matter how hard you try to be good. So no matter how much you love somebody like that, it just isn't worth it!"

Yes, Fiona was thinking behind the concealing fern. *Definitely time for some further improvements in Starry's appearance. Now that perhaps she has gained some wisdom.*

Starry paused for a long moment, and Victor continued to stare at her, as if he knew she was about to tell him something very important.

"But . . ." Starry finally continued, "That doesn't mean you should run away from *love.* You just got to be careful about who you give that love to." Starry's eyes went deep and dreamy. "But love itself is so good, Victor. I hope you will always remember that. It's . . . it's a very great mystery—kind of like music you think you can hear, but that you know doggoned well doesn't come from anywhere on this old earth."

Victor studied her face carefully, as she was still bent over his shoes. Her multicolored hair fell around her face, and Victor reached up and placed a tentative finger into the middle part of Starry's hair, where it was a rich, shiny brown. But Starry didn't seem to notice, because her eyes were glazed over, and she was still trying to put words to something that no human mind could ever comprehend and no human voice would ever be able to speak.

"Like music from someplace else, Victor," she said, with the most sincerity in her voice that Fiona had ever heard, and yet at the same time, the words were drowning in a syrup of perplexity.

"Nook!" Victor said suddenly—he had yet to learn how to pronounce his L's—"Nook!" he repeated, pointing into the sky over Starry's shoulder. Starry looked, and so did Fiona, to where the new moon was rising—a mysterious, silver globe that seemed to rise right out of the lake itself, even with the daylight not yet fully gone.

"Yes, honey," Starry said to Victor, in a voice that matched his excitement. "Look! It's the moon!"

"Moom!" Victor repeated, clutching his hands together in delight.

"Hey, Victor," Starry yelped happily. "That's it! That's what love is like—it's mysterious and far away, and we can never even really touch it—never hold it tight and at the same time, never let it go." Here, Starry paused, and Victor stared at her face, seeing something in it he had never seen before. But of course, he had no words to describe it. Finally, a moon-shining tear slid down Starry's face, but her mouth smiled. "But we can hear it sometimes, honey. Like music. Music from beyond the moon."

Then Starry grinned, pleased with herself, and Victor clapped his hands together in the glow of her strange excitement. Quite suddenly, Starry's face changed, returning again to the thing she couldn't say. But no more tears traced a shining path down her face. Instead, Starry's face almost glowed—much like the new moon so high up in the heavens. "But you listen to me, Victor—if that music ever dies away and you can't hear it anymore, then you just got to hold on real tight to what it sounded like. Never forget it. And always remember you were real blessed to hear it at all."

Victor had focused on Starry's strange words and her different face as long as he could. His attention span was short, and besides, he didn't understand most of what Starry was saying or why she looked the way she did. So he looked down and discovered a small ant bed near his shoes, and his attention flitted right away as he stooped to watch the tiny ants scurrying around. While Victor studied the ants, Starry continued watching the moon, but her face was at once as content and peaceful as Fiona had ever seen it. Fiona smiled to herself and went back to watering the plants.

Music from beyond the moon, huh? Fiona was thinking. *Well, for goodness sake, Starry—who would have thought you could have such . . . poetic . . . thoughts? But of course, that was just fanciful thinking!*

But in spite of herself, Fiona thought of J. Roy. *Music from beyond the moon, indeed!* Because there hadn't been any magic about it, really. J. Roy was just a man—a man whose shirts she washed and ironed, a man who left his dirty socks in the middle of the bathroom floor. A man who paid little or no attention to her, but who had always—always—touched her shoulder as he left the dinner table with his belt loosened. Music? No. Not really. Just something comfortable.

But then Fiona remembered what would happen when she heard his footsteps on the back porch, when he came home from a long, hard day of working on the docks. The sound his feet made on the old wooden boards and the faint creak of the lowest step. That always brought a tiny ripple of pleasure to Fiona. Very tiny! *But music?*

When Fiona looked back at Victor and Starry, Victor had lost interest in the ants and was holding out his hand to the sky. Starry, smiling, reached up and took it. But Victor pulled it away, shaking his head and then once again, holding out his hand. Toward the moon. "'Becca," he said.

"What did you say, honey?" Starry murmured. "You want that? Well, I'm sorry, but you can't have it. It's too far away. Listen, now, and see if you can hear the music." But still, Victor held out his hand, gazing solemnly at the moon. And then it dawned upon Fiona not only what Victor had said, but that he was holding out his left hand—and Victor was certainly most strongly right-handed. His left hand. The hand he had used to reach out and grasp Rebecca's tiny fist.

"But it sure is pretty, isn't it?" Starry asked, and Victor nodded, smiling.

"'Becca," he whispered.

Chapter Nine

Love-Oak, Florida—Six years later
1930

Myra never held a tea so that everyone could meet Rebecca. Instead, she and the baby simply dropped out of sight, as far as the community was concerned, staying always within the quiet sanctuary of the house, and with her precious baby in her arms every single minute. Doc himself never mentioned Myra or Rebecca in public again, and if anyone happened to ask about them, purely out of Christian charity or even normal curiosity—disguised as courtesy—he just smiled and shook his head. People never really knew what to make of that, but Doc was such a beloved healer for everyone in the community, people finally decided that whatever went on in his own house was certainly his business and none of their own.

Regardless of their good intentions, gossip had gotten around years ago. Someone said that they heard the little baby Doc and Myra adopted in Jacksonville was the subject of a court case—that the natural mother had changed her mind and wanted the baby back. But since the adoption had been finalized, the courts certainly would have to be involved. They figured that's why Myra wouldn't take the baby out of the house. She was afraid someone—a private detective or something like that—had been hired to kidnap her precious child, returning her to the birth mother, because the mother thought the courts would never overturn a formal and finalized adoption.

But of course, Myra knew nothing of the gossip or speculation about any supposed problem, since she could not . . . *would not* . . . believe that her baby was adopted at all—was anything other than her own flesh–and–blood child. No one would have dared say a thing to Myra about it, and besides, they never had the opportunity, since Myra never went out of her house, not even to church.

Every time Fiona took Victor to town with her, he looked all around, searching, Fiona supposed, for baby Rebecca. Sometimes, he would look at Fiona with a questioning expression in his eyes and say, "'Becca?"

Fiona always tried to soothe him, since he was far too young to understand what was happening. "No, honey," Fiona would croon. "She's not here today," and even though Victor seemed disappointed, he never argued.

After years of Myra's self-imposed isolation from the community, Doc drove out to the fishing camp one afternoon and talked for a long time with Glory, after which he received her somewhat reluctant blessing for his hiring Jubilee to do all of the shopping for the family and to help Myra out around the house. "Not helping with the child," Doc emphasized. "Myra will do that herself. But everything else—shopping and light housekeeping and laundry—that sort of thing. Just part-time, you understand," Doc said to Glory.

Of course, Glory wasn't happy about losing Jubilee full time at the restaurant, but she had to agree with Doc's argument. Jubilee's work for Myra would be so much better for her future—cleaning fish really wasn't going to prepare Jubilee for any kind of a better job when she grew up, such as being a domestic helper or maybe even a nurse's aid. Also, Glory figured quietly that since Jubilee's work for Doc wouldn't be full time, Jubilee could manage both jobs just fine.

So every weekday, as soon as Jubilee was through at the restaurant, and all day on Saturdays and Sundays, as well, she went straight over to Doc and Myra's house, where she helped with housework. Myra taught her how to dust and run the vacuum cleaner, and once or twice a week, she gave Jubilee a detailed grocery list so that she could do all of the family's shopping. The one thing Myra never allowed was for Jubilee to take care of Rebecca. That was Myra's and only Myra's job. At the restaurant, Starry took up the slack Jubilee's afternoon work had left, putting away the chairs and tables and sweeping down the pier after every lunchtime.

As time went by, Jubilee shared with Glory something of her days in Doc's household. She told of how, when Doc came home in the evening, he would politely inquire of Jubilee just how things had gone that day, and Jubilee would always tell him, "Just fine, sir!" He never pressed for any details, but went straight into the living room, sitting down in his comfortable chair and opening the newspaper.

Jubilee was careful to obey Myra's strict instructions that she not talk to anyone in the grocery store or the mercantile about anything that went on in Doc's house—not about Doc himself or Myra, or, especially, Rebecca. And if anyone in town asked her about any of them, Jubilee—who had been carefully coached by Myra herself—simply smiled, shook her head, and ran her fingers across her lips, as if she were zipping them shut. Finally, people stopped asking and took for granted—though no one said so, of course—that Myra was no longer a part of the community at all. Doc, on the other hand, carried out his duties in such an exemplary fashion that people began to suspect that Myra had shut *him* out of her life, as well as the entire community.

Jubilee knew better than to repeat any kind of such gossip to Glory, but she did share little things she thought were unimportant. Because Jubilee knew that she was safe in talking to her aunt. Glory would never, ever repeat anything she heard—usually not even to Fiona. So on occasion, Glory pried a little and Jubilee told her everything that was going on. That Rebecca was growing fast—growing and turning into a beautiful little girl. But Miss Myra would not allow Jubilee to even touch her—not for anything in the world. That Doc always kissed both Myra and Rebecca when he came in from making his rounds. That he always greeted them with, "How're my girls today?" in a happy-sounding voice. And that even if Rebecca tried to hug him or sit in his lap or talk with him, Miss Myra would whisk her away, saying that she needed her bath, or it was time to brush her hair. Rebecca tried to protest, but it did no good. So, Doc would simply go sit down in his chair and read the evening newspaper. And sometimes, Jubilee thought she saw tears. "Not the running-down-your-face kind," Jubilee said, "but something in his eyes, if you know what I mean."

Glory knew exactly what she meant.

"Please don't say a thing, Aunt Glory, about what I tell you—I sure don't want to lose that good job!" Jubilee would always admonish, but Glory knew something else that Jubilee didn't even have to tell her—Doc paid Jubilee too well for her work, probably out of his sense of relief at knowing that Jubilee was there with Myra and Rebecca every afternoon. She also knew that Jubilee liked working for Doc's family a lot better than she did working at the restaurant. "It's lots better than this job," Jubilee said once, "where I don't get paid nothing."

"Don't get sassy," Glory warned, but Jubilee set her chin a little bit, even though she obediently replied, "Yes, ma'am," in a falsely subdued-sounding voice.

Of course, while Rebecca was growing, so was Victor, but he suffered none of the constant restraint imposed upon Rebecca. From the very time Victor was old enough, he would unlatch the screen door and slip away from Glory and Fiona and go outside alone, to play in the palmetto bushes and in and around all the scrub palm trees behind Fiona's cottage. Fiona tried everything within reason she could think of to keep him inside with her, where he would be safe. She twisted a wire around the door latch, but he soon untangled it. She put a bell on the door, so that whenever he opened it, she would know, but he managed to pry the small clapper out of the bell, so that its warning was mute. Finally Fiona gave up, in a way, always watching him when he was outdoors, but not letting him know that. Agreeing to let him out to play, but impressing upon him the bounds of his new-found freedom.

On rare occasions, Victor ventured as far as a large live oak tree beyond which Fiona had sternly forbidden him to go. Fiona was always happier when Victor went with Old Man to the Trading Post, which was often, or when he sat beside Starry on the end of the pier, where she would read book after book to him. Because then, he had adults around to watch out for him. But what he loved the most of all was going out into the brush. Alone.

"There's nothing but marsh land beyond that tree, Victor," Fiona admonished, and she had to warn him only that once, for her warning voice fired his imagination—the imagination that had been fed so richly by the Seminole stories Old Man's grandson Dave always told him. And he could actually *see* bottomless pools of quicksand waiting to suck his slender body all the way down to hell itself, and the wicked, triangular heads of snakes that would sink their yellow fangs deep into his flesh. If he thought hard enough, he could feel the smothering mud in his lungs and the needle-sharp, poisonous fangs striking deep into his leg. Thus, did he graduate from supervised activities, like fishing from the end of the pier with Mr. Owen (Fiona refused to let Victor go out in Mr. Owen's boat) and listening to the old Seminole stories and, of course, the indoor puzzles and games that Fiona and Glory could supervise—but above all, he loved the great outdoors just beyond his back door.

"Why on earth you want to play out there in all that wildness is just what I can't understand," Glory complained to him more than occasionally. "Plenty of other places to play," she mumbled at him. "Don't see what's so interesting to you out there in all them weeds. Liable to be snakes, you know! Do you get snake bit, don't you come running and hollering to me, not after I done told you and told you not to go out there!"

He knew about the snakes. And he knew about the quicksand, but he could never know, nor could he have explained to Glory, exactly what drew him so forcefully into the brush. And more than once, he envisioned himself running back toward the house, with snakes dangling from his legs—hundreds of them!—and him squalling and hollering for Aunt Fiona and Glory, and Glory standing there with her hands on her broad hips, clucking her tongue and saying, "I done *told* you and *told* you not to go in them weeds! Now look what you gone and done!" But so far, that hadn't happened.

"You got to take that boy in hand. You just *got* to!" Glory would fume, and all the while she was admonishing Fiona, Victor was running at top speed toward the deep weeds and the palmetto bushes. "He gonna run all over you one of these days, don't you get him straightened out right now."

But Fiona simply smiled and shook her head at Glory's stern warnings. "He's just being a *boy*, Glory. And I won't take that away from him. Why, you're the very person who told me when Victor first came that we couldn't make him into a girl. And you were right."

"Well, don't say I didn't warn you," Glory muttered darkly. "Growing up to be a wild child, I tell you!" But Glory was wrong—Victor was certainly not wild. He was simply highly imaginative, and he circulated through his confined worlds—the Trading Post and the smooth surface of the lake beyond the pier, and the sun-warmed planks outside of the restaurant door, where he sat with Starry while she read to him.

So the days and then the months and then the years passed. Fiona forgot to worry about Victor's mother coming back, and they all settled into their lives together. But time did pass, even though they almost didn't realize it at all. Glory was the one who expressed it best. "You know, 'til we had Victor, I never realized how fast time goes by!" she said. She and Starry and Fiona were sitting at the kitchen table, dutifully shelling a huge paper sack full of butterbeans that Mrs. Owen had brought by to them. Starry, as usual, said little, because she simply enjoyed listening to Fiona and Glory.

"My husband may like fishing," she had said. "But I'm the one who knows how to grow a garden!" So, carrying the big sack of fresh-picked butterbeans from her garden as her "ticket" into their kitchen, Mrs. Owen had been "all eyes," as Fiona said later. "Why, she almost drove herself crazy, trying to look around and see everything she could see."

"Lordy! Ain't it the truth?" Glory laughed. "Them old eyeballs just swiveling around and around—made me want to grab up that dirty dish towel and throw it in the drawer. And all those dishes in the sink! I'll swear, I thought she was gonna pull out her glasses and put 'em on, so's she could see better." Starry smiled at Glory's vivid description.

"But she sure did bring us some good butterbeans," Starry ventured, causing Glory and Fiona to blush about their unkind words. "And maybe she just doesn't know she does that—snooping around, I guess you'd call it."

"I guess so," Glory replied. "Somebody ought to tell her."

"How about you?" Fiona laughed.

But before Glory could answer, Victor came tearing through the kitchen, grabbed a handful of cookies from the jar, and headed out the back door on a dead run.

"Don't let the door . . ." but Fiona's admonition, the one she had made at least a hundred times, was interrupted by the loud *bang!* of the slamming door.

"'Bye!" he hollered on his way down the back steps, and the women could hear the chains clanking on his new bicycle as he pedaled away.

"Oh, well!" Fiona said. "He knows exactly how far he's allowed to ride. And besides, he'll be back in school soon, so he better know how to follow orders." They all fell silent again, and the only sound was that of pea pods being popped open and peas plopping pleasantly against the side of the bowls they held in their laps.

"Like I said, I guess I never did know how fast time goes by 'til we got that boy, and now, he's not so little anymore," Glory said. "Seems like yesterday we was trying to make a diaper for him out'n an old sheet, and now he's growing up right in front of our eyes. Just look at him—out there on a real bicycle, all by himself."

"But what about Jubilee? You've seen her growing up, haven't you?" Starry asked, tossing another handful of pea pods into the trash bag.

"Don't seem so much that way with her," Glory said. "She got so much of her growth right at first, she hasn't changed that much. Gotten taller, is all."

"And filled out," Fiona reminded her.

"When Victor's mama brought him here, were you all expecting him to stay for so long?" Starry asked, surprising both Glory and Fiona, who seemed to have put aside any questions about that.

Starry didn't notice the glance that went between Glory and Fiona, and she went on. "I mean, she's sure been sick for an awful long time, hasn't she? Years?" Starry's innocent-sounding question hung in the quiet air of the kitchen, and Glory and Fiona each waited for the other to answer Starry's question. Finally, Fiona said, "Well, truth of the matter is we never heard much from Victor's mama. Kind of lost touch with her, I guess you would say."

"But that's terrible!" Starry pronounced. "Just dropping off her child like that, all those years ago, and then not even staying in touch."

"We just don't know the circumstances," Glory interjected. "But everything's okay just the way it is, isn't that right, Fiona?" Fiona nodded enthusiastically.

"But doesn't Victor ever ask about her?" Starry said, raising her eyebrows and becoming truly interested in the subject of Victor's mother.

"Well, we're not a close family," Fiona explained.

"Oh," Starry said, although she still carried a small frown in between her eyebrows. "You'd think she wants to know he's okay," she added. "I saw you making a birthday cake this morning," Starry said. "So I know it's Victor's birthday again, and I think his own mama would at least send him a card or something." And neither Fiona nor Glory had anything to say about that. Because, not knowing his exact birthday, they had simply selected a month and a day that seemed to be appropriate, given that Victor was probably around eighteen months old when he had come to them. Or so Doc had surmised.

Even though they were always so careful not to talk about Victor's mother where he could hear them, they must have failed that day. Because later in the afternoon, when Fiona and Victor were alone in the kitchen, the question Fiona had always feared popped right out of Victor's mouth. "Where's my mother?"

He took Fiona completely off guard, and while she certainly hesitated, she took a deep breath and tried to make her voice sound completely matter-of-fact. "She had to go away, honey," Fiona replied, using the same voice she used when she read fairy tales to him . . . *She had to go away . . . and so the princess and the handsome prince lived happily ever after. The End.*

"But where'd she go?" Victor asked.

"She went to someplace for people who are real sick," Fiona answered, still reeling from the suddenness of Victor's questions.

"When will she come back?" Victor asked, and Fiona noticed that he did not ask, "*Is* she coming back?"

"I don't know, honey," Fiona sputtered, turning to the sink and running water, just to try and distract herself from the conversation.

"Okay," he said simply, but then he added, "Maybe she turned into a bear, like in the Seminole story." Fiona didn't respond to this idea, but she made a mental note to try to restrict the time Victor spent at the Trading Post. Fiona knew, of course, that Old Man never spoke a word, so it was his grandson, Dave, who was telling Victor all of those fantastic stories, probably while Old Man sat nearby and nodded solemnly. It would be easy for Victor to think that Old Man himself was telling the stories, that much Fiona knew for sure. Victor knew stories about witches who turned themselves into owls at night, one about a beautiful bride who turned into a bear-bride for a bear in the forest, and especially, tales about the panther, who was the "strongest medicine" anyone could imagine.

Initially, Fiona had worried that Victor would take some of the tales literally, and now that he had suggested that perhaps his own mother had turned into a bear, she felt that she had to say something to straighten out Victor's thinking. So she said, "Honey, all those tales David tells you— you know, of course, that they aren't real, don't you?"

"I guess so," Victor admitted.

"You *guess* so?" Fiona wanted to make sure that he knew the difference between things that were real and things that were imaginary.

Victor glanced up at her. "I know about stories," he explained patiently. "Like that book Starry gave me, where the moon talks to people."

"Oh." Fiona's carefully thought-out explanation went flying right out of the window, and without speaking, she wondered, *What's the difference between a storybook and what David's telling Victor?*

"Don't worry, Aunt Fiona," Victor said at last. "I know you won't turn into an owl and go off every night, eating the hearts of dead animals."

Fiona shivered.

But suddenly, Victor's face lit up, as if he had stumbled upon some truth for which he had been searching. "Oh! I'll bet I know what happened to her. To my mother," he amended, and his smile was miraculous to behold. "She turned into a panther! That's what happened! Oh, I'm so glad!" With that, he left the table and went out to the back porch, once again letting the screen door slam behind him, leaving Fiona to shake her head and to wonder if these stories were a curse . . . or a blessing. What Fiona didn't know—couldn't know—was what Victor was seeing in his imagination, *My mother, the beautiful panther. I heard her purring in the bushes. I know her gentle jaws and raspy tongue. I will see her again, if only I look for her hard enough.*

After supper and the sharing of Victor's candle-studded birthday cake, Fiona was relieved that Victor had said nothing more about his mother. She stood alone in the kitchen, scraping the last of the icing on the platter with her finger and putting it into her mouth. One slice of cake remained, and she felt an absolute compulsion to eat it—to consume it with great reverence, almost as one would consume a wafer in the church—a sacrament, that's what it was, that tiny slice of Victor's cake.

Victor! How is it that you're growing up so fast? What's going to happen when you finally go out into the world as a grown man? Such a cold and cruel world? How can I stand by and let you grow up and move out from under my protection? The thought was too horrible, so she grabbed up the piece of cake and stuffed it into her mouth, exactly as if, by eating it, she could erase the birthday, his questions about his mother, and the simple fact that Victor was growing up—too fast.

For the very first time, Fiona could understand Myra and all the years of her reluctance to let anyone or anything take Rebecca away from her constant vigilance. Fiona wished that she could do the same thing, keep Victor with her every minute of every day. Not let a single soul into the safe and beautiful world she had worked so hard to create for him. But you couldn't do that, she reminded herself. Couldn't cage up a human being, no matter how young and vulnerable. And one of these days, Fiona was sure that poor Myra would reap some terrible results with Rebecca. She was certain of it, because one of these days, Rebecca would grow up, and what on earth would Myra do then?

Ironically, the phone rang at that very moment when Fiona was thinking so hard about Myra and Rebecca, and Fiona, in her typical fashion, had gathered scrub buckets and cleaning rags in preparation for getting three cabins ready for new arrivals. Working hard was always Fiona's way of dealing with troubling thoughts. But when the phone rang, she dropped everything in a clatter.

"You okay?" Glory called from the porch.

"Fine!" Fiona yelled, grabbing the receiver.

"Fiona?" the voice was unfamiliar to her. "This is Myra." After a long silent hesitation, she added, "Rebecca's mother."

"Why, yes, Myra. How are you?" Fiona's mind was racing. No one had heard a single word from Myra in years, and now here she was on the other end of the line.

"Fiona, I just wanted to tell you to make your . . . Victor . . ." Myra almost spat the name. "Make him stay away from here!" Myra's voice was trembling. "Make him stay away from *my daughter!*"

"What?"

"What I said!" Myra harrumphed. Myra slammed down the receiver, making Fiona jump at the sound. Fiona looked at her own receiver, as if its very appearance would provide her a clue as to what Myra was talking about. But just at that moment, Victor came through the kitchen.

"I want to talk with you," Fiona said in a trembling voice. "Have you been going down to Doc's house and bothering Miss Myra and Rebecca?" Fiona's voice was so loud and so accusatory that Glory came from the porch and stood in the kitchen door, frowning.

"I just wanted to play," Victor defended, his pale eyes flaring up with a flash such as Fiona and Glory had never seen before.

"So you *have* been there." Fiona's voice was heavy with accusation.

Victor dropped his gaze and studied the toe of his shoe. "I just wanted to play with 'Becca," he repeated in a sullen tone.

"You can play with Rebecca at school," Fiona said. "But that's all."

"She won't play with me at school," Victor muttered. "She runs so fast, I can't keep up with her." His ears burned at such an admission.

"You chase her around?" Fiona asked, slightly alarmed.

"Just a little bit," he confessed.

"Well, I don't want you to go to Doc's house after school or on the weekends at all," Fiona said. "Do I make myself clear?"

Victor didn't answer, but his ears reddened even further.

"I said, do I make myself clear?"

"Yes," Victor finally muttered, and then, sensing that his scolding was at an end, he sidled slowly toward he back door and then darted outside, running across the porch and jumping down the steps, while the door slammed noisily. And Fiona realized that she had not even corrected him, insisting that he say, "Yes, ma'am" to her.

"What was all that about?" Glory asked, as if she hadn't been standing right there almost the whole time.

"I guess he's been riding his bike down to Doc and Myra's and wanting to play with Rebecca. But he won't do that anymore."

"Well, I thought this was the way it would be," Glory muttered under her breath, leaving Fiona wondering what she meant by that.

Later that evening, Fiona put the cake platter into the sink, turned off the kitchen light, and went straight to Victor's room. The light from the lamp in the hallway fell across his bed, and he was sprawled on his stomach, his surprisingly large feet sticking out from under the sheet, somewhat dirty feet that he had failed to bathe. One arm dangled over the edge of the mattress, and his sleeping face was cushioned by the pillow. She studied him—the light illuminating the blonde hair and a few precious curls still there, right at the back of his neck. Without even approaching his bed, Fiona could detect his aroma—health and soap and skin and some innocence that was still left. But another aroma, one she had not noticed before. The unmistakable aroma of a healthy, young male.

Her Victor—he had been so little and so dirty and so alone and afraid, and she had gathered him in her arms and had taken him into her home and her heart—had made him clean and filled with good food, and he had been happy with that. With her. Why couldn't it just stay that way?

As she stood in the doorway, Fiona's thoughts began a wild fantasy of their very own, one in which she imagined them all—herself, Glory, Starry, Old Man, Doc—and yes, even Rebecca—as small planets fixed in their orbits, moving around each other but never into each other's paths.

All separated by some kind of cosmic distance. They were gentle, kind, and mostly polite with each other, and in a way none of them could have explained, they loved each other. But their smiles were always at a distance—a distance they all needed.

And then there was Victor—and he wasn't just another small, new planet that formed its own path, but a brilliant comet that danced in fiery splendor as it soared among the spaces between them all. A beautiful, fiery comet.

Where would it go?

Chapter Ten

Love-Oak, Florida, 1940

"Time! You stinking old thief!" Fiona spoke out so suddenly that Glory almost dropped the bowl of butterbeans she was shelling. They had been sitting on the porch in a rare hour of relaxation, with the restaurant closed for the afternoon and with all of the reserved cabins cleaned and waiting for new fishermen. For long minutes, Fiona had been looking out over the banisters toward the lake, saying nothing. Still, Glory could almost *feel* Fiona's mind working on something or the other.

"What's that?" Glory asked, righting the bowl between her knees.

"I said, 'Time! You stinking old thief!'" Fiona repeated. "Now who on earth said that? I know I read it somewhere."

"Blamed if *I* know," Glory muttered. "You're the one what's got your nose in a book whenever you have a few minutes."

"I just can't remember who said it. And maybe it didn't say *stinking* and *old*," Fiona quarreled with herself. "Maybe I added that myself."

"Sure does sound like you," Glory smiled. And then she added, "What's it mean anyway?"

"Means time goes by too fast."

"I knew *that*," Glory answered. "Maybe not in those words, but I surely did know that already."

"He's almost grown," Fiona whispered, as if she were afraid to hear the words herself.

"Victor?"

"Of course, Victor," Fiona responded. "Why, sometimes, I think I hardly know him at all anymore. He's so tall, and sometimes, I don't even recognize his voice. And I don't know that look in his eyes anymore."

"That's the way it's supposed to be," Glory assured her. "Little ones are supposed to grow up and get to be big folks theirselves."

"Even Jubilee?" Fiona said, as if she were suggesting that Jubilee should somehow be exempt from the process of growing up into full womanhood. Or trying to draw Glory into the conversation on a different, everyday level.

"Sure enough that one!" Glory laughed. "Men coming around all the time. Look just like cats after a bowl of cream."

"But don't you mind?" Fiona asked.

"No. Time was I thought she'd never, ever grow out of that huffing and puffing and rolling her eyes and sighing. I sure don't mind seeing that go."

"She's a full-grown woman now, so maybe she'll get married," Fiona said, still trying for some reason to draw Glory into the same vague sense of dissatisfaction she herself was experiencing.

"What are you really going on about?" Glory always had a way of cutting through whatever shield Fiona tried to build around herself and her feelings. At those words, Fiona felt tears come up in her eyes, but she blinked them away quickly, before Glory could notice them.

"I don't even really know!" Fiona admitted, and it was certainly as true a statement as she was capable of making. "Just a sad, sad feeling. So sad, I could just die!"

"I know," Glory answered.

"Do you really?" Fiona asked, with doubt in her voice.

"Yep—reckon I do," Glory sat back in the rocking chair, with her hands, for once, resting idly on the rim of the bowl in her lap.

"Something or other just sets you off. Could be some little thing not even worth a hill of beans. Just the way light shines on the lake sometimes, or a dog barking 'way far off at dusk." Fiona listened carefully, as Glory put into words the very sadness she felt, but not put it into words either, because that wasn't really possible. Still, Glory was coming close. Fiona listened.

"I don't rightly know how to say it," Glory went on. "But it's something every woman knows. That's for sure." Glory stopped and looked at Fiona over the tops of her glasses. "Sometimes, it has to do with young'ans growing up." Glory's final words touched a terrible ache deep inside of Fiona, so much that she almost felt like wailing. But instead, she said. "I'm going to miss him." Fiona was surprised at hearing her own words and wondered if her voice betrayed the deep, sad feelings she was experiencing. "And I don't quite know how to say it, either" she added.

"I think you're saying it just fine," Glory said, and went back to shelling butterbeans.

" All those long years that I worried about Victor's . . . mother . . . coming back and taking him away. And now, it's *time* itself that's doing it!" Glory said nothing for a few moments, but then a deep chuckle escaped her throat.

"What's funny?" Fiona asked, ready at the drop of a hat to have her feelings hurt.

"I was just thinking that maybe you need yourself another man," Glory giggled, while Fiona's mouth fell open in surprise and her eyebrows gathered in storm clouds. Fiona jutted out her chin and was ready to respond with venom, but she was interrupted when Jubilee came riding up on her bicycle, stopped at the front steps, and looked up at Fiona and Glory with a worried expression on her face. And the sight of Jubilee, a fully grown woman, saddened Fiona even more, for some reason. Because Jubilee was really quite lovely, but in a still somewhat petulant sort of way. Her legs were long and slender, she had developed a formidable bosom, and she had also taken to wearing lipstick and earrings.

"Whatchu doing here this time of day?" Glory demanded. "Aren't you supposed to be at Doc and Miss Myra's?"

"That's what I come to tell you all," Jubilee said, swinging one leg off of the old bicycle she rode. "Miss Myra, she's sick something awful. Doc's taken her up to Gainesville, and Miss Myra said she wouldn't go at all, wouldn't leave Rebecca. So they had to take Rebecca with them, and that's why I'm here and not there. Nothing for me to do with nobody home."

"When did this happen?" Glory asked, leaning forward in her chair.

"Yesterday afternoon," Jubilee said, glistening with the thrill of spreading bad news.

"I knew Myra wasn't well, or at least, that's what I heard," Fiona said. "But Doc has taken her to Gainesville, you say?"

"Yess'm," Jubilee nodded. "And he said he doesn't know when they'll be back. But he called Miss Myra's sister over in Tampa and told her to come."

"I wonder why," Glory mused. "If Rebecca went with them to Gainesville, there's no need for Miss Myra's sister to come."

"He said someone should be in the house, to watch out after it. And he whispered to me—so Miss Myra and Rebecca couldn't hear him—that if Miss Myra had to stay in the hospital over to Gainesville, he would be bringing Rebecca back so she wouldn't be missing so much school."

"Rebecca without Myra?" The words slipped out of Fiona's mouth before she could even think them.

"That's what the sister is for," Jubilee explained.

"And now that they're gone, I suppose you'll spend all your time in the afternoons hanging out around that old pool hall down by the creek. Hanging out down there with all those no-count *men*." Glory fairly spat the last word, and Jubilee's face lit up as if there were a light bulb behind her eyes. But she got herself under control and cast her eyes demurely at the ground. "No, ma'am, Aunt Glory," she denied while a smile still stuck to the edge of her bright red lips. "I'm gonna be going to church. That's what I'm gonna do." Before Glory could challenge Jubilee's open and obvious lie, they all heard a loud *whoop!* from the other side of the house, and Victor came tearing up to the porch on his bicycle, going fast and with his long legs stuck out in front of him.

"Look out, Ju-bee!" he yelled, using his childhood name for her.

"Victor! Be careful!" Fiona yelled, as Victor put his feet down on the pedals and slammed on the brakes, sending a shower of sand up from the driveway. He stopped, sweating and grinning at Jubilee, who twittered almost prettily. But Glory was frowning at her, and so she lowered her head and eyes and tried to hide her smile. Whenever Victor saw Jubilee, there was always a burning question behind his eyes. About Rebecca. But time after time, Fiona saw him blink it away, and that's exactly what he did now.

"Supper ready?" Victor called—far too happily, Fiona thought—dropping his bike and bounding up the steps. "I could eat a bear!" Jubilee giggled, and Glory frowned harder. Fiona saw Victor swallow his question about Rebecca. Saw him put it deep inside of himself, in a place where he thought it couldn't hurt him. Where he may have thought he could forget it.

"Well, come on inside," Fiona said, brightening despite knowing of Victor's pain. Because when Victor—*her* Victor was home, the sad feeling dispersed like an early morning fog, and her chest, instead, was filled with a glorious sunshine. Victor followed her into the house, leaving Glory still frowning at Jubilee.

"Where have you been anyway?" Fiona flinched as the screen door slammed hard behind Victor. He glanced at her and shrugged his shoulders at the loud noise. "Down at the Trading Post," he said. "Did you know that Old Man and Miss Arabella have a son—a grown man, I think. And he's coming home for the first time in—I guess—years."

"Where has he been?" Fiona asked. "I never heard anyone say anything about another *son*. You sure they didn't mean David? He's a grandson."

"This is their son," Victor said. "He's been up in New York—some kind of school for preachers, I think."

"Well, I know they're happy about him coming home."

"I can't wait to meet him," Victor said, following Fiona into the kitchen. "I never met anybody from as far away as New York before. So what's for supper?"

On the porch, Glory wasn't through with Jubilee. "Don't you be acting like that around that boy," Glory warned.

"Like what?" Jubilee asked, turning her most innocent gaze upon Glory. "And what *boy*? All I see is a *man.*"

"You know exactly what I mean!" Glory stormed, and Jubilee turned her bicycle around and prepared to ride away. "You stay away from him," Glory snarled.

"But he's sure a man," Jubilee laughed, cutting her eyes at Glory, as if just to annoy her.

"Yes, he's a man, as you say" Glory agreed. "*And* he's *white*! So you leave him alone. You hear me?"

"Yess'm," Jubilee said, but she was still smiling.

"Else I'll take a broom to you, girl!" Glory said, her jowls shaking in anger.

"Yess'm," Jubilee said, before she hopped upon her old bicycle and pedaled away fast—just as if the devil himself were chasing her.

"Lord, help us!" Glory muttered, before she picked up the bowl of shelled butterbeans and went inside.

No one, other than Rebecca's teachers at school and Jubilee, knew anything at all about Rebecca and no one else had even seen her, not since that day all those years ago when Fiona made such a terrible mistake in the drugstore. But Fiona and Glory knew how distressed Myra had been when she lost Rebecca to school every year. Jubilee herself had told Glory how every single year, Myra simply sat all day long in a chair by the window, watching for her Rebecca to come home. Sat there and said nothing, ate nothing. Just waited.

Now, Myra was ill, and if anything happened to her, what would happen to Rebecca, that young woman Myra had kept so sequestered? Like some exotic, fragile orchid in a greenhouse?

Over the next week or so, Fiona learned what was happening through Glory, who learned everything from Jubilee, including the arrival of Myra's sister, Irma. Doc arranged for David—Old Man and Arabella's grandson—to meet her bus from Tampa and take her to the house, where Jubilee was waiting, just as Doc had instructed her.

When Jubilee told them about Irma's arrival, she detailed the older woman's dress, shoes and hat, and wrinkled her nose as she described the shopping list Irma gave to Jubilee right off.

"She put canned figs on her list!" Jubilee exclaimed. "Can you imagine?"

"But didn't you help Miss Myra put up figs last year, right from that tree in her own yard?"

"I sure did," Jubilee confirmed. "But those weren't good enough for *her*! She didn't want *FIG PRESERVES*"—here, Jubilee pursed her lips and affected what she took to be Miss Irma's accent. Then she continued, "No! Her Majesty wanted the canned kind, not preserves, and Lord have mercy, they were so expensive, I almost fell over when I saw the price!"

"But you bought them, didn't you?" Glory inquired suspiciously. "Like she told you to."

"Yes, ma'am," Jubilee said. "Just liked to have killed me, is all."

"Has anyone heard from Doc? When are they all coming back?"

"Today," Jubilee said. "Or at least, Doc and Rebecca are coming. I don't know about Miss Myra."

Doc came home long enough to leave Rebecca with her aunt Irma and Jubilee, and then he proceeded, over the next few weeks, to take Myra all over the northern and central part of the state, to one specialist after another. Every time Myra had to leave Rebecca again, she was even more upset over that than she was about her own failing health. Rebecca, on the other hand, seemed strangely resilient regarding Myra's illness, and she was properly obedient to her aunt Irma, who usually simply sat around all day, crocheting.

"What will Rebecca do without me?" Myra wailed, and at first, Doc knew that she meant how she hated going to her doctor's appointments, leaving Rebecca with only Irma, the spinster sister, to care for her. And with Jubilee—who came every afternoon, to shop for groceries and to make sure Rebecca did her homework. When supper was ready—cooking was the only thing Miss Irma did, other than crocheting—Doc usually came home, depending upon whether he had taken Myra to yet another hospital out of town or whether she was still at the hospital in Gainesville, where doctors were working hard to diagnose and treat her illness.

After Jubilee's initial negative reaction to Miss Irma, they all got along well, mainly because Miss Irma bothered neither girl—simply sat in the rocking chair by the window, crocheting one doily after another. Jubilee speculated to Glory that, by the time Miss Myra got well, all the chairs and tables in Doc's living room would be topped by so many crocheted doilies, they would look just like wedding cakes.

But as Doc took Myra to one specialist after another and got the same unhappy news from each and every one of them, he began to realize that when Myra talked about "leaving Rebecca," she meant it in a more permanent way. When Doc brought Myra home for the last time, he also brought packets of a powder that relieved her pain. The powders worked, but they also left Myra in a half stupor most of the time, and some nights, she would dream that Rebecca had died, and she would scream and cry until Doc had to give her an injection to make her sleep.

"Spooks me something awful," Jubilee confessed to Glory. "She sure is sick, and nobody seems to want to talk about it."

"Maybe it's just too uncomfortable for them," Glory suggested. "You shouldn't be so critical. They're doing the best they can."

Whenever Jubilee came around, Glory noticed that Victor hung around, as well. He didn't necessarily enter into their conversations, but he passed through the kitchen several times, and when he did, Jubilee lit up and giggled.

"I done told you about that!" Glory threatened.

"I'm sorry, Aunt Glory," Jubilee sounded truly contrite. "He's just the handsomest man I ever saw in my whole life."

"You're asking for nothing but trouble," Glory warned again. "Maybe you shouldn't come over here so often."

"But I have to have somebody to talk to about Miss Myra and what all's going on in that sad old house," Jubilee argued. For a moment, Glory hesitated, because she did like to know, herself, and the only way she would find out anything was through Jubilee. "Well, you just watch your eyes, is all," Glory issued a final warning. "Colored girl like you can get into a heap of trouble making eyes at some white man. Even a young one. You know that."

"Yess'm," Jubilee said, but when Glory turned away, Jubilee smiled.

Over the weeks, everyone in town heard about troubles at Doc and Myra's house, by that strange way news has of circulating through small towns and communities. But they knew none of the details, as did Glory and Fiona. Still, one by one or a few at a time, they started coming to the back door at Doc's house, whispering, tiptoeing, and bringing casseroles and pies and freshly baked bread. They always refused Irma's invitation to come in—politely, of course—because they were reluctant to enter the house, knowing as they did of how Myra had made it into a sanctuary where she could be safe with her Rebecca. Somehow, they felt that to intrude into that *sanctum sanctorum* now that poor Myra was so ill would be akin to sacrilege.

And so eventually, in the hush of that house of illness, in the half sleep of the blessed narcotics, and in the presence of more crocheted doilies than she had ever imagined, Myra passed away quietly, and the last word she ever spoke was "Rebecca!"

Some people said it was a blessing, because Myra had suffered so terribly—more from knowing she would, at last, have to leave Rebecca, than from the actual physical debilitations of her illness, whatever it had been. Some of the younger and middle-aged women in town quietly speculated that Doc would certainly remarry, after a decent period of time of course. But then they would always comment on the terrible task of trying to be a stepmother to Rebecca, to that young woman who had been so smothered. For surely, she would just *go wild!* And they lowered their voices more and more, until they spoke about it not at all. At least, not until after the funeral.

Chapter Eleven

A large crowd gathered at the old Love-Oak Cemetery for Myra's funeral, many because of their respect for Doc—their beloved and only doctor. But just as many came out of pure curiosity about Rebecca, anxious to see the mysterious young woman who had grown up so hidden from the community—from life itself. On the funeral day, they gathered early and kept their whispered comments low and sedate, as was befitting the occasion, but when Doc's familiar car pulled into the cemetery driveway, and the preacher looked up alertly, all the people craned their necks to see it.

Doc stepped out and opened the passenger door, holding his hand inside to help Rebecca out of the car. When she appeared, there was a nearly inaudible intake of breath among the crowd, because Rebecca was nothing short of elegant—slender and graceful and wearing a black dress that left her tanned arms bare. She was also wearing a black veil that almost completely hid her face, and a quiet murmur went through the people gathered there, a brief, communal wondering if the veil was, appropriately, in mourning for Myra or if perhaps there was something wrong—disfigured—about Rebecca.

But as soon as Doc and Rebecca made their way up the aisle that had been left between the sections of folding chairs, people could tell that the veil was a lightweight one, and they could all see the face of an incredibly beautiful young woman behind it. She kept her eyes cast down, and Doc kept his arm around her shoulder, as they went forward and took their seats in the front, beside Irma, who had already been seated. Some people whispered that Doc himself was tearless because he had lost his beloved Myra so many years before, when their own baby girl had died. Certainly every person in the entire community knew that Myra had refused to believe that "this" Rebecca was not the baby to whom she had given birth. But truthfully, some of them had even forgotten it themselves.

Far back in the rows of seats, Fiona touched a tissue to her eyes and looked at Victor, who was sitting tall beside her. In their day to day comings and goings, Fiona hadn't really noticed his height, but on a recent day, when he was standing beside her, she realized that her eyes came up only to his shoulder. Additional tears tried to spring to her eyes, upon this incredible realization, but she blinked them back.

How has this happened so fast? This man beside me was a lost little child, and the young woman beside Doc was a tiny baby in a frilly bonnet and a dress festooned with ribbons .Oh, too fast! Too fast!

Standing at the back of the crowd with Jubilee fidgeting slightly beside her, Glory had nearly the same thoughts. *Just look at Victor, how he has grown, and how he is looking so steadily at Rebecca. Fiona probably won't notice that, because she just don't want to know they're old enough to be a man and a woman and perhaps in love. But I know that Victor has loved her for many years. And now that Myra is gone—Myra, the overprotective mother, the jailer, really—Rebecca will be free for the first time in her life. And what will happen between those beautiful young people?*

Jubilee's fidgeting broke Glory's reverie. They had been standing in the far rear and slightly to the side. For after all, they were neither family nor friends. Nor were they White. So they were in attendance, out of respect for Doc, but not really there. Something to which Glory was accustomed, but to which Jubilee rankled.

"Can't we go to Doc's house after this is over?" Jubilee queried in a whisper.

"We sure can," Glory confirmed. "We're going to serve the food and make sure everyone has what they need."

"How about what *I* need," Jubilee asked in a stage whisper.

"Hush!" Glory spat back at her. "You're asking for trouble, missy! You're asking for trouble!"

As the service progressed, Fiona thought that the look in Victor's eyes wasn't something you expected to see at a *funeral,* for Heaven's sake! But Victor was a young man now, and whatever she had failed to teach him, he would have to learn by himself. On the other side of Victor, Starry sat resolutely, wearing a tasteful navy-blue dress with a narrow white collar and a bit too much lipstick, Fiona thought. But Fiona said nothing, of course. But she did notice Starry craning her neck, so she could see Doc, and looking at him in a most peculiar way. But surely, Starry would never "make a move" on poor old Doc, at least not at his wife's funeral! So she watched Starry most carefully, and Victor, as well— and the way he looked at Rebecca. Then Fiona rebuked herself, *Stop thinking about those kinds of things! After all, this is Miss Myra's funeral, for Heaven's sake! Doc will take good care of Rebecca for Myra's sake if for no other. He won't allow her to be gallivanting all over creation, and especially not out to the camp, to see Victor. And I don't think Victor would dare to go to Doc's house, not after the fuss Myra put up. But Starry . . . well, that was a different thing.*

The service was short and lovely, with the minister using the familiar verses out of Proverbs about the qualities of a *good woman,* and when he finally said "Amen," Doc arose and waited until Rebecca and Irma preceded him down the aisle. But about halfway down, Rebecca suddenly turned back and moved into the sheltering arm of her father.

But just as Rebecca—leaning against Doc—passed Victor and Fiona, Victor reached out suddenly behind Fiona and brushed Rebecca's hand with his own. When Fiona realized what had happened, she was struck with the gesture, so reminiscent of that day in the drugstore when Rebecca was an infant and Victor just a toddler, and he had reached out and grabbed her baby fist. Rebecca glanced at him in a startled manner, started to smile, but quickly regained her composure and passed on by with her eyes cast down.

And yet, in that fleeting instant, Fiona saw something in both their eyes that she had never seen before. She didn't know how to describe it, even to herself. Briefly, Fiona wondered if that glance had been Victor's very first contact with Rebecca, since that long ago time when Myra told Fiona to keep him away from her daughter. All those years.

And yet?

After the funeral, people gathered at Doc's house, moving quietly and carefully around, speaking to each other in soft tones and accepting the punch Glory and Jubilee were serving. Glory kept her eyes down and her presence unobtrusive, but Jubilee smiled openly and looked right into people's faces, especially when she offered drinks on a tray to Victor.

"Thanks, Ju-bee," he said, a little too loudly, and then his eyes slid right back to Rebecca, who was sitting beside Miss Irma, quietly accepting condolences. Jubilee glanced at Victor again and then at Rebecca, and her eyes blazed, but she said nothing. With the veil she had worn to the funeral now removed, everyone could see quite clearly that Rebecca was absolutely beautiful in every way. Her dark eyes seemed to dance with light, even in such a somber environment, and her small mouth inadvertently turned up into a smile at the least provocation. Obviously, Rebecca was unaccustomed to being around so many people, but she seemed to take the occasion in stride, thanking people for their condolences and for coming to her mother's funeral.

Throughout the entire visitation, Jubilee continued to serve punch and cookies, but what she was really doing was watching both Victor and Rebecca openly, watching as Rebecca smiled and looked up to find Victor staring right at her. Once, Jubilee saw Rebecca's cheeks flush to a delicate pink when Rebecca looked at Victor.

Fiona was watching, as well, and she noticed the quick glances going back and forth between Victor and Rebecca. But she also noticed that Starry, on the other hand, was conducting herself in a most proper manner, conversing genially and quietly with the others, and making no attempt to draw Doc aside or to talk with him. Later, Fiona would have to remember to compliment Starry on her demeanor.

For weeks following Myra's funeral, people in the community seemed to hold their breath, collectively, wondering what would happen. They figured, rightly so, that any young woman who had been so firmly sequestered might go *wild*, once she gained her freedom. And they all said silent prayers for their beloved Doc and Myra's sister, Irma.

Who knew what things would be like at that house. Who knew?

But if anyone anticipated any sort of meeting between Victor and Rebecca—now that Rebecca was *free*—those anticipations seemed to go unsubstantiated because Rebecca's routine seemed to change not at all. Victor glimpsed her only infrequently as she left school, but every chance he had, he watched her—as if he could never get enough of looking at her. Still, he didn't go to Doc's house again, even with Myra now gone. Yet he often rode his bicycle close enough to watch Rebecca, but without anyone else knowing about it. And although Jubilee managed to glimpse Victor a few times herself, she just smiled and said nothing.

As usual, Jubilee came to meet Rebecca at school most afternoons and went home with her. Rebecca's aunt Irma stayed on, almost as if she were a faint shadow of Myra, and Doc always came home as soon as he had taken care of all his patients. Their lives seemed to have changed very little.

Chapter Twelve

Soon, Fiona forgot to think about Rebecca, just as she had eventually forgotten to think about Victor's mother. Or the way Victor had stared at Rebecca. Because, even with Jubilee's part-time help at the fish restaurant—begrudging as that help was—work continued to pile up for them all—especially for Glory. Starry tried her best to step into the breach with a polite determination that surprised Glory, but not Fiona. Because Fiona had been aware for some time that she was seeing a marvelous change in Starry, one for which Fiona took full but silent credit. All the years of working to make Starry into a *real lady* were, at last, beginning to pay off. Because some time ago, Fiona ordered new dresses for Starry from a catalog—sweet, conservative housedresses with white piqué on the sleeves and a modest touch of lace around the neckline. Fiona had been especially careful to remember that Starry was, indeed, still a younger woman so she needed something a bit more frilly, a little softer, than what Fiona and Glory wore. And those new dresses had been merely the beginning of a very slow but absolutely glorious transformation for Starry.

After living in that bare little Number Seven cabin for so long, Starry decided to make curtains for the one small window—pale blue checks, a fabric of which Fiona approved heartily. But when Starry first mentioned making some curtains, Fiona had immediately imagined that Starry would choose bright red velvet with a gold braid trim, the thought of which set her heart racing.

"Let me help you pick out the fabric for your curtains, Starry," Fiona said with a smile.

"Well, yess'm," Starry said after a long moment. "I think I'd like that a lot." So the fabric was selected, and Starry sat at Fiona's old treadle sewing machine every evening for almost a week, pushing fabric under the metal foot and concentrating so hard that most of the time, Starry's tongue stuck out of the side of her mouth. She stitched her fingers right into the fabric only once, and while Starry cried openly, Fiona helped to disentangle her skin from the needle, gently plucked the stray threads out of Starry's fingers, and applied a Band-Aid. Even though Starry cried with pain, she said, "doggone!" only one time and cursed not at all.

After the curtains were hung—and Fiona had to admit that they were

beautifully made and absolutely perfect for the small cabin's only room—
Starry cut out pictures of flowers from Fiona's old Ladies' Companion
magazines and tacked them neatly to the walls, and at the last, she bought
two small throw pillows from the general merchandise store in town and
placed them carefully on her bed. Starry told Fiona that she had chosen
the pale blue color for the pillows because then they matched both the
curtains and the flower pages on the wall, and Fiona nodded in approval.
So Fiona watched Starry's pleasure and her development of "good taste"
with great satisfaction, noticing that Starry's face had finally begun taking
on a tranquil expression that softened her eyes and made her skin take on
a younger and more vibrant tint, especially since Starry had switched from
her purple-toned lipstick to that delicate and petal-like cherry red. So all in
all, Fiona was greatly pleased with Starry. And Starry never mentioned
Middy, something else that Fiona took as a sign of Starry's rehabilitation
from a man Fiona regarded as nothing more than a tattooed derelict.

But Fiona also watched carefully to see if Starry and Doc would start
keeping company, and that would have been far too early, too soon after
Myra's death. That didn't happen, even though Fiona was sure Starry was
hoping it would. Still, Starry did start dating, and Fiona heaved another
great, worried sigh. She could only hope that Starry had gained some
wisdom about herself and that she wouldn't start going out with any man
who reminded her of Middy. Still, Fiona also knew that such "bad boys"
often attracted women, and she never could understand that. Perhaps a
love interest between Starry and Doc wouldn't be so bad, after all, when
the time was right. Right now, it was far too soon after Myra's passing.

"Did you know that Starry's going out on a date tonight?" Fiona
asked Glory.

"And?" Glory could be completely exasperating.

"And . . . don't you wonder about it?" Fiona asked.

"She's going out with that Billy-fellow who works at the mercantile,"
Glory said.

"How did you find out about that?" Fiona asked, exasperated. "I
thought for sure she'd finagle a date with Doc, if she went out with
anyone."

"Too soon for Doc to be seeing any women," Glory pronounced.
"And I found out because Starry herself told me. I imagine she'd tell you a
lot more things too, did you be a little less judgmental around her."

"Judgmental?" Fiona exclaimed. "Why, you're the one who hardly
has a kind word to say to her."

"But I'm honest," Glory fired back. "You . . . you always act so
polite, but deep down, you think first chance she gets, she'll up and run

off with some other piece of trash." Fiona couldn't reply to that, because she suddenly realized that it was absolutely true.

"And besides," Glory went on. "She's not like she was when she first come here. She's got a lot more of that self-esteem stuff, I think they call it. Thinks more highly of herself, is what it means, but in a good way. So I wouldn't worry about her, if I was you. But after some decent time has passed, Doc sure better watch out for her!" Glory added, laughing.

And as it turned out, Glory was right—at least partly. Starry went out with that "Billy-fellow" only one time and then never again.

"How come you don't go out with him again?" Fiona hadn't wanted to ask that question, but she couldn't stop herself. She had been standing beside Starry at the end of the pier, waiting for Mr. Owen's boat, with Starry looking out over the lake and, as usual, dangling her feet above the water. But there was something different now about Starry. Fiona could sense it, but she just didn't know what it was. And, being Fiona, she meant to find out.

"I'm not going out with him again," Starry said at last.

"But why not?" Fiona meant to get to the bottom of it. Starry waited before she answered, and it wasn't until they both heard the far-off put-put of Mr. Owen's outboard motor that Starry stood up and looked directly at Fiona.

"He didn't treat me like I was a *lady*," Starry said, and the lift to her chin told Fiona that Glory had been right, most certainly. Starry had gotten "that self-esteem stuff" sure enough.

"I'll just wait for a man who *will* treat me like a lady," Starry added, and Fiona immediately thought of Doc, but she said not a word. After all, Glory had probably been right. After a decent amount of time, Doc sure better watch out!

Eventually, even Glory stopped harrumphing around Starry all the time, and every weekday morning, when Starry handed over the pan filled with perfect filets, Glory even said, "Thank you."

"Yes ma'am," Starry would always chirp, grateful for the somewhat reluctant courtesy Glory was showing to her. But despite their best efforts, Glory and Starry had a hard time keeping up with serving all of the people who came to the restaurant. A few times, they even ran out of fish and coleslaw and had to turn away paying customers, something that set Glory's teeth on edge.

"Well, that's it," Glory fumed. "We've just got to get us some more help in here, that's all. I know Jubilee wasn't one to do much, but it made a difference, and now, we have to bring in someone else."

"But hasn't Victor been helping out too?" Fiona asked.

"Oh yes," Glory agreed. "He's awfully good about helping out. He washes all those big pots and pans and sweeps off the pier—whenever he isn't out in the boat with Mr. Owen or down at the Trading Post with Old Man, or out riding all over creation on that bicycle—or wherever he goes on that thing—but we need somebody who can work around in a kitchen without setting it on fire or spilling hot grease all over himself!"

And Fiona was thinking, *He will be young only once in his whole life, and I don't want to see him working in that kitchen like he was in a cage. And he's growing up so fast. Too fast. Childhood is already behind him, and he's turned into a young man. He needs his freedom.*

She knew that it wouldn't be easy to find someone to come for only a few hours every weekday, and who on earth would be willing to work for the small amount they could pay? But one afternoon, when Old Man came to mow the lawn—Fiona still paid him to do that, even though Victor himself always did the mowing—Old Man simply pushed the mower around the yard, and Fiona paid him. On that day, Fiona studied Old Man carefully, and while she said not a word to him that day, she approached Glory later about an idea she'd had. "What about Old Man's wife?"

"What about her?" Glory asked, not making any connection.

"I was just thinking that maybe we could hire her to help out with the restaurant."

"We don't even know her," Glory complained.

"We know *him*," Fiona said. "And that's enough for me."

"But doesn't she work at the Trading Post?"

"I don't know. We can ask," Fiona said, ever more comfortable with the thoughts of Old Man's wife working for them, but then she exclaimed, "Goodness! I don't even remember her name!"

"It's Arabella," Glory said, matter-of-factly.

"And just how do you know that?" Fiona asked.

"Don't know," Glory said. "Just heard somebody say it one time."

So the next day, Fiona walked down to the Trading Post, a place where she had never been, and Victor walked along with her.

"I like coming here," Victor volunteered as they drew closer to the restaurant and the Trading Post beside it. "Feels like another home to me, if you know what I mean—growing up on the stories David tells about the Seminoles. Good stories—like the Deer Girl."

"Deer Girl?" Fiona asked.

"Oh, she was really a deer who turned into a girl with beautiful eyes,"

Victor said, completely accepting of something so magical. "Or maybe she was really a young girl who turned into a deer—I'm not sure."

"Goodness!" Fiona exclaimed, thinking to herself that she really should have encouraged Victor to read more when he was younger—read good old time-honored fairy tales she'd heard from her own grandmother. Something that would have balanced out these fanciful things David had told Victor for years. Something truly gentle and Anglo-Saxon, like Jack and the Beanstalk—

> *Fee, Fi, Fo, Fum*
> *I smell the blood of an Englishman*
> *Be he live or be he dead,*
> *I'll grind his bones to make my bread.*

Fiona shivered and smiled to herself—well, maybe not that particular one. And besides, it was too late for fairy tales. Far too late, for Victor, who towered above the short Fiona, leaning down his shining head to her when she spoke and smiling his beautiful smile at her.

When they went inside the Trading Post, Fiona was somewhat uncertain, noting the somewhat musty aroma of the place and gazing around her at all of the things for sale, mostly for tourists. The lighting was very low, and native baskets were filled with wares designed to part the tourist from his money, like small shells and pebbles gathered from around the lake and labeled, "Magic shells and stones—they will bring you good luck and cure all of your ailments." And the aromas were foreign to Fiona, as well—the still-green aroma of the woven baskets and the old dust of a thousand stories.

Victor, however, walked in with complete familiarity and went right to where Old Man was sitting in a dim corner, in a tilted-back chair, and with his eyes closed. Victor put his hand onto Old Man's shoulder, and the heavy lids flew up immediately, the black eyes snapping alert.

"Aunt Fiona wants to talk with you," Victor said, and Fiona noticed the soft tone of Victor's words, as if the words themselves could somehow reach out and bruise the old man. Just as Fiona was ready to speak, she noticed a shadow moving behind the taller baskets near the wall, and because Fiona already felt somewhat uncomfortable in the Trading Post, she hesitated. The shadow moved again, and Fiona could see the outline of a young woman—Rebecca? But what on earth would she be doing at the Trading Post?

A soft giggle floated out into the musky air. *But what could make me think it's Rebecca? What would she be doing in a place like this?*

Victor had seen the shadow as well and had heard the giggle, but even though he smiled, he kept his eyes on Old Man.

Fiona took a deep breath and stammered, "We need some help out at the restaurant down at the fishing camp, and we wondered if your wife . . . I'm, sorry, I can't seem to remember . . ."

"Miss Arabella," Victor interjected, still gazing in the direction of the shadow.

"Yes . . . Miss Arabella . . . would like to come and work for us, only for two or three hours each weekday? We can't pay much, but we certainly do need the help." She didn't expect Old Man to answer, of course, but she did expect to see some shift in the eyes—some indication that he had heard her. She received none. However, when those deep, black eyes tilted to gaze at Victor, Fiona certainly did see a change in them. Right in front of her own eyes, they became even deeper and soft . . . almost as if they were made of melted chocolate, and the sides of the mouth turned up ever so softly. And Fiona was somewhat startled. She thought to herself, *If anybody ever asks me what love looks like, I will remember this. I will remember these eyes. He loves Victor like a son!*

Old Man broke her strange reverie when those same dark eyes shifted to the shadow behind the baskets. Fiona heard a soft footstep, just as Old Man's eyes swiveled back to Victor, where they stayed for seemingly long minutes, riveted right into Victor's very heart. Old Man heaved a sigh and shook his head slowly.

"No?" Fiona blurted, surprised by the negative response, but a faint rustling behind the baskets indicated that whoever had been there— Rebecca?—had now slipped away. Old Man's eyes stayed riveted on Victor, and then slowly, they shifted to Fiona. The great head nodded once, and so the answer was given. But for a breathless moment, Fiona wondered, *But exactly what was the question?*

The next day, Old Man came walking down the sandy road, Arabella walking beside him but not touching him. Fiona had been on her way to clean one of the cabins, and she saw them coming from a distance. Old Man, in his typical fashion walked as straight as an arrow, his chin up and proud eyes staring straight ahead. Arabella tripped along beside him, plump and smiling. When she saw Fiona, she threw up a hand.

"Hello, Miss Fiona," Arabella said. "I don't know why my husband has brought me here, but I am glad to meet you." Fiona came forward, balancing the pile of clean towels and sheets on her hip, and extended her hand to Arabella.

"Hello, Arabella," Fiona said. "Yes, we need someone to help in the restaurant every weekday—probably from around eleven in the morning until two in the afternoon, or whenever we get everybody fed. Would you like to have the job?"

Arabella glanced at Old Man, who nodded almost imperceptibly.

"Yes, thank you," Arabella said. "Since my grandson is helping out at the Trading Post, I have more time on my hands than I care to have. I'd like to take the job."

Behind Fiona, Victor came wheeling up on his bicycle.

"Hi, Miss Arabella!" he said, genuinely happy to see her. "Are you going to be helping out around here?" Victor was clearly delighted at the prospect.

"I believe so," Arabella said, glancing at Fiona.

"Well, that's just great," Victor laughed, and the next instant, he was off on the bicycle, pedaling down the road and with the breeze ruffling his pale hair. Old Man's eyes shifted for a moment and then resumed their impassive stare at absolutely nothing. In an effort to fill in the uncomfortable silence that followed, Fiona offered, "Victor tells me that you have a grown son who's going to come home soon." Arabella's face brightened considerably.

"Yes!" she said, her word filled with joy that Fiona could well understand. Because some day, Victor, too, would go away, and if she knew he were coming back home, that same joy would fill her own heart. But at the same time, the mere thought of Victor's someday leaving her sickened her heart and brought unwanted tears to her eyes.

"And what is your son's name?" Fiona asked, more to cover up her own discomfort than for real information.

Arabella drew herself up and stuck out her chin in motherly pride. "My son is Wahali," she almost sang out. "But where he is studying . . . in a monastery far away . . . he is known as Brother John."

Fiona was thinking, *A monastery? Does Arabella even know what that is? And do I?*

"Well, either name is beautiful," Fiona murmured. "I'm happy he's coming, and I'm so happy you'll be helping us out here."

The first day Arabella came to work in the restaurant, Fiona was worried about how Glory would take to the idea. Glory certainly knew how much they needed help, but after all, Glory was simply Glory, and Fiona never knew quite how she would take anything new. But to Fiona's surprise, Glory saw Arabella coming down the road, and she merely said, "Well, it's about time! Starry and me been going crazy, trying to get everything done. And Starry, she's slow as molasses, you know!"

And so Arabella came to work in the restaurant, going straight to the kitchen, where Glory put her to chopping cabbage for coleslaw.

"Now you be sure you chop it real fine," Glory directed. "Don't want no chunks in there." Arabella merely nodded and continued chopping. Starry had already prepared the fish filets, and Glory was in the process of battering them when she suddenly turned to Arabella and said, "And what's it like being married to a man who never says a single word?"

Arabella stopped chopping and glanced at Glory, who was standing with one hand on her hip, as if demanding an answer. Arabella smiled. "I'd say it's a blessing!" she said finally.

After a few moments of surprised silence, Glory started chuckling under her breath. Arabella heard her and started giggling softly herself, and within minutes, they were both laughing so hard that Arabella's tears were threatening to fall into the cabbage.

"Lord have mercy!" Glory exclaimed, wiping her face. "I reckon that's so! I sure do reckon that's so!"

Chapter Thirteen

Weeks passed, and slowly but surely, the changes everyone in the community were expecting to see in Rebecca's life started happening. All of a sudden, Rebecca seemed to realize that she was free for the first time in her life—free from an unhealthily intense and smothering love that in a few more years, surely would have stunted her personality. At first, she had been like a bird that had been kept in a cage for so long that, when the door was propped open, the bird didn't seem to know that it could fly away. And almost like the poet Lord Byron wrote in *The Prisoner of Chillon,* "My very chains and I grew friends/So much a long communion tends/To make us what we are—even I/Regain'd my freedom with a sigh."

Perhaps Rebecca didn't even know enough about freedom to sigh about it, but she slowly caught on to her new circumstances and began celebrating her newly found liberation by quietly ignoring anything her aunt Irma asked of her.

"You just wouldn't believe it," Jubilee told Glory one afternoon. "Rebecca isn't *rude,* exactly, but she just pretends she doesn't hear a thing her aunt Irma says to her."

"Like what?" Glory asked, trying not to seem too curious for details, but definitely feeling curious to the extreme.

"Well, like yesterday—Miss Irma told Rebecca to put a barrette in her hair, to keep it out of her face."

"And?" Glory persisted.

"Rebecca didn't pay a bit of attention. Just pulled her hair over her face even more, and then . . ." Jubilee paused for dramatic effect, and Glory heaved an impatient sigh. "And then," Jubilee repeated, relishing Glory's silent curiosity. "And then she looked at me, and her eyes was just dancing with some kind of mischief in 'em. And . . . she stuck out her tongue!"

"She did *what?*" Glory was shocked.

"Stuck out her tongue," Jubilee repeated.

"At her aunt Irma?"

"Yess'm, that's what she did!"

"And what happened then?" Glory stammered.

"Miss Irma didn't see it, 'cause of all that hair in Rebecca's face."

"Lord have mercy!" Glory breathed, frowning and trying to match such a childish gesture with the serene, well-mannered young lady at Myra's funeral. "Lord have mercy!" Glory repeated. "She sure must have a whole big bunch of anger all bottled up inside her, to do something like that."

Jubilee's voice crept into Glory's muddled thoughts.

"There's more." Jubilee's voice was low and devoid of its typical surliness.

"More?"

"Victor comes around." Jubilee spoke so softly that Glory heard only Victor's name.

"What?" Glory pressed. "What's that about Victor?" Glory studied Jubilee's face, trying to determine the look in her niece's eyes.

"Victor comes around," Jubilee repeated, louder.

"Comes around where?"

"Doc's house. He rides his bicycle right up to the screen porch, and Rebecca sits on the porch and they talk through the screen, so Miss Irma doesn't catch on, because I don't think she'd like Rebecca talking to a *boy*."

In her typical manner, Glory used a feigned anger to cover her surprise. "You can get that look off your face, missy!" she snarled at Jubilee.

"What look?" Jubilee was sincerely perplexed.

"I've seen you looking at Victor yourself," Glory's voice was fairly dripping with venom. "You just forget all about that. You go to Doc's and do the job he's paying you to do, and stop snooping. Doc don't pay you to snoop."

"You're wrong, Aunt Glory," Jubilee sputtered. "Snooping is exactly what Doc pays me for!" After Jubilee huffed herself away, Glory stood thinking for long minutes. *Nothing wrong with Victor going over there and talking with Rebecca,* she mused silently. *It was Myra who didn't want him anywhere near there, and she's gone now. And if that aunt of hers tries to do the same thing, that will be terrible. Surely, Doc himself won't try to keep such a tight hold on that girl, and if he does, he's in for trouble, sure enough.*

After supper that night, Victor left right away, hopping onto his bicycle and disappearing, as usual. Glory and Fiona cleared the table and started washing the dishes.

"Jubilee tells me Victor's going over to Doc's," she said, in a matter-of-fact manner, and for long moments, Fiona said nothing, just continued washing plates, rinsing them, and passing them to Glory for drying. "You hear me?" Glory finally asked.

"I heard you," Fiona answered. "Well, we knew things were going to change after Myra passed on," she stated. "And Victor's been wanting to go play with Rebecca for a long time."

"*Play?* You think he wants to go *play* with her?"

"Well, yes," Fiona said. "Play."

"Too old for playing," Glory mumbled, wondering what could be wrong with Fiona that she couldn't realize Victor and Rebecca were far too grown up to play in the innocent way of children. "Way too old for playing. Got a young *man* and a young *woman* here. And that's what you don't seem to realize."

"Don't go making something out of nothing, Glory," Fiona said, and Glory simply shook her head. *Because when a mama won't let herself know her young'an's grown, that's just as bad as what Miss Myra did to Rebecca.* But Glory said nothing more, because she knew Fiona wouldn't be able to hear it.

The next morning, while Jubilee was chopping cabbage for coleslaw, she muttered, "Doc's bought her a bicycle."

"That's nice," Glory answered, determined to turn a cold shoulder to Jubilee's gossiping. But she was thinking, *Well, if he's bought her a bicycle, it's for sure and certain he isn't going to keep her too close. Not going to make the same mistake poor Myra made. And maybe Victor won't have to go all the way over there to see Rebecca. I'd be willing to bet anything that HERE is the first place she'll come.*

But Glory was wrong about where Rebecca would go on that new bicycle, because she didn't come to the camp at all. Not at first. She rode that bike as fast as possible and far beyond the confining yard—all over town and far out into the countryside as well. But not to the camp. Because whenever she was out on the bicycle, Victor was usually on his own, right beside her. Everyone noticed, but no one said anything, believing that it was long past time for Rebecca to have some freedom—and some company. Victor didn't have an easy time keeping up with Rebecca, because she always rode so fast, adoring the feeling of her hair blowing off of her forehead and the green whir of palmettos as her fast-spinning wheels moved down the sandy paths.

Rebecca's mind was more on freedom than it was on Victor, and Victor did his best to keep up with the initial expending of Rebecca's pent-up energy.

Finally, one afternoon when Victor came in almost worn out and with his cheeks reddened, he confessed to Glory, "I've ridden all over creation with her, and I want to talk, want to just *be* with her, but before I can turn around, she's off and gone again, and she won't stop!"

"Be patient, Victor," Glory advised. "Let her get that out of her system. It's been a long time coming."

And Rebecca's aunt Irma, at the same time, was making exactly the same complaint to Doc—"I just can't keep up with that girl! She's out the door and gone before I even know about it!" Her whining was accompanied by a crochet needle that just went faster and faster. "It's just come down to that fact. I can't keep up with her!"

To Doc's credit, he did everything he knew to do, to try and keep up with his suddenly free and highly energetic daughter, without absolutely forbidding her to leave the house, because he strongly suspected that such an order would only have spurred her to open rebellion and sneaking out whenever she could. So Doc's solution was to purchase another bicycle—for Jubilee, so that she could ride with Rebecca and "keep an eye on things."

So keeping her eye on Rebecca became Jubilee's full-time job—keeping up with Rebecca and Victor as they raced through town and out into the countryside. That threesome on fast bicycles soon became a regular sight all around Love-Oak, and the townspeople smiled and nodded about it—for after all, it was certainly time that Rebecca enjoyed a bit of freedom. But Victor wasn't happy about it at all.

"If only Jubilee didn't have to go with us all the time," he complained. But only Glory noticed that Victor seemed to have a very dark cloud hanging over his head. And still, Rebecca rode her bike all over the countryside and just as fast as she could go.

Doc's house had a large, windowed pantry right off of the kitchen, and Doc hired a carpenter who enlarged it into a bedroom for Jubilee, so she could live right there in the house with them and keep an eye on Rebecca—for Irma's sake. When the room was finished, Doc bought a nice bed with a spread that matched the curtains at the window and put a small chest of drawers in the room, as well. Jubilee was thrilled. For the first time in her life, she had a place of her very own, one she didn't have to share with younger brothers and sisters, or with a mother or an aunt. And to make things even better, Doc gave her a check for her work at the end of every week. With her first paycheck, Jubilee bought herself a store-bought dress, the first she had ever owned, and she was so pleased with it that she put the hanger right on the curtain rod—wouldn't put the dress into her small closet, because she wanted to be able to see it with her own eyes anytime she chose. And she got Starry to go with her to the dime store, where she bought the first lipstick she had ever owned. And with

Starry advising her on the color, it was, of course, a little too bright.

If Rebecca thought for a moment about Victor, no one ever knew. And when Jubilee dreamed about him, no one ever knew that either.

And all the while, Rebecca's aunt Irma crocheted doilies.

Needless to say, Glory hated losing Jubilee's part-time, free labor in the restaurant, but she and Fiona had privately agreed that Jubilee wouldn't be working at the restaurant for long, anyway. Too many men were flitting around her, and Glory privately thought that sooner or later, Jubilee would fall for one of them and either get married or else—Lord forbid! Glory always thought—find herself in a "family way," and the man would be long gone, leaving Jubilee to face the same trials and tribulations Glory's own mother had faced. And too, although Fiona didn't know about it, there was the matter of Jubilee's interest in Victor. Glory was happy for that opportunity to be diminished.

Chapter Fourteen

Fiona shouldn't have been at all surprised the first time she saw Rebecca and Victor come whizzing past her kitchen window on bicycles, with Jubilee pedaling hard right behind them, struggling to keep up—but she was. Aside from the reception after Myra's funeral, where Rebecca had been quiet and withdrawn, obviously clothed in grief, Fiona had not seen her at all. But she had certainly heard about Rebecca, Victor, and Jubilee's fast forays into the countryside.

As the bicycles whizzed past the window, Fiona saw Rebecca throw back her head and laugh out loud at the wind rushing past her, and with her black hair streaming out behind her.

Right on around the house they all went, and Fiona went into the living room and looked out of those windows to see Rebecca starting to take the path that led around the lake, using her long legs to their greatest advantage, but then turning abruptly and bicycling into the myriad small paths that meandered through the thick palmetto brush and, at last, back to the yard outside of Fiona's kitchen window. Rebecca's laugh drifted in through the open window and filled the silent kitchen, and Fiona recalled the soft giggles coming from deep in the shadows behind the baskets at the Trading Post.

Even though Fiona knew, through Glory—who knew through Jubilee—that Rebecca was "running wild" following Myra's death (or that's what her aunt Irma called it), and that Doc had hired Jubilee to keep up with her—and also that Victor was certainly tagging along with the two—she hadn't expected them to come this way, and she couldn't imagine why Rebecca had pedaled so far away from her own home and had gone tearing around the small paths near the lake and then back to Fiona's own back yard. But Victor had disappeared. Where was he?

Then Fiona saw Victor coming around the house from the other direction, coming to a laughing, braking halt right in front of Rebecca and stood there, staring at her, until Jubilee came huffing up on her own bicycle and stopped, as well.

From the kitchen window, Fiona studied the three young people— Victor as strong and beautiful as some young Nordic god—the way she had seen them pictured in books—tall for his age, and square jawed, with almost no trace of boy softness left in his face, his body strong and brown as a berry from the Florida sun, and his hair bleached out almost pure white by the same sun. At that moment, Victor was so beautiful, Fiona caught her breath.

And then she looked at Rebecca. Where Victor was fair, Rebecca was dark haired and dark eyed, and the tan on her skin was a beautiful shade of olive. She sat quietly and completely relaxed on her bicycle, smiling at Victor, and Fiona couldn't help but notice her long arms and legs, the perfect shape of her young body. Behind Rebecca, Jubilee sat on her own bike, looking like some kind of ebony goddess herself, but pouting and puffing, obviously winded from trying to keep up with Rebecca and—yes!—*glaring* at Rebecca, who was quite obviously the only person of interest to Victor at that moment.

Fiona regarded the scenario of healthy young people, almost as if she were studying a painting in a museum. Without speaking a word, she told herself what she was seeing. Youth and energy, and—yes—perhaps even passion. And with Jubilee smoldering in the background. Had she ever had such feelings? Silently and mesmerized by what she was seeing, Fiona searched back through her memory and found . . . nothing. Not even for J. Roy.

Rebecca's dark eyes were sparkling with light from without and within, and she locked her gaze on Victor as if she would never want to see anything or anyone else, ever again. Rebecca smiled and opened her mouth to speak, but no words came.

Because she suddenly needed to be with Victor. Breathe the same air he breathed, walk where his feet had trod upon. After all the days of pedaling all over Love-Oak and beyond, it was as if she were really seeing him for the first time. And there he was, right in front of her this time, instead of behind her. He was blocking her way. Tall and bright looking as another noontime sun, his skin glistening with sweat and the male aroma of him surprising her nostrils.

Rebecca knew instinctively in that very moment that Victor would never look the same to her. Would never be "just Victor." And Fiona almost felt the same thing. Because Fiona remembered how he had looked only that very morning—not really a young *man* at all, but a great, gangling boy, with bright, innocent eyes filled with excitement at once again going out on the lake to fish with Mr. Owen. But now, Victor didn't even look like the same person—not the same at all, not when he was smiling and looking at Rebecca.

So Fiona stood silently, watching a pivotal point in Victor's life and in her own, watching him turn into a man right in front of her eyes. And she thought that all her hard work had paid off—that Victor's life had been everything she had hoped it would be.

But now there was something Fiona had not considered . . .

Rebecca.

And Jubilee?

Rebecca suddenly laughed and pedaled away on her bike, with Victor scrambling to his own bike and taking off after her.And Jubilee trailing badly and still smoldering with some kind of a fire Fiona had never seen in her before.

After that first surprising time, Rebecca came to the camp almost every single day, and she and Victor went wheeling off on their bicycles, with Jubilee hot eyed, grumbling, and trailing behind them. And every time Rebecca pedaled past the restaurant at the near end of the pier, Glory noticed her, as well.

Rebecca was certainly no longer a child. She was almost as tall as Victor, though she was a couple of years younger, and, if Glory admitted it, she was absolutely lovely in such a young, reckless way. She always wore clean shorts and soft cotton tee-shirts and her dark hair pulled back into a ponytail and tied with a bow that matched the color of her shorts. She was graceful and slender and always spotlessly clean, and even her perspiration, generated by the bicycle riding, held the faint aroma of soap and talcum powder. These were some of the things about Rebecca that Glory suspected had so entranced Victor. And Glory noticed Jubilee, as well. Always trailing behind. Always left out. Always black.

Well, that's just the way the world is, Glory thought to herself. *But I'm going to keep an eye on her. She's overripe and angry and jealous. And that's dangerous.*

Almost every day, Rebecca was around, Jubilee trailing discontentedly behind her, walking along beside Victor as he carried the suitcases and fishing gear for the fishermen who reserved cabins, and when Victor was out fishing, Rebecca helped Arabella to fold paper napkins, a task that always gave Arabella plenty of time to gaze at Rebecca to her heart's content—as Rebecca chatted endlessly and innocently about a movie she had recently seen, or especially about the newsreels that preceded the main film at every theater.

"Did you know that the Germans have invaded Poland?" she asked Arabella one morning.

"No, I didn't," Arabella said. "What does it mean? And where is Poland anyway?"

"I don't know," Rebecca confessed. "But Papa says it's going to mean war, sure as you're born. And speaking of my papa, here he is!"

As Doc's car pulled into the driveway beside Fiona's house, Rebecca ran to him.

"Papa! You left so early this morning, I didn't get to see you!"

Doc gathered his slender daughter into his arms, inhaling the fresh air clinging to her hair and face. "I'm sorry, honey—a patient needed me." He glanced around—"And where is Jubilee?" he asked, slight concern in his voice.

"I'm right here!" Jubilee shouted. "I stay with Miss Rebecca, just like you tell me," Jubilee defended herself before she could be accused of neglecting her duties. Jubilee didn't add, *It's what you pay me to do, and I do it. But if you only knew how hard it is for me to stand back, like some kind of slave or something and watch all the things that go on between Rebecca and Victor. Her skin darker than his but still White. And me black as an old crow.*

"Okay," Doc said, relieved. "I just wanted to speak to Fiona for a minute or so." Fiona, who had come out onto the porch, waved at Doc as he came walking across the yard.

"How about some nice cold tea?" Fiona asked.

"I'm afraid I don't have time," Doc explained. "I just wanted to make sure that Rebecca wasn't getting under foot with all Glory and you and . . . Starry have to do. I can't keep up with her, what with the practice and all," the doctor explained. "And Irma won't even try, bless her heart. I just don't want Rebecca and Jubilee to wear out their welcome with you folks."

"Not at all," Fiona lied with a laugh. Because she meant to make sure that Jubilee was with Rebecca and Victor all the time, and that way, she wouldn't have to worry. And besides, what could she say to Doc if she wanted to give him any warning? That Victor and Rebecca were "making eyes" at each other? How silly! They were still far too young for any such thing. *Weren't they?*

But still, she added, "In fact, I'm really happy to have someone for Victor to be friends with, especially when there's no school. And since you have Jubilee helping to watch out for Rebecca, she has to watch out for Victor as well, and that's a big help to me and Glory . . . and Starry, what with all the work we have to do." Doc noticed that Fiona was speaking of Rebecca and Victor in a way that showed she had thought almost everything out. Just as he had done. But then, as if Fiona could read Doc's thoughts, she added, "Children their age can get into all sorts of things," Fiona said, smiling. And Doc nodded solemnly in agreement, but *Children?* Fiona noticed the slight frown on his face, and she thought, *Oh, I'm glad I'm not trying to raise a girl-child in this day and age, especially not one like Rebecca!* But as Fiona walked with Doc toward his car, chatting lightly about the weather, she saw him glance around, as if he were looking for someone.

Starry?

Actually, Glory did as much watching out for Jubilee as Jubilee did for Rebecca, because Glory wanted to make sure that her niece was doing a good job and earning every cent of the money the doctor paid to her on Friday evening of every week. But Glory also knew that Jubilee was probably in love with Victor herself, and in a way that would never be suitable for anyone concerned. She could only pray that Victor didn't feel the same about Jubilee! *What would this world come to, if Coloreds and Whites started falling in love with each other? Chaos, that's what!*

Glory was truly fond of all three of the young people, and in the afternoons, she spread newspapers on the picnic table in the shade and dished out freshly fried fish and potatoes onto the center of it for Victor and Rebecca. Alongside that, she always put plenty of steaming hot hushpuppies and served it all with a big pitcher of sweet tea that had condensation from the hot air running down the sides of the pitcher. For Jubilee, Glory fixed a paper plate of fish and hushpuppies, taking the plate and leading Jubilee to sit beneath a nearby tree. If Glory hadn't watched Jubilee closely, she would have sat right down at the table with Victor and Rebecca. *And whoever heard of such a thing!*

After they were completely sated with such a good dinner, Rebecca would spread a soft, old quilt in the grass in the shade, and that's where she and Victor would fall asleep side by side, almost as soon as their heads were down. Jubilee leaned back against the tree and tried to sleep, as well, but Glory fussed at her about it.

"Doc ain't paying you to sleep!" she admonished. "You gets to sleep on your own time, not his'n!" So Jubilee would lean against the tree, fanning herself with an old comic book and trying to stay awake. Glory looked out of the restaurant door from time to time, checking to make sure that all was as it should be with the youngsters.

They're almost of an age, she thought to herself. *And it's purely dangerous to put two healthy young folks so close to each other all the time. Even sleeping beside each other, for Heaven's sake!* And, as she studied the sleeping forms of Victor and Rebecca from the vantage point of the kitchen doorway, studied their fresh, unblemished skin and shining hair, she projected her mind into the future. *It just don't look right, young man and young lady lying there together, even if they do still think of themselves as youngsters, which I really doubt. And even if that quilt is spread right out in pure daylight—right in sight of God and everybody else!*

And what is going through Jubilee's mind, watching those two together? Lord help us all!

Chapter Fifteen

For that entire summer, Victor and Rebecca were together almost every day, with Jubilee always in attendance, of course.Fiona and Glory let Victor slack off with helping at the camp, because they agreed that he needed a summer of riding his bike, swimming in the lake, and being in the good company of charming, energetic Rebecca. At least, that's what Fiona thought.Glory herself wasn't so sure.

"He won't be a child much longer," Fiona mused in a theatrical voice, and Glory responded, "I don't think he's much of a child *now!*" Because Glory was still noticing signs that Fiona chose not to see and didn't want to hear about how Victor and Rebecca bumped gently against each other as they walked along laughing, and how Rebecca tossed her head so that her dark hair went flying around in a most delightful manner. Jubilee noticed all of that, as well, though she said nothing to Glory about it. She didn't have to.

"Listen, Jubilee," Glory said to her one morning late in the summer. "You making sure you stay right by Miss Rebecca every minute? Every single minute now, you hear me?"

"Yess'm," Jubilee answered. "That's what Doc told me to do, and that's what I get paid for doing." Then she added, "I do a good job."

"I'm sure you do," Glory said. "But do you have any idea of why I'm reminding you about how important that is?"

"I . . . think so," Jubilee answered, smiling.

"Well, just what do you know?" Glory asked, frowning. Jubilee covered her smile with her hand and whispered, "I know Rebecca and Victor are in love with each other—and I can't blame Rebecca one little bit." She didn't add, *How I wish he'd look at me like that!* But she didn't have to. Glory knew, anyway, and gave Jubilee the most vicious frown she could muster.

But of course, Jubilee was absolutely right—Rebecca, young, lithe, filled with energy, and quite beautiful, was flirting outrageously with Victor, who mostly seemed to walk around in a trance—absolutely stunned by this new experience—this thing called *love,* with his eyes lit up in a new light and always with a secretive smile on his face. He spent hours in his room every night, writing something down, and Fiona snooped one day when he was out, and found that he was writing poems. All about Rebecca. Her hair. Her eyes. Her smile. Fiona blushed and wished, for the first time in her life, that she hadn't snooped.

But she didn't worry. After all, they were so young.

As the summer went on and the weather became oppressively hot and humid, Rebecca brought her bathing suit and towel rolled up and secured to the handlebars of her bicycle. Victor, who hurried through his breakfast, always came running out of the house, waiting for Rebecca to arrive. And when she did, Victor's face looked as if the sun had come out from behind a cloud. They smiled and whispered together, softly bumping into each other from time to time. And Jubilee stood by and watched. And waited.

Rebecca went into Starry's cabin—Starry had told her to feel free to use it for changing her clothes—and when she came out, she wore a brilliant blue one-piece bathing suit that showed off her graceful shoulders and long, tanned legs. And when Rebecca put on her bathing cap, she always turned this way and that, as she tucked her long hair into the cap, glancing from time to time to see if Victor was watching her. And he usually was, with a look Glory easily recognized and Fiona didn't.

Jubilee, sitting in the shade, fanned herself with a cardboard Jesus fan Glory accused her of stealing from church. Of course, Jubilee denied such a theft completely, but when Glory wasn't watching, she smiled as she fanned herself. Jubilee, the hawk, watching absolutely everything Rebecca did.

"I don't know why I can't go swimming with them," Jubilee finally complained, with a whine in her voice.

"You do too know why!" Glory fumed. "Because it isn't done." Certainly, Jubilee could understand exactly what Glory meant, because no matter what friendships grew up between black people and white people, they never mingled, socially, not even to go swimming together in a lake. Jubilee said nothing else, but Glory could still sense something smoldering in her niece, and she worried. So Glory watched Jubilee—and Jubilee watched Rebecca and Victor swimming every afternoon, watched the frolicking, the splashing and laughing and heard Victor's shouts and Rebecca's squeals as they dunked each other beneath the crystal-sparkling surface. Soon, they waded up on the shore near the pier.

"Hi, Miss Fiona!" Rebecca called, waving to Fiona on the porch. Then she whipped off the bathing cap, glancing around to see if Victor was watching, as the cascade of rich, black hair fell around her shivering shoulders. Rebecca's lips were tinged blue with cold. And Victor was watching. Victor was always watching.

"You children get dried off and into dry, warm clothes," Fiona barked. "It isn't very smart of you all to get chilled!Remember polio!"

Rebecca was still glancing around at Victor, who was wading ashore. Fiona was sure that Rebecca was simply another child to him, but innocence could be dangerous, and so she was glad, once again, that Jubilee was watching them every single minute.

One morning toward the end of the summer, Arabella said to Fiona, "My son called me long distance last night, and he's supposed to come early next week."

"Victor told me you had a son who would be coming," Fiona said. "But you never told me you and . . . your husband . . ."—Fiona didn't want to call him Old Man to his wife—" . . had a son . . . another son . . . much less that he was at a minister's school way off in New York."

"Well," Arabella ventured. "I guess it isn't the kind of thing you would talk about very much. And they don't call themselves ministers," she added, frowning. "Call themselves monks."

"Monkeys?" Fiona exclaimed, puzzled.

"No, monks," Arabella corrected her. "I'm not sure of what that means, but that's what they call themselves."

"And he's coming! Isn't that *wonderful?*"

"Well, Miss Fiona," Arabella hesitated. "He wants to stay in one of your cabins, if that's okay with you."

"Why?"

"Says he has a lot of thinking to do. Meditating, he calls it, and he needs some privacy. And besides, he doesn't want to put me and his papa out any. You know how grown sons can be."

No, I don't, Fiona thought to herself. *But one of these days, I'm sure to find out.*

"He said he'll pay whatever you ask," Arabella added, proudly.

"That's not necessary, Arabella. Just pick out whatever cabin you want him to have. And I'll make sure it's fixed up extra special."

"How about Number Five," Arabella said. "It has that beautiful hibiscus right by the front door. Wahali will like that!"

Kind of close to Starry's own cabin, Fiona was thinking, but she didn't say anything. *I hope he won't be very handsome—although I'm sure Starry will flirt with anything in pants. Even a monk.*

"Wahali—it's an unusual name," Fiona ventured. "Does it mean something special?"

"Yes, it means 'eagle.' "

"That's lovely," Fiona exclaimed. "And Cabin Five will be his."

Maybe I can put the new reservation for next week into Cabin Six and make some sort of a barrier between Starry and . . . this Wahali . . . this eagle-man.

Then, Fiona couldn't help but ask one more question. "And what is your husband's real name?" Fiona felt awkward with such a question, but it seemed an appropriate time to ask.

"His name is Koi." Arabella smiled. "It means 'panther.'"

Arabella returned to the restaurant kitchen, and Fiona could hear Glory, Starry and Arabella talking excitedly about the impending arrival of Arabella's son. On her way back into the house, Fiona happened to glance at the quilt spread out in the shade of the largest live oak tree, where Rebecca and Victor would have their lunch.They had both changed out of their wet bathing suits and were wearing shorts and tee-shirts, and they were sitting on the quilt, eating fried fish with their fingers and laughing about something. She couldn't hear what they were saying.

Some distance away, Jubilee sat under another tree, fanning herself with the cardboard Jesus fan. As Fiona watched, Rebecca leaned toward Victor and said something to him. This time, he did not laugh, but he looked at her long and hard and then shrugged his shoulders. Something—Fiona couldn't tell what—changed right then and there in the angle of his neck and the way he tilted his head back and looked high up into the tree. Fiona sighed and went back inside.

"God bless Doc for hiring Jubilee," she said aloud to no one at all.

Later that afternoon, a rain shower drove Victor and Rebecca in from under the trees and onto the front porch swing. Jubilee followed, of course, perching herself on the far end of the banister—in exactly the same place where Old Man had kept his voluntary sentry-duty that night all those years before when Starry had first come—and Middy.

Fiona was sitting at her desk in the living room, making out a list of the things she would do to make Cabin Five even more special, for Arabella and Old Man's son. Her desk was so close to the window overlooking the porch that Fiona couldn't help but overhear everything that Victor and Rebecca were saying to each other, even though they had obviously been in the middle of a conversation as they had come to the porch.

"It's what you and I call God," Victor said.

"As in 'Our Father?'" Rebecca asked.

"That's the one," Victor assured her.

"Then why do they call Him Great Spirit?" Her question was an honest one, but the words had hardly left her mouth when her eyebrows drew down and she asked, "Do you like those stories the old Seminole grandfather tells?"

"He's not *my* grandfather," Victor protested. "And anyway, it's David who tells the stories."

"Not my grandfather either," Rebecca said. "But everybody calls him grandfather—Old Man, that is—because he's the oldest person around here. Did you know that he is one hundred and one years old?"

To that information, Victor made no response. But he continued talking, as if he hadn't heard Rebecca.

"Did you know," he asked, "that the panther was the very first creature the Great Spirit put on the earth?"

"Even before he made Adam and Eve?" Rebecca asked.

"I think so," Victor replied, but the tone of his voice indicated that he wasn't sure.

"Would you like to kiss me?" Rebecca's question came right out of the blue, both for Victor and for Fiona, who held on to the chair in which she was sitting to keep herself from running out onto the porch and snatching Victor away from Rebecca—*my Lord! Rebecca is only a child! What on earth could give her such a notion?*

"Kiss you?" Victor was clearly perplexed. "Do I want to?" Fiona couldn't really tell whether Victor was asking the question of Rebecca—or of himself. But Fiona took a deep breath and made herself release the grip on the edges of the desk chair.

"Well, do you?" Rebecca repeated. "Look, I'm a girl, and you're a boy, and that's what girls and boys do!" Petulance and downright irritation in her voice.

"Of course I want to kiss you!" Victor almost snarled. "But you aren't supposed to *ask,* for Heaven's sake! The boy is supposed to do that!" But even as Victor spoke the words, his eyes were somehow fixed on Rebecca's mouth, the soft, sweet mouth, and he felt his body leaning forward, almost involuntarily.

What about Jubilee? The thought lasted such a short time in Victor's mind, because suddenly nothing mattered—nothing except Rebecca. At the desk on the other side of the porch window, Fiona closed her eyes and wondered if she could possibly remember the first time J. Roy had kissed her. And she certainly could. Here she was, a very-late-middle-aged woman—a widow, for Heaven's sake!—but with the surprising memory of J. Roy's soft, young lips on her own. A kiss of how long ago? Forty, fifty years? And yet she could still feel it—as real as it had been that warm spring afternoon so long ago, when J. Roy, strong and handsome and with his eyes brimming with her image, leaned forward, his spearmint breath against her face. And the electrifying touch of their mouths. A clean, dry, pristine little kiss—hardly more than a pressing of their mouths together. But there it was, alive and well remembered after so long. At the desk, Fiona's heart gave an involuntary *thud*, and she blushed and opened her eyes, feeling that she had somehow gained a great gift in remembering something like that about J. Roy. Still, she avoided looking through the window onto the porch.

After Fiona's precious moment of electric silence, Rebecca's voice broke in, "Well, if that's the best you can do, I'm going home!" Rebecca jumped up out of the swing, ran into the yard in the pouring rain, and went bicycling off in a huff, with a startled Jubilee trailing behind her— trailing badly, because Rebecca's energy was fueled by hot anger, while Jubilee's was fueled only by a passive fear of losing her good job and by a reluctance for an end to the intimate moment she had witnessed between Victor and Rebecca, imagining herself in Rebecca's place. Because Jubilee was almost as adept as Glory in pretending to be interested in one thing— in this case, her Jesus fan—while truthfully, she was observing something else. And, at that moment, hating Rebecca with all her heart.

Fiona stayed at the desk, pretending to sort through papers she had already sorted, but she glanced through the window from time to time, watching Victor where he sat alone in the swing.

Oh Lord! When did they get to be old enough to be kissing, for Heaven's sake? I should get somebody—some man—to talk to Victor about . . . about Nature and what all kind of trouble it can lead to. But who could I get? Not Old Man, for sure— he never says a word. Maybe Doc? But if Doc knew Rebecca and Victor were kissing, wouldn't he be terribly upset about it? Well, there's only one answer—Glory and I will have to do it ourselves. There's simply no one else. Not right now, not when I'm sure Rebecca has hurt Victor's feelings so badly. But soon!

Fiona heard Glory and Starry come up on the front porch. Obviously, they were done at the restaurant for the day, and Fiona needed to talk to Glory as soon as possible. They needed to map their strategy— decide how best to bring up the subject of Nature and how to explain it to Victor.

As she came up on the porch, Starry said, "Hi, Victor—where'd Rebecca go?"

"She went home," came the sullen reply.

"Oh," Starry said, glancing at Glory, who merely shrugged her shoulders. After a hesitation, Starry added, "Anything wrong?"

"Just that I don't understand girls," Victor said, and Fiona was completely surprised to hear his voice *break!* Was he trying not to cry? Or was he simply at the age where his voice was a child's one moment and a man's the next? A man's!

My Victor? My beautiful, pink little boy? Why, it couldn't be possible! Especially not now—not with war breaking out across the ocean. Not with that monster Hitler marching. No! My Victor cannot become a man. I cannot bear it. And what was wrong with the way he kissed Rebecca anyway? What does she expect, for Heaven's sake? And how does a boy learn to do such a thing . . . properly?

After supper that night, Victor excused himself from the table, went down the back steps, across the damp yard and into the palmetto brush.

"I hate it when he goes out there so close to dark," Fiona said as she finished the last of her coffee. Although she had watched Victor closely during supper, she could see no complete devastation in his face or manner. Just a bit more of the quietness she knew to be a part of his own individual personality.

"No way to stop him, though," Glory said, shivering slightly at the thoughts of Victor walking into the swampy area, so close to dark.

"I wonder why Arabella's son is coming," Starry said, musing over the question that had obviously been on her mind, while she used the tip of her table knife to trace the small green flowers on the oilcloth tablecloth. "Wonder why any *monk* would leave a monastery?"

"I'm sure I don't know," Fiona answered.

"And how come he wants to stay here, instead of with his mama and daddy?"

"I don't know that either," Fiona said. "But when he comes, we have to just let him alone—he said he wants to 'meditate,' whatever that means, and whatever it is, I suspect it needs peace and quiet."

Suddenly, Fiona herself changed the subject completely, turning to Glory. "We have to talk to Victor," she said, the tone of her voice indicating the seriousness of her thoughts.

"Talk to him?" Clearly, Glory didn't understand.

"Yes, we have to talk to him about . . . nature. You know," Fiona fumbled for words. "About boys and girls—men and women—what can happen between them."

Glory grumbled. "So you finally realized there's something that could get to be dangerous between Rebecca and Victor? Didn't I try to tell you?"

"You did," Fiona admitted. "I just didn't see how it could be, with them being so young."

Starry spoke right up, startling both Fiona and Glory. "They're not too young. Why, I had my first man when I was only thirteen," she said matter-of-factly, drawing a frown from Glory and a sharp intake of breath from Fiona.

"What?" Fiona gasped. "Thirteen?"

Glory sat stony faced, glancing only once at Fiona, as if to say, *See? You can't make a silk purse out of a sow's ear, and if I ever saw a real sow's ear, it's this one sitting right here with us! Doing such as that and her only a child!*

"Yep," Starry sighed. "He was my own step-daddy."

"Oh, my Lord!" Fiona wailed. "You were just a child!" Glory was somewhat startled to hear her own words coming out of Fiona's mouth.

"I sure enough didn't look like a child!" Starry laughed a strange, perhaps embarrassed laugh. "Why, I never even wore lipstick or curled my hair, but I sure got me a full figure a year before that! A year before he . . ." Fiona held up her hand, unable to stand hearing anything else from Starry, but she did remember watching Rebecca when she and Victor were coming out of the lake that noontime—remembered Rebecca's relatively flat chest and long, slender legs and hips so narrow, they almost weren't hips at all. Somehow, remembering that childish, stick-like figure felt encouraging to Fiona. No "full figure" there. Not yet, anyway.

"So you think *we're* the ones supposed to talk to Victor about the . . . birds and the bees?" Glory asked, deciding simply to ignore what Starry had said. "And how come you're including *me* in that *we*? Why, I never even had me a boyfriend! What you think *I* can tell Victor?"

"I can help tell him," Starry offered, drawing a strong flinch from Fiona. "Why, I was telling Victor all about love when he was just a little thing—could barely keep up with walking beside me." Fiona remembered that time—when she had been watering the porch plants and overheard Starry telling Victor something about . . . about *music from beyond the moon.* That was exactly what Starry had called it.

"You told him that love was like music from beyond the moon," repeated Fiona, drawing a sharp glance from Starry.

"Yess'm, I did," Starry confessed, with a worried frown drawing her eyebrows together.

"But what did you mean by that?" Fiona pressed.

"Well, I'm not sure if I remember right," Starry started in. "But I think it was because love is so mysterious, and we don't know where it comes from, and maybe . . . we don't know where it goes, when it goes away." Starry's voice trailed off to a whisper on the final words.

Fiona knew that Starry was thinking about Middy, yet again. And how many years had it been since he deserted Starry? Left her on the porch like an old girl-dog he didn't want anymore? From that memory, Fiona's mind went back to the night of the storm and the arrival of precious Victor in their lives. Somehow, an expression about him being like "a puppy nobody wanted anymore" came rushing into Fiona's memory—but who had said it? Did *anyone* say it? Or had she merely thought it?

And besides, Fiona was thinking, *that isn't the way love works! Love doesn't make a grown man mess around with a thirteen-year-old child.*

Love doesn't make a man walk away and desert a woman, leave her standing there on the porch of an old fishing cabin.

Love doesn't make a mother put her precious little boy in the yard of two old women and walk away from the flesh of her flesh and bone of her bone.

No.

Love stays. Love hangs on, no matter what.

Love comes home at night, smelling a little like fish bait and with the warmth of sunshine on his skin.

Love wears a beat-up old hat and leaves his dirty socks in the middle of the bathroom floor.

Love snores at night—snores in his own home and in his own bed, and with his own wife beside him.

Love isn't any music from beyond the moon. It isn't mysterious at all. In fact, it's really perfectly simple—love is an old Victrola with cracked and fuzzy-sounding records to play on it, but the songs are familiar.

The songs are the ones we all know.

Fiona had said nothing aloud, but she was embarrassed to feel tears filling up her eyes. She stood up suddenly, gathering her plate and Glory's and putting them in the sink, where they clattered against the porcelain.

"*I'll* tell him," she said.

Chapter Sixteen

Fiona didn't want to waste any time before talking to Victor, especially because she felt that she had to take advantage of Rebecca's being angry with him and, consequently, avoiding hanging around the camp all day every day.

So the next morning, right after breakfast, and right after Glory had left for the restaurant, dragging along a frankly curious and reluctant Starry behind her, Fiona said to Victor, "Stay here in the kitchen with me a little minute, honey. I need to talk to you about something." When Fiona sat back down, with a fresh cup of coffee, Victor still had that innocent expression in his face, yet he wore right between his eyebrows a faint, perplexed frown.

"Is everything okay?" he asked.

"Yes, everything is fine," Fiona replied. "But it's time for me to tell you some things, that's all."

"About my mother?" Victor asked, and his question hit Fiona as hard and as suddenly as an unexpected tidal wave. She had anticipated many things regarding this talk, but Victor bringing up the subject of his mother was not something she had even considered.

"Well, we can talk about your mother, if that's what you want to do," she sputtered, trying to recover her stability and stirring more sugar into her coffee than she really wanted.

"Okay," Victor said, waiting expectantly.

"So, what do you want to know?" Fiona asked, stirring and stirring her coffee.

"Well, to start with, who was she?"

"Your mother was my sister's daughter," Fiona said easily, because of all the years of saying it. After all, perhaps that was the absolute truth, or, as Glory had once predicted, Fiona had finally come to believe it herself. But what difference could it possibly make?

"Why did she leave me with you and Aunt Glory?" he asked.

"Honey, she was sick, and that's all I know."

"Did she die?" Victor asked such a simple question, and not a trace of emotion permeated his voice.

"I don't know," Fiona confessed. "I just don't know."

"But you should know, shouldn't you? If she was your own sister's daughter?" Now Victor's eyes were fixed on Fiona's face, and she was speechless for a moment. Was he questioning whether his mother was really her niece?

"I should, but I don't," Fiona said at last.

"If she didn't die, then she left me because she didn't love me," Victor pronounced.

"Oh, I'm sure she *did* love you," Fiona protested. "But she was sick, and so she couldn't take care of you. She brought you to me and Glory because she knew that we would love and cherish you forever." The partial, yet profound, truth of that statement almost made Fiona choke.

"Do I look like her?" he asked, once again with great simplicity in his voice.

"Well, I don't rightly know," Fiona explained. "We weren't a *close* family, Victor—I saw your mother only for a few moments, the night she brought you to us, and the light was dim, so I really don't know exactly what she looked like."

"Can you find out if she died?" Victor asked, and Fiona realized that his mind was simply stuck on that question—*If she didn't die, then maybe she left me because she didn't love me.*

"I don't know how to find out," Fiona said. "My sister—your grandmother—passed away long ago, and there's no one else for me to ask." Victor said nothing, and Fiona felt the urge to go on, to assure Victor that his mother had loved him very much. "She loved you, Victor. You have to believe that."

"Okay."

"Okay? What do you mean *okay?*" Somehow, Fiona meant to find a conclusion that left Victor with complete assurance. But how could she do that? *Make up another lie? And had it really been a lie, to tell everyone that Victor was my great-nephew? Why I can't even remember what is the truth and what is something I simply wished into being. Perhaps I should have let Doc call the authorities. Perhaps I should not have been so intent on keeping Victor for myself. But how could I have let him go? And what would have happened to him? Someone else— some stranger—some foster mother—would have told him, "Your mother abandoned you. She didn't want you. She didn't love you"* Fiona was struggling hard to keep the tears from coming, but the thought of what would have happened if she had let him go almost broke her heart. And now, his own heart was probably breaking anyway.

"I mean it's okay that I don't know," he said. "I don't want to hurt you, and maybe talking about it does just that." Those were his words, but there was pain in his eyes. Fiona could see that so clearly. He started to get up to leave the table.

"Wait!" Fiona yelped. "That wasn't what I wanted to talk to you about." *Yes! Change the subject. Don't think about what could have happened. It didn't happen, and that's all that matters. Glory and I have been his family, and so has Starry, and Old Man, and Mr. Owen, and Arabella. We love him, and we've given him more love than any one woman—even his mother—could have given. That's all that matters.*

Victor hesitated and then he sat back down and folded his hands on the table.

"I wanted to talk to you about . . . you and Rebecca," Fiona said, with her face turning a slight shade of pink, whether from the subject of Victor and Rebecca or from the agony of knowing that everything she had tried to do for him simply wasn't enough. He still wanted to know about his mother—that old pull of blood!

"What about me and Rebecca?" Victor asked and Fiona looked for resentment in his voice, but there wasn't any.

"Well, you're both growing up so fast, and . . . Rebecca . . ." Fiona's voice ground to a halt, because she wasn't about to let Victor know that she overheard Rebecca asking him to kiss her, for Heaven's sake!

"What about Rebecca?" he asked. Fiona bit her bottom lip and searched for the words she needed to say, but words that would not send Victor into an uncharacteristic fit of anger or rebellion. That talk about his mother had been more than enough for one day.

"She's quite beautiful, isn't she?" Fiona asked, for want of anything better to say at that point.

"Yes, she is beautiful," Victor mumbled, his words soft and what . . . regretful? Pained? "But she's really mad at me right now." Victor's eyes held a look of pain that Fiona had never seen before—or had not noticed. Her heart lurched.

"She is lovely," Fiona said softly. "And she won't stay mad at you forever. So what I need to ask is if you know *something* about . . . romance?" Then she altered her question to try and be more specific— "About *love?*" Victor's face reddened, making his pale blue eyes gleam like neon. *And was this even necessary? Weren't both Rebecca and Victor still children? It was that kiss—that's what has me worried. But why? Really?*

"I know something about love," Victor said, looking down at the tabletop. And then he glanced up at her with familiar mischief in his eyes. "I know that I *love* Glory's fish and hushpuppies!"

Fiona couldn't help but laugh. "Oh, honey—we use that word for so many different things! I think it's one of the great downfalls of the English language that we have only that one word for . . . everything." But then she reduced her laugh to a mere sad smile, and she suddenly reached across and put both of her hands over Victor's. "You need to be careful," she whispered. "When a . . . man, even a very young one," she amended. "When he's around a beautiful young woman—especially one who is . . . *willing* . . . he can . . . lose control. And it can start with something as simple as . . . *kissing*," Fiona explained quietly, watching Victor's face to see if he connected her remark with what Rebecca had asked of him when they were supposedly talking in private on the porch. "Do you understand me?" she added quickly. "You just have to be so careful . . . of *love*! Do some more growing up, honey. And be careful in the meantime."

Victor was studying the tablecloth, and his jaw was working slowly, as if he were grinding up something too big to swallow.

"It's okay, Aunt Fiona," his voice was strong and filled with warmth, as if the words might purge something inside of him. "I know what you're talking about, and I'll be careful. I promise. Besides," he added. "She's still mad at me." With that, he got up from his chair with a movement of great finality, planted a warm peck of a kiss on Fiona's cheek, and left the kitchen. The back screen door banged, and she heard him whistling as he hopped on his bicycle and pedaled away.

"Well, so much for *that!*" Fiona said to the empty kitchen.

When Starry stuck her head around the doorway from the hall, Fiona wasn't the least bit surprised to see her there. Because Starry had a way of eavesdropping that always made it seem purely accidental—at least to her—and this was no exception.

"How did it go?" Starry asked, her face all innocent looking. Fiona immediately wondered exactly how much of the conversation Starry had heard. Enough to make her question Fiona's story about Victor's mother being her own sister's child?

"Okay, I guess," Fiona answered. "It's sure not easy to talk with a young man . . . about things like that."

"That's why I offered to do it," Starry said gently.

"But Starry . . ." Fiona started in and then stopped.

"I know, I know," Starry said, smiling. "I didn't use good judgment myself, so how could I be one to talk with him?"

"I guess so," Fiona confessed, reddening. She just wanted to be alone in the kitchen, to plunge her hands into warm, soapy water and focus on nothing more complicated than doing the dishes. Yes, that was what she needed—something mundane and simple, something no one had to figure out or worry about. Fiona got up from the table, picking up her cup and hoping that the gesture would let Starry know that the conversation was over. But of course, such small signals were always lost on Starry.

"But somebody like me knows all about pitfalls, Miss Fiona," Starry said at last. "So I know all the warning signs."

"Well, let's just see what happens," Fiona mumbled. "Let's just see."

And I know about pitfalls too, Starry, Fiona thought. *I know what it's like to love a child so much that you will do anything . . . say anything to keep that child safe and happy.*

And I also know what it's like to really love a man and not even know it. But Fiona said nothing—simply took her coffee cup to the sink and started washing the dishes, turning her back on Starry, who finally took the hint.

During the next week, Victor never brought up the subject of his mother again, something for which Fiona was most grateful. Her mind had whirled this way and that, trying to decide exactly what she should tell Victor, if he brought up the subject again. But she prayed fervently that he wouldn't. And he didn't mention Rebecca either, though her absence—and Jubilee's—had left a peculiar silence around the camp.

Fiona was happy to see Victor going fishing almost every morning with Mr. Owen and spending many afternoons at the Trading Post, with Old Man and David. Only briefly did Fiona wonder how on earth Old Man had transmitted all of those old Seminole stories to his grandson, David, when Old Man himself never spoke a word. But Fiona didn't ask many questions. Seminole stories were the least of her worries, and all she knew was that she'd had no proper answer for Victor about his mother and that Rebecca hadn't come to the camp for that whole week, something for which Fiona was strangely grateful. But Fiona watched Victor carefully, and she couldn't deny that there was a strange, new sadness around his eyes. Certainly, *he missed both Rebecca and Jubilee. They had all been together almost the whole summer. That's what it was,* Fiona assured herself. *He misses his friends. Perhaps I was silly to give Victor that warning speech about love. In fact, I'm sure of it. I simply jumped the gun.*

"He's too quiet," Glory said.

"What do you mean?" Immediately, Fiona was defensive, especially when Glory told her something she noticed herself and said nothing about.

"I wish he had somebody to talk to," Glory added.

"He has *us*," Fiona protested.

"I mean a *man*," Glory amended. "I wish he had a man to talk to. 'Cause he's hurting, even if you don't want to see it. No way in this world he's going to talk to *us* about something like *that*."

"Like what?" Fiona insisted, although she meant not to say a single word.

"Love," Glory stated, quite simply.

This time, Fiona made no reply, but she knew that Glory was right. Victor needed a *man* to talk to about Rebecca. And so, in spite of all her protestations to herself, Fiona felt as if she were waiting for an afternoon thunderstorm to break, because the air was heavy and silent and filled with some kind of strange expectation.

Fiona enlisted Starry's help in making sure that the Number Five cabin was in good shape for the arrival of Arabella's son—Wahali or Brother John, depending upon whether you thought of him as a Seminole or as a monk. Fiona and Starry washed, ironed and rehung the curtains at the single window of the cabin he would occupy, and they sorted all through the stack of clean towels and sheets, selecting the whitest sheets and the least threadbare towels.

On the day Wahali was to arrive, Arabella came to work very early, bringing a beautiful piece of Seminole patchwork to hang on the wall of the cabin her son would occupy. Hand stitched in white on black, Fiona at first thought that it depicted Christian crosses, but with an extra piece above the cross tie. But Arabella told Fiona that the "crosses" were the Seminole symbol for trees, so that when her son was lying in bed, he would still be reminded of the beautiful live oak trees all around him in the darkness. While Fiona and Starry hung the patchwork piece on the wall, Arabella stood in the doorway, turning her head this way and that, watching their efforts. When, at last, the tapestry was hung to her satisfaction, Arabella smiled broadly. "Good!" she said, glancing once more at the beautiful tapestry created by her own hands, stitch by single stitch, and then she nodded and went off to the restaurant to help Glory. Fiona and Starry noticed that she was wearing a new dress, one sewn of the softest batiste, with fine lace edging the collar and the sleeves, and in a shade of turquoise that enhanced Arabella's dark hair and olive complexion. She also wore a smile that seemed absolutely chiseled between her slightly rouged cheeks, and she never lost that smile the whole morning. Starry took one look at Arabella's new dress and worried that she would spill something on it, so Starry brought out one of her own aprons for Arabella to borrow.

When the taxi from Wasachoossee finally pulled into the driveway, Arabella came fairly leaping out of the kitchen, leaving a whole bowl of shredded cabbage half done. Glory didn't realize what had happened, and she hollered, "Hey! Wait a minute! All this here cabbage gonna go brown on us!" But Fiona, who had come from the porch to greet the occupant of the taxi, called to her, "No, Glory—don't say a thing to her. This is her *son!*" And the word tasted so beautiful in Fiona's mouth that she felt tears spring up in her eyes.

The tall, stately young man who slowly unfolded himself from the back seat of the taxi didn't look like a monk to Fiona—but then, she wasn't sure of what a real monk would look like anyway. She had imagined a hooded robe, but Wahali was wearing khaki trousers and a white cotton shirt with the sleeves rolled up. He may not have looked like a monk to Fiona, but certainly, he bore his Seminole heritage, in his blue-black hair and deep, olive complexion. He was taller than either Arabella or Old Man, broad of shoulder, and his eyes were perfect replicas of Old Man's—deep, dark, and unreadable. And yet there was a slightly different look, a tilted-down angle to his eyes that gave his entire face a look of deep sensitivity and . . . yes, compassion.

Starry had come up behind Fiona, and they simply stood back and smiled, while Glory peered from the doorway of the kitchen, and though Fiona said not a word, she was thinking, *Oh, most certainly, he is his father's son!* Starry, on the other hand, touched her hair to make sure it was all in place, regretting for a moment that its bright red color was gone, and thought, *Jeepers! That's the most gorgeous man I have ever seen in my life!*

Wahali threw his arms wide, and Arabella literally barged right into his chest. The broad shoulders bent down to her shorter height, and he lifted her right off of her feet and swung her around, as if she were a beloved child. Once again, Fiona felt tears coming up in her eyes, and she glanced at Starry, whose face had turned a bright red.

"Starry!" Fiona exclaimed in a rough whisper. "I see that look on your face. You behave yourself!" But then Fiona laughed, and Starry had the decency to cast her eyes down to the ground. But her smile remained fixed. "Isn't he simply *gorgeous?*" Starry whispered.

"Oh, he is that!" Fiona agreed. "But he's also a *monk*, just you remember that!"

"Yes. Ma'am, I'll sure remember that," Starry agreed. "But the question is, will *he* remember it?"

"Oh, Lord have mercy on us!" Fiona whispered at last.

"And isn't *Wahali* the most beautiful and mysterious name you've ever heard in your life?"

"To you, his name is Brother John, and don't you forget it," Fiona whispered roughly, and then she repeated, "Lord have mercy!" and this time, it was definitely more of a prayer than an exclamation.

When Wahali had fetched his single leather valise from the taxi and he and Arabella went walking away toward the cabin they had prepared for him, Fiona turned to Starry. "You go in there and help Glory with that coleslaw. We sure can't expect much out of Arabella today."

As Starry went reluctantly toward the kitchen, casting yet another glance toward the cabin, Fiona went back toward the cottage, where a load of towels was churning away in her dancing-all-over-the-porch washing machine. But just before she reached the front steps, she stopped once more, gazing as well toward the cabin where Brother John and Arabella were entering. Her head tilted up toward his face, and his head bent down gently toward his mother.

Son! She heard the word echo so beautifully in her mind, and she glanced at her watch, wondering when Victor would come home for lunch. At least, when Rebecca had been around, Fiona could look out of any window and see them together, either having lunch on the old quilt or else playing in the lake like two beautiful dolphins. Of a sudden, Fiona was so hungry—yes, *hungry* to see his face, his pale hair and beautiful blue eyes, to breathe in the clean, healthy aroma of him—she could hardly stand it. *Son!*

The first night Brother John stayed at the camp, he walked away from his cabin just before dusk—on his way, Fiona figured, to have supper with his parents. *What a happy time for them all,* Fiona thought, but then right away, she began wondering, *I wonder why he chose to live so far away as New York state? And how did he decide to become a monk, of all things!* These were questions that Fiona certainly knew were none of her business, but her curiosity was such that she knew, at some future point, she would gently and delicately ask Arabella about it.

Around about ten o'clock that night, Fiona was turning out the lamps in the living room when she saw Brother John walking along the lakeshore in the moonlight. He was wearing khaki shorts and a pale blue, open-necked shirt—and he was barefooted, walking along in the very edge of the lake water. Without even thinking, Fiona turned on the porch light, went down the steps, and joined him at lakeside.

"I wanted to tell you," she started out. "If there's anything you need, just let us know."

"Thank you," he replied simply, and then he gazed out across the lake where the early moonlight was shimmering on the water. "Hard to believe, isn't it, what's going on in Europe?"

"Yes," Fiona agreed.

"Just think," he went on. "Right across this lake is a small peninsula of land, and then beyond that is the ocean itself. And across that body of water is Europe. And war."

Fiona didn't know what to say, so she said nothing.

"Hard to believe," he repeated, softly.

"Yes," Fiona agreed. "Well, if you need anything, let us know."

"Thank you," he said again, and Fiona retreated into the house, leaving Brother John—Wahali, the Seminole—gazing out over the lake in the moonlight.

Chapter Seventeen

Wahali made a very congenial but quiet guest at the camp. Every evening, he walked to Arabella and Old Man's house in the early dusk, for supper with his parents. Arabella continued her work in the restaurant, but instead of working quietly, as she had done before, she chattered almost endlessly about the meals she prepared every evening for her family, and every few minutes, she would peer out of the kitchen door at Cabin Number Five. Because even if she didn't see her son, she seemed to find deep comfort in simply gazing from time to time at the cabin where he was staying.

"Oh, it's so nice to have a young man to cook for—one with a big, healthy appetite!" she laughed, returning from her latest glance through the kitchen doorway and going back to chopping cabbage. Glory thought that perhaps Arabella didn't even realize that she was chopping cabbage at all.

"Tonight we're having pork chops and scalloped potatoes, just as he likes."

"Where'd you get enough meat rations to buy pork chops?" Glory wanted to know, because with the war going on in Europe, everyone had to ration meat and sugar and, especially, gasoline.

Arabella's eyes misted up instantly. "Abby, that sweet little waitress down at the Trading Post, gave me all her meat rations. Said she'd been saving them up for something important because she doesn't care much for meat anyway. And when she heard our son was coming home for a visit, she wanted us to have them. She said something else, too," Arabella added, and then she went silent, glancing at Glory.

Glory sighed. "What did she say?" Glory's voice was weary. *Why couldn't folks come right out and say what they wanted to say?*

Arabella giggled. "She said she hoped I didn't mind, that she was *in love* with Old Man!"

"What?" Glory exclaimed.

"Well, she laughed when she said it," Arabella added.

"Why, he's old enough to be her own grandpa," Glory said.

"I know," Arabella laughed again. "And she knows it too. I think it was just her way of saying how much she cares for him. Nothing more than that."

"I would certainly hope so," Glory added, laughing a little herself.

"Anyway—that sweet little lady gave me so many rations, I think I can serve meat almost every single night Wahali's here," Arabella exclaimed. "She's the one who came when Rowena left. It's been a long time now. Maybe sixteen or seventeen years ago—and my, how time does fly!" Arabella added, and Glory kept on battering filets and slipping them into the hot oil, where they bubbled and released their oily perfume into the hot air. But as soon as Arabella mentioned Rowena, she fell silent, remembering the long-ago night when Old Man went out in the storm and brought that precious girl home with him. But truthfully, this was probably the very first time Arabella had thought of that night again, because the only answer she ever had from Old Man when they disappeared was that tight mouth and the kind eyes, and the gentle nod that had said, "She's all right." More than that, Arabella did not know. *Could* not know.

"But anyway," Arabella finally went on, "tomorrow night I'm fixing fried chicken and biscuits." Glory, who was getting somewhat weary of hearing about Arabella's planned menus, decided to broach the subject that was really on her mind.

"Just what does a monk do, anyway? And how'd your son get to be one?" she asked. Because Glory was a good church-going woman, a strong and loyal member of the local African Methodist Episcopal Church and thereby interested—in a polite but quite suspicious way—about anything to do with a religion other than her own. She remained skeptical whenever any of the Seminole people talked about the "Great Spirit," and privately, she wondered if they were talking about the same Lord God Jehovah, the Our Father, of her own church.

"Well, I don't know *everything* about it," Arabella confessed, sensing some of Glory's carefully concealed skepticism. The chopping slowed, and Arabella looked off into the distance, as if she were struggling to remember exactly how it all happened.

"Wahali was always . . . different," she explained, almost as if she were talking to herself. "In some ways, he was much stronger than Awan—that was his older brother, David's father. But in other ways, he was not so strong." Glory kept battering fish the whole time Arabella talked, but she realized that her simple question had opened up a whole store of memories for Arabella, and she almost regretted having asked about Wahali and the monastery. But Arabella was almost like a mysterious recording—one that couldn't be stopped, and once she got started, she reeled off a story such as Glory never expected.

"Wahali fell in love when he was very young," Arabella said, wistfully. "And the girl he loved, Sawni . . . drowned." The word struck Glory with a sense of being underwater, not being able to breathe, suffocating. She put down the fish filets and rinsed her hands, while Arabella went on, "For a long time, I thought Wahali would take his own life, as well. He disappeared into the swamp, and for two long months, we never knew what had become of him. Oh, it was terrible!" Arabella almost wailed. "I imagined everything—him being eaten by alligators or bitten by water moccasins or lost . . . forever."

Arabella went back to chopping cabbage, as if the story had ended.

"What happened?" Glory asked, even though she really didn't want those words to come out of her mouth.

"He came home," Arabella said simply. "He was dirty and eaten up with mosquito bites, and he had a fever that lasted for a long time. But he came home."

"And then went to New York?" Glory asked, because somewhere, there had to be a connection between the story Arabella was telling her and the original, simple-sounding question Glory had asked.

"He heard about a lake in faraway mountains, and somehow, he became completely obsessed with going there. And so he went."

"And?" Glory couldn't stop herself from asking for more.

"And now he has come home." Arabella's face lit up with such a glow, it almost seemed to Glory that a huge candle was lit behind her eyes. "He has come home."

Glory went back to battering fish filets and sliding them into the hot oil, but she wore a puzzled frown, because the story didn't make any sense. Still, she didn't ask any more questions—didn't want to blow out with the breath of a question that beautiful light from within Arabella's eyes. But she did glance over to where Arabella was working. "Lord have mercy! Arabella, you're chopping enough cabbage to make a whole washtub full of coleslaw! Here, gimme that knife and you start mixing in the dressing for that cabbage. We'll have to put the rest in the icebox."

Aside from walking down to Arabella and Old Man's cottage every evening for supper and waving happily to Arabella, as she went in and out of the restaurant kitchen during the day, Brother John—Wahali—kept pretty much to himself. Sometimes, Fiona would see him wading along the edge of the lake, with his shirt unbuttoned and blowing open in the breeze off of the lake, revealing a strong hairless chest. At those times, Fiona would glance around to see if Starry was in sight, but so far, Starry had not sought out his company, and Fiona was happy about that turn of events. *Heaven only knows what kind of trouble a woman like Starry could churn up, if she got to going after a man like him. I just hope he's worldly enough to see it coming, if it comes at all, that is.* But most of the time, Fiona would catch only a glimpse or two of him before he walked on along the edge of the lake, disappearing around a bend of palmettos and live-oak trees that put him out of her sight. Sometimes, many hours would pass before she saw him come walking back along the lake. And Starry was never around.

Every morning, as soon as Fiona was sure that Wahali had gone out, she would go into his cabin, to make up the bed and leave clean towels. But every time, the bed was already carefully made, and only one towel had been used. Not really meaning to snoop, exactly, she sometimes took a moment to look around the small room, to see if she could find anything that might give her some insight into the life of a *monk*—and she wasn't even sure of what a monk was or what he did. But on the bedside table, she found only a plain wristwatch and a small Bible, and in the bathroom, there was only the bar of soap she had provided.

One morning, about a week after Rebecca had so abruptly stopped coming to the camp and Wahali had arrived, Jubilee came wheeling up alone on Rebecca's bicycle and . . . wearing Rebecca's bright blue bathing suit. And her very womanly figure was almost spilling out of the suit that belonged to the slender Rebecca. A rolled towel was propped on the handlebars, and Jubilee came riding up and even threw up an arm in greeting to Fiona, who had been sweeping off the porch, before she propped the bike at the side of the front porch, unrolled the towel, and took out Rebecca's bathing cap.

What on earth! Fiona's mouth fell open, and she hastened to the restaurant kitchen to tell Glory, because, as Fiona properly realized, this was something for Glory to deal with. After all, Jubilee was *her* niece, not Fiona's. Jubilee saw Fiona head straight for the kitchen, and she wasn't surprised. She knew exactly what to expect but squared her shoulders and started putting on the cap.

Glory came charging out of the kitchen like a runaway train engine, and all she lacked for showing her terrible anger was twin puffs of indignant smoke coming from her nostrils.

"What're you doing here?" Glory bellowed, approaching Jubilee, who simply smiled and continued tucking her hair under the bathing cap. "And why are you wearing Miss Rebecca's bathing suit? Lord have mercy, girl! Tuck yourself back in at the top. Your womanhood's spilling out all over the place!" The words came flowing out of Glory, and all the time she was shaking her head, as if denying what she was actually seeing with her very own eyes.

"Doc took Miss Irma and Rebecca over to Gainesville today," Jubilee said. "I think they went shopping."

"But what on earth are you doing?" Glory demanded.

Jubilee jutted out her chin and stared straight into Glory's eyes. "I've come to go swimming with Victor," she said, her voice cool and strong. "Where is he?" For a brief moment, Glory was rendered speechless, and she was so shocked that she was almost surprised to see her own hand—calloused and work worn—coming flying out from under her apron and connecting with a loud smack as she slapped Jubilee's smug face. The sound of the hard slap resounded in the still air, and Glory was only halfway aware of Fiona and Starry watching from the porch and Arabella, who was peering out of the kitchen door at the altercation.

The slap swung Glory all the way around, and then her glowering face was once again, right up against Jubilee's. Jubilee had resisted stumbling backwards from the slap, but she put her hand on her stinging cheek. But even though she had tears in her eyes, her voice was still strong when she repeated, "I came to go swimming with Victor."

"You get out of here," Glory stormed. "You get right back on that bike of Miss Rebecca's and go on back to Doc's, where you belong. And you better be hoping there won't be no crosses burning on Doc's lawn tonight! And cover yourself up!"

When Fiona had hastened to the kitchen to get Glory, she left the broom leaning against the steps, and Glory grabbed it, and holding it like a baseball bat, she was fully prepared to use it on Jubilee.

For a long moment, Jubilee glared back at Glory, but Victor's voice interrupted whatever was going to happen. He had come from inside the cottage, where he had been sequestered in his room, as was his recent custom.

"Rebecca here?" he yelped, looking all around, almost not even noticing Jubilee and Glory. "Is she?" he asked again.

"Rebecca's not here," Glory snarled, still staring at Jubilee and holding the broom.

"What's going on?" Victor asked.

"You wanta go swimming?" Jubilee said, smiling at Victor and only glancing at Glory and the broom.

"Sure," Victor responded easily. "But where's Rebecca?"

"Won't I do?" Jubilee asked in the most brazen voice any of them had ever heard and putting her hands on her hips, as if she were posing for a bathing suit photo.

"Well . . . yeah," Victor finally answered, but his frown indicated that something was going on he clearly didn't understand. "Why are you wearing Rebecca's bathing suit?" he asked, innocently.

"Because she's a fool!" Glory hissed, shaking the broom and taking another step toward Jubilee. "You get out of here, you brazen hussy!" Glory once again drew back the broom, and this time, she connected solidly with Jubilee's provocatively thrust-out hip.

"Ow!" Jubilee yelled. "You can't do that!"

"Watch me," Glory yelled back, and with that, she swung the broom again and hit Jubilee a second time, only this time much harder, and then she watched almost in sympathy as Jubilee's face crumpled into tears. She hopped back onto Rebecca's bike, the towel falling to the ground, the bathing cap still only halfway on, and her ample bosom threatening to pop right out of the bathing suit. She pedaled away with a vicious pumping of her long legs, looking back only once, with a terrible frown.

"What happened? What's the matter?" Victor asked, sincerely perplexed.

"Nothing," Glory muttered. "Absolutely nothing at all. This time," she added under her breath.

"I wish Rebecca had come," Victor muttered.

"So do I," Glory answered truthfully.

After what they all privately called "the Jubilee episode," Victor seemed even more lost without Rebecca around. He paid little attention to Wahali, the strange guest who carried no fishing gear and never took a boat out on the lake. But the one thing Victor didn't miss was Rebecca telling him that his kisses weren't done right! *If that's the best you can do, I'm going home!* Her cruel words echoed endlessly in his ears, and he wanted with all his heart to get to her—grab her shoulders and kiss her so hard and so long that her knees would buckle.

In his pain and anger, Victor turned down several invitations to go fishing with Mr. Owen, and his solitary daily bicycle rides took him only as far as the Trading Post, where he sat on a wooden box, watching Old Man pretending to sleep, and occasionally studying the few tourists who came into the shop. One day, however, a woman who had been giggling ever since she set foot into the shop glanced over at Victor and said loudly to her companion, "Oh, look! There's a *blonde* Seminole! I've heard about those!" Victor didn't care enough to bother correcting her, but after the two women left the shop, he saw Old Man's stomach jiggling as he tried to suppress his giggles.

But one day during that first week that Wahali was at the camp, he came into the Trading Post to say hello to David, his nephew. And when

Old Man saw Wahali come in, he got up out of his chair, went over to his son, and clapped him on both shoulders. Wahali clapped his father's shoulders back, and both men smiled and nodded their heads at each other. Then Old Man went back, sat down in his chair, and closed his eyes, as if nothing had happened.

Wahali looked at Victor. "I'll bet you're Victor," he said. "My mother told me about you, but I'm afraid I haven't had the chance to meet you yet." Victor felt strange, hearing words coming out of a mouth that was so similar in shape to Old Man's mute one.

"Hi," Victor sad, getting up from the wooden box and extending his hand. "I've heard about you too," he said. "I've heard you're a monk, but I don't know what that means."

Wahali laughed at the frank and honest remark. "Well, I'm ready to walk back to the camp, so why don't you walk along with me and I'll tell you about it."

"I've got my bike," Victor explained, envisioning how hard it would be to push it all the way back, along the sandy shore of the lake.

"Leave it here with my father," Brother John volunteered. "You can come back for it tomorrow. Is that okay, Pop?" Victor almost laughed out loud, hearing Wahali address Old Man in such a manner, but Old Man didn't seem to notice. He didn't even open his eyes. Simply nodded his head.

So Victor and the monk walked back along the lakeshore, the monk with his pants rolled up and Victor wearing the shorts he always wore when he wasn't in school.

"It's nice to grow up in a place like this," Wahali ventured. "What with the lake and the sky and the quiet."

"Yes," Victor agreed. "You grew up here too, didn't you?"

"I did." Wahali grew silent for a few moments, and then he spoke with sadness in his voice. "Enjoy this while you can, Victor. One of these days, it will be all gone."

"What will be gone?"

"This beautiful wildness," Wahali said, sweeping his arm in a gesture that took in the lake and the shore and the Australian pines and palm trees growing nearby.

"Why do you say that?" Victor asked, trying to imagine all of it *gone*.

"Because people will find this place and every other place like it," Wahali said. "They will see that a great deal of money is to be made, and they will change it all, to attract tourists. Many, many tourists."

"We already have tourists," Victor argued, feeling vaguely alarmed, but not understanding why.

"Not like the tourists that will come in the future. So many of them! They will want to have an 'experience.' And nice places to sleep, and pools to swim in. And fantasy worlds to live in, for a little while. Palm trees will be lit by artificial colored lights, even at night, and music will be piped in electronically. And no one will be able to hear the birds or the lapping of the water anymore."

"How do you know all of this?" Victor didn't want to ask, but he couldn't help himself, because he simply couldn't imagine such a change in this place of such rare beauty.

"Some of us . . . Seminoles, that is . . . can see the future, and that's what I see happening. It's very sad." What Wahali was saying really didn't make any sense to Victor, but if Wahali was really worried about it all changing, there was one question Victor had to ask. "So why did you leave here?"

Once again, the frank and open way the younger man spoke impressed Wahali with its simplicity and honesty. For long moments, he didn't answer, and Victor thought that, perhaps, he had asked too personal a question. But then Wahali cleared his throat. "I was running away." It was a simple answer, but one Victor didn't expect.

"What from?" Like Glory's questions to Arabella, Victor's mouth asked something that hadn't first gone through his mind. "If it's so beautiful here, what were you running away from?"

"What everyone runs away from, one way or another," Wahali said in a low voice. Victor thought about the words, but they conjured up no understanding for him. "Love," Wahali said finally, then added simply, "Running away was the right thing for me to do. What I didn't know was that I was really running *toward* something. I ran away from love, but I found Love."

"I'm not sure I understand," Victor confessed.

"I'm not sure I do either," Wahali laughed.

"So what kind of love did you run away from, and what kind of Love did you find? And how did you become a monk? And what does a monk do anyway?" Victor was smiling easily, the questions rolling out of his mouth faster than Wahali could think about them. They walked for several more minutes before Wahali spoke again. "A monk prays and meditates," he started out. "And in my case, works in the monastery bakery. I make bread."

"You work in a bakery?" Victor laughed. It was hard for him to envision this tall, well-built Seminole young man kneading bread dough.

"I do," Wahali said.

"What about meditating and praying?" Victor asked.

"I do that while I'm making bread," Wahali said.

"And what kind of love did you run away from," Victor continued. "And what kind of love did you find . . . in a bakery?"

Wahali laughed. "That will take some explaining, Victor. We can talk about that another time." Wahali's words seemed to close the door on further discussion, so Victor said instead, "I wouldn't want to run away. There are too many things here I love and I would never run away from them."

"Like what?" Wahali asked. "Or perhaps I should say . . . like *who*?" He had amended his question because, with the afternoon light, the monk could see the blonde whiskers sprouting on Victor's chin. *Ah!* he thought. *The boy is really a man.*

Victor blushed. "There're just lots of things here I wouldn't want to leave—the lake, for one thing."

"There's a lake where I live," Wahali offered. "It isn't like this one, of course, but it is very beautiful anyway."

"Where is it?" Victor asked, tossing a pebble into the water.

"In some mountains called the Adirondacks, far away up in New York state. And the lake is all that's left of a glacier that came through there many thousands of years ago. The glacier carved out the lake bed and then melted, so the water is deep and very cold, but it is a beautiful lake anyway."

"I'd sure like to see something like that," Victor said. "Only lake I've ever seen is this one."

"Perhaps some day you can come and visit," Wahali offered.

"I'd like that—but only for a visit." Wahali did not reply to this statement, because instinctively, he knew that more would follow it. And he was right. Victor offered, "My mother left me here, and so this is where I want to stay for now. Maybe one day, she will come back."

"She *left* you?" Wahali couldn't manage to keep the surprise out of his voice.

"Yes," Victor whispered so softly that his voice almost became as one with the faint lapping of the water on the lakeshore. "When I was a baby, my mother left me with my Aunt Fiona—really my great-aunt—and she never came back." Victor's voice had thickened, and still, Wahali waited for him to say more. And he did. "You talk about running away from love, but I think that maybe she *didn't* love me, and that's why she ran away and left me," Victor whispered. Still, Wahali didn't speak. Finally, Victor went on, "I don't even know if she's alive or dead, but one thing I do know for sure—if she really loves me, she will come back." Then Victor suddenly added, "Please don't say anything to Aunt Fiona about this. It makes her sad to talk about it."

"Maybe your mother will come back," was Wahali's only comment. And after a while, he added, "And maybe not. Maybe she left you *because* she loved you."

"What do you mean?" Victor demanded, both anger and curiosity in his voice.

"I mean exactly that," Wahali said slowly and very carefully, "Maybe she left you *because* she loved you."

"Well, that sure doesn't make any sense!" Victor spat, and then he said no more. And Wahali was thinking, *Of course it doesn't make any sense to so young a man. But some day you will know that possibility. I certainly would not wish it for you, but I believe that one of these days* you *will leave someone, simply and purely because you* do *love her. But I will not tell you about that, because that too, is sad. And you do not need to hear it. Yet.*

The monk and the young man walked on in silence, but as they approached the camp, Victor mumbled. "I didn't mean to be rude."

"It's okay. I don't think you were rude at all," Wahali replied. "If you like, we can talk more another time."

"I'd like that," Victor said. "But I don't want to talk about my mother—whoever she is. Or *was*," Victor added.

"Okay," Wahali said simply. "We can talk about my lake in the mountains. I'd like to tell you all about it. And about what I *found* when I ran away."

"That's fine," Victor agreed. And so they parted in comfort.

Chapter Eighteen

But there certainly was no comfort at Doc's house. While Wahali and Victor had been walking along the shore and speaking of things Victor really couldn't understand, Rebecca had been sitting erect and defiant in her father's living room, with Doc himself on one side of the room and Aunt Irma on the other. Doc's face was red with restrained anger, and Aunt Irma's face was as white and pasty as biscuit dough.

"Jubilee tells me that you and Victor were kissing," Doc said, his frown covering the whole of his forehead, and Aunt Irma nodded up and down in agreement with his anger and in time with her crocheting needle. "Is this true?" he demanded.

Rebecca met his gaze with a solid stare. "Yes sir, it's true," she said, her voice strong and carrying a tone of utter and complete defiance. What Rebecca was really thinking was that if she ever got her hands on Jubilee, she would strangle her, right on the spot.

"We kissed. But only once."

"What on earth were you thinking?" Doc stormed, but as soon as he asked that question, he realized that he didn't need for Rebecca to answer. He *knew* what she had been thinking.

"From now on, you are confined to this house," he shouted. "Confined! Do you hear me?"

"Yes, sir," Rebecca answered, still retaining her cool demeanor, but her thoughts were like wild birds flying blindly around a cage they didn't know was there. *A prison, that's what this house is. Again!* Rebecca thought, but in the face of Doc's terrible anger, she said nothing.

"No more running around on that bicycle like a wild woman," he bellowed. *No more freedom, no more wind blowing my hair. No more Victor!*

"Listen," Rebecca finally spoke, "you need to know that I was the one who invited that kiss. I really kissed him more than he kissed me." Somehow, Rebecca had to take the blame from Victor. She simply had to.

"Invited it? How?"

"I asked him," Rebecca replied, her tone of voice indicating the answer was perfectly simple.

"I don't care," Doc growled. "I don't care how it happened. The fact of the matter is that it *did* happen, and it won't happen again. Do you hear me?" Doc's face was turning an alarming shade of red, and in light of his obvious fury, Rebecca retreated somewhat. "Do you hear me?" Doc bellowed again.

"I hear you," she murmured, and she glanced over at Aunt Irma, who was still crocheting and avoiding eye contact with either Doc or Rebecca.

"Then that's that," Doc pronounced, and without another word, he left the house, revving the engine on his car and driving away so fast that sand spewed from under his wheels.

As Victor and Wahali walked along the shore, neither of them heard the engine as Doc's car raced along the sandy road paralleling the beach. But when they parted, and Victor approached the cottage, he saw that Doc's car was parked in front of the porch, with the driver's door standing open. His heart gave a hard lurch, and as he ran toward the cottage, his only thought was that someone was so sick or hurt that they had to call the doctor and that he had run inside so fast, he forgot to close the car door.

But when Victor burst into the living room, he saw Doc and Fiona sitting quietly together, while Glory poured coffee for them. Both Fiona and Glory looked healthy—worried, perhaps, but healthy. Victor's only clue that something was wrong was Jubilee, who was standing in the corner of the room, her arms wrapped around herself and her head down.

"It's all your fault!" Jubilee looked up and yelled as Victor came into the room.

"What? What happened?" Victor asked, perplexed.

"You all kissing!" Jubilee wailed.

"What?"

"What I said," Jubilee insisted. "I saw you and Rebecca kissing. So don't you dare say it didn't happen!" Glory put down the coffee pot and went to the corner where Jubilee was standing with her arms crossed and her chin jutting.

"Come on. Let's go in the kitchen." Glory wrapped her arm roughly around Jubilee's shoulders and pushed her from the room, but as Jubilee left, she glanced again at Victor—and smiled at him—the strangest smile Victor had ever seen, and his head was whirling with the effort to comprehend everything that was going on. He could only gaze, horrified, first at Jubilee's retreating smile and then at Doc and Fiona.

"This is true, isn't it?" Doc asked, and the rough tone in his voice carried the full volume of fatherly concern. Fiona looked down into her coffee cup, her face a bright red. Victor straightened to his full height and took a deep breath. "Yes, sir," he said to Doc. "Rebecca and I kissed while we were sitting in the swing." Deep in his heart, he wanted to protest that it had all been Rebecca's idea, that she had not liked it at all, that his ignorant failure in that kiss had led to her being so mad and staying away for almost a whole week. But Victor couldn't say that, because he would not betray Rebecca, no matter what. No matter how terrible he was at kissing.

"I was afraid of something like that," Doc said. But then he looked at Fiona. "I assume some responsibility for this," he said. "I let her go running off all over creation. I just didn't know how to stop her." He thought for a moment and then added, "And it's not Jubilee's fault either. She did what she was supposed to do. She did what I *paid* her to do." Fiona continued staring into her coffee cup, but her mind was racing, remembering Jubilee's turning up on Rebecca's bike and wearing Rebecca's bathing suit. *And what was that all about? And Doc hasn't said a single thing about that.* Fiona wondered. *And why was Glory so mad at that girl?*

Doc's gaze stayed on Victor. "What's going on between you and Rebecca?"

"Nothing, sir," Victor's voice rose in his own defense and in Rebecca's. "We're good friends, or we were, until she got so mad at me. Why, I haven't even seen her in over a week." That was as much as Victor was willing to say in his own defense.

"Yes, well . . ." Doc arose, putting his cup on the table.

"Victor?" Fiona's voice was gentle. "Why don't you go ahead, and let me speak with Doc in private?"

Victor looked from one of them to the other, and Fiona was unable to read whatever emotion showed on his face. Without another word, he went down the hallway to his own room, closing the door behind him and wondering why he felt so terrible, especially after the way he had tried to defend Rebecca. And what on earth was Jubilee doing? Why did she tell Doc about that damned stupid kiss?

And especially, *why now?* Old Man's son, David, had taught Victor about the "why now" question. He said that if you ask that question about anything and keep on asking it, you will get to the bottom of any problem. And to the answer of any question. So, in spite of the shock of the moment, that question kept flying around in Victor's mind. *Why now? Why now?*

In the living room, Fiona tried to smooth things over. "Listen, Doc, you know how children are. I don't think there's anything to worry about. Victor and Rebecca are just friends." But as soon as the words left Fiona's mouth, she realized that she was expressing wishful thinking instead of facing facts.

Wahali had been headed for his own cabin, but just as he got to his door, he saw Victor break into a frantic run to the cottage—a run that bespoke of more than youthful exuberance, and so instead of going into his own cabin, he walked rapidly on toward Fiona's cottage, coming up onto the front porch just as Glory led Jubilee into the hallway and then into the kitchen. Quietly, he let himself in the screen door and stood there, not wanting to eavesdrop but merely to be there, if he could be of help to anyone.

"They're okay," Fiona repeated, but her words had lost their fervor. "I know that Victor's a good boy, and he would never do anything to hurt Rebecca. And besides, they're too young to be serious, don't you think?"

But Doc didn't answer her question. Instead, he said, "I'm sorry Jubilee is so upset." Doc's voice was low and miserable. "Rebecca simply scares me to death lately. I don't exactly know how to put this, but I think Rebecca is . . . infatuated . . . with Victor, and I'm worried. And then when Jubilee told me this morning what had been going on . . ."

"But don't lots of young girls get what they call puppy love?" Fiona tried to argue.

"They do," Doc confirmed. "But . . ." His voice trailed off, and Fiona didn't know what to say in that long silence that followed.

"Surely, it can't be all that serious," Fiona finally said. "They're just youngsters," she repeated. Fiona glanced up and saw Wahali standing in the doorway, but she was so caught up in the topic of conversation, she failed to acknowledge his presence.

"Maybe," Doc replied, "But it's more than just what Jubilee told me. I've seen this coming ever since Myra passed away. Rebecca just isn't the same girl she was." He sighed deeply. "She's rebellious and rude to Irma, she goes around slamming doors and pouting and—now this infatuation. And Irma's so disgusted, she's threatening to move back to Gainesville. Why, I'm almost at my wits end."

"It's a hard age," Fiona agreed, and she searched back in her memory. She had once been Rebecca's age, but she couldn't remember being angry or—Lord forbid!—disrespectful. If she had been "mouthy," as her mama had called it, she would have gotten the backs of her legs whipped with a sharp switch—hard.

Doc's voice came low and wrapped around a sigh. "I have to forbid Rebecca to see Victor," he sighed. "I have to forbid it . . . and if that doesn't work, I'll have no choice but to send her away. Send her to a boarding school."

"Boarding school?" Fiona's voice rose. "Is that really necessary? Forgive me for saying so, Doc, but aren't you making a bit of a mountain out of a molehill?" Fiona spoke as gently as possible, because she was sure that her words would be offensive to Doc.

"Maybe I am," Doc admitted. "But if I can't make her stop seeing Victor, then I don't know what else to do, to be truthful about it. Irma hasn't been able to control her, and she never agreed to live with us forever—only while Myra was . . . sick." Doc stopped and rubbed his forehead. "If things don't get better, Irma will leave. I know it. And now *this*. I can't have Rebecca running wild all over creation. And kissing boys. Kissing Victor. Irma won't put up with that, and Myra wouldn't either." The last few words were almost a wail, and Fiona's heart went out to him.

"Maybe I shouldn't have come here," Doc confessed, looking about as miserable as Fiona had ever seen. "I've already made up my mind what to do about Rebecca, and I'll do whatever is necessary. But oh, I miss Myra so much."

"I wish there were another way," Fiona said softly, wanting to go over to the couch, sit down beside Doc and put her hand over his. But that wouldn't have been proper, would it? Doc continued, "This will be best for everyone. Rebecca will simply have to obey me in this—my absolutely forbidding her to see Victor—or she will have to suffer the consequences. I *will* send her away, if I have to."

"What about . . . Jubilee?" Fiona asked, changing her question at the last moment, because what she really wanted to ask was, "What about Victor?" But she didn't dare.

"I'm bringing in a woman who used to work for Irma in Gainesville," Doc explained. "She'll take over for Jubilee, and Rebecca won't be allowed to go out of her sight. But please tell Jubilee that I don't blame her for any of this. She did what she was supposed to do."

When Wahali realized just what kind of a conversation he had intruded upon—even with the best of intentions—he backed out of the door, went quietly down the steps, and retreated to his own cabin.

The hardest thing Fiona had to do was to tell Victor, which she did just as soon as Doc left.

"Honey, Doc doesn't want you and Rebecca to be together. At all," Fiona added.

"But why?" Only Victor's pride kept him from weeping. It had been one thing when Rebecca got mad and didn't come to the camp, but he lived in the certainty that she would somehow forgive him that terrible kiss and come back. He was sure he could do better, if only she would give him a chance. And with all his heart, he wanted that chance. With all his heart, he wanted to be with Rebecca.

But with Doc forbidding them from being together, it was a whole different thing. While he swallowed back the tears that tried to come, he could almost inhale Rebecca's soap-and-powder scent, the aroma of lake water in her hair, the sweetness of her sun-warmed skin.

"I heard what you said about Rebecca and me just being friends," Victor confessed.

"Well, I hope that's the truth," Fiona argued, chastising herself for not waiting until Victor's room door had closed before she uttered those words he was now throwing back at her.

"It's not the truth," Victor said. "I love her. I've loved her for a very long time." And Fiona didn't say anything, but she recalled Glory's very words. *Sometimes, love comes early.*

"You love her? Do you even know what that means?" Fiona asked.

"I know what that means," Victor said. "And I *do* love her. And I mean to be with her."

Victor's words frightened Fiona. "Honey, Doc's her father, and he has to do what he thinks is best," was all Fiona could think to say.

"He doesn't know what's best," Victor's voice reflected a terrible anger. "He doesn't know what's best for Rebecca and me."

"Well, be that as it may, you have to do what he has demanded," Fiona argued, trying to bring the whole conversation to an end.

"We'll just have to see about that," Victor mumbled, and Fiona countered with the final terrible thing she had to tell him. "If you go against his wishes, he will send her off to a boarding school," Fiona warned, hating the words and trying to speak them in such a soft tone that Victor would be spared the threat behind the words.

"*Boarding* school?"

"That's what he said," Fiona added. "That's exactly what he said."

"But why?" Victor repeated, for clearly this whole episode was beyond his understanding—or perhaps beyond his *wanting* to understand.

"He means to keep the two of you apart," Fiona explained, but in the back of her mind, she, too, was wondering what on earth could have prompted Doc into considering such a drastic solution. Was Doc going to repeat Myra's mistake—a cruel mistake that used love as its excuse?

"He wouldn't do that," Victor argued with himself. "He wouldn't send her away, no matter what he says." And then, his frown cleared. "Maybe he knows he can't keep us apart, no matter what. No one can!" He fairly spat the words.

"Please, Victor," Fiona begged. "Please don't challenge Doc. He just may send her away, and that isn't fair to Rebecca."

At last, Fiona felt that she had uttered words that caught Victor's entire attention, but rather than seeing any degree of acceptance in Victor's eyes, she saw instead a thousand wheels turning, as Victor started thinking about ways to get around Doc's terrible edict.

"Just let's give Doc time to cool down a little bit," Fiona said. "To be truthful, I don't really know why he's reacted this way, myself. Let's just give him some time. Maybe he'll reconsider."

"He can't do it," Victor said yet again, but only as if he were talking to himself. "He can't keep us apart." Fiona realized then that Victor was no longer listening to anything she said, and that he would not give in to Doc's strange requirements. But she didn't really understand why. Victor and Rebecca may have thought that they were in love, but they were too young to know what it meant. So thinking, Fiona left Victor's room, left his now silent anger and the sudden and inexplicable wall he seemed to have put up around himself. A wall against *her*.

So she sought out the sanctuary of her own kitchen. Filling the sink with warm, soapy water, she started washing dishes that she had taken right out of the cabinet—dishes that were already clean. The other thing Fiona couldn't understand was the way her tears dripped into the sudsy water and disappeared. Just like that.

For the rest of that week, Victor remained uncharacteristically withdrawn, and Fiona still thought that Doc had probably overreacted— *way* overreacted. She also thought that perhaps a few days of thinking it all over would bring her around to see it Doc's way, or that Doc would reconsider. But neither happened. The one thing Fiona did believe was that if Doc wasn't careful, he'd clamp down on Rebecca so hard, he would simply drive her into flagrant and open rebellion. Maybe even make her run away. Fiona had heard of those things happening, and the way Myra held on to her was bad enough, and now, perhaps Doc was going to make the same mistake. Poor Rebecca! But despite her worries about Rebecca, Fiona was even more worried about Victor. He was pale with a suppressed anger and almost completely silent, and she knew that he was in pain, even though she couldn't see that deep place in Victor's heart where his love for Rebecca surprised him by its very intensity. Because that place held only the image of Rebecca. Her smooth arms, the deep brown eyes. Her hair sparkling with droplets of lake water. Her slightly crooked smile and the way she tilted her head when she was silently laughing at him. Even that terrible little kiss and the unbelievable softness and warmth of her lips and the sweetness of her breath against his.

Rebecca, on the other hand, was filled more with anger than with direct thoughts about Victor. And most of her anger was directed at Jubilee, who made it a point to stay as far away from Doc's house as possible. Rebecca didn't know about Jubilee's wearing her bathing suit and riding her bike and going to see Victor, but she did know that Jubilee had tattled about the kiss. That meaningless little kiss! *Or was it meaningless? If it had been so terrible, why do I yearn so much to repeat it? And was it really so terrible? My very first kiss from a boy. A man .And why am I thinking only of Victor's face, his mouth, the sky-colored eyes?*

And why was her own papa going to make a prisoner of her? She had been a prisoner all her life, and now, having tasted freedom, she knew that she could not live without it. Ever.

Predictably, Glory, too, blamed everything on Jubilee. "It's all your fault! You see what happens when you try to be somebody you're not? Try to mess around with a White boy? And why'd you have to go and be such a tattletale? You want to be a white girl that bad? Trying to mess around with Victor? Whoever heard of such a thing?" Under Glory's withering accusations, Jubilee went into what Glory called her "stone-face" stance at first, but then she couldn't hold in her words any longer.

"Well, Aunt Glory, I'm paying for it, sure enough! Doc locked up Rebecca's bicycle . . . and mine, as well . . . in that little garage behind his house," Jubilee complained. "And that woman he's gotten to watch Rebecca is the meanest looking old bat I ever saw in all my life."

"That's no way to speak of your elders," Glory scolded. "Doc is doing what he thinks is right, and we've no business talking about any of it." However, Jubilee knew full well that Glory really wanted to hear about it, so she went on, trying to keep the whiny sound out of her voice.

"Her name is Murphy," Jubilee said. "Did you ever hear of any woman being named something like that?"

"Well, no," Glory had to admit. "But I'll bet her name is *Mrs.* Murphy, and that's what you should call her, if you ever have the chance to talk with her." Jubilee heard the subtle hint in Glory's words, and she nodded her head, knowingly. "I'll bet she's way too big to fit in that cute little bed that used to be mine," Jubilee said.

"She stout?" Glory asked, trying to pretend that she wasn't really interested.

"This big!" Jubilee shouted, holding her arms as far apart as she could. "Way too big for that pretty little room." At the thought of the room she had lost at Doc's house, Jubilee's eyes filled up, but Glory didn't have any sympathy for her.

"Serves you right!" Glory pronounced. "Serves you right, you having to go back to living with your mama." And then Glory added one more verbal barb. "And serves you right that you have to go back to cleaning fish. 'Cause you know good and well you wouldn't have said a thing to Doc about any silly little old kiss—unless you was just eat up with jealousy! You can argue that you were just 'doing your job,' but I know better. You can't fool me, missy, so you might as well stop trying!"

Starry hadn't been at home when Doc made his visit, but, of course, she picked up immediately that something important had happened.

"What happened?" she asked when she came in. "I saw that handsome monk—Brother John? I can't remember his Seminole name— going to his cabin, and then I saw Doc leaving, and when I came in through the kitchen, Jubilee was crying and Glory was standing there with her arms crossed, just staring at her with the meanest look I've ever seen."

"Doc's forbidden Rebecca and Victor from seeing each other," Fiona said, praying that she wouldn't have to rehash the whole thing for Starry's benefit. But of course, she did.

"But *why?*"

"Because Rebecca and Victor *kissed*," Fiona whispered—just in case Victor was in his room and able to overhear their conversation.

"Kissed? Is that all?"

"That's all, thank the good Lord," Fiona said. "But Doc just went into a knee-jerk like I've never seen before and said if he can't control Rebecca, he's ready to pack her up and send her off to some boarding school. And there's more. He's hired some older woman to make sure Rebecca stays on the straight and narrow."

"Kissed? That's all?" Starry repeated, seemingly focused on that one element and nothing more. "And how did Doc even know about that?"

"Jubilee told him, which of course, she should have done," Fiona added, somewhat defensively. "It was her job to keep up with Rebecca, after all. Only thing I can't figure is why she waited over a week to say anything to him about it."

"So Jubilee did her job, and now there's no job for her to do? That's too bad! How's Victor taking it?"

Fiona heaved a deep sigh. "He's angry. Angrier than I've ever seen him," Fiona confessed.

"But he *does* know, doesn't he? You told him everything?"

"Of course, he knows. And yes, I told him absolutely everything."

"Pretty soon, he'll probably act like he doesn't care. Of course, he does care, but he won't want to let anyone know that!"

"I think you're right, Starry. But what should we do?"

"We shouldn't *do* anything. Leave him alone—give him some room."

Fiona sighed yet again. "I think you're right, but it's hard! I want to make everything better for him." Fiona was close to tears. "I want to grab the whole world by the tail and make it be kind to him."

"Well, what you gotta do right now is just leave him alone—hush your mouth. Let him talk if he wants to talk, and if he doesn't, then accept that." For long moments, Fiona stared silently at Starry, and finally, her shoulders relaxed and she sighed. "How'd you get to be so smart, Starry?" Fiona asked, wiping her eyes on her apron.

"Honey, you want to know anything . . . anything at all, about that old male ego, you just ask me! I've run headlong into it so many times, it's a wonder I have any skull left at all!"

Despite herself, Fiona smiled, and as Starry just nodded, Fiona thought that Starry looked very wise and . . . yes . . . *pretty*.

Chapter Nineteen

Starry knew how fragile feelings were between Glory and Jubilee, and she thought it was all because of Jubilee telling Doc about the now infamous kiss. So over the next few days, Starry quietly and bit by bit took over the job of cleaning and filleting all of the fish every single day. Jubilee, of course, was only too happy to relinquish her most hated of all jobs, and at first, Glory grumbled about Jubilee "getting away with things" and not having to "pay a price," but eventually, Glory became somewhat mesmerized by the daily chores and seemed to forget about Jubilee. The only thing Glory watched for was for Jubilee making excuses to spend time with Victor. But eventually, Glory seemed to forget about that, as well.

For one thing, Victor was seldom around. He took to riding his bicycle even more than usual, and Fiona insisted that no one would try to get him to talk about Rebecca, even though all of them were wondering if he was honoring Doc's decision that they not see each other. "If Victor has anything he wants to say, he'll say it!" Fiona insisted.

Too, even though from time to time Starry cast sidelong glances at Wahali when he left the camp to walk along the lake, she never made any attempt to talk with him or to call his attention to herself in any way. Fiona thought that perhaps Starry was too old to try to attract Wahali, or else, he simply couldn't be attracted at all, by anyone. Or perhaps Starry had finally gotten some good sense and figured that there was enough going on at the camp, without her adding to the worries.

And no one really noticed when Arabella went to Wahali's cabin late one afternoon and talked to him for a long time. Because after all, she was his mama.

On the day before Wahali was to go back to New York, he was setting off to walk along the lakeshore when he saw Victor coming down the gravel road on his bicycle.

"Hey, Victor," Wahali called. "You want to go for a walk?"

A walk was probably the last thing in the world Victor really wanted to do, but it was certainly better than going into his room and staying there, seething and petulant. As Victor approached Wahali, he said, "I guess you heard everything about Doc coming to see Aunt Fiona."

"Yes, I did," Wahali admitted. "I'm sorry. I just wanted to help if someone was sick or hurt, but I guess I walked in on something private." Victor said nothing, just looked out over the lake and kept walking, but the silence itself was saying something, sure enough, and Wahali walked ahead, simply waiting for Victor to speak.

"I don't know what to do," Victor confessed. Wahali kept his face in a careful mask of polite disinterest, waiting for Victor to say more. If he would. And the surmising had been accurate. When Victor spoke again, his voice was raspy with emotion. "I don't know how to live without her. I feel just like the sun has gone behind a big cloud, and I've never felt so cold and alone in my life."

"Well, that's the way of it," Wahali agreed gently.

"We did kiss," Victor confessed, as if he hadn't heard Wahali. "But it wasn't my idea—and it sure made her mad. She told me, 'If that's the best you can do, I'm going home!'" Here, Victor raised his voice into a falsetto, both imitating and perhaps chiding Rebecca's painful words. Then he went on in his normal voice but one dripping with misery. "And that one stinking kiss was what caused all the ruckus. I don't even know what was wrong with the way I kissed her. I'd never done it before." This time, Wahali allowed himself to smile. "It does take some practice," he said. "I remember wondering how it was done—where the noses went, and such as that."

"You did?" Victor was surprised, believing as he did that he was the only person in the world who had been ignorant and awkward and uncertain. And Wahali smiled privately. *What a joy it always is, when a young person thinks his experience is completely unique, that no one else in the whole world ever experienced such a thing, and then he finds out that it's really only part of a very common human condition.*

"Did any girl ever tell you your kiss was no good?" Victor asked.

"Not exactly," Wahali said, his tone taking on the quality of an older brother, one who has experienced more of the world than the young man who was depending upon him for guidance . . . or comfort . . . or something. "But it gets much better with practice. It really does."

"Some practice we'll get now, with us not allowed to see each other at all," Victor spat, just as something inside of his heart gave a terrible, aching lurch, causing him almost to gasp with the pain of it.

"You miss her terribly," Wahali's simple words cut through everything unspeakable Victor was feeling.

"I didn't even get to say goodbye," Victor whispered.

"Well, you really didn't want to say goodbye anyway, did you?" Wahali asked. Victor shook his head.

"Doc's scared, Victor," Wahali offered.

"We didn't do anything wrong," Victor said. "And we *wouldn't* have."

"Doc doesn't know that."

"Doc doesn't trust me." It was partly a question and partly the solid pronouncement of a truth.

"I'm not sure," Wahali offered. "Perhaps it's something else, something we don't understand."

Victor was silent. "If we'd done something really bad, I could understand, but we didn't. And we wouldn't have."

"Again, Doc doesn't know that." Briefly, Victor wondered if Wahali was taking Doc's side, but somehow, he could not feel resentful about it. "Be patient," Wahali advised cautiously. Victor stopped walking and studied Wahali carefully. Then he almost snarled when he asked, "And what do you know about it? You're a *monk*, for God's sake!"

"Yes, for God's sake, I am most certainly a monk," Wahali laughed. "But I wasn't always."

"You had you a girlfriend?"

"I had me a girlfriend," he said quietly, loving to hear the reflexive pronouns that were such a distinctive element of Love-Oak speech patterns.

"What happened to her?" Victor's direct question made Wahali flinch a little. "Did you leave her? Did you leave her because you *loved* her?"

That harsh question, of course, was a reference to what Wahali had said about Victor's mother—that perhaps she left him precisely because she loved him. But the question was so angry and delivered with such a snide tone of voice that it stung Wahali's heart. Still, he understood the anger that was almost overwhelming Victor.

"No, she left me," Wahali whispered. "She died," he added softly.

Victor couldn't fully grasp the idea, because he didn't want to grasp it. Everything in him rebelled against the mere thought of it. *Rebecca!*

"I'm sorry," Victor mumbled.

"I am too," Wahali answered. "But it happened."

"Do you mind if I ask how?"

"Yes, I mind, but I'll tell you anyway." They had stopped walking along the edge of the lake, and Wahali moved farther up the shore, finding dry sand for sitting. Victor sat beside him, wanting to hear what Wahali had to say and yet not wanting to hear at all.

"She drowned," Wahali said simply. "Right here in this very lake."

Victor couldn't imagine such a thing. In his mind's eye, he saw Rebecca—saw her swimming, her arms taking strong, lazy strokes and her long, well-muscled legs kicking up the water behind her. Then he saw a look of sudden terror on her face, saw her beautiful head slowly sinking beneath the surface of the lake, saw her lithe body sinking to the sandy bottom. His muscles lurched silently, preparing to do whatever he had to do, to save her—muscles that responded only to Victor's imagination.

"Is that why you went away?" Victor had to say something, anything, to take away that terrible image, and the almost overwhelming desire to charge into the lake, trying to save a figment of his own imagination. And those were the words that came out of his mouth, unbidden.

"Yes. At first, it was why I went away." Wahali looked at Victor, trying to gauge how much to tell him. "When my Sawni died—that was her name, Sawni—I wanted to die too. More than anything, I just wanted to die. She drowned, and I wanted to drown, as well, and I planned to make it happen. But then I thought of my mother, and I knew that if I drowned myself right here in this very lake where I lost my Sawni, my own mother might find my body. I couldn't let that happen."

Victor said nothing, but he looked out at the familiar lake and realized that he would never see it quite the same way again. That he would always be able to see a beautiful young Seminole girl sinking to her death beneath its surface.

Wahali continued, "So I decided to find another lake in which to take my life. One too far away for my mother to see my dead body."

"New York?" Victor asked, and Wahali nodded.

"A woman came into the Trading Post one day, and she was talking to another woman—loudly, you know, the way most of the tourists talk—and she said something about a place high in the Adirondack Mountains in New York, where she and her husband had gone on vacation the year before. Talked so loudly about a lake that was there. And once I lost my Sawni, I thought back at how intently I had listened to that woman and how her words had stuck in my mind. And suddenly, I believed that God had let me overhear her conversation just so I would know about *that* lake." Wahali sighed. "I took it as God's will that I go find that very lake and do what I had to do to be with my sweet Sawni." Wahali paused, lost in the agony of his memory. "So I took all of my savings and bought a bus ticket."

"Did you tell your parents where you were going? Or why?"

"Oh, certainly not, and I regret that with all my heart, even today. I caused them so much agony. I didn't even know until I came home again that they thought I was lost in the swamp. I shouldn't have done that to them." Again, Victor was silent. He could not imagine doing such a thing to Fiona. Or Glory. Or even Starry. He could envision them sitting around the kitchen table, wondering where he was, crying and holding on to each other. The thought almost brought tears to his eyes. "So what happened? You didn't . . . drown yourself?"

"Obviously," Wahali smiled. "When I got to that town, I saw those magnificent mountains for the first time. I spent all the next day just staring at them. I had never imagined such beauty, because I grew up here, the same as you, and all I knew were flat marsh lands and palm trees and a horizon that might reach all the way to the moon. The next day, I found the lake that woman talked about, and I was ready to do . . . what I had to do. The lake was big—much bigger than our lake here—and deep and dark and colder than anything I'd ever known. And completely surrounded by those wonderful mountains. Mountains that shut out the rest of the whole world."

"Then what happened?"

"I rolled up my pants and waded into it, at first. To see what it was going to be like. It was so cold my feet went numb. I loved that feeling, because that's what I wanted, to be numb all over. Especially my heart."

"And then?" Victor waited, almost holding his breath. Wahali leaned back on his elbows and smiled.

"I met a monk," he said, as if there were music in those words themselves. "He was walking on the shore of the lake, and when he saw me, he walked right out into the lake where I was standing—didn't even take off his sandals. Didn't even hold up his robe—just walked out to me. We talked. He was kind and gentle, and eventually, I told him what I was going to do, even though I really didn't want to tell him anything. It seemed to me that the words poured out, and I couldn't stop them."

"And he talked you out of it?"

"No. He just listened while I talked *myself* out of it. We stood there for a long time, both of us practically freezing to death, but he never left me. And one thing he said—out of many things he said to me that day— one thing struck me like a bolt of lightning. Blasted open my very heart!"

"What was it?"

"He said that I was *blessed!*"

"Blessed?"

"That I was blessed to have known *love*—that some people go through their whole lives without ever really knowing it, without giving it and without getting it. And if that happens, they have failed at the one and only thing God sent them here to do."

"*Do?*" Victor wanted to scream the word, but he managed to hold down his voice, because screaming would have been like shouting in a church.

"*Do*," Wahali confirmed. "God sends us here to love each other, and we try to do that—best to *give* it, but some are blessed enough to *receive* it, as well." Wahali closed his eyes and lifted his chin toward the sky. "Even if we lose it. Even if we try to kill it, or it succeeds in killing us. Even if it laughs in our faces while it rips out our hearts and leaves us to bleed to death. We are blessed!" Wahali's voice had risen, not in anger, but in passion at his own words. Somehow, Victor wondered if Wahali were still trying to convince himself. Victor frowned and shook his head. "And that's why you didn't drown yourself?"

"That's why," Wahali said, opening his eyes and smiling at Victor. "And because of something else that monk told me, that love never ends. Never. And you can't really kill it, no matter how hard you try. Because love has existed since before time began, and it will still exist when the earth and the stars and the moon have all turned to dust. When everything is gone, only Love will be left."

"Are you talking about God?" Victor asked.

"I am talking about God and about life itself, which is a great gift God gives to us."

"And that's why you became a monk." Victor sighed. "And did you find it? Love?"

"Oh, indeed! I found it, but it was there all the time. I just couldn't see it." Wahali closed his eyes again and said, "'For thy love is better than wine.'"

"What?" Victor had never heard such words.

"That's in the Bible," Wahali said, with his eyes still closed. But Victor couldn't imagine such words appearing on the tissue-thin pages of a holy book.

"Song of Solomon," Wahali said easily, again looking at Victor. Victor was still thinking about that when he heard his own voice, and the surprising words he spoke seemed to have come from some place outside of his own thinking. "I don't think I know much about love."

Wahali made a soft snorting sound. "Of course you do! You've been surrounded by it most of your life. Fiona and Glory, Mr. Owen and . . . my pop."

Victor's mind was filled with the faces of the women who had raised him. He could see Fiona's blue eyes and blonde, corkscrew curls. He could also see Glory's dark-skinned face and those soft, beautiful eyes. But then Victor finally heard the rest of what Wahali had said. "Your pop?" Victor queried. "Your pop loves me? How on earth do you know that?" Victor thought of the solemn man who never spoke a word.

"I can see it in his eyes," Wahali answered. "He loves you."

"Yeah . . . maybe so, but maybe my own mother didn't."

"I told you," Wahali repeated his earlier words, words that Victor, in his pain, had just thrown back at him, "Maybe she left you *because* she loved you. That would be the hardest thing in this world to do. Only love could have made her do something that broke her heart. Love alone can make you do something like that."

Victor said nothing, but he felt a strange and completely foreign stirring of warmth toward his mysterious and unknown mother. He pushed that feeling away quickly. In that, he was so very much like Fiona. Instead of looking at the new feeling, he simply laughed.

"That's not the kind of love I mean," Victor whispered, his face reddening.

"I know what you mean," Wahali smiled.

"It's a pain, isn't it?" Victor's words surprised Wahali.

"What's a pain?"

"Love."

"Oh yes, it's certainly *that* all right," Wahali admitted. "But it's the only thing that matters. The only thing." Wahali took a deep breath, as if saying those words had tired him out. And then he added, "Now, do you want some advice?"

"I don't think so," Victor growled.

"I don't mean about *kissing* or even about *that* kind of love." Wahali laughed and turned a deep shade of red. "You'll have to learn all that for yourself. But if you don't want advice, just let me think out loud to you. Okay?"

"Okay," Victor mumbled, unconvincingly.

"Keep loving Rebecca. By all means, keep loving Rebecca, but from afar—for now. You and Rebecca must do what Doc has demanded. So keep each other only in your hearts and wait."

Victor listened carefully, and the more Wahali said, the more Victor's chin jutted and his eyes narrowed. When Wahali looked at him, he actually flinched at the glare in Victor's eyes.

"Well, that was a *pretty* speech," Victor spat the words and turned away.

"You're angry," Wahali stated the obvious. "And I don't blame you. You're in love, and now your beloved has been taken away from you." Victor blinked rapidly, determined not to allow childish tears to come up in his eyes. Wahali realized that, quite possibly, Victor would lash out at him, but he felt bound to speak the words in his heart. "Open your eyes,

Victor—look all around you at all the love. Be patient. Wait. And some day that very special kind of love will be yours, and you will never be the same."

"God's love?" Victor's voice still held the sound of barely controlled rage, and his words almost held a curse in them.

"God's love? No! You don't have to *wait* for that. You've always had it. God's love doesn't *come*—it doesn't *arrive*—it just *is* and *was* and always will be, forever and ever." Wahali laughed out loud, a strong, delighted laugh such as Victor had not heard from him before. "Your love for Rebecca is a very small reflection of that great Love."

Victor listened, waiting for the words to simply wash over him, like little waves in the lake. Wash over him and be gone. But that didn't happen. Wahali's words sank deep inside of him and diffused some of the terrible anger, making it vanish as if it had been smoke. He was almost surprised when he heard his own voice asking a question that seemed not to have passed through his mind at all, "Why did you come back here?"

Wahali drew a breath that was possibly a sigh of relief that Victor had controlled his rage—had not reached out and punched Wahali right in the face. "You can't repeat what I'm going to tell you." Wahali would be taking a risk in what he was about to tell Victor, especially given Victor's anger, but it was a risk he was willing to take.

"Okay," Victor said, in simple assurance but with a slight edge in his voice. Wahali continued, "I came back here to see my mother and father because I'm leaving the monastery."

"Leaving? Why?"

"I'm joining the army," Wahali said gently. "And I don't want my mother to know. Not yet anyway. But I wanted to see her again—and my pop—before I sign up."

"But why are you leaving that . . . monastery? I thought you really liked it there. The lake and all? And *love* and all?" Victor's voice was sing-song, the last of his terrible anger slowly dissipating.

"Because this war is going to get worse. This is my country, and I love it. So if the time comes when my country needs me, I'll fight for what I believe in." Here, he hesitated, and then grinning broadly, he thumped his chest once and announced in a loud voice, "After all, I'm a *warrior*, you know!"

Fight for what I believe in . . . Victor's entire being seemed entangled in those words, and once again, he heard himself speaking, but he didn't know what the words were going to be. "If your . . . Sawni . . . had not died, and if someone—anyone—had tried to keep you away from her, what would you have done?"

Wahali was caught completely off guard by Victor's earnest question. He had never considered such a thing, because Sawni's drowning had put an end to any other way of thinking, had put her in a place far beyond his reach, something he had accepted long ago. For long moments, Wahali said nothing, and then he realized that, above all, he had to be completely honest with Victor.

"I would have found a way. I'm a warrior, you know," Wahali repeated.

And maybe you're not the only one, Victor thought, remembering the tourist who had pegged him as a "blonde Seminole." *Maybe you're not the only one!*

When Wahali and Victor got up and started to leave the lakeshore, Wahali stopped for a long moment and looked out over the lake. Then he stretched out his arms, tilted his head up toward the heavens, and closed his eyes.

"Sawni," he whispered. "Sawni, my beloved!"

Chapter Twenty

On the day of Wahali's leaving—but only Victor knew that he was not going back to his monastery—Arabella's eyes were red and swollen, and she carried a huge wad of tissues in her apron pocket when she came to the restaurant to chop the cabbage for that day's coleslaw. Glory had suggested that she not come in to work, since her son was leaving, but Arabella came anyway.

"Better for me to stay busy," Arabella explained. The night before, she had used the very last of the meat rations, treating her son to a real steak dinner. Almost like a last meal, Glory thought when Arabella, in typical fashion, described the meal in detail.

When the taxi arrived, Glory and a sniffling Arabella came out of the kitchen. Starry walked quite deliberately to the far end of the pier and stayed there, and Fiona came down from the cottage porch. "We hope you'll come again," Fiona said. "It's been so nice having you here."

"I'd like to come back—my time here has been a special blessing," Wahali answered, glancing at Victor and raising his hand in farewell. Then, without another word, but having bear-hugged the weeping Arabella thoroughly once more, he got into the taxi. Victor watched it disappear down the sandy road.

For a week following Wahali's departure, Arabella came to work with tears in her eyes and from time to time, as Arabella was chopping cabbage, Glory would hear her issue forth a deep, deep sigh. But Glory didn't ask her about it, because Glory already knew Arabella was grieving for Wahali. And Glory knew, as well, that if she started talking with Arabella, the tears would spill over into the coleslaw.

Victor, as well, realized Arabella's silent grief, and he wondered how much more worried and sad she would be if she had known that her son was not going back to the monastery, but to basic training to become a soldier. And in Victor's many long and solitary walks around the lake, he heard Wahali's voice over and over again—"I would have found a way." Other times, Victor was simply *gone,* and none of them knew exactly where he went.

Whenever Victor was at home, a deep and uncomfortable silence hung over the cottage, a silence that all of Fiona's fussing around and hard work could not dispel. At the supper table, each one of the women—Fiona, Glory and Starry—tried to raise a topic of conversation that would include Victor, but that never worked. He sat at the table and ate his supper in silence, and if any of them asked him a direct question, he seemed to be lost in thought and had to travel a long way to get back to what he had been asked.

After supper one night, Starry came up with what she thought might be a solution. "I know love-sickness when I see it," Starry pronounced while she was helping Fiona with the dishes. She had waited until Victor had already headed out of the back door, as was his after-supper habit.

"You know," Starry began, speaking to Fiona, but glancing at Glory, who was still sitting at the table finishing her coffee. "I've been having headaches, and I think I'll go see Doc about them. He'll be in his office tomorrow afternoon, and I'll see if he can give me something to make them not hurt so bad." Starry had phrased her statement carefully, hoping not to draw any suspicion from Fiona or Glory, but of course, that didn't work.

"I'm surprised you waited this long," Fiona said. "Ever since Myra passed on, you've been looking for some way to be with Doc, and if having a headache is the way, then I guess you'll have to go ahead." For the first time, Fiona's voice carried no hint of disapproval, and her acceptance of the words encouraged Starry to be more honest. Glory said nothing, simply sitting there watching Fiona and Starry closely.

"Well, I guess it isn't *all* about a headache," Starry whispered, drawing a very small harrumph from Fiona and a frown from Glory—not for Starry's headache, but for Fiona's small sound of disapproval.

Starry went on. "I want to talk with him about Victor and Rebecca. See if I can say or do something to make him change his mind about them."

"I think you're wasting your time," Fiona said. "If Doc had been going to change his mind, I think he would have done it already."

"It just doesn't make any sense," Starry said. "Doc's such a reasonable and intelligent man about everything else."

"I know," Fiona said. "This really isn't like him, but then I've never been a parent to a *girl*, so I can't really say anything against him. But I sure do hate to see Victor so unhappy."

"Being unhappy's a part of life," Glory said. For several moments, the women said nothing else, but then both Fiona and Starry came to a silent, mutual decision not to address Glory's remark. Starry mused, "I hate to see him unhappy too. I sure do wish Jubilee was still working for Doc. She could tell us what's going on."

"She would tell *me*," Glory said. "And then I would be the one to decide what I wanted to share." And what Glory didn't say was *Lord have mercy on us! Two white women thinking they know what unhappiness really is. Why, they don't have a clue.*

"Yes, of course," Starry agreed with what Glory had said. "But we still pretty well got the gist of things, eventually. And where is Jubilee anyway? What's she doing?"

"Lord only knows," Glory mumbled. "Lord only knows what that one's doing." *Because that's a girl who's headed for trouble, sure enough. Headed for trouble, big time.*

"You really think you can say something that will make Doc change his mind?" Fiona asked Starry, a hint of wishfulness in her voice.

"Don't know," Starry answered. "But I'm sure gonna try."

"Making a mistake," Glory pronounced, getting up from the table, taking her coffee cup to the sink and glaring at Fiona. "I told you a long time ago you couldn't make a little girl out of that boy. But you sure did try hard enough. Made him mind his manners all the time and be so sweet. It wasn't natural! But he's a man now, and you can't control him." Fiona and Starry stared at Glory, as if she were telling them something they didn't know. "He's a man," Glory repeated. "And it's right that he's *acting* like a man."

Fiona sputtered, "But having good manners doesn't have a thing to do with being a boy or a girl," she protested, stung by Glory's accusation. But those words weren't enough to dispel Fiona's anger. So she couldn't resist the impulse to say, "And when did you get to be such an expert on *men?*"

"I got ears," Glory snorted. "And I got eyes, and that's all I need." Then, she added, "Victor's a man now, and he's in love. I know that 'cause I got eyes and I got ears."

"And what do you know about love, Glory?" Fiona's soft tone belied the accusation in her question. "Aren't you the very one who told me you wouldn't *allow* love in your life?"

Glory stared back at Fiona, and immediately, Fiona felt guilty for having divulged something of their private conversation with Starry. Then Glory set her chin. "Just 'cause I know what a creek looks like don't mean I gotta fall in it."

Starry frowned. "Huh?"

Indeed, if Jubilee had still been living at Doc's house and being paid to keep up with Rebecca, she could have told Glory plenty about what was going on. Because at night, as soon as Doc's house was perfectly quiet and all the lights were turned off, Rebecca would get out of bed, where she had pretended to be sleeping, and go to the window, when she heard a small pebble ping against the glass. It was Victor. Every single night, it was Victor.

So she crept silently onto the screened-in back porch and stopped, watching Victor come up close to the screen. He never came into the porch itself, perhaps out of a half hearted attempt to obey Doc's edict, no matter how unfair he thought it was. Or perhaps it was because both Victor and Rebecca were afraid they would be caught, and Doc would keep his word—send her away.

But for this time, they were together again—through the screen, yes—but whispering back and forth, and every night they met in such a way. The first time, when Rebecca put her face close to the screen, she was surprised to feel herself propelled backward in memory—back to a day when she was very small but had somehow escaped Myra's ever-present watchfulness and had gone onto the porch alone. There, she had pressed her face against the screen and looked out into the open back yard. Her moment of freedom was short-lived, because Myra missed her right away and, almost in tears, Myra scooped her up and took her back inside, to what had already become a sort of benevolent prison for her. But in that brief, beautiful moment, Rebecca breathed in that peculiar, rusty aroma of the screen. It was a scent she would never forget.

So that the first of many nights when Rebecca and Victor whispered to each other through the screen and even put their hands on it up, palm to palm, Rebecca was filled with a rush of emotion—some of it old and confined, some of it new and exciting.

"I miss you!" Rebecca whispered, realizing as she heard her own words that she wasn't sure of whether she missed Victor himself or else the freedom she had enjoyed with him for those few precious weeks. But how could she separate those two?

"You know when I first started liking you? I mean, really liking you?" she whispered to Victor. "It was when you never complained, no matter how fast I rode my bicycle. You never told me to slow down, and you never, ever tried to make me stop. You never once said, 'Come back!'"

"Why would I do that?" Victor whispered back. "I love seeing you with your eyes shining and the sunshine in your hair. And I even like having to chase after you," he added.

"You like for me to be *free*," Rebecca answered.

"It's more than like," Victor whispered back. "It's *loving* you—and because of that, I love everything you love."

"I love you, too, Victor," Rebecca murmured against the screen.

And so, for a long, lovely hour or so almost every night, Victor and Rebecca were together, as if the screen wasn't even there. The encounters left them both yearning for each other and for a return to the way they had been—innocent and free and unfettered by edicts. Or by screens.

"I'll come back," Victor always whispered. "I'll come back every night until I find a way for us to be together—really together."

"Yes," Rebecca murmured. "Promise me, Victor!" And she was thinking, *This house has become a prison. Again!* And although Rebecca did not speak aloud, Victor could see the unspoken words in Rebecca's eyes.

"I promise!" Victor whispered, meaning it with all his heart. And so later, as he reluctantly made his way down the long gravel road toward home—a road lit only by moonlight—he renewed that very promise to himself. And to Rebecca. *I'll find a way.*

When Starry prepared to go to Doc's office the next day, she took special pains applying her makeup, and she brushed her chestnut hair until it shone. Selecting a reasonably sedate navy-blue dress with a lace collar, she buttoned the dress and frowned at herself in the mirror. Then, unbuttoning the top three buttons, she aimed a spray of perfume right into her cleavage. She was supposed to be seeing Doc about a headache, but one never knew what parts of the body a physician would choose to examine. The thought brought a flush of blood to her cheeks, and she quickly re-buttoned the dress.

She put on lipstick and powder, but while she was looking in the mirror, she was also trying to plan what she would say to Doc to bring up the topic of Victor and Rebecca. Starry certainly couldn't remind him of Myra's over-protectiveness. One didn't say ill things about the dead. But how to bring up the subject? She didn't know, but as she left her cabin and headed for Doc's small office beside the post office on Main Street in Love-Oak, she determined that she would find a way.

When Starry entered Doc's office, she found herself in a very small waiting room containing only two chairs. The bell over the door had announced her arrival, and Doc came out of an interior room, drying his hands on a towel.

"Starry?" he asked, wiping his hands and adjusting his glasses.

At that point, Starry almost lost her nerve, and unknown to her, she took a quick backwards step.

"Don't go," Doc said gently, coming forward and standing close to her. "Are you ill?"

"No," Starry stammered—and then she reconsidered. "Well, I have these headaches, you see," she murmured, drawing her eyebrows together in a small frown. Before she could even think, Doc moved forward and placed his hand on her forehead. Involuntarily, she felt herself lean into his touch. His hand was warm and soft and smelled of soap.

"No fever," Doc pronounced, and when he removed his hand, Starry stopped herself from a small forward lurch—as if her whole being longed to follow his touch.

"Come into my office and let's see what we can do for you," Doc said, stepping back, opening the door to his inner office for her, and indicating a chair in front of his small desk. As she took the seat, Doc came to her side, picked up her wrist, and looked at his watch as he took her pulse. Starry tried to take a deep breath, to stop her pulse from racing.

"A little fast," Doc murmured. "But nothing to worry about, I'm sure." And with those words, he gave Starry a small smile that increased her pulse even more. Then he pushed up the sleeve of her sedate dress and fastened a cuff around her arm. When he pumped up the cuff, Starry's head began to pound, but again, she took a deep breath and tried to relax.

"Pressure's a little high," Doc said, removing the cuff and taking a seat behind his desk, where he scribbled down information before pulling his glasses down on his nose and looking at Starry over the rims.

"Are you worried about something?" Doc asked. And before she could answer, he added, "Tell me about these headaches. And when you get them." His voice had the effect of drawing words right out of Starry's mouth, even if she didn't know what those words would be.

"Well, sometimes I'm worried about . . . things."

To that, Doc said nothing, just leaned forward over his desk and looked straight into Starry's eyes, waiting. "Well," Starry went on, as if Doc had argued with her. "I worry about everyday things. You know," she added.

"What things?" Doc asked, and he kept his gaze riveted onto Starry's face.

"Little things," Starry repeated, lowering her eyes from Doc's steady gaze.

"What little things?" Doc persisted, noticing Starry's hands in her lap and the way she was twisting her fingers.

Starry had every intention of telling Doc that she was worried about

Victor, but when she opened her mouth to speak, she was surprised at her own words. "Like what's going to happen to me?" As soon as the words left her mouth, she felt the tears spring up in her eyes. Doc took a tissue from the box on his desk, held it out to Starry, and she took it and blotted her eyes. "Just look at me—I'm forty . . ." Here, Starry stopped and took a deep breath. "I'm thirty-nine years old and living in a borrowed cabin at Fiona's, and I don't have anything in this world to call my own. Except for a couple of dresses," she amended. Her face crumpled, and she jammed the tissue against her nose. "And no future," she wailed. "No hope of anything any better."

It wasn't what she meant to say at all. Not at all. And here she was, blubbering and acting a fool and spilling out her heart to a man she hardly knew.

"Oh, that isn't what I meant to say," she exclaimed. But Doc still studied her with a rapt attention that was both comforting and frightening.

"I don't know much about you, Starry. How you came to be living at Fiona and Glory's or anything like that." Now, Starry studied Doc's face as intently as he had been studying hers.

"I loved the wrong man," she finally whispered, dabbing at her nose and determining to share nothing else personal with Doc.

"Were you married?" Doc's question came so softly and unexpectedly, Starry almost gasped.

"No," the word was so terrible that Starry felt a bitter taste in her mouth, but Doc's expression never changed. She thought that her confession of being with a man without being married to him would bring a scowl of disapproval, but that didn't happen.

"Do you still love that wrong man?" Doc dropped his eyes to his desktop, and he fiddled with a stubby pencil, staring at it as if it were the most important thing in the world.

"No," Starry said, and there was no bitter taste to the word this time. Doc picked up the pencil and began writing.

"Well, sounds to me like you just need to think about what you want out of life and start working toward that." Then Doc seemed to have been embarrassed at such a statement, so he hastily added, "How long since you've had your eyes checked?" Doc's question came in the same tone of voice he used in asking the more personal questions, and in making such a pronouncement about what she should be doing with the rest of her life, Starry was surprised to realize that she wanted more of those personal questions. And more of his advice.

"Long time," she answered.

"Well, you need to get them checked," Doc said, still writing. "Here's the name of a good optometrist in Gainesville. Be sure you make an appointment and go see him."

"You think that's what is causing my headaches?" Starry asked, taking the paper.

"Could be," Doc smiled the words. "At least, that's something we should check out and eliminate as the problem. Anything else bothering you?"

Once again, a simple question, tacked on to a seemingly dismissive tone in Doc's voice, surprised her, and she took a deep breath, reminding herself firmly of her original purpose in coming to see Doc.

"I'm worried about Victor," Starry whispered.

At her statement, Doc removed his glasses and rubbed a hand across his eyes.

"I'm sorry," he said. And nothing more.

"I don't suppose you could see your way clear to let Victor and Rebecca see each other again?" There. Starry had said what she came to say.

"No. I'm sorry."

"But why?" Starry didn't mean to ask that question, it simply dropped out of her mouth. Doc looked at her with weary eyes and waited for several moments before he answered.

"I can't explain it," he said at last. "Now you go and get your eyes checked, and see if you need some glasses. If the headaches persist, come and see me again." *Come and see me again.* Starry hung on to the words.

"Thank you," was all she could manage, but as she got up to leave, Doc said, "Thank you for caring about Victor and Rebecca. You're a good lady, Starry. A really good lady."

It wasn't until Starry got out onto the sidewalk and into the bright noontime sunlight that she really heard what Doc had said. *He called me a lady! He called me a really good lady.*

Somehow, she couldn't just go home after hearing that. The words were too beautiful. They had to be relished. And tasted. And pondered upon. Those precious words and the others. *Come and see me again.* So Starry walked partway around the lake, breathing in the sweet, clean air and feeling the warmth of the sunshine on her shoulders. And she heard a voice from deep inside of her heart, a voice that sounded suspiciously like Glory's—*Goodness gracious! What's going on around here? Love just dripping like manna from Heaven. Hanging around all over the place—like Spanish moss in the old live oaks. Victor and Rebecca. Starry . . . and Doc. What's going on? Is it contagious? Lord, I sure hope not!*

"Well?" Fiona asked as soon as Starry came back home from her visit with Doc and her ensuing long walk around the lake.

"I tried, but I didn't have any luck," Starry said, feeling her cheeks flaming. Fiona peered at her closely.

"It's only what I expected," Fiona said. And then she peered at Starry's face even more closely. "But it sure looks like you had some luck about *something*. And if it wasn't about Victor, then what was it?"

"I don't know," Starry answered honestly. "I really don't know."

Chapter Twenty-One

But even while Starry was busy reliving her time with Doc, feeling his warm, gentle hand on her forehead and hearing his words over and over again. *"You're a good lady,"* and *"Come and see me again,"* and while Victor was silently and desperately trying to formulate a plan for being with Rebecca ("I will find a way!")—right in the middle of everything—in the midst of all the *love* that was in the air—some mild and newborn, some more matured and deeply intense, some felt but denied ripening—the whole world changed.

Forever.

On that lazy Sunday afternoon, Victor was down at the Trading Post with Old Man and Arabella. Glory was sitting on the front porch with Starry, with Glory dozing off from time to time and Starry looking out over the lake—somewhat longingly, Fiona thought. There were times—and this was one of them—when Fiona really felt bad for Starry, who was getting older and had no husband, no children, no family—and all because she had put all her eggs into one basket. A basket named Middy. And after all, Starry really wasn't that unattractive—not since she was wearing decent clothes and letting her hair be its natural color—a deep, russet chestnut that Fiona thought was really quite lovely.

More than once, Fiona had mentioned Starry in her prayers. "Father, please let some nice man come along for Starry—someone who will appreciate her for who she is." But so far, Fiona's prayers had gone unanswered, even when she thought that perhaps Doc was the answer to her prayer for Starry. And truthfully, Starry had been somewhat evasive about her visit with Doc and her attempt to question his edict regarding Victor and Rebecca. Still, Starry's cheeks had more color in them, and she seemed to be resting in a strange, new contentment that Fiona couldn't quite figure out. Could only hope that this was a new beginning for Starry.

On that fateful Sunday afternoon, Fiona left Starry and Glory sitting on the porch and went into the pantry right off the kitchen where she discovered that some homemade fig preserves had oozed out from under the lids and needed to be cleaned up. That was a small blessing to Fiona—no problem figuring that out. No problem knowing how to take care of it. She had just wrung out a dishcloth in warm, soapy water when

Victor came racing on his bicycle up to the screen door on the back porch. He didn't even get off the bike—just yelled out, "Turn on the radio! Turn on the radio!" and then he was off and gone again.

Glory and Starry, who had seen Victor come tearing around the side of the house at breakneck speed, came into the kitchen.

"What's he yelling about?" Glory asked. Without answering, Fiona turned the small black knob on the radio on the kitchen counter.

The garbled, frantic voice that came into the kitchen was a stark and confusing contrast to the usual Sunday afternoon radio programs the women sometimes enjoyed, and for several minutes, they stood, straining their ears, trying to catch the meaning behind the almost hysterical words. "Pearl Harbor—sneak attack—Japan." They stood, frozen in disbelief, as did most Americans who were simply enjoying a quiet Sunday afternoon.

"Hawaii?" Glory asked, pronouncing it "Hawa-yaa. Where's that?"

"I'm not sure," Fiona said.

"Across the ocean, but not toward Europe," Starry answered. Fiona and Glory looked at her, somewhat startled, and then they all fell silent once again. The radio announcer continued to report the terrible news, with his voice breaking from time to time, and Fiona, Glory and Starry sank silently into the chairs around the kitchen table, saying nothing but listening as hard as possible.

"This terrible attack," Fiona moaned. "Now there will be war. Oh my God—Victor!"

"He's too young," Starry whispered. "He's only sixteen."

"Please, God!" Fiona replied, without worrying about whether her words made any sense at all. God Himself would know what she meant.

"Where *is* he?" Fiona yelped. "Where *is* he?"

"Out on his bicycle, just like always," Glory said. "Nothing's changed *here.*" But as soon as she said that, they all knew that Glory was wrong—everything had changed. Absolutely everything.

They sat in the kitchen together for hours, listening to various accounts of the devastation and of the many lives that were lost. They listened in disbelief, forgetting to make a pot of coffee or to start preparing supper.

Finally, the late afternoon sun came into the window over the sink in a long, lonely-looking finger—the particular ray of sunshine Fiona had always hated, but she didn't know why. It was that time of day—the dying sun and dark coming, and the way that slant of light cast something almost like a pall over everything. When she was in high school, her teacher had read a poem to the class about "a certain slant of light," and Fiona, still a child back then, had gotten goose bumps all over her arms, because she had discovered that somebody else in the world *understood* exactly what Fiona had felt—still felt but could not put into better words, all those years later.

Fiona got up from the table to turn on a lamp, just to partially dispel the loneliness of the ray of sunlight lying across the edge of the sink, and as she turned on the light, the back door burst open and Victor came running into the kitchen. His face was glowing red from having ridden his bicycle so hard, and the rush of cool air around him bore the perfume of fresh air and green fronds. His eyes burned almost a neon blue, and his mouth was grim. "I heard it on the radio down at the Trading Post," he gasped. And then he added, "Bastards! Stinking bastards!" His voice deep and raspy and bitter in a way Fiona had never heard before. Fiona almost automatically told Victor not to use such language, that it wasn't worthy of a gentleman, but then she thought better of admonishing him.

Because Victor was absolutely right. *Bastards! Stinking bastards!*

Chapter Twenty-Two

The very next day—December 8—President Roosevelt declared that the United States was at war with Japan. While they all sat in the kitchen listening to the radio broadcast, Glory rocked slightly from side to side in the chair, moaning under her breath, and Fiona studied Victor as if she could never get enough of looking at him. She wondered how something that happened so far away could utterly change her beautiful boy in a flash. For she thought that his entire face had suddenly grown into more manly planes, and the bony protuberances that supported his pale eyebrows had strengthened and asserted themselves above the neon blue of his eyes. On his chin, the few straggling blonde whiskers had grown into a small multitude that shone in the pale light from the window.

Fiona noticed that Starry, too, had a different look about her. She had pulled her thick hair back into a band, without much regard to how it looked. And more importantly, at least to Fiona, was the fact that Starry had failed to repair the chipped polish on her fingernails—the first time, ever, that Fiona had seen her without perfect nails. Because Starry's work of cleaning and filleting the fish for the restaurant was hard on her manicure, and she had a cigar box full of polish, files, clippers, cotton pads, and so forth, just for maintaining her nails. Usually, she worked on her nails every single evening, while they sat around listening to the radio programs they had always enjoyed *A Date with Judy* and *Amos 'n' Andy*—but with that last show, even though they all laughed heartily at the antics of Amos and Andy, Glory sometimes shook her head and muttered, "Don't know why they have to sound so dumb all the time!"

But the program that struck the most fear into them was *The Shadow*, and when that disembodied voice came on—"Who knows what evil lurks in the hearts of men? The shadow knows!"—Glory would put her hands over her ears. But now, the radio stayed tuned to the news most of the time, and truthfully, none of them could really remember when—such a short time ago—they had laughed and listened and prickled with goose bumps over *Gangbusters*, without another care in this world! It all seemed so long ago and far away. And now, if *The Shadow* program ever came on again, they all *knew*, without any doubt, what evil could lurk in the hearts of men.

Sometimes, just as Fiona was falling asleep, that voice would come into her head. . . "Who knows what evil . . ." and she would say a fervent prayer for the safety of all the good American soldiers and an even more fervent prayer that Victor—her Victor—would not become one of them.

On that Monday night following the attack on Pearl Harbor and the President's announcement of war, Victor waited, as usual, in the shrubbery just outside Doc's screened porch. And when Rebecca sneaked onto the dark porch, her first words to Victor were, "You didn't come last night."

"I know. I'm sorry," Victor whispered back. "The attack." And he added nothing more, because Rebecca—and everyone else—knew what that terrible word now meant.

"What will happen?" Rebecca whispered. "Will you have to fight in the war?" The abrupt question erased all of the carefully planned words he had rehearsed, the words that would have told her that he now had two duties to fulfill—his duty to her, as his beloved, and his duty to his country. And how he meant to fulfill them both.

"Yes," he answered, and her silence told him everything he needed to know. "I have to go," he explained. "I *want* to go."

"No!" A louder whisper that made Rebecca cringe against her own voice and glance uneasily toward the kitchen door.

"Yes," Victor said, and the word carried all of his resolve.

"What if you . . . don't come back?" she asked.

"Oh, I *will* come back," Victor whispered. "Because I will have *you* to come back to." Rebecca put her hand against the screen, and Victor placed his against it from the other side.

"I'll wait for you, Victor," Rebecca tried to stifle a sob.

"I want more than that," Victor whispered. "I need more than that to come back to."

"What do you mean?"

"I will come back to you as my wife. I want us to be married before I go."

He waited for her hand to withdraw from the screen. But it didn't.

"Yes," Rebecca whispered. "Oh yes—but when? How?"

"Two weeks from right now. Two weeks from this very night. Come onto the porch, just like always, but then come outside. I'll be waiting behind the shed. Be careful!" he admonished. "Before then, put some oil on the door hinges so they won't make any noise. But don't let anyone see you do it."

"All right. But how will we get to . . . wherever we're going?" she asked.

"I don't know yet," Victor answered frankly. "That's why we have to wait until I get everything figured out. I think we're old enough to be married in Georgia. Bring your birth certificate and be careful—if Doc catches us, he'll send you away." Rebecca knew that Victor was right—they had to be very careful. There was a long silence between them then, with Victor thinking about how he could get the two of them across the state line and into Georgia and with Rebecca wondering where her birth certificate was. Probably in her papa's valuable papers file, in the drawer of his desk. And just thinking about what she and Victor were planning on doing brought tears to Rebecca's eyes. She took a deep breath.

"I lied to you," Rebecca whispered, and Victor was startled by her words. In his imagination, he and Rebecca were already on a Greyhound bus, crossing over into Georgia. *Rebecca lied? About what? About marrying me?*

"You lied?" Victor whispered back.

"Yes." Rebecca's face, partially hidden behind the rusted screen, suddenly took on an elfin quality, and her dark eyes sparkled. "I lied about that kiss," she confessed. And then her beautiful mouth—the mouth speaking those confusing words—broke into a smile. "It was a wonderful kiss," she whispered.

"Why did you lie?" Victor couldn't stop the words, remembering the agony he had suffered.

"I don't know," Rebecca replied. "Maybe I thought it would be more like the kisses you see in the movies. You know, with us wrapped up in each other's arms and music playing. Or something like that. When it wasn't, I wanted to hurt you. I'm sorry. What I really want is for you to kiss me again and again and never stop."

As Rebecca whispered, the porch light suddenly came on, and without even thinking, Victor ducked down into the shrubs around the porch.

"What're you doing out here?" Aunt Irma's voice, raspy with sleep.

Victor's heart was pounding so hard, he felt that Irma would be able to hear it. But Rebecca answered Irma in such a calm and relaxed way, she dispelled any fear he may have felt, "I'm just sitting out here by myself, Aunt Irma," she said. "Looking at the stars."

"You can see stars from inside the porch?" Irma asked.

"A little," Rebecca said, tilting her neck and making sure that she could glimpse a small sliver of nighttime sky between the porch roof and the shed where her bicycle was securely locked away.

"And who are you talking to?" The hair on Victor's neck bristled, but Rebecca kept her calm demeanor.

"I was reciting poetry, Aunt Irma," Rebecca said. "Saying poetry and looking at the stars just seem to go together, don't they?"

"Humph," Irma grunted. "You weren't going to go out, were you?" Irma's voice was filled with skepticism.

"Oh, no, ma'am," Rebecca assured her. "You can look at the screen door and see it's still latched." Irma peered at the screen door and saw that Rebecca was telling the truth. "Well, you better get on to bed," Irma said, as if she were somehow disappointed that she hadn't caught Rebecca trying to go outside. "It's awful late," she added, standing by the kitchen door, obviously determined to wait until Rebecca was inside the house and in her own bed. "Sitting out here in the dark, looking at stars and saying poetry. Whoever heard of such a thing?"

So while Victor crouched noiselessly in the shrubbery, Rebecca stretched slowly and strolled behind her aunt into the kitchen, turning off the porch light as she went and not even glancing at the side of the porch where she knew that Victor was hiding. The door lock clicked firmly into place.

Crouched in the dark, Victor felt something strangely familiar in the far reaches of his mind when Rebecca went inside of the house. *A skirt that moved from side to side as someone—who?—walked away from him.* The image stirred a vague sadness in his heart, but he didn't know why.

While Victor was making his solitary way home that night, his mind was filled with whirling thoughts and images that flitted about like a flock of nervous sea birds—flying in all different directions and with no evident thought of where they would land. First of all, he had to provide for Rebecca, and he didn't know how he would do that. True, he had a small amount of money in a savings account—supposed to be to help pay for him to go off to college some day. It would be enough to get them to Georgia, where they could be married and find a small place to live. Perhaps they could take a room in a boarding house. That thought pleased him, because it meant that when he went off for army basic training, Rebecca would be in a safe place while she waited for him to come home . . . come home from *where?* That was what he didn't know. But once he was in the army, there would be money for him to send to her. Not much, perhaps, but enough. It would have to be enough.

And while Victor was walking in the dark toward home, the small world around him was going on at another pace. Fiona was lying awake in her dark room, wondering as she did every evening, exactly where Victor went when he "went out," and why. If Glory was to be believed, he was somehow with Rebecca. And Doc must not know about that, or he would have done something to stop it. But how could Rebecca and Victor meet, without Doc knowing? *Oh, if only he were still a child!* She thought, fretfully. *I could forbid him to go out at all. I could keep him here, safe and with me. But no—he grew up and became a man. And now, I can't stop him from doing anything he chooses—going to war or seeing Rebecca. Whatever the future holds, maybe I just don't want to know.*

Glory, also unable to sleep, had tiptoed out of her room and was sitting on the darkened front porch, looking out at the lake and at the fish restaurant on the pier. In the nighttime air, they both looked eerie and somewhat unreal, and Glory was thinking about almost everything at once—Jubilee, and what would happen to her, if she kept trying to overstep the place where she should be. With her own kind. Because after all, that was the way things had always been done. And more, it was the law. And Victor—now a grown man and how little and vulnerable he had been when he first came to them. How she had loved him. How she loved him still.

Starry, too, was lying awake in her tiny cabin, where a sliver of moonlight came between the curtains and rested upon her pillow. Starry was thinking about Doc, feeling his warm, soft hand on her forehead, hearing his gentle voice advising her to decide what she wanted for the rest of her life. And the answer was that she wanted *him*. But it was also more. She wanted to do something . . . anything . . . to help with the war effort. How could she simply keep on filleting fish and making coleslaw when her country was at war?

And what Starry decided that night was something she wanted to tell Doc about. So she would go back to see him one more time before she put her plan into action. Briefly, she wondered if she was being a good patient who wanted to tell him that his advice had been well taken, or was she simply hoping that he would place his warm hand upon her brow one more time? Starry didn't know the answer, and truthfully, she didn't really care. The main thing was that she had a plan, and it was one that didn't entertain the slightest interest in having Middy . . . or any other man like him . . . to come back into her life. But Doc? Well, that was something different. And maybe—just maybe—she should be the one to take the first step. Let him know that she wanted to get to know him better. Starry wasn't sure, but she would bet almost anything that Myra had been very cold to him. And for a very long time. Because there was something small and sad in his eyes that told her this truth. So perhaps his heart was simply asleep—anesthetized like a patient on a table? If so, then Starry would be the perfect one to wake him up. To life. And to love.

Wouldn't she?

Chapter Twenty-Three

In the Trading Post the next day, Old Man sat, as almost always, in his chair in the corner. His eyes were closed, but he was not sleeping. Instead, he was listening to two tourist women talking in low tones to each other about the terrible attack on Pearl Harbor.

"Sally's boy is stationed in Hawaii," one of the women whispered to the other. "At Hickam Air Force Base. Did you know that?"

"No! Has she heard from him? Is he all right?"

"She doesn't know. It's terrible, the waiting. She just doesn't know."

Old Man did not open his eyes, but because he was living up to his name more and more—a much older man now and more dream laden than ever—he could see, imprinted on the insides of his eyelids, the face of his son Wahali. Old Man snorted softly. *For him to think that I didn't know what he was up to! That I couldn't tell just from looking at him that he was going to find a way to get into this war. The way Wahali looked at his mother. The silent pain in his eyes. And the resolve.*

"Dream laden," the words echoed in his somnolent mind.

But when Old Man slipped into yet another dream, it was not one about his son or about the war. It was his grandmother's old fable about twins. He could hear her own voice in his dream—*"Long ago, a great hunter left his chickee to hunt for food. While he was gone, a panther came and killed and ate the hunter's wife, who was great with child. The panther left behind only her great womb, and the hunter, in his grief, took the womb and placed it in a hole in the ground. When time was done, twins emerged from the solitary womb. One of the twins became lightning and the other became thunder. Together, they lived out their lives high in the sky, always fighting with each other. This is why twins must always be separated. Always. Because if they are together, there is always great danger."*

He was awakened by a loud laugh from a tourist in the Trading Post shop, but not before his grandmother's face appeared at the very end of his dream. *"Two,"* she said to him, pressing her finger into his chest, so that when he awakened, he could still feel her strong finger against his chest, right over his heart.

Dream laden.

But it was no dream that the world had begun changing all around them. Most of the young men went right off to army training—and some too young and some too old lied openly in order to go to war. A few of the older men, whose real ages were found out and some who were simply too old to try and fool anyone, sat around outside of the barber shop in town every single day, telling and retelling stories of their exploits in World War I, their gnarled hands simulating bombers descending upon the enemy, and their wrinkled lips imitating the sound of screaming engines and falling bombs. Somehow, that incredible, undying spirit, though encased in bodies too old for war, was comforting to people in the town.

Other changes had come about, and those changes were what Starry was depending upon. As the area emptied of young, able men, young women began tying scarves around their heads, donning shapeless overalls, and signing on for various shifts at the converted manufacturing plant near Gainesville, although no one knew what the plant was being used for now—something hush-hush to do with the war. And one of those women, though not such a young one, was Starry.

Glory immediately suspected that something was up with Starry, and she shared that curiosity with Fiona. They both watched and saw that Starry was quietly and quickly teaching Arabella how to clean and filet the fish, and they knew it wasn't at all like Starry to try and shirk her work. On the contrary—Glory always thought that Starry seemed to take some kind of a perverted pleasure in gutting the fish, perhaps imagining that she was doing the same thing to the stepfather of so long ago who had forced himself upon the thirteen-year-old girl-child. But whatever the impetus, her strokes with the knife were savage but accurate.

So without saying a word to anyone, Starry showed Arabella all of the techniques, and when Arabella was proficient, Starry made her announcement right after the Kaltenborn news program went off the air. "I've taken me a job at the plant," she said. "And what that means is I'll be living with a friend in Gainesville during the week—or whenever my shift turns out to be." When no one spoke, she continued, "There's a bus runs from the post office here up to the plant every day, but it's a long ride and no need for me to be here all the time."

Fiona's first question, of course, was, "A friend? A woman friend or a man friend?" Starry sighed in a little disappointment. "A woman friend, Miss Fiona. You know I'm a good girl!"

"Where'd you meet her? How'd you hear about the job in the plant?"

"Her name is Mikela, and I met her a long time ago, when Middy and me were working a song-and-dance routine in a bar up north of

Gainesville. Hadn't seen her in years, of course, but one of the fishermen who came here about a year ago turns out to be her uncle, and I gave him my address here, so he could give it to her and she could write to me, if she wanted to."

"And she wanted to," Fiona answered.

"Sure did. Said she was happy to know where I was and what I was doing, and she also asked me about Middy. So I told her I didn't know where he was and didn't really care. Then she went on about the job she had in a plant and how important it was to the war effort. Got me to thinking, that letter did."

"Uncle?" Fiona's mind seemed to be lagging behind Starry's words.

"Yess'm?"

"I said, 'uncle?'" Fiona repeated.

"Yess'm, her uncle," Starry repeated, somewhat puzzled.

"A *real* uncle, or maybe the kind of man some girls call 'uncle,' just for decorum?"

"Oh, Miss Fiona—a real uncle, to be sure. His younger brother was Mikela's daddy—the one who owned the bar we worked in for a while. He got run over by a truck and died, so Mikela's uncle sort of took over looking after her."

"And what kind of job is it you'll be doing in that plant?"

"I don't know," Starry confessed. "It's all real secret, so I won't know until I get there. One thing I do know is that the pay's real good, and lots of women are working there—you know, women whose men are off at the war or who don't have a man anyway and need to earn their own living."

"So the only time you'll be here is when you're off from work?"

"Yess'm. There's an extra bus that goes back and forth between Love-Oak and some other towns around here and the plant, and I'll use that, whenever I have some time off."

Fiona was silent for a long time, and then she whispered, "We'll miss you, Starry."

"I'll miss you all too. But it sure feels good for me to be doing *something* to help with the war!" And her words sank into Fiona's heart. *Something! There had to be something she could do! Something beside stomping on empty cans to flatten them out!*

When Victor heard the news about Starry, he made a mental note. He and Rebecca would have to be careful not to take the bus that went to the plant, but the regular bus that went right to Gainesville—and then on to Folkston, Georgia. This was just one more cog to be accounted for in the wheel of Victor's plans.

On the day before Starry left, she went to see Doc. The small waiting room in his office was empty, and once again, he seemed surprised to see Starry there.

"Are you ill again?" he queried in a concerned voice. "Those headaches come back?"

"No," Starry whispered, hoping against hope that he would come forward and put that gentle, warm hand on her brow. But he didn't. So she continued, "I just wanted you to know that I've taken your advice about making plans for my life."

"Oh?" Doc asked. "And?" While his words were few, his mind was filled with knowledge about Starry that perhaps she thought no one else knew—that she had arrived at Fiona's camp in the company of a man who, as the story went, simply left without her. But of course, Doc said nothing. After all, that was only cheap gossip. But he was reasonably certain that was the "wrong man" Starry had spoken about before.

"I'm going to work in the plant up near Gainesville," Starry said. "I'm going to help with the war effort."

"Yes, I've heard that plant was hiring women to work there."

Starry waited, hoping he would say something else. And he finally did. "I wish you good luck, Starry." Her name was honey on his tongue, and Starry felt a tremor go through her. Doc looked down at the floor.

"When do you leave?" he asked at last.

"Tomorrow afternoon," Starry replied. "There's a bus goes right from here to the plant."

"Then may I offer to pick you up at Fiona's and give you a lift into town?" Doc asked. "Actually, I need to go out your way and check on the Allen boy. Stubborn case of measles." And then he added, "Thank goodness, the government gives me extra gasoline rations. What time does your bus leave?"

"Three-thirty," Starry said. "And I appreciate the ride. I'll have a suitcase to carry and it's a long walk."

"Three o'clock, then," Doc said, and he gave Starry a crooked smile that left her weak in the knees, but with a knowing look in her eyes.

That next afternoon was blustery and rainy when Starry came running down the path from her own little cabin to Fiona's cottage. She held a rain slicker over her head and the old valise Fiona had loaned to her bumped heavily against her thigh. She came up onto the porch, grinning, dropped the valise and the slicker from over her head, and twirled around, showing Glory and Fiona her baggy overalls—her working uniform in the plant for making . . . something. Under the overalls, however, Starry wore a bright red and white polka-dot blouse and she had her hair tied up in a matching red scarf.

"Ta-da!" she twirled happily, with Fiona and Glory looking on approvingly. Victor had come out onto the porch and retreated to the corner, exactly the place where Old Man had guarded them all from Starry and Middy, those long years ago.

"You're a working woman, Starry!" he laughed. "And you're helping our country win this war. Wish I could help too," he said, somehow relishing the secret he harbored. Fiona blanched at his joyful voice and his willingness to "work" for his country, but all she could picture was her beautiful Victor, wearing a uniform and marching away—away from Love-Oak and *her*.

"You're too young," Fiona snapped, without really meaning to.

"I *know*, Aunt Fiona," Victor snapped back.

"Just don't you be in any hurry," Fiona murmured, and she didn't notice that Victor was not smiling. Right at that moment, Doc's car came turning into the driveway in front of the porch, and he pulled as close to the front steps as possible. Starry, in too much of a hurry to give hugs all around, simply blew kisses toward them, put the slicker back over her head, and dashed down the steps to the car.

Victor turned his face away and pretended to look up into the rain clouds. He could not . . . would not . . . meet Doc's eyes, not with what he was planning.

"How is Rebecca?" Fiona called to Doc, and as soon as the words left her mouth, she regretted them. This wasn't the time or the place for her to inquire about Rebecca. But Doc smiled, waved and shouted, "Fine. Just fine," before he put the car into gear. Just as the car pulled away, Fiona saw Starry's arm slip around the back of Doc's seat and the slight twitch of surprise in Doc's neck. And then Starry's face, grinning at her through the rear window.

Lord help Doc if Starry really decided to go after him!

But suddenly, the porch seemed too quiet. Fiona was wondering just when Starry had become such a vital part of the little camp. It hadn't been that long since the rainy afternoon—one exactly like this—that Starry and that despicable man, Middy, had come running across the yard and up onto their porch. That was when they'd first gotten Victor. So it *had* been a while. Just didn't seem like it.

Fiona glanced over to where Victor was sitting on the wet banister, staring up into the gray clouds. Was Glory right? Was something going on?

Chapter Twenty-Four

The day after Starry's departure, Arabella came to work as usual, but she spoke almost not at all. Such silence was unusual for the ebullient Arabella.

"You okay?" Glory ventured.

"No, but that's all right," Arabella responded, and Glory rightfully figured that whenever Arabella got ready to say what was on her mind, she'd spill it out. Finally, after sneaking tissues from her pocket to wipe her eyes and nose while she was cleaning and filleting the morning catch, Arabella spoke the words she dreaded, herself, to hear. "I got a letter from Wahali—he's left the monastery. He's in army training."

"Left the monastery?" Glory tried to make her voice sound surprised, but truthfully, she had never understood why anyone would want to go to a place like that anyway.

"Gone to army training," Arabella repeated. "When he's done with training, he gets to come home for a few days, and then . . ." Arabella's voice trailed off.

"And then he'll go off to war," Glory whispered.

"Yes," Arabella hiccoughed. "Then he'll go off to war."

"What does Old Man say?" For a moment, Glory had tried to remember Old Man's Indian name, because they had all agreed not to call him Old Man to Arabella. But the name had been strange sounding, and Glory had forgotten it, if she had ever really known it. Usually, they just said "your husband," but this time, Glory forgot. And besides, she had also forgotten that Old Man never said a word of any kind. This would probably be no different.

Arabella looked at Glory with her eyes full of misery. "He says nothing," Arabella reported. "But I know his eyes, and they are proud. His eyes say that his son is a *warrior!*"

"When will he get home?" Glory asked, already beating eggs for the fish batter and trying not to stare at Arabella's tragic face.

"I'm not sure. Whenever he's done with training. I don't know when that will be."

"Well, I'll pray for you all," Glory said. "And I'll pray especially hard for Wa . . . Wa . . ." She tried again and then gave up. "For Brother John," she said finally.

But Glory didn't have much time to pray for "Brother John," because only two days later, Wahali called Arabella long distance and told her that he would be coming home on leave the next day, now that his basic training was completed. And that's all anyone could think of, especially because of Arabella. She had gone into a state of mixed-up joy and despair, because they all knew that he would be going overseas as soon as his leave was over, but she busied herself by going around to everyone she knew, shamelessly begging meat rations. In only one day, she gathered enough to buy three frying chickens and a small round steak. That cut of steak would be too tough for simply broiling, so Arabella planned on making smothered, braised steak out of it. And she discussed the recipe endlessly, to the point where Glory finally whispered to Fiona, "In all my born days, I've never had a piece of anything called 'smothered steak' in my life, but I'm just sick to death of hearing about it."

At last, the taxi brought Wahali home, and when Arabella saw him, she cried harder than ever, because he was lean and tanned and broad of shoulder and decked out in a uniform, so that none of them could have recognized him. Arabella came charging out of the restaurant kitchen, fairly flying over the uneven boards of the pier, and once again, she was swept up in his arms, where she wept openly against his chest, the buttons on his uniform jacket burning into her cheeks.

"Why?" Arabella sobbed against his uniform. "Why couldn't you stay *there*, where you were safe?" Hearing that question, Fiona and Glory turned aside, because they couldn't bear to hear the anguish in Arabella's voice. But his answer was calm and quiet, and both Fiona and Glory heard it clearly. "Mama, I was a monk, and I loved it. But I'm Seminole, and I'm American."

For this visit, Wahali stayed in his mother and father's house at the far end of the lake, and whatever he'd been thinking so hard about when he stayed in the cabin and spent so many hours walking up and down the lakeshore seemed to have been resolved by the wearing of the uniform and the trim fitness of his body.

Victor, who was on hand to help carry Wahali's duffel bag, stared at the fine uniform and the short haircut and the bright shine in Wahali's eyes. Victor tossed the big bag up onto his shoulder, ready to take it all the way down the lakeside to Arabella's house.

"I can take that, Victor," Wahali said, having shaken Victor's hand and clapped him on the shoulder.

"No," Victor insisted. "I *want* to do that for you. It's the least I can do." As Arabella, Wahali and Victor started off for the cottage, Wahali asked Victor, "You want to take a walk with me after supper? I can tell you all about basic training."

"That would be swell," Victor responded, expanding his chest a bit.

Fiona and Glory overheard that and looked at each other without smiling.

"You ever wonder why Victor's so interested in basic training?" Glory asked, but Fiona didn't answer. "He's too young, isn't he?" Glory persisted, asking questions that Fiona didn't even want to think about. "I mean, without permission?"

"Yes," Fiona snapped. "He's too young." *But somehow I fear that will not stop him!*

Glory went back to the restaurant kitchen, and Fiona sat down in one of the rocking chairs on the porch. Her mind was so full of swirling thought, she almost felt dizzy. *I wonder, did I ever feel what Victor is obviously feeling about Rebecca? And about that stinking war and finding a way to get right into the middle of it?*

The answer was *no*. She could never understand the male impulse to fight—the closest any woman could come to it was the truly savage impulse to protect her young. And Lord knows, she had never felt about J. Roy the way Victor seemed to feel about Rebecca. *Did I miss something?* Fiona asked herself silently. *Did I miss something important? And did J. Roy know I didn't love him enough? Did he want more from me than I was able to give?*

The questions depressed her terribly, and as always, she retreated to the scrub buckets and mops and went about cleaning two of the cabins that needed it. *This will do it,* she thought, *the aroma of pine oil and bleach and the sunshine smell of clean bed linens. Yes, this will certainly do it.*

When Arabella, Wahali and Victor got to the house, Old Man was sitting out on the porch, watching as they came across the lakeshore and into the yard.

"Hi, Pop!" Wahali shouted, going to his father, bending down, and embracing him gently. Old Man's eyes were cloudy, and for a moment, he seemed confused. He looked at Wahali for only a moment before he turned those great, dark eyes on Victor.

"Two," Old Man said, his voice as raspy as an old, broken hinge.

"What?" Wahali asked him. "Pop! You spoke!"

"He's been saying that one word for a couple of days now," Arabella said. "It's the first thing I've ever heard him say, and I don't know what it means!"

"Pop?" Wahali kneeled down in front of his father. "What are you saying, Pop?"

Old Man's eyes stayed riveted on Victor.

"Two," he repeated, raising his hand and pointing directly at Victor.

"Two?" Victor parroted. Old Man nodded his head emphatically and then closed his eyes, resting his hands on his chest. Wahali looked at Arabella, and she simply shook her head. Victor took Wahali's duffel bag from his shoulder and placed it on the porch.

"Miss Arabella, do you mind if I take a little walk with Wahali . . . I need to speak with him privately." Victor asked, and Arabella looked from Wahali to Victor and back again. Wahali didn't wait for her answer but turned and went back down the porch steps, clapping Victor on the shoulder to follow him. Together, they walked across the yard and went slowly along the lakeshore.

"What's up, Victor?" Wahali asked when they were beyond hearing distance to the house.

"I probably won't be here when you leave," Victor explained. "And after I'm gone, I want you to tell Aunt Fiona and Glory, so they won't worry."

"And where are you going that they don't know about?" Wahali asked, frowning.

"Rebecca and I are running away to get married. And after that, I'm joining the army myself." For long moments, Wahali and Victor walked side by side, with neither of them saying anything. Finally, Wahali spoke.

"I wish you all the best," he said.

"Aren't you going to try to talk me out of it?" Victor was surprised at Wahali's quiet acceptance of his plans.

"No," Wahali laughed. "Because it wouldn't do any good, would it?"

"That's right!" Victor almost yelled.

"But aren't you too young to join the army?" Wahali asked.

"Yes, but I'll forge Aunt Fiona's signature."

"That's been done before, plenty of times," Wahali admitted, just as a breeze suddenly picked up, rippling the surface of the lake and setting the palm fronds to rattling. Silently, Wahali raised his face to the night sky, and Victor, watching him, could almost envision a white egret feather nestled firmly in the GI haircut. The breeze stopped and then started again, a hot, fervent breeze with small threads of icy air intertwined in it. "Weather front coming in. Or a storm," Wahali pronounced.

At the same time, in Arabella's kitchen, the voice on the radio warned of a tropical storm that was approaching from the Caribbean and would probably come ashore somewhere around St. Augustine. Arabella heard, but she really didn't care. Her heart was simply waiting for a pan full of golden cornbread to be finished baking. For her son. In the skillet, the smothered steak simmered gently.

On the lakeshore, Wahali turned to Victor, reaching out and shaking his hand. "Good luck to you. And to Rebecca," Wahali said, and then he turned and walked back toward the house, leaving Victor standing by the lakeside.

Victor stood alone for a long time, knowing in his heart that he had passed through some kind of a door inside of himself and that it had closed behind him, forever. But it was such a beautiful door!

His thoughts were interrupted by a rustle in the palmettos, and he called out, "Who's there?" His voice was soft, but it contained a tone of alarm.

"Just me," Jubilee said, standing up among the palmettos.

"Ju-bee?" Victor's mind was racing between being glad to see her and being worried that she had overheard everything he and Wahali had been saying to each other. "What are you doing here?" Victor laughed.

"I followed you," Jubilee said. "I follow you lots of time and you don't even know it." Victor gazed at Jubilee's familiar face—familiar, yet not familiar, for in his mind, he always saw a child's face, but Jubilee was certainly no longer a child. She was a young woman, a beautiful young woman—or at least she would have been beautiful, if she could have softened her scowl and loosened the hardness of her chin.

"You followed me? But why?" Victor stopped worrying about what Jubilee might have overheard, and he simply concentrated on the slightly anguished face of his old friend. Right in front of Victor's eyes, Jubilee's face lost its hard-edged, petulant expression, and her eyes softened to the point where Victor halfway expected them to melt and run down her cheeks, along with the stray drops of rain that had started to fall.

"Because I love you so much, Victor. You must already know that." Jubilee sighed, looking down at the ground, as if she couldn't bear to look at Victor's face for another moment. "Will you kiss me?" she asked. A simple request, with resignation stitched in and around it. The same sort of question Rebecca had asked him not so long ago.

"Of course, Ju-bee," Victor said, and before she could speak again, he leaned forward and kissed her cheek.Immediately, tears flowed down her face.

"Why don't you love me, Victor?" she asked. "Because I do love you so much."

"I do love you, Ju-bee," Victor answered.And then he added, "But not in *that* way. I love you as my friend."

"Even after I told Doc about you and Rebecca kissing?" she inquired, her eyes still cast down.

"Even after that," Victor assured her. But her next question took him completely by surprise—"Would you love me *that other* way if I was a white girl?" Victor waited before he answered, searching his own heart and mind, and seeing in his memory the wonderful face of Glory—the mahogany skin, the tiny, tight curls of hair, the warmth of her arms, her deep, kind eyes.

"If you were a white girl, Ju-bee, I would still love you the same way—as my friend," he proclaimed, feeling a warmth in his chest as these words came out, because he knew them to be the absolute truth.

Jubilee's hand came up, and she cupped Victor's face for a brief moment. "I'll always love you, Victor. Always," she whispered, and then she turned and walked away into the darkness.

Victor watched her go, and something deep inside of him felt a moment of grief.

Oh, Ju-bee! What did you hear me say this night?

From his chair on the porch, Old Man heard the weather report from the radio in the kitchen. And more.

Victor didn't hear the news about the storm, because he was once again on his way to Doc's house, where later, he and Rebecca would whisper through the screen. But not for much longer.

Chapter Twenty-Five

On the following Tuesday, Fiona, Glory and Victor sat at the kitchen table after supper, listening to the radio, especially to the news about the war. But also the weather, and at the same time, listening to the rising wind.

"I hope Starry gets home okay," Fiona said.

"She supposed to come tonight?" Glory asked.

"That's what she said. But of course, with the plant running day and night, I guess we should just expect her when we see her. She's only been there a week."

Victor was listening, but in a strange, new way, knowing as he did that this would be the last time he sat around the kitchen table with the two women who had raised him, who had taken him into their home and their hearts. The ones who had soothed his nightmares away and bandaged his scraped knees. He thought of Starry and added to himself, *The one who read so many books to me.* All the women who loved him and had never left him. For a brief moment, he thought about his *real* mother, and he finally realized in the fullest sense Fiona and Glory were his real mothers. Finally and for all times.

His glances at them, as they talked about the worsening weather and about Starry, were guarded, and he bit the inside of his cheek to keep tears from springing up in his eyes. And then he thought about Rebecca, could almost feel her slipping into his arms. After the long weeks of being with her only through the screen of the back porch, he ached to hold her, to bury his nose in her hair, to feel the warm softness of her body against his. To lie beside her on the lakeshore, just as they had done before—breathing in the sunshine aroma of her skin. No sunshine now—just a storm coming and coming fast.

But some small part of his mind was also on Jubilee. Exactly what had she overheard when he was walking on the lakeshore with Wahali?

Victor was reasonably certain he'd failed to mention anything about *when* he and Rebecca planned to run away. And besides, wasn't Jubilee supposed to be his friend? Surely, she wouldn't say anything, even if she knew. And she didn't know.

"Honey," Glory's voice broke into his reverie. "What on earth you thinking on? It's like you're not even here."

"I'm sorry," he whispered, looking at the tablecloth.

Glory continued, "You sitting there, so dreamy-like and looking 'rond this room like you never saw it before in your life. What's going on with you?" Glory had a way of going right to the primary question, without what she called "pussyfooting around," which is the way Fiona always asked questions—or rather, resisted asking them, tried so hard not to ask them, because she really didn't want to know the answers.

"Nothing's going on," Victor mumbled. Glory and Fiona exchanged glances, both of them knowing that wasn't the truth.

"Sure coulda fooled me!" Glory mumbled, getting up and gathering the supper dishes from the table. As Victor started to stand up, Fiona reached across the table and put her hand over his. "What is it?" she asked, staring down at the tablecloth, herself, because such directness was uncomfortable for her.

"It's okay, Aunt Fiona," Victor smiled. "It's really okay." Because he did not want to hurt her—this gentle woman who had taken him into her own home and her own heart, when his mother simply had left him. *Walked away and left him.* But he knew full well that what he was going to do *would* hurt Fiona—would wound her to the very center of her being, the way it would hurt any woman.

Because there was no woman on the face of this earth who had any idea of what it was like to be a man.

Even while Victor sat at the kitchen table, looking right at Fiona's downcast eyes and declaring that everything was "okay," his leather valise was packed and hidden beneath the palmettos outside of his own bedroom window. Without realizing it, Victor heaved a deep sigh that didn't go unnoticed by either Fiona or Glory. Quickly, he stretched out his arms and gave a mock yawn.

"I'm going out for a walk," he announced, keeping his voice casual.

"In this weather?" Glory queried.

"I've always liked walking in the rain," Victor smiled. He stood up, reached over and embraced Fiona, and then he went to the sink and embraced Glory. Neither of the women said a single word when Victor left the kitchen, closing the door behind him and went across the back porch and out into the rain.

The silence in the kitchen went on for several minutes, with both Fiona and Glory frozen in place and neither of them willing to meet the gaze of the other. Finally, Glory turned back to the sink.

"This is different," she said to no one in particular. "This time, I think he's really *gone.*" And she didn't hear Fiona's whispered reply, "I know."

Even while Fiona still sat at the table and Glory stood at the sink in mutual silence, the front door burst open, propelled by the force of the rising wind and banging against the wall.

"Victor?" the two women asked simultaneously. But it was Starry who came into the kitchen, dripping with rain and with her hair blown in all different directions.

"Wind like to have blown us to pieces!" Starry declared, trying to smooth her hair in place. Behind her, standing in the doorway was another woman, a little younger, perhaps, than Starry and also dressed in the so-called uniform of women who worked in the plant—"Rosie the Riveters" they were all called. Both of them wearing dripping rain slickers.

"This here is Rowena," Starry said. "She didn't have any place to go while her shift is down, so I invited her home with me. I've told her all about Love-Oak, and she said she wanted to see it. Rowena, this is Fiona and Glory," Starry hesitated, then. "Where's Victor?" she asked.

"Out," Fiona and Glory said simultaneously, glancing at each other. "Hi, Rowena," Fiona said politely. Glory nodded her head without turning to look at either Starry or Rowena. "You all walked from town in this wind and rain?" Fiona asked. "I thought maybe you'd stay at the plant, what with the weatherman saying there's stormy weather heading this way."

"No. They said anybody who lived close enough should go home— see to their houses and things like that. Too, some of the men who work there have families to take care of. Men who can't go into the army, that is," she added. "We caught the bus and got to the post office, and then Doc happened along and gave us a ride." Starry's face turned a furious shade of red. She looked at the floor and smiled at the linoleum. Behind her, Rowena gave a short giggle and then put her hand over her mouth.

"So he knew you were coming?" Fiona couldn't stop the words.

"Yess'm," Starry confessed, still looking at the floor. "He really didn't just happen by—I talked to him on the phone this morning. But that was before Rowena here said she could come home with me."

"I think he wasn't expecting me," Rowena muttered, joining Starry in gazing at the floor.

"Well, I guess not," Fiona got up from the table and lit the stove under the kettle. Absently, she motioned to Starry and Rowena to sit down. Starry took their sopping raincoats and tossed them onto the back porch.

"Well, he sure didn't seem to be himself," Starry said. "But I think he was happy to see me—at first. I was standing in front of the post office, right where I told him I'd be, and Rowena here had gone into the ladies' room for a minute. And when she came out Doc just seemed really surprised, is all. Hardly spoke a single word all the way here."

Fiona remembered seeing Starry's arm snake its way around the back of Doc's seat when he drove her to the bus that first time she went to the plant. *And maybe Doc is smart enough to be very careful around a woman like you, Starry,* Fiona thought silently. *Honey, bless your heart, you're simply so . . . so willing!*

At this point, Starry's friend, Rowena, pulled off her scarf, and blonde curls with small streaks of silver in them popped out along her forehead, but still, she said nothing more. Fiona, fiddling with the cups and saucers, wondered, *Is there something wrong with this woman? Is she simply lacking good manners? Or maybe she's simple-minded? And if she is, how can she be trusted to work in a government plant?*

"Did *you* think Doc was acting sort of funny?" Starry asked Rowena, who seemed startled by the question.

"Oh, I'm sorry—what did you say?"

"Well, you wouldn't have noticed anyway," Starry said. "Because you don't know him. Or *do* you?"

"No," Rowena said simply. Fiona was wondering, as she occasionally had wondered, if Doc ever "saw" other ladies, now that Myra had passed on. Ladies who lived out of town, because Doc was a good man and a respectable one, but he had to be lonely, for Heaven's sake. And he had been a widower for a long time now. Could he *know* her from someplace else, and was that why he was surprised?

Fiona pushed aside her thoughts—no way for a good Christian woman to be thinking!—she silently admonished herself. When they were all seated around the kitchen table, with the radio droning in the background, and with their fresh cups of tea before them, Fiona broached her first polite question to the visitor. "And where are you from, Rowena?" she asked, stirring only the smallest bit of sugar into her tea. Glory had said absolutely nothing, ever since Starry had brought her friend into the kitchen, but Fiona knew that Glory was often a bit timid around strangers.

Rowena smiled, and Fiona thought that perhaps she wasn't at all simple—just tired, maybe. Because she truly had a pretty smile. "I used to live near here, but then I moved up to a little place north of Gainesville." Without actually staring at this Rowena-person, Fiona could tell that she was close to tears. *Yes, she's definitely tired!*

"I'm glad Doc gave you all a ride," Fiona said. "Wouldn't want to think of you walking all that way in the rain. Will there be enough room for the both of you in that little cabin, Starry? Or . . . Rowena . . . can stay in another cabin, if you like."

"My cabin will be fine," Starry assured her. "There'll be plenty of room, and I'd welcome some good company, with this storm and all. That okay with you, Rowena?" Rowena smiled at the tablecloth. "Fine," she said.

"Now where did you say Victor was off to?" Starry queried, stirring her tea absently.

"Out." Again, Fiona and Glory spoke in unison.

"Well, he always did like going out in the rain," Starry sighed. Fiona glanced at Starry sharply, but Starry didn't seem to notice. *Why didn't I know that?* Fiona silently questioned herself. *Why does Starry know that, and I never did?* As always, Fiona's next statement was far removed from what she was thinking. "Did Doc say anything about Rebecca?"

"No," Starry said. "Why?"

"Nothing, I guess," Fiona replied. "I've just had kind of a feeling about her lately."

"No, he didn't say anything about Rebecca. Goodness, that Doc sure is a nice looking man!" Starry said, making Fiona wonder how Starry's mind had jumped right from her question about Rebecca and into what a handsome man Doc was. But then, that was certainly Starry.

"Sweet, too," Starry added, drawing a slight frown from Glory, and the whole time, Rowena simply stirred her tea, looking into the cup and saying nothing. *Tired!* Fiona thought.

The howling wind disrupted the conversation. "We better take care of everything right now, before this weather gets any worse," Fiona advised. "Glory, you need any help getting the tables and chairs at the pier put away like you want?"

"Weather felt like it was turning bad," Glory said. "So Arabella helped me batten down all the hatches before she went home."

"When is Arabella's son—the monk—supposed to go back?" Starry asked. "I'm just wondering if the taxi will be running tomorrow or the next day."

"He still has a few days, I think," Fiona answered. "And I'm glad he's at home with Arabella and Old Man with this storm coming. They're both getting too old to handle those heavy shutters and drag all the porch furniture around. And they will all sure enough be in the wrong place, far as lake water is concerned, does the wind come in from the east."

When Starry and Rowena had gone down to Starry's cabin—putting their raincoats back on and also holding newspapers over their heads in the downpour, Glory spoke for the first time. "What do you think?" Glory asked, speaking so low that Fiona had trouble hearing her over the water she was running into the sink.

"About what?" Fiona asked.

"Don't you wonder about her?" Glory asked, and when Fiona turned from the sink and looked at the back of Glory's head, something in her mind tried to *click*. But it was just too much trouble, what with the wind howling and the rain peppering against the kitchen window.

"What about her?" Fiona asked in a somewhat frustrated whisper.

But some kind of faint fear tried to edge its way into her mind. She remembered the night Starry and Middy had first showed up and how she had even latched the screen door when they were on the porch. What was it she had been so afraid of? She couldn't remember.

"Haven't you noticed?" Glory asked.

"Noticed what, for goodness sake?" Fiona asked, but she felt her heart give a little skip of a beat. Glory leaned close. "Haven't you noticed how much that woman and Victor look alike?"

Fiona's mouth formed the word *NO* before she really even had a chance to think about Glory's question, so the two of them stood at the sink, looking into each other's eyes, until Fiona finally made up her mind. "Have you lost your mind?" Fiona snarled. "Why, they don't look a thing alike!"

"Maybe he looks more like your *niece?*" Glory asked, lifting one of her eyebrows until it almost disappeared into her hairline.

"I just wish he would come on back home," Fiona mused. "I hate for him to be out in this weather, no matter how much he likes walking in the rain."

But the evening progressed, the weather got worse, and Victor still had not come home. Fiona went to bed, but she couldn't sleep. *Where is he? Maybe he's with Rebecca—some way. I'm almost sure that's where he's been every single evening. And how on earth can Doc not know about that? Or maybe Victor went to see Old Man and Wahali and decided to stay there, what with this storm getting so bad. But they have a phone. Couldn't he call to let us know he's okay?*

"He's gone," Glory said. Could she be right?

Once, during the night, Fiona thought she heard voices just under the howling of the wind and pounding of the rain, but she soon dismissed it as an overworked imagination. *Just imagine that! Glory thinking . . . that friend of Starry's and Victor looked like each other. Ridiculous. And saying that about him being gone. That isn't true. He can't be gone—he's my precious son!*

Chapter Twenty-Six

Victor was grateful for the early darkness brought on by the storm, and he lowered his head against the rain and walked resolutely down the flooded, sandy road. Every step he took, leaning against the increasing wind, brought him closer to Rebecca, and he imagined approaching the back yard at Doc's house, getting so close to Rebecca, and he was sure that the sun would break through and flood the earth with warmth. When he was so close to Rebecca!

But some kind of dim light appeared ahead of him around a curve in the road, and he knew it wasn't his imagination playing tricks on him. It wasn't his imaginary sunshine, it was car lights. Quickly, he stepped into the thick palmetto bushes beside the road and ducked down, lowering his head so that the lights would not reflect off of his face in the darkness. Still, he could see light bouncing off the trunks of live oak trees and creating a strange shimmer in the air, because of the driving rain. As the car neared where he was hiding, he peered through the dripping fronds and saw Doc's own car, driving slowly through the downpour, wipers crazily trying to clear the windshield. He could make out three shadows in Doc's car—one in the passenger seat beside Doc and—he couldn't be sure—perhaps another person in the back. Doc and who else? Perhaps Rebecca and the old aunt? But that didn't make any sense. Then Victor became focused on the fact that, whoever was in Doc's car, Doc himself was away from home, and Victor was on his way to claim Rebecca.

Tucking his valise under his arm, he resumed trudging down the flooded road, glancing behind him several times for Doc's car returning. Because Victor didn't know where Doc was going or why. And who were the other two people in his car? Perhaps some distraught parents of a sick child. But not Rebecca. He was almost sure of that.

At the same moment Victor started walking again, Arabella felt Old Man get out of bed with a soft grunt and pad across the room in the darkness. As always, she said nothing, but she wondered what had aroused him from sleep. The wind? Surely not. The hard rain pelting against the windows? No. After a few minutes, she heard the back door open and then close, heard the cruel gust of wind blow the pages of the calendar on the wall.

"Mama?" Wahali standing in the doorway to her bedroom. "I think Pop went outside. Shouldn't I go with him?"

"No. Let him go," Arabella replied sleepily, and then for a brief moment, she thought about those words. Hadn't they been the bedrock of their long marriage? *Let him go. Because what else could I have done with a man like him? That wildness in him is what I love the most—knowing that I could never tame him to hearth and home. Nobody ever succeeds at caging a wild animal, for either the creature goes silent and then quietly dies—retreating somewhere deep inside of himself, where no one can see his living death until the breath is gone from him. Or else he tears up teeth and claws, seeking freedom, even gnawing away parts of his own body to escape confinement.*

"I think maybe he heard something," Arabella said to Wahali, who hesitated for only a moment and then nodded and went back to bed. "Maybe he heard something," she repeated to herself. *Maybe the panther called to him again. So let him go.*

Fiona told herself that it was the blowing wind that was keeping her awake, but she couldn't quite fool herself to that extent. Again, she thought she heard voices coming from another room, but no matter how hard she listened, she couldn't hear them again. She tossed and turned for almost two hours, trying to get comfortable. But no matter. She couldn't fall asleep, and she kept hearing Glory's voice and the words Glory spoke, but now, as if she were hearing them for the very first time—*Maybe he looks more like your niece.*

Fiona sat straight up in bed, staring into the darkness, as if she might find something there to see—something to make everything clear to her. But whatever wanted clarification, it was something she didn't want to know. That was the only thing she was completely sure of.

When she finally got up and went down the dim hallway toward the kitchen, she was surprised to see, in addition to the small nightlight they always left burning, another light, a soft but brighter light coming from under the kitchen door. She pushed it open and saw Starry and Rowena sitting at the table with their hands folded, as if they were simply sitting there and waiting for her.

"I'm sorry," Rowena looked up first. "Did we wake you?" Fiona didn't answer right away. She just stood in the doorway, wondering. In the kitchen corner the drenched raincoats were piled.

"What's the matter? Did you all get scared by the storm and want to come back here?" But while she spoke, hearing her own words as if they came from someone she didn't know, Fiona was studying Rowena's face. *Have I seen that face before? Have I heard that voice in my own back yard? In the middle of the night? Is this the poor excuse for a mother*—her mind almost spat the word—*who ran away and deserted her own child and then sent a puny little package of worn-out old clothes for that beautiful little boy*—*sent it by Old Man and put in a note that said, "Be god to him"?*

Starry had not said a word, had only sat there, with the most miserable look on her face that Fiona had ever seen. Obviously, Starry had been crying.

"What's wrong?" Fiona asked. And then again, words she didn't even think came to her as she looked at Rowena. "Who *are* you?"

"I'm so sorry," Starry's voice broke. "I didn't know." Starry's voice was not even defensive sounding—only deeply sad. "We were just lying there, waiting to fall asleep and listening to the wind and rain, and Rowena here told me." Here, Starry's voice broke off.

Still staring at Rowena, Fiona asked, "Told you what?"

"No, Starry," Rowena interrupted. "Let me tell her. I'm the one who did it."

"The one who did *what?*" Fiona's heart was pounding, but she didn't know why. Then she blurted, "Has something happened to Victor?" And her voice rose a terrible octave.

"No," Starry assured her. "Not that we know of anyway. Didn't he come home?"

"No!" Fiona almost yelled. "Do you know where he is?"

"No," Rowena answered.

"I said, 'Who *are* you?'" Fiona's voice was shaking, and she wanted to sit down, as well, because her knees were weak and her head was spinning. But she was determined to remain standing, so she could most properly look down upon this strange woman who was sitting at her kitchen table.

Starry was snuffling softly, and when Rowena looked up at Fiona again, absolute misery was on her face. "I'm his mother," Rowena murmured.

Fiona sat down then, because her knees would not hold her up. *So there it is then. The one person I have feared for all these years. And*—*how strange*—*I'm not afraid of her at all.*

"I didn't know," Starry bawled. "I'm the one brought her here, and I didn't know."

"NO-O-O!" Fiona's voice was almost like a long, extended, never-ending growl. She had never felt such anger—and for the first time in her life, she could understand the kind of passion that could turn a normal human being into a *murderer.* And the next words Fiona spoke were completely unknown to her, until she heard them. "You can't have him! I will kill you with my bare hands, before I let you take him away from me!"

"I know," Rowena hiccoughed. "I know I can't have him. I just wanted to see him. I *had* to see him."

"Isn't it a little late for that?" Fiona growled, and she was shocked to find that she loved saying cruel words. She wished that she had a full vocabulary of terrible, horrible, gut-bursting words she could hurl at this miserable wretch. But instead, she said, "Why *now*? Why, after all these years? Did you just suddenly remember that you had a son—a beautiful, wonderful son—and you walked away and left him in my yard? Did you just now remember *that*?" Oh, where were the words she could use like daggers, drive them into this cruel witch's heart and laugh at her agony? Dance on her blood as it poured out?

"I've always remembered," Rowena sobbed quietly. "I always knew where I left him. Because I *selected* you and Glory. I *chose* you."

"That's a lie. That's a dirty, stinking lie. You didn't even know us." Something was replacing the terrible anger, something stronger, something cold and quiet . . . and deadly.

Rowena continued, "I worked in the restaurant down by the Trading Post. I heard people talk about all kinds of things. And one day, some ladies came in for coffee, and they were talking about you. And about Glory—what good people you were and how kind. They talked about how hard you all worked to make a success of the fishing camp, and all I could think about was wishing my little boy could grow up in that kind of place—a clean, beautiful place with grass and trees and clean sheets on the bed."

"You saw our cottage? This cottage?"

"When I got off work one day, I walked up here and saw it. Saw the clothes you all had hanging on the clothesline—saw a pair of red socks." Here, Rowena tried to smile. "Guess that doesn't sound like much, but I figured anybody who would wear red socks must have a good sense of humor." Fiona remembered the socks clearly, how Glory had fussed at her for buying something so frivolous. "You get them mixed in with the pillowcases, we all gonna be sleeping on pink."

"You left him with us because of red socks on the clothesline?"

"Yeah, I guess so," Rowena confessed. "That and wanting him to have things better than I could give him. And knowing you were good people."

"So you dumped him and ran off," Fiona stated, flatly and with no emotion in her voice. Where was the anger? Where had it gone? Why was she in her own kitchen and in the company of such a miserable excuse for a woman?

"I left him with you all," Rowena said. "Tore my heart out to do it, but I knew it was the best thing for him."

Suddenly, Fiona didn't know what to say. Everything she had always feared about "the mother" coming back for Victor had come to pass, and yet she didn't know what to say, so when she finally spoke again, the words were a complete mystery to her, until she heard them with her own ears. "What does Old Man know about this?"

"It's not his fault," Rowena whispered. "It was all me, and me alone who decided to do this."

"And what do we do about Victor now? Now that you're here?" Fiona murmured.

"Who?"

"Victor—your son. No—*my* son," Fiona explained.

"Nothing," Rowena said. "I'll just leave as soon as I can. I probably shouldn't have come, but I wanted to see him—just once—so bad. When he comes home, we don't have to tell him anything, just let him think I'm a friend of Starry's. Maybe that's best."

"I don't know," Fiona said. "You've sure enough opened a can of worms now, and I have to think about what's best for Victor." But within minutes, Fiona knew that she couldn't keep this truth from him, couldn't live the rest of her life knowing that she had concealed such a thing, that she had robbed him of what was probably the one and only chance to know his own mother. And as far as what this would do to Rowena, Fiona was surprised to realize that she simply didn't care. There she was, sitting at her own familiar kitchen table, listening to the wind and rain from the storm, and this monumental happening was sitting right there with her.

Starry sat silently, remembering when she and Rowena first were assigned to the same shift at the plant. Starry had liked Rowena right away, but she couldn't have said why. On their coffee and lunch breaks, when they shared their sandwiches, Starry talked about Love-Oak Lake and the fishing camp and Fiona and Glory and Victor. Rowena had leaned forward in such sweet attention, Starry had felt a glow of happiness—that anything she could say would be of such kind interest to Rowena. Little did she know that she was telling Rowena about her own child.

"He didn't come home," Fiona said. "Glory thinks he *gone*."

"Gone where?" Starry asked through her tears.

"We don't know," Fiona answered, and she was suddenly comforted by knowing that Victor—her precious Victor—wasn't a helpless little child any longer. Wherever he was, he was a *man! And suppose he isn't gone at all. Suppose Glory's wrong, and in a little while, Victor will come through that door and tell us he stayed at Old Man's last night. And what will I say to him then . . . "Victor, I'd like for you to meet your mother"?*

While they all sat in mutual silence, Glory came into the kitchen, blinking her eyes. She hesitated, looked around, and then said, "Well, what in the name of Heaven is going on here? Almost in the middle of the night?"

"This woman, this Rowena, is Victor's mother," Fiona said flatly, anticipating Glory's surprise. But again, what she expected to happen didn't happen at all.

"*I* knew that," Glory laughed. "I knew that yesterday evening, the minute I laid eyes on her. Sure don't know what took you so long."

Starry interrupted Glory's laugh. "Miss Fiona, I didn't know anything about Rowena being your niece," Starry murmured. "I promise you, I didn't know. And you didn't say a thing, when I brought her in last night." Rowena frowned, not understanding what Starry was saying.

"It's okay, Starry," Fiona finally answered. "And I guess it's time for truth all the way around—Rowena here isn't my niece, at least, not that I know of. I made up that story so the authorities wouldn't try to take Victor away from us."

Fiona's eyes met Glory's, and both of them were remembering what Glory had predicted so many years ago—*Maybe you'll get to where you believe it yourself.* And how right Glory had been. But what would happen when Victor came home? If he knew this Rowena was his mother? *All the fears about Victor's mother coming back for him, and now, here she is. But where is Victor? And who are we to him now?*

Rowena interrupted Fiona's thoughts. "Thank you, Miss Fiona and you too, Glory," Rowena said. "Thank you for loving my son and taking such good care of him. I knew I had done the very best thing for him, when I left him with you. No matter how hard it was."

"It was the right thing to do," Fiona murmured, wondering with all her heart whether that was a true statement. *Because who knew where this would lead? Would it open up another world to Victor? Perhaps one that would take him far away from her? But wasn't Glory right? Wasn't he, even now, already gone? Gone far beyond wherever he had gone on all the other nights?*

Rowena sighed. "I think I better go now. Whenever Victor comes home, he doesn't need to see me here. He wouldn't even know who I am, and there's no need for him to know. Ever." Rowena sighed deeply, and then she added in a whisper, "But if I could know that my baby—my other child—had been so well cared for, I'd be blessed indeed."

When those words reached Fiona and Glory's ears, at first they had no meaning. Starry looked up sharply and then glanced at Fiona and Glory, wondering what was happening. She thought they hadn't even heard the words, but then those very words froze all their thoughts.

Other child?

"Other child?" Starry asked, while Fiona and Glory sat with their mouths literally hanging open.

"I wanted to ask him about her," Rowena whispered. "But I just couldn't."

Other child? Her?

The women sat in complete silence, Rowena looking down at the tablecloth, and Starry, Glory and Fiona all staring at each other. Starry's eyes were still filled with tears, as if she didn't really understand what was being said. But Fiona and Glory's eyes were simply mirrors of confusion and then shock.

"Other child?" Fiona finally whispered, drawing Rowena's stare away from the tablecloth and to her own face.

"My little girl," Rowena whispered, the words clouded in absolute misery. And then she gazed back at the tablecloth and added, "I don't know if . . . *he* . . . recognized me."

"Who?" Starry asked, although she probably already knew the answer to that question, and she almost cringed to hear Rowena's response.

"The doctor," Rowena whispered. "I gave my little girl . . . my baby . . . to the doctor and his wife. The very night she was born."

In the terrible silence that closed in behind her words, everything seemed to stop. Rain no longer sounded on the roof, and the wind died away so that instead of creeping in around the kitchen window and gently moving the curtains, the very air seemed to reverse . . . to suck the breath right out of them all. Take away everything required for life to go on.

Then, in the middle of that vacuum, that out-of-this-world silence, Fiona heard her own voice—low and saturated with a misery she had never heard in anyone's words.

"I want to make sure I understand this," she took a gulping breath, as if she had been swimming underwater for a very long time and then had broken through to the surface and spilled out the terrible words, "You left your little boy with Glory and me, and you left your baby girl with Doc and his wife." It wasn't a question, only the cold, logical words that built a wall of pure agony around Fiona's heart.

"I did," Rowena whispered. "I did," she repeated.

"Rebecca." Fiona whispered.

The only other sound was Glory's murmured prayer, "Oh, Lord have mercy on us!" and Starry's deep sob.

Chapter Twenty-Seven

By the time Victor reached the back yard at Doc's house and crouched down behind the car shed, the downpour was diminished a little, but the wind still whipped the palmettos and scrub palm trees into a frenzy of crackling fronds. He sat close to the back wall of the shed, trying to fit himself in a place where the overhang of the tin roof would shield him from the rain. But with the wind whipping back and forth, and changing directions as if it couldn't make up its mind what it wanted to blow completely away, he could not escape. He simply turned up the collar of his rain coat and held it tight against his neck. And waited.

In her own room, Rebecca tiptoed around as quietly as possible. She had closed her bedroom door, but she knew that her aunt Irma or Mrs. Murphy could open it at any moment, and without knocking at all.

She had complained to Doc about their habit of simply bursting into her room without even the courtesy of a knock, but Doc didn't take her side at all. "You gave up a right to privacy when you had that kissing session with Victor," Doc replied to her complaint in a voice that was at once both bored and slightly angry.

"It wasn't a kissing *session*," Rebecca pleaded. "It was just one kiss, and I *asked* him to kiss me!"

"That doesn't matter," Doc growled, and then just by looking in his eyes, Rebecca knew that he had shut his heart against her voice, so that she felt as if she had fallen backwards into a cage just like the one she had grown up in—but that had been her mother's cage—a terrible, smothering place where Rebecca had been imprisoned by her mother's unyielding, all possessing love. But this cage, this cage that kept her away from Victor, was made of her father's own anger.

So that as Rebecca sat on the side of her bed, with her packed suitcase carefully concealed underneath—in the event that Aunt Irma or Mrs. Murphy simply opened the door and came right in—she thought back and remembered the feeling of her hair blowing in the wind as she rode her bicycle at breakneck speed. And the electric feeling of Victor's warm skin when his suntanned arm brushed against her own. And the one small kiss and the incredible sweetness and softness of his mouth. And more—she remembered that when Victor kissed her, he had not even held her shoulders with his hands—so that for that one glorious moment, she had been *free* in both body and spirit.

At nine PM, Rebecca turned off her bedside lamp and crawled into bed fully clothed, pulling up the coverlet so that her clothing couldn't be seen by anyone who happened to peek into her door. And there, she waited, listening to the soft, metallic tick of the clock on her table, watching with half-closed eyelids as the second hand moved around the face ever so slowly. She knew that Victor was already outside behind the shed, waiting for her—waiting in all that rain and rising wind. Rebecca smiled the deeply contented smile of a woman who knows that she is loved by a man.

Once, her bedroom door cracked open, and she quickly shut her eyes, even though her head was turned away from the door.

"You asleep?" Mrs. Murphy's rasping voice, soft enough not to awaken Rebecca if she had been asleep. For long moments, the lamp from the hallway cast an arm across her bed, and Rebecca held her breath. Then the door closed softly, and the light was gone.

Thy kiss is sweeter than wine, she heard her heart whisper.

Chapter Twenty-Eight

When Old Man walked out into the rain and wind that night, he stopped near the gravel road upon which Victor had approached Doc's house only an hour before. He stood listening, but he heard nothing, other than the wind in the palm fronds and the gurgle of rain water running from the road into the drainage ditches on either side. Water dripped from the Spanish moss hanging from the live oak trees, and the final wind of the storm blew the hanging moss into wavering hanks of witches' hair.

Something had called to Old Man, something he now couldn't seem to hear. But then, his hearing had been going bad lately, so that he looked slightly perplexed at Arabella whenever she said something to him in such a low voice that he couldn't hear. Whatever had called him must be answered. That was the only truth he knew.

But the gravel road wasn't the right way. He knew that, as well.

So that, while Victor was crouching behind the shed in Doc's back yard, waiting for Rebecca, Old Man walked calmly across the soggy ground and deep into the low forest of palmettos, until he disappeared into the sodden darkness, his heart strangely light and happy within him. Behind him, the lights of his own home still showed through the windows, and he knew that his wife and son would sit up and wait for him to return.

But return from where?

As he walked on in the rain, he tried to remember exactly what had prompted him to go out in the middle of the night. *Had the panther called him? He didn't think so. Had his grandmother come to him again in a dream and asked him to go out into the storm?*

That sounded right. And then a single word echoed in his mind—TWO. But what did that mean? Vaguely, he remembered pointing at Victor and saying the word, hearing the raspy squeak of his long-unused voice.But he couldn't remember what he had meant by it. Still, he knew it was important. Very important. Perhaps it had something to do with twins.

With the rain streaming down on him and plastering his hair to his skull, he walked until he came to the edge of Fiona's fishing camp, where a faint light shone from one of the cabins. From far away, he could see two people—two women—sitting across from each other at a small table in front of the lone window. Their heads were bent toward one another. They were talking, but he couldn't hear what they were saying, and besides, he was too far away to see exactly who the women were. In the rainy darkness, that light in the window seemed to beckon him, but he rebelled against the impulse to seek warmth and shelter and to join the women.

Instead, he walked on, coming upon the even deeper forest of palmetto shrubs behind Fiona's cottage. Here, no light.

But something.

TWO.

Again, the word echoed in his mind, and he heard his grandmother's voice saying that twins must always be separated, else danger would come. *What danger? And not twins. Simply TWO. Two who must be separated. It is the Seminole way. Separate the lightning and the thunder, and all will be peaceful.*

For long minutes, he stood at the edge of the trees behind Fiona's cottage, trying to remember something that struggled so hard, trying to enter his memory—something trying to be born. Then came a sudden tightness in his chest that pushed at his breath, even as a woman's body contracted and pushed to give birth.

Strangely, his arms suddenly held a baby. Or was it a panther cub? The squeal he remembered was the same. Which was it? Was he an Old Man trying to remember something important? Or was he twelve years old again—hardly old enough to call himself a man—and was he holding a tiny panther cub and feeling its rib cage rising and falling? Watching its baby mouth curl into a tiny snarl?

He was surprised when he heard a deep sob escape from his own lips, a sob that had no root in his heart, no meaning, but a cleansing sob, nonetheless. The tightness in his chest somehow wasn't so tight any longer, and he turned away from Fiona's back yard, walking off through the brush and seeking . . . seeking.

Something.

He walked for a long time and finally came to the deep ravine at the edge of the swamp. Here, he stopped. The torrents of rain had filled the ravine with rushing water that gurgled and whispered, but over that sound, he heard a faint cry of some kind. *A baby? Who would take a little baby out in weather like this?*

Slowly, the tightness in his massive chest came again, compressed his heart, this time harder and more insistently. He sank to his knees at the lip of the flooded ravine and pressed both of his fists against the tightness . . . against the pain. His heart! *Was it bursting?*

But then he forgot all about his heart, because he felt something in his hands—had his heart simply come bursting through his chest and now rested in his own hands? When he looked down at his fists, fully expecting to see his red, bleeding heart in them, he saw, instead, that each hand held a mewling, squirming panther cub.

TWO. TWINS. And one must die. That is the way of it, he argued with himself. *But which one? Which one? Two that must not be together. Which one must die?*

As he struggled with the terrible question, he curled his arms around the cubs and nuzzled the sweet, damp fur before he tucked them safely inside of his shirt. Then he sank down gratefully against the side of the ravine to think. *Must think! So much depends upon the right decision.*

Inside his shirt, the cubs stopped their squirming and quietly cuddled against the warm, bare skin of his chest, and he cradled them against his heart and rocked back and forth, ever so slowly. The cubs began to purr—rhythmic and steady.

And while he waited in wonder, trying to remember what he was required to do, the purring of the cubs seeped its way right through the skin of his warm chest, where his heart thudded off-beat and ominous.

He thought, *So this is it, then. This is good. This is enough. My son will come searching, and he will find me here. Perhaps tomorrow. Perhaps tomorrow's tomorrow, that place closed in the eye of the night. But he will not find the cubs. Their mother will have come by then and taken them away. Oh, I can see her eyes when she finds them.*

See the love in her eyes!

And even while Old Man was imagining such a beautiful thing, he saw the panther-mother herself approaching him, moving silently on her great padded feet. Saw the soft, yellow eyes. Smelled the wild richness of her fur. He smiled. *Panther-mother, Great Spirit.*

She came so close that he could breathe in the warmth of her softly snarling breath, gaze into the Love in her eyes. Knew that she could see right into his very soul and that she loved what she saw there. She began leaning gently against him, covering him with her own warm body, and he was filled with her greatness, her beauty, her goodness. Her love. He felt her warm fur around his wet shoulders, and he laughed at the silent, incredible beauty of it all. Felt the panther-mother gently nudging her way into his shirt, where her cubs—and his soul—were waiting.

Love has come!

So that when, at last—in one horrific lurch—his own heart stopped beating, he smiled as he felt the warm, rhythmic purring of the cubs coursing through his dead veins.

Chapter Twenty-Nine

Victor, still crouched behind the shed and with the rain dripping down his back, heard Doc's car when it pulled into the yard. So whatever house call Doc had been making hadn't lasted long enough to suit Victor.

He watched as the headlights of Doc's glared through the gaps in the boards of the shed, blinding bars of light that Victor watched carefully.After the car stopped, the engine ran for several more minutes, and Victor wondered why Doc was just sitting there with the engine running, using up his precious gasoline.Then the bars of light shining through the shed abruptly disappeared, and Victor heard the motor shut down.Still even more long minutes went by before he heard the car door open and Doc's slow footsteps across the gravel driveway and up the back steps.The door to the screened porch opened with its usual squeak—so Rebecca had forgotten to oil it—but the kitchen door never closed behind Doc. Or at least, Victor didn't hear it, if it did.Still, the wind was high and rain still dripped from the shed roof, so perhaps he simply didn't hear the door to the kitchen open and then close.

Victor strained to see the face of his watch. Eleven thirty. Only half an hour more and Rebecca would come onto the porch, and this time, she would not wait for him behind the screen. This time, she would come out.

His mind raced past the embrace they would relish, past the warmth and softness of her body against his, the damp perfume of her hair. Instead, he concentrated on where they would go to catch the bus to Gainesville and then from there into Georgia. Where could they stay to be out of the storm until the bus arrived for them? They certainly couldn't catch the bus in front of the post office, because someone might see them. What people in town knew about Victor and Rebecca's plight, was unknown to Victor, but they must not take any chances.

About two miles outside of town, there was a small grocery store where the bus would stop if someone flagged it down. That's where they would go. But how would he keep Rebecca dry and warm in the meantime? They would certainly be soaked to the skin by the time they walked far up the dark highway to the store. No way to get around that. And would she be able to walk so far? Well, that didn't matter. He would carry her. Pick her up, cradle her close to his heart and walk to where they would begin their lives together.

He reasoned that once they got on the bus, it would be dark inside, and they would have dry clothes in their suitcases. Surely, that late at night—or early in the morning—they could slip out of their wet clothes and into dry ones without anyone noticing. Suddenly, Victor's mind attached itself to the vision of Rebecca unbuttoning her sopping blouse and sliding her slender arms out of the clinging sleeves. He felt the blood rushing to his face and pounding in his ears so loudly that it even shut out the last sounds of the rain. He shook his head and tried to think of something—anything—else. So he projected even further . . . He and Rebecca already married and living in a small, neat apartment. He wore an army uniform and kissed her goodbye as he went off to the war. In his dreamlike state, Victor heard her say, "Oh, please don't go." And he manfully replied, "But I must!"

In the rain-soaked darkness behind the shed, Victor's heart swelled at the picture in his mind. And the beautiful words almost brought tears to his eyes. He would have to leave Rebecca—but she would wait for him. When he came home, he would be coming home, with honor, to *her*. To his great love. To his wife

He looked at his watch again. Eleven forty-five. Only fifteen minutes and his new life with Rebecca could begin.

But those last fifteen minutes seemed to drag on for hours.

Doc eased himself into the rocking chair on the back porch. He had always relished sitting in the complete darkness and looking out over the yard, but he had not done that in a long time. Because for many years, mostly when Myra let him know emphatically that she wanted to be alone with Rebecca, he had sat there. Alone. So the porch ceased to be a sanctuary and became, instead, a place of greatest loneliness. Where he was always alone. Except for the smoke from his pipe.

Alone.

He had quietly accepted it all, but now, on this night, he was deeply troubled. *Was that her? Was that the mother of my daughter? Why didn't I come right out and ask her? If only I hadn't been so afraid, I would KNOW.*

Myra's gone. Nothing can hurt Myra now.

Because on that other stormy night so long ago, he had glanced at the woman only briefly. Then somehow, she simply ceased to exist. But how could that happen? For the first time, he was completely honest with himself. Myra's deep and desperate beliefs had become his own. That's what his love for Myra did to him.

Doc sat quietly for long minutes, forcing himself to remember the things he had forgotten in his determination to create a world in which his Myra would be happy. And he had been successful. Because Myra had been deliriously happy—with Rebecca.

But without him.

Then he thought of Starry—what a perfect name—because of the way her eyes sparkled and lit up . . . for him. He felt her warm forehead beneath his hand and the gentle way she had leaned into his touch. Taking a deep breath, he could almost, once again, inhale the fragrance of her hair.

How pleased he had been when she phoned and told him she was coming home for the weekend. So easy for him to offer her a ride, to see her eyes—shining for him.

But then, that other woman was with her. The shock of seeing her again, after all these years. Not even remembering what she looked like that night long ago. As Doc sat in the darkness of the porch, the knowledge of what was real—what he knew to be absolute fact and also what he only strongly surmised. A strange but logic-based fact—came back to him. He wept silently.

I didn't even know why I reacted so strongly about Victor and Rebecca, but now I do. It only makes sense, Fiona calling me to check up on a little boy she later claimed was her great-nephew. And on the very same day Rebecca came to us. It made perfect sense—but maybe I just didn't want to know. Maybe I finally thought that we really did get her in Jacksonville, or maybe I even came to believe that she was our own. Maybe I entered Myra's make-believe world and didn't even realize it.

Oh, Myra! I tried so hard for you. I tried so hard!

When Rebecca slipped silently out of her room and onto the screened porch, right at midnight, Doc *felt*—rather than saw or heard—that someone or something was moving close to him. He held his breath, because after the terrible onslaught of so many long-denied, half-forgotten memories, he felt strangely vulnerable. And weak.

"Rebecca?" His own voice startled him, bursting out as it did on the silent porch and in the darkness and tinged with a plaintive sound he didn't even know existed.

In the darkness, Rebecca came to a stunned and immediate halt and stood with her shoulders hunched up, as if she could draw herself into her skin like a turtle drawing into his shell.

Doc's rising out of the chair was only a whisper of sound, his body like an unfamiliar stalk that existed only to hold up his throbbing mind. And then his arms, without any thought, wrapped around his beautiful daughter, and he sobbed quietly into her hair. Rebecca dropped her suitcase with a thump on the porch floor and stood stiff and confused while Doc wept.

"Where's Victor?" Doc asked, finally. Because the terrible truth of what was happening in the here and now had slowly nudged aside the terrible memories. *But who really knows?* That question had no answer.

Victor, waiting for Rebecca behind the shed, heard the thump as she dropped her suitcase. He held his breath. His heart hammering and pulse throbbing behind his eyes. Then he heard Doc say his name, and he knew that all his carefully thought-out plans for running away were gone. All gone. But he would not let Rebecca face her father alone. He would come forward like the man he really was and try to defend her.

So Victor stepped out from behind the shed, walked across he yard, and opened the door to the screened porch. Almost at once, Doc reached out with his other arm and swept a rain-soaked Victor into his embrace, the same embrace that held his daughter. Holding both of the young people to him, Doc choked out the words, "I'm so sorry!"

Victor hardly noticed that Doc was holding both of them and not letting go. Doc, with his head down between Victor and Rebecca, crying like a little child, and Victor crazily wondering what would happen to him and to Rebecca? Would Doc really send her away to a boarding school? And if he did, how could Victor keep on breathing? How would life possibly go on?

Everything about Victor was focused on Rebecca. The way she seemed to fit perfectly into his arms, even while they were both locked in the strange embrace of her weeping father. He breathed the soft aroma of her body, a perfume that crept through the fragile fabric of her clothes, the electricity that passed through his fingers where his hand was pressed against her arm.

Would I do anything for her? Yes! And would I die for her, if that's what was required? Oh, yes! A thousand times over. Would I die to be with her, if she were dead? Yes.

He thought of Wahali, and for the first time, he could fully understand why Wahali wanted to drown himself. Anything to be with his beloved. Anything.

Wherever Doc sends Rebecca, I will find her. I will go with her. The resolve was comforting. Outside, the rain stopped, and the wind died down, almost as if all Nature were holding its breath, waiting to see what would happen.

Finally, finally, Doc raised his head, gazed silently into the faces of the beautiful young people.

"Don't send her away," Victor pled, before Doc could say anything. "It's all my fault. Please don't send her away."

"'I won't," Doc whispered. "I won't. But for now, Victor, you need to go on home."

"But what's going to happen?" Victor's voice almost held a pleading tone.

"I don't know," Doc confessed. "I only know that you need to go home. Someone is there with Starry. Someone you need to meet." More, Doc could not say. More, he would not reveal to these young people who were obviously so deeply—and so horribly—in love.

"Don't send Rebecca away," Victor asked yet again, and once more, Doc assured him, "I won't. I promise you that."

"You want me to go home?" Victor wasn't sure what that meant. *I have no home without Rebecca. Can't Doc understand that?*

"There's someone you need to meet," Doc repeated.

"Who?" *Who can matter to me more than Rebecca?*

"Just go home, Victor. Come back tomorrow—if you still want to— and we will all sit down and talk."

With that, a weary Doc started to lead Rebecca into the kitchen, leaving her suitcase on the porch floor, right where it had fallen from her hand. But Doc turned back to Victor, almost as an afterthought.

"Be strong, Victor," he whispered, while Victor tried to understand the strange light in Doc's eyes. "Be strong and remember that love wounds us all." Without warning, Starry's face appeared to Doc, and he had to restrain himself from adding, "*It wounds us all and leaves us as if we were dead. But then it comes again. And heals us.*"

With that, Doc reached back and closed the door, and Victor glimpsed Rebecca's face over Doc's shoulder. Through tears, she smiled at him, and Victor felt his heart physically break right within his chest.

Chapter Thirty

Walking back along the flooded road, Victor wondered why he was going home, as Doc had asked him to do. Who could be at his house that Doc wanted him to meet, and what difference could it possibly make, no matter who it was? Did Doc think he was a simple child, to be ordered about, to be told where to go and when?

As he walked, Victor's anger built, and he resolved that he would be with Rebecca, no matter what. After all, Doc had promised that he wouldn't send her away, and he trusted Doc to keep his word. But what did Doc want to talk about that had to wait until tomorrow? *If I still want to? What kind of question is that? Does Doc really think that anything he could ever say would keep me away from Rebecca? Did he think I would accept being sent home like a naughty child? What a fool! Of course, I will come back tomorrow!*

As Victor approached the cottage where he had grown up, he was surprised to see a light on in the kitchen at such a late hour, glowing through the window and falling in a crooked slash over the soaked grass. Victor stepped right in that pool of light, looking up at the kitchen window and wondering why anyone would be up in the middle of the night.

Silently, he watched Fiona go to the sink and run water into the kettle. She was making tea. But why, at this late hour? Was she waiting up for him to get home?

He studied her silhouetted figure in the window, with his own imagination—his own memory—filling in what he could not see. Fiona's soft face, her smile. He could almost feel her warm hands cupping his own face, which is what she did whenever she had something important to tell him, something that required her to look deep into his eyes.

Watching her, he wondered what she would say when he went inside. Surely, she would ask where he had been, and perhaps he should simply say, "I tried to run away with Rebecca and marry her, but Doc stopped us." Victor almost laughed aloud at the thought, and he would have laughed, if it hadn't been such a deep and fresh wound in him, if he hadn't been focused so hard on what he would say to Doc tomorrow and of what he would do—because he certainly would do something—if Doc refused to listen.

So instead of thinking any more about what Fiona might ask, he simply went onto the back porch and from there to the kitchen. He didn't try to be quiet, because Fiona was already up. In typical fashion, he let the screen door slam.

But nothing could have prepared him for the sight that greeted him. Fiona was standing at the stove, with her hand on the teakettle, and Glory, Starry and some woman he had never seen before were sitting at the kitchen table, just as if they were preparing to have lunch together, but the time was most certainly well after midnight. When he came into the room, all of the women looked at him as if they had been waiting for him all of their lives.

"Victor!" Starry sounded out the anxiety all of the women seemed to wear on their faces—even the woman Victor didn't know. Fiona came across the room and stood close to him, looking up into his face. "Honey, where have you been? I was so worried about you."

"You needn't have worried," was all he said, because he was watching the women, realizing very slowly that something was going on. Something he didn't know about.

Did Doc phone ahead of my getting home and tell Aunt Fiona about what happened tonight? Do they all already know that Rebecca and I tried to run away?

Once again, Starry spoke, but her voice came to him as if he were dreaming: "Victor?" As she spoke his name, she indicated the stranger sitting beside her. Victor glanced at the woman. She was older than Starry, and there was something familiar about her that he couldn't place.

"No, Starry!" Fiona interrupted. "Let me. I'm the one who should do this."

"Do what?" Victor asked, and just as he had imagined when he stood in the yard, Fiona reached up, put her warm hands on either side of his face, and looked right into his eyes.

Then she spoke slowly and distinctly, as if he were still a very young child. "Victor, this woman is Rowena. She's your mother."

The words touched his ears, exactly the way tiny pebbles thrown against a window make a sound, but the sound has no meaning of its own. Fiona's eyes filled with sudden and uncharacteristic tears, and he finally tore his gaze from her and looked at the strange woman sitting beside Starry, who indicated her, palms up, as if she were going to say, "TA-DA!" But instead, she said nothing at all.

Your mother. Your mother. Your mother.

In that moment, everything and everyone else in the room

disappeared, and as if he were looking through a cardboard tube, the woman's face became the only thing he could see. Victor stared at her—stared, mesmerized, into his own eyes. Or at least, eyes so similar to his own that, had they not been framed by the soft features of a woman's face, he would have sworn that he was looking into a mirror. And where the kitchen lamplight fell upon her, he saw the familiar contours of his own face, yet one devoid of the harder-edged, masculine jaw and forehead.

"Rowena," Fiona went on doggedly. "This is Victor. Your . . . no, *my* . . . *our* son." As Fiona spoke, she glanced at Glory, and at the last word, Fiona's voice tried to break, and she took a deep breath and shook her head. Her voice would *not* break, and neither would she. She would not allow it.

At that moment, the whole room—that warm, familiar kitchen, suddenly became a vessel of memory. Became . . . *the aroma of the soaked grass and the sight of the rain-blackened bark of the tree and the hot agony of unshed tears. A hand pushes down upon his shoulder, her voice says, "Stay!" and he almost tastes the moist richness of the biscuit she presses into his hand.*

He sits in the wet grass, watching her skirt sway as she walks away, hearing a rustling in the palmettos and the comforting growl of the panther. And another face—an angular face with the kind eyes that looks out from between the dripping fronds—Old Man. Old Man looking at him. Looking after him. Old Man and the panther. And he, himself, who has no name, holding on to the biscuit as if it were life itself. Then sleep—heavy, unwilling sleep—and arms that lift him. Trembling arms.

The skirt gone and the biscuit gone and the soothing warm water of the bath. Soft voices of Fiona and Glory, fussing with each other, but at the same time crooning to him and telling him that everything is going to be all right.

Victor stood silently, looking outward at this stranger who was his mother, looking inward at the memory. At the same time, he waited for something to arise from the depths of his heart. But nothing came. Staring into the face of his own mother, he waited for something. Anger? Relief? Joy?

Starry's voice broke through his muddled thoughts. "You're sopping wet, Honey. I'll get you a towel." With that, Starry went out into the hallway and then into the bathroom, leaving Victor staring at Rowena—with the indistinct images of Fiona and Glory hovering somewhere around the periphery of his awareness. All of them encased in a silence colored gold by the light of the lamp.

Rowena stood up, leaning her hands against the edge of the table, as if standing had been too great an effort for her to make. Still, Rowena and Victor said not a word to each other. They simply stood there, staring at each other, with whatever words they would have spoken dead on their tongues.

When Starry came back with the towel, she looked from Rowena to Victor and back again, then at Fiona where she still stood near the door and at Glory, who had her chin down on her chest and was rocking slightly back and forth in her chair and moaning something low and indistinct.

Victor took the towel and wiped his face and arms.

"Sit down, Victor," Starry asked, unable to endure what seemed to be an emotional standoff among them all.

"No, thank you," Victor responded, his voice so un-characteristically cold that Starry almost shivered. Rowena sank back into her own chair, as if she were simply unable to stand any longer, but although Victor's legs were trembling, he remained standing, somehow beginning to feel the very first feeling of any kind since he'd left Rebecca.

And the feeling was this—he liked looking *down* on Rowena, on this short, curly-haired woman who had his own eyes in her face. Victor's mouth opened, but no words came out.

"Sit down, Victor," Starry repeated in a stronger voice, and somehow, her words seemed to dislodge the terrible silence. On the stove, the kettle began to whistle, and Fiona moved as if in a dream, taking the kettle from the stove and pouring water into the waiting teapot.

Victor sat—but with no more comprehension than a dog that had been trained to mindless obedience. Fiona poured tea for them all, and Victor watched—stupidly—as Glory put spoonful after spoonful of sugar into her tea and then forgot to stir it.

"There's more," Starry's voice broke the silence. "You need to know everything." She looked right at Fiona and then at Glory—"He needs to know everything," she repeated.

Everything? Wasn't this enough? Wasn't this more than anyone could bear? What more could be said?

Starry continued, "I think I know where you were tonight, Victor. And it's time for you to know *everything*." Neither Fiona nor Glory spoke, but at Starry's words, Rowena looked directly at Victor, with her chin held high and her eyes—his own eyes—boring into his face.

"Go ahead and say whatever you need to say to me," Rowena whispered. "I want to hear it."

"I don't care what you want," Victor's usually soft voice came across in a restrained growl. Under Victor's icy gaze that went on and on and in the terrible echo of his voice, Rowena crumpled. Her voice squeaking, she managed, "You were my baby. My own little baby. I loved you."

The words hit Victor as if someone had thrown a bucket of icy water on him but still, he said nothing.

"I *still* love you," Rowena muttered.

For long moments, Victor simply sat, looking at Rowena. Starry glanced at Fiona and at Glory, but they both seemed determined to let these words run their course.

"You left me," Victor stated, simply, but there was such a terrible bitterness in the words that Starry could almost feel it on her own tongue.

"I know," Rowena whispered, and again, there was something in the words that Starry could almost taste. Deepest sorrow—and strangely, some kind of resolve. Rowena continued, with agonized words, "I wanted you to have things better than I could give you." At the same time Victor heard Rowena's words, he also heard in his memory, Wahali's words as well—*Maybe she left you because she loved you.*

"Wait a minute. This can't go on!" Starry yelled, making Glory twitch in her chair and Fiona look at her in open-mouthed surprise. "Victor has to know *everything!* Who's going to tell him?"

Victor frowned and stood up.

"What's *everything?*" he asked in the same rasping voice. "Tell me *what?*"

Still, no one spoke, and Rowena studied him for long moments, her eyes blazing with a faint glow. Finally, she said, "Oh God! Love is terrible."

"No, it isn't!" Victor contradicted her immediately. "It's beautiful. It's wonderful!" He almost added Wahali's other words, *Even if it laughs in our faces while it rips out our hearts and leaves us to bleed to death . . .* but he didn't, because tomorrow he would go back to Doc's and they would talk. Doc already promised that he wouldn't send Rebecca away, and somehow, Victor would find a way to be with her. He was sure of it.

"It's about Rebecca," Starry said, having despaired of Fiona's telling Victor the terrible truth. It should have been Fiona's responsibility. Or her agony. But Fiona still said nothing, and Glory closed her eyes, her moan becoming louder and the swaying of her body increasing. Rowena was beginning to look around at the other women, with a perplexed frown on her face.

"*What* about Rebecca?" Victor ordered, looking around at any of them—all of them. These women! *Has something happened to her? In the short time it took me to go home, as Doc ordered me to do? What a fool I was to leave her there!*

"WHAT ABOUT REBECCA?" Victor bellowed. Starry met his frantic gaze, and Starry was finally the one who spoke the words that would break his heart.

"Rebecca's your sister, Victor. Your *sister.*" Starry's head drooped, as if the sheer weight of the words made her body bow under the burden of them.

"*What?*"

Fiona put her hands over her face, as if she could not bear to watch the agony of what Victor was now going through. Glory's eyes snapped open, focused on Victor, and all her love for him seemed to bleed out from under her eyelashes. Starry raised her head and stared at Fiona and Glory. Rowena looked around at them all, frowning and shaking her head. And to Victor, she added, "But aren't you glad to learn that you have a sister? I thought it would help. Why, I thought you'd be happy."

Later, Victor would have no memory of leaving the kitchen, of running across the back porch and dashing out into the rain-saturated night—and certainly no memory of the door slamming noisily behind him.

Chapter Thirty-One

"What happened?" Rowena's question hung in air that still resounded with the slamming of the door. "What's going on here? Did I say something wrong?" No one answered her, but all eyes, full of accusations and horror, were fixed on her face.

"You wouldn't understand," Starry finally said to Rowena, and she had to bite her tongue to keep from saying more, because she knew that Rowena was completely ignorant of everything she had done, everything she had caused. Starry then turned to the mute and frozen Fiona and Glory and ordered, "You all stay here. I'm going after him."

"Let me go with you!" Fiona managed to yelp, but Starry stood her ground.

"No. I'm going alone. I think Victor's had his fill of us all, but maybe he'll tolerate me. If I can find him," Starry added. As she reached for the door, she added, "I know what he's going through."

And that was true. If anyone among them had experienced the full agony of lost love—the heart-crushing pain—it was Starry. But now, she had to remind herself of that fact, because her pain had almost completely dissipated in the certain glow of her deep and growing affection for Doc.

While Starry's mind was filled with Doc's face, she also thought of Victor and what surely must be the most terrible loss he had ever known—far more than having lost his mother—and Starry's mind had leaped back to her own loss of Middy, as well.

So Starry was also completely relieved to step outside into the darkness and the rain-washed air. She inhaled deeply, as if to dispel all of the anguish she had been breathing in the kitchen, and without even thinking, she headed toward the pier and started to walk along the lakeshore. She didn't call Victor's name, because even if he heard her calling, she didn't think he would answer. But as she went along the familiar shore, she saw that there were no footprints in the rain-pocked sand.

He didn't come this way.

She turned back and gazed at the cottage, wondering how any one building of any kind could contain everything Victor had experienced in those few short minutes. Then she looked down the row of small cabins, straining in the darkness to see if anything moved.

Nothing. Only the light she had left on in her own cabin, a soft light that showed through the window.

Where has he gone? Where would I have gone, if such things had happened to me—especially when I was as young as Victor?

Suddenly, and without any logic whatsoever, she knew he was wherever his mother had left him, all those many years ago. But where would that be? Starry had always envisioned an attractive young woman who was Fiona's great-niece, knocking on the front door and holding the hand of a well-mannered and well-dressed, blonde toddler. A little boy. Victor. And when the mother had to leave, Starry imagined her kneeling down and explaining to the child that he must stay with his aunt Fiona. Just for a little while.

Obviously, none of that had happened, and Fiona wasn't even Victor's great-aunt. It was all a fiction. But what *wasn't* a fiction was Victor's love for Rebecca. That was the one reality they all had to face, for Victor's sake, if for no other.

If Starry could have found Victor at that moment, he would not have been able to tell her exactly where he was or how he got there. He had lunged, strangely blind and deaf, across the back yard and around the side of the cottage—with no conscious thought of where he was going—all the way around to the far side yard, to the very tree where his mother had left him when he was a baby. Everything about that rain-dampened place called out to him in his blindness, and he returned, not only to that place, but to that moment of the gentle face of Old Man peeking at him through the palmettos, the lullaby-growl of the panther-mother who told him that she would stay with him forever.

Now, huddled beneath the same tree—but a tree grown taller over the years—Victor bent over against the pain and began rocking back and forth—in the manner so well learned from Glory—*his* Glory. One of his mothers. The low moan came naturally to him.

If only . . . if only . . .

If only she had not come. If only we had been more careful, Doc would not have caught us. Right now, Rebecca and I would be on the dark bus, traveling through the night and on our way to Georgia.

He could almost hear the deep roar of the engine and smell the faint exhaust fumes and the strange, musty aroma left behind by many travelers.

She would be my beloved!

We would have been married. We would have been lost in our great love and our great innocence that would have protected us from everything.

The agony of his frustrated thoughts caused him to rock more forcefully and to moan more deeply.

Children.

The idea burst upon him. Oh, not children! Not innocent ones to reap the punishment for this terrible love.

That's why Doc was so determined to keep us apart.

He knew.

Victor rocked and moaned and finally put his head down, while the words of the Song of Solomon, introduced to him by Wahali, washed over him, unbidden—bringing his agony into the full light of words. Wahali had quoted only one line—"For thy love is better than wine," but Victor, entranced by the idea that the Holy Book should contain words of such passion, had looked up that Book himself, and had been both shocked and gladdened at more of the words. "Behold, thou art fair, my love; behold, thou art fair; thou hast doves' eyes." And also, "Behold, thou art fair, my beloved, yea, pleasant: also our bed is green." How hard he had worked to memorize those lines, and others, so that one day, he would be able to speak them to Rebecca. But now, the words flowed through his mind and poured themselves out, impotent, upon the rain-soaked ground . . . "Many waters cannot quench love, neither can the floods drown it . . ." and at the last, "For love is strong as death."

Somehow, the words he would have spoken put him into a trance, so that his eyes fixed themselves on the faint glow of light from the porch at the back of the cottage. He watched in awe as someone began walking. Walking toward him. Rebecca! Wearing a white dress and holding a bouquet of flowers, smiling at him and stepping carefully through the wet grass. Rebecca's laughing eyes, the tilt of her head, her smile. So sweet! So sweet! The agony slowly becoming a faint but familiar blossom of pleasure.

Then, a voice whispering his name.

Caught up completely in the vision and in the deep, abiding blooming in his body, Victor stood shakily and held out his hand to her. To his beloved.

"Victor?"

Starry.

Her hands reaching out for him, her arms gathering him in, his head bending down to her warm shoulder. Her crooning voice, her breath against his ear. He leaned his weight against her, felt her stutter-step for balance, and all the while, her voice—soft, soothing, almost breaking in shared agony.

When, at last, she gently pushed against him, sent his weight back to his own legs, she clutched his hand.

"Come on," she said.

"Where?" he croaked, but the word had no meaning.

"Come," she repeated, and slowly Starry led an unsteady Victor around the front of the cottage. "They're in the kitchen," she explained. "They won't see us."

So step by step, Starry led Victor around the front of Fiona's cottage and down the sandy path to her own cabin, where light from the small lamp in the window welcomed them in. But the first thing Victor saw in Starry's small cabin was a traveling bag sitting on the floor—*Rowena's?*—and he turned his face away from it. Starry led him to a chair at the table, and then she went into the tiny bathroom, where she kept a hot plate.

"I don't want any tea!" Victor snarled, suddenly becoming more awake and aware of what was going on around him, and with the last, lingering tendrils of his dreaming falling away.

"I don't want any stinking goddamned tea!" he shouted.

"I'm not going to give you any tea, Victor," Starry snarled back at him. "Stinking, goddamned, or otherwise! Here," she added, as she poured amber liquid into a small glass and handed it to him.

"What is it?"

"Bourbon," she said. "Drink it."

Victor drank, loved the burning, wanted it to consume him completely. Wanted it to destroy his heart, leave him lying on the floor with acrid streams of smoke coming from his chest.

He sat silently, staring at Starry, and feeling that he was hanging on the edge of a cliff built of words—words! And he didn't want to hear any more of them. Didn't want to hear anything Starry had to say—or anything else. Or anyone else. He wanted to cling forever where he was hanging and not fall into the abyss. The words had come. He had been helpless to stop them. And they had come from Starry, this woman who now stood in front of him, holding his empty glass.

"More?" she asked in a soft tone.

He shook his head. That wasn't what he wanted. He didn't want bourbon, he wanted to rip off his ears—gouge out his eyes—go blind and deaf. His breathing seemed to stop. His mind exploded into a kaleidoscope of garish, swirling colors with no pattern, no meaning. He felt that his mouth was hanging open, with his own breath—tainted with the aroma of bourbon—curling like smoke into his nostrils. He sat back with an expulsion of breath and felt that his lungs would never fill up again.

"I wish I knew what to say to you," Starry murmured, as if she instinctively knew that Victor didn't want to hear any more words. "But I don't," she added, sitting in the chair across the small table from him. ."You're hurting so bad, I can almost feel it myself, but I still don't know what to say."

"Don't say anything," Victor snarled.

"Yes . . . well," Starry whispered. "Men are like that."

It sounded like an insult, and Victor was in no mood to be insulted.

"Men are like *what?*" he demanded, looking into Starry's eyes and suddenly seeing the soft blue in them—and the pain those eyes were reflecting from his own—and from another, different pain that was foreign to Victor.

"Men don't like to feel helpless," Starry said, taking a small sip of bourbon herself.

Crazily, Victor wondered for a moment what Glory would say, if she knew that he and Starry were sitting right there in her cabin, drinking what Glory called the "devil's brew." He almost laughed, but it would have been a laugh born of something he didn't want to feel, and so he swallowed it down.

"Here," Starry said, tipping the bottle and pouring more of the amber brew into his glass.

"What makes you think I'm helpless?" Victor demanded.

"Oh, you aren't really helpless," Starry said. "But you're in pain, and that makes you *think* you're helpless. You're no different from any wounded animal, Victor," Starry went on. "And that means you have to watch so carefully, that something . . . or someone . . . doesn't take advantage of you."

"And how did you get to be so stinking smart?" Victor asked in a harsh tone, downing the drink Starry had poured for him.

"I know all about wounded animals," she replied simply.

Then Starry paused for a moment before she added, "I used to be one."

Victor studied her carefully, but he said nothing more. Starry slowly twirled the empty glass between her hands. "No one can wound you so horribly as someone you love. Or rather, someone you used to love."

"I love her. I will always love her. I'll love her as long as I live!" Victor spat, and at the same time, he struggled to keep the tears of anger and frustration from coming. Starry hesitated only a moment before she went to kneel beside Victor's chair. And when Starry reached up and put her arms around Victor, he suddenly, heavily, leaned into her embrace, burrowing his face in her hair, much as he had done when he was a child, and stifling back a sob.

"Oh, God!" he finally bellowed. "You and that stinking music from beyond the moon. You were right." But Starry didn't hear Victor's words, because she was caught up in her own surprised emotions at that moment. Because Starry was a woman, and she longed to comfort Victor, to give him the warmth and comfort—the supreme warmth and comfort—that only a woman could give to a man.

But in some strange way Starry would never understand nor even remember, she was holding Victor close to her, to comfort him, but more. Much more.

Somehow, she was also holding and consoling herself—her old self, the last fragment of a long-ago self she had almost forgotten—and all the years with Middy. Years in which she yearned for comfort, needed it so desperately, from him.

And never got it.

Years in which she tried with all her being, over and over and over again, to please him, somehow.

But she never did.

How hard she tried to bring a smile to his face, a smile for *her*.

But he never smiled.

The agony rose up in her chest like evil bile she could not swallow down again, and for a moment, she thought that she would be sick all over Victor. Instead, she swallowed hard and gripped Victor's shoulders even harder—not in passion, but in the last and dying throes of a long-ago agony.

Victor shifted in his chair and stood up, bringing Starry up with him, their eyes burning in mutual pain, so that Victor gazed at Starry's trembling mouth and then brought his lips down to hers, his arms vice-like around her. His kiss was hot and sweet and vicious, and tasted of his agony. Starry leaned into the kiss, at first to comfort Victor—but then not to comfort, but to punish. She backed away from their mutual agony, and as she did, Victor's hand brushed against her breast.

"Oh!" Victor whispered, and Starry heard everything that one word held—agonized delight, passion, confusion. Starry's mind was racing. Was that the kiss of a young man in terrible pain, and was that intimate touch the blundering move of an innocent boy? Or was Victor—her precious Victor—reaching for her the way a man reaches for a woman?

Her own response had surprised her.

"I'm sorry?" Victor murmured, asking. He looked down at the floor, his voice husky and plaintive. But then he raised his head and looked right into Starry's eyes, and she could see that his gaze held no regret. For a moment, his look almost took Starry's breath away, and she briefly wondered how many times she had looked into his eyes and had always seen the *boy*—and never the *man*.

But quite suddenly her own agony fulfilled itself, and it was Middy's face Starry saw, and not Victor's. She gasped and was surprised to hear her own voice. "Why did I think I deserved someone like Middy?" Starry asked, and when she spoke, she knew the words for the first time, heard them for the first time as they blundered—along with Middy's indistinct face—into the blue magic of this moment with Victor. She had not even thought the words, but there they were, spoken right out into the air, and she was helpless against the additional flood of words that followed. "Whoever I was *then*, I'm not that person anymore. I deserve better. I will *have* better."

Victor heard her words, but they had no meaning for him, and so he remained silent. Waiting.

Starry stopped speaking, her own words having come from some place inside her that she had never known existed. The Truth—the Truth was always there, was always smiling and whispering to her from inside her own beating heart, and she hadn't even known it. Slowly, Middy's face dissolved from her imagination. And Victor's face replaced it.

Her hands came up and rested against Victor's chest.

Gently, she pushed him away.

"I didn't mean . . ." Victor stammered, silently longing for Starry to put her arms around him again.

"I know," Starry said, smiling. "I know, Honey."

"What are you talking about?" Victor finally asked. "Who were you talking about?"

"Nothing. Nobody," Starry smiled. *Truth!*

"Who's Middy?" Victor asked, wanting to push aside whatever stood between him and Starry. Wanting her.

"No one," Starry smiled again, feeling complete delight at the words. *Truth!*

"Someone you loved?"

"A long time ago," Starry admitted. "When I was somebody else." *Another Truth. Another beautiful Truth.*

"Love died," Starry added almost dreamily, in her first, full taste of a freedom of the heart she had never known existed. "It really died," she repeated, smiling at Victor and shaking her head.

"No. Love doesn't die," Victor protested, wanting to believe it.

Not knowing what to do with his hands, he allowed them to hang at his sides, clumsy and useless. Somehow, his wounded mind was stuck on those strange words about music from beyond the moon that Starry had spoken to him all those years ago and on the words Wahali had spoken.

"What?" Starry was perplexed by Victor's statement.

"Love." Victor almost sobbed the word. "Love doesn't die!"

Starry longed to hold Victor in her arms again, but something far stronger kept her from it. Somehow, Doc's gentle face seemed to appear before her, and when she spoke again, her eyes were shining with a new Truth.

"Maybe you're right," Starry admitted. "Maybe it doesn't die. Maybe it just goes somewhere else. And waits for you."

Chapter Thirty-Two

In the quiet kitchen, Rowena still looked from Fiona and Glory and back again.

"What?" she repeated, frustrated and confused, and Fiona looked at this woman—this woman who did something long ago that she thought was for the best. And she had been almost right. Almost.

"Victor was . . . friends . . . with his sister—Rebecca." It was all Fiona could manage.

"Well, that's good, isn't it?" Rowena asked, still perplexed.

"More than friends," Glory muttered.

"More than friends?"

"They were in love," Glory said, and then she looked accusingly at Fiona. "I told you that a long time ago," she said. "But you didn't want to believe it."

"I wonder if Starry has found him yet?" Fiona asked, unable to address the accusation Glory had flung at her—and in front of this total stranger, too.

"In *love?*" Rowena clearly couldn't believe what she was hearing.

"They didn't know," Fiona said. "*We* didn't know."

"Old Man knew," Glory said in a matter-of-fact voice. "And Doc knew too. That's why he was so against them seeing each other."

For Fiona, everything began to make sense, especially Doc's strong reaction to the simple kiss Victor and Rebecca had shared.

"Why didn't Old Man tell us?" Fiona whined. "Why didn't Doc?"

"You ever heard Old Man tell anybody anything?" Glory growled.

"No," Fiona admitted.

Again, the kitchen was filled with silence. Then Fiona gave a deep sigh. "Well, we did everything we could," she said at last, and Glory nodded. "We sure did that."

"We couldn't protect him from everything," Fiona added. "But we did our best, and that's all anybody can do." For the moment, Fiona and Glory had forgotten that Rowena was even in the room.

"That's all anybody can do," Rowena parroted, and Fiona and Glory both nodded.

Fiona didn't say anything else, but she nodded to herself. *We all did our best—even Rowena. And we all loved him, some in one way and some in another. But we still love him. We always will.*

By the time they persuaded an exhausted and tearful Rowena to climb into Fiona's empty bed, Fiona and Glory had already reached a silent agreement. They would wait up, in case Victor came home.

They would have a long wait.

Later, when the first light of dawn was coming across the lake, making a mirror of its surface and reflecting the delicate gray of the sky, Victor walked back toward Fiona's cottage—toward home. He had left Starry's cabin, with the pain beginning to find some sort of a place to curl up inside him and rest, still throbbing but no longer stinging him almost to tears. Somehow, the deepest anguish seemed to have fallen into a troubled slumber inside of him.

He crept slowly around the side of the house, came in the back door—noiselessly—and tiptoed down the familiar hallway, hoping not to awaken Fiona or Glory. The door to Fiona's room was standing open, and he peeked inside. Someone was sleeping in the bed, but he knew instinctively that it wasn't Fiona. She never went to bed until he was home. And safe.

So it had to be Rowena asleep there. It had to be his own mother. He could see only the side of her sleeping face, but in it he saw the ravages of pain. *Love did that to her, too,* Victor suddenly thought. *It ripped out her heart, so at least we will always have that in common.*

He remembered looking into her eyes for the first time. Saw his own eyes, but also saw an accumulated misery of so many years, a misery he had known only so recently, but that he would carry forever. So that he knew the words he would speak, if she were awake. *When I have lived as long as you have lived and love has broken my heart as many times as it has broken yours, my eyes will look the way yours looked this day.*

He closed the door noiselessly and padded silently down the hall toward the living room, where he could see a low light burning—a small lamp that usually sat on top of a bookcase was now placed in the open window that looked out toward the lake.

A light in the window. For him.

When he looked through the window toward the front porch, he saw both Fiona and Glory asleep in side-by-side rocking chairs, slumped, so that they leaned against each other. Like bookends.

Fiona was dreaming that she held a fretful baby in her arms. She swaddled it in her apron and crooned to it, holding it close to her own warm body and rocking back and forth to sooth it. Giving the baby her own warmth and nurturing it with her love.

Glory was dreaming about the sunshine on the dock outside of the restaurant door, where Jubilee, who was just a toddler in Glory's dream, looked up and smiled at Glory with shining eyes. *My child!*

Standing so close to the familiar porch, Victor drank in the image of these two women—his mothers. *This is what love looks like,* Victor said to himself, *As long as I live, I will remember this moment.*

And he did.

In his heart, he once again heard Wahali's words. "Love doesn't die, you know." And this time, he added Starry's words—"It just goes somewhere else. And waits for you."

Victor's love for Rebecca—his beloved—was dying a slow and terrible death. But in another way, he knew that he would carry Rebecca in his heart forever. Both as the great love of his life. And, eventually, as his sister.

His blessing.

And his curse.

But here on this old porch, in the earliest light of dawn, was love, as well. A different kind, but love nonetheless.

When Victor walked quietly out of the back door of *home*, walking out of the house where he had once been a child, he knew for the first time that he was a man.

Perhaps this leaving would be his last, because once he joined the army and went far away to fight in a terrible, bloody war, he might never come back, at all.

But then again, perhaps he would survive. Perhaps he really had a long life ahead of him, and this was only one day of it.

That early morning, Victor left home to go to war, to keep the enemy away from his lake and away from his sister, and away from his sleeping mothers.

He was blessed. He had known love.

And Love itself was somewhere, waiting for him.

He would welcome it, no matter what it ever did to him.

Chapter Thirty-Three

Hours later that same night, Victor waited alone beside the dark road for the bus to Gainesville, waited to enter the unknown world in which he would be a man. In his aloneness, the full symphony of love and agony played out in time to the fierce beating of his heart.

Perhaps that's what Fiona and Glory were really warning him about, when they cautioned him not to go too far into the swamp, where they told him about monstrous alligators that were waiting to catch him unaware and to lock him in their terrible jaws. Carry him deep into the black water and hold him until he was no longer alive.

Because isn't that what loving Rebecca had done to him?

No.

At the last, Wahali's strange words were the ones Victor carried with him into adulthood—"God sends us here to love each other, and if we can do that, we are blessed. Even if we lose love. Even if we try to kill it, or it succeeds in killing us. Even if it laughs in our faces while it rips out our hearts and leaves us to bleed to death, we are blessed."

There was only one other person in all of Love-Oak who would have understood. Starry. Because while Victor waited for the bus that would carry him far away, Starry was lying awake in the small cabin she called home, alone in whatever strange vigil she was keeping. Her tears were for Victor's pain. But Victor and Rebecca were both very young, and they had many years left for love to chew them up and spit them out before they finally found out what love was all about.

But they would find it. Starry was sure of that. And in only a few hours, she would go to Doc, to comfort him and to love him with all her heart.

Fiona and Glory still snored softly in their chairs on the front porch, waiting faithfully for Victor—who was not coming home. Rowena slumbered fitfully in the unfamiliar bed, wondering—but not knowing that she was wondering—if there could have been another way, other than leaving her children behind. She would never know the answer.

At the other end of the lake, Arabella and Wahali sat silently in their kitchen, not yet knowing that Old Man would not be coming home either, that true to what Old Man envisioned, Wahali would find his father's body in the ravine that very morning, would see the deep footprints of the panther-mother all around and would correctly guess that the Great Spirit had sent her to fetch his father's beautiful soul.

Wide awake, Starry watched through her window as the moon slowly faded away in the earliest light of dawn. In daylight, she wouldn't be able to see it, but it was always there.

She smiled to herself as, once again, she heard the music.

Acknowledgements

Thanks to Julie L. Cannon and Kisha Day for initial editing and to Craft DS for digital retrieval (www.craftds.org)

Paraphrased Seminole legends are based upon the book, *Legends of the Seminoles*, copyright 1994 by Betty Mae Jumper and Peter B. Gallagher. Used by permission of Pineapple Press, Inc.

About Augusta Trobaugh

Augusta Trobaugh earned the Master of Arts degree in English from the University of Georgia, with a concentration in American and Southern literature. Her first novel, *Praise Jerusalem!,* was a semi-finalist in the 1993 Pirate's Alley Faulkner Competition. Trobaugh's work has been funded through the Georgia Council of the Arts, and she has been nominated for Georgia Author of the Year.